Boring Stuff

2023 © Þom Rhodes

All rights reserved. No part of this literary work may be reproduced, cloned, reincarnated, smuggled, or distributed without the written permission of the publisher/author. Brief quotations, reviews, critical reviews and other non-commercial uses permitted by copyright law. For permission requests, please contact the publisher, by forming a summoning circle with ground Ethiopian coffee and sacrificing a potato using an obsidian knife. Failure to abide by copyright law will result in 4 members of the Onyx Spire showing up to your house on a black wyvern and unleashing a dozen undead bards in your bedroom. Do the right thing, and don't be ignorant.

This is a work of pure fiction. Any relation to historical events, real people, actual places, are used for fictitious reasons. Names, characters, and places are unfortunately the bi-product of the author's own imagination, and any similarities to other works or media is purely coincidental.

Printed by Amazon KDP in the United States of America.

ISBN: 9798371882028 (paperback)

Imprint: Independently published

First published on January 1st 2023, first printed edition 2023.

Edition: 2-ß

No potatoes were intentionally harmed in the writing of this novel, but some were cut into wedges, fried, and topped with melted pepper jack cheese and bacon. They asked for it, they had shifty eyes.

BLOOD OF THE FAE
One Last Adventure: Book 2

Þom Rhodes

This book is dedicated to Devin Spearwalker
For being the best family I could've asked for.
For always pushing me to be a better version of myself.
For never giving up on me.
For never letting me give up on myself.
Thank you.
The world needs more brothers like you.
These books wouldn't be possible without you.

01.

Days had turned into weeks, and weeks had turned into months. When was the last time he'd seen the outside world? He could smell the dry summer air blowing through the sorghum and oats beyond the walls of his tiny room, but he hadn't seen the fields in almost a year. The scratches on the wall near the window counted the two hundred and fifty two sunrises he had witnessed from the room. He might've missed a few due to stormy weather or heavily overcast days, but he felt he was close enough to being correct.

It was the farmers' fault, he figured. They were the ones who had been cutting down the trees to make room for their corn and wheat fields. He only did what any normal, calm, reasonable person would do with the reckless destruction of nature. He burned down their homes and ruined their soil. If anyone was to blame for his imprisonment in the dungeon in Goldenveil, it was those farmers.

Much to the cheers of the farmers and the other residents of Eastonbrook, Duke Kearnis and the arbiter of the Calinsahr Duchy were swift in handing down the punishment for the supposed crimes. To spend the rest of his life wasting away in the bowels of Artinburg Castle in Goldenveil, that was what they decided, and for two hundred and fifty two days, he'd been sitting and waiting, when he wasn't pacing or staring at the light through the narrow window. At least, he had counted two hundred and fifty two days.

"Meal time, you damned cat," one of the guards called harshly before shoving a tray of dried meat, boiled beans, and stale bread through a slot under the heavy iron door.

He sat up from the dirt-stained pad made from blankets he was allowed to use as a bed, and looked at the miserable food for a moment. "Any news from the outside?" his voice called in return, before slowly moving on his hands and knees towards the door.

"Nothing that concerns you," the guard replied in an irritated manner, "not since you're going to be spending the rest of your life in that hole. Forget about the outside world, it's forgotten about you."

"What's my name?" he inquired, picking up the cold, dried meat that was clearly leftovers from a soldier's rations.

"What? It's Lorvin," the guard responded, clearly annoyed. "Why would you ask something like that?"

He shrugged as he answered, "just curious. If you know my name, it means you haven't forgotten me yet."

"Trust me, I've tried," the voice of the guard came from further away.

As he chewed on the tough chunk of meat, Lorvin pressed his ear to the door, listening in on whatever went on beyond his tiny room of stone and steel. The footsteps of the guard drew close once more, and a metal mug of stale wheat ale was hastily shoved through the delivery slot as well. Lorvin picked up the slice of bread and dipped it into the urine-hued liquid before biting into it.

"What did he ask?" a guard with a softer voice asked, far away from Lorvin and the door.

The gruff voice responded in a manner that implied an indifferent shrug. "Damned cat wanted to know what's going on outside. Why does he care? He's never going to see the outside of that cell."

There was a brief pause as the younger-sounding voice chuckled a bit. "They might have to execute him," she continued darkly. "Going to have to make room for war prisoners somewhere, somehow."

"War prisoners?" Lorvin heard the older man ask, the tone confused.

"You didn't hear? There was an attack on Albinasky Keep just over a week ago. It's just a rumor in the barracks, but I hear we might be going to war against Elgrahm Hold."

"Why attack them? Did the duchess finally declare her independence? Aren't we busy already with Anslater?"

"The rumor is that Lady Eisley stole something from the king. Something important. Now, she's refusing to return it, and has murdered the king's proxy to her land. The king, and Chancellor Ai'phalkahn, are all fired up about it."

"So, is the keep still standing?"

"No one returned," the younger voice went solemn for a moment. "Either they were captured, or…"

"No one survived," the man finished the thought for her.

Lorvin shook his head as he chewed on the meat some more. "I hope it's true, and I hope no one survived." he said loudly after swallowing a bit of the hard meat. "King Borlhauf is an idiot if he thinks he's respected north of the border with the Free Region."

"Shut up, you damned cat!" bellowed the older male guard.

"Lady Eisley's sheriff would have definitely treated me better than this," Lorvin answered with a heavy dose of mockery, "but I know him. So, that helps."

"Would you be quiet?" called the softer, female voice.

"You're going to be conscripted into the main army, sent to the front lines, and killed on behalf of a tyrant," Lorvin said with a smirk. "Why should I listen to you?"

Heavy footfalls could be heard approaching the door of the tiny cell that Lorvin called home for the time being. Keys rattled, and the lock was thrown open angrily. When the iron door was yanked open, the brooding form of the male guard stood in the narrow hall, dressed in his usual chainmail shirt and leather trousers.

"What did you say, you damned cat?" the guard questioned with a snarl from his weather-worn face.

"I said," Lorvin stood up slowly, holding the mug of old ale in his hands. "You're going to get killed in a war anyway. Why should I listen to you?"

"Listen, and you better listen good, cat," the guard spat on the bare feet of the prisoner. "Arbiter Paur only said you're to spend the rest of your days in this jail, he never said I couldn't speed up the process."

"Hmm?" Lorvin tilted his head, and a devilish smile crossed his face. "I didn't hear you. Could you speak up?"

The guard growled and pulled the metal baton from his belt. "I think I've had enough of your mouth, damned cat," he sneered, pointing the iron bar at Lorvin.

"Oh thank the gods," Lorvin rolled his eyes and grinned, "I was just getting ready to leave."

"What?"

Without adding anything else to the conversation, Lorvin hurled the remainder of the wheat beer into the face of the guard. Caught by the surprise of the liquid attack, the guard stepped back as he tried to clear his eyes. Lorvin, using all of his might, crashed into the guard's chest with his shoulder and threw the man into the opposite wall. Pulling the baton from the hand of the guard, while spinning on his heels, the inmate heaved the ale-drenched guard into the cell like a sack of potatoes. Stumbling and stunned, the guard could barely turn around before the cell door was slammed shut and locked behind him, with Lorvin standing in the hallway holding the keys.

"Let him out of there, right now!" the female guard ordered, holding her baton threateningly towards Lorvin as she charged down the hall.

"Why?" Lorvin asked, facing the younger guard with a maddened expression on his face while tucking the keys into the rope belt around his long, unclean tunic.

With the iron baton in his right hand, Lorvin rolled slightly to the right as he stepped backwards, parrying the wild, overhead strike from the rushing woman. He drove his left palm into the throat of the guard as her hasty momentum carried her forward in her blocked attack. The sound of bones cracking filled the air as Lorvin brought the baton in his hand down against the elbow of the woman, forcing her to drop her own weapon and reel away in pain.

He never killed anyone, and he wasn't going to start now, but he couldn't let the woman chase him or free her companion. So, as she staggered backwards down the hall, Lorvin swept her right knee with a vicious kick from his shin, then stomped upon the woman's left ankle as she collapsed from the blow to her knee. A gut-wrenching popping sound filled the air when Lorvin smashed her ankle once more with another hard stomp, this time grinding his heel into the bones of the guard. She wasn't dead, but she definitely wouldn't be walking soon.

Shrieks of pain, and furious shouts flooded the hallway as Lorvin took off running. He followed the hall past four other cells, turned left at a junction, and sped down a narrow flight of stairs. Despite the lack of torchlight, his feline eyes adjusted quickly to the darkness, allowing him to run flawlessly through the unlit depths of the castle.

Honestly, he had no idea where he was running to. He just knew he needed to escape. Lorvin had no map, and only the memory of being dragged to his cell with a canvas sack over his head, but he had determination.

Or maybe it was rash foolishness?

No, it was definitely determination.

Unless, it was indeed rash foolishness.

He grinned as he raced through the dark tunnels under Artinburg Castle, picking his path based upon what he knew from the layout of the city, and the sunlight that often entered his tiny room. Down another set of stairs he charged, then, upon hearing the sound of rushing water, pulled a heavy iron grate from the floor. The freed drainage vent crashed to the stones, the hefty metal thundering loudly as Lorvin dropped through the hole in the floor. His feet landed on a narrow ledge next to a stream of putrid, warm water flowing through the lowest levels of the castle and under the city of Goldenveil.

Following the rancid fluid through the clammy tunnels, Lorvin found himself at the mouth of the tunnel that jutted out from the cliffs that the city was built upon. Though covered in a web of iron bars and a securely locked gate, the inmate could see the light of the midday sun, and the shimmering bay far below the torrent of sewage.

He paused for a moment in the light that poured in through the drainage grate, looking at the mess of dirty, matted, dark silver and black fur that coated his body. Lorvin hadn't been allowed to have a proper bath in his entire stay in the cell, only given a bowl of warm water and a musty cloth once a month. As he looked over himself near the barrier to his liberty, he realized how dirty he had truly gotten while locked up. Even the ragged old tunic he had been given was stained and torn so badly it looked like it had held beets and knives at some point.

"This just won't do," Lorvin muttered, running his fingers over the warm metal of the grate that kept him from freedom.

Without delay, the prisoner used the stolen keys to etch a quick sigil into the opposite walls of the tunnel, where the grate was fastened into the hewn stone. A simple sketch of a cracked stone, with a fire rune carved into the middle of the broken symbol.

Rage-filled howls began to draw near from the passageways the inmate had already traversed. Torchlight and shadows closed quickly with the prisoner, who stood examining his hasty carvings on the walls of the tunnel.

Lorvin took a deep breath and closed his eyes as he began to pray. "Oh Chaugnah, god of stone and soil," the prisoner whispered, despite the guards rushing to find him, "pardon my destruction and grant my freedom from this pit. See me safely through the trials ahead."

As the dungeon guards appeared around the final corner, their voices rising in anger upon seeing the fleeing prisoner, the markings in the stone flared to life with a brilliant white flash. A sudden explosion of dust and stone debris boomed through the tunnels, shaking the walls and forcing the guards to their knees to prevent being knocked over by the force of the blast. The huge metal grate tumbled down the cliffs, blown free from the end of the sewer, rattling and clanging as it struck the rocks on its path to the azure waters of the bay.

"What are you—," one of the guards began to shout to the prisoner who stood on the very edge of the broken stone where the drainage grate once sat.

"You're going to threaten to stop me," Lorvin cut the man's furious words short, "and I'm going to ignore you. Then, you're going to try to claim that jumping from here would be insane, but rather than listen to you ramble on and on, I'll just assure you all, that I'm perfectly content with my divine madness."

Amid the shouts from the guards, Lorvin ran at full speed and leapt from the end of the tunnel. With the rush of the bay's waters coming up to greet the fleeing prisoner, the sound of leathery wings filled the air, and a massive black shadow dropped from the sky. As Lorvin fell, and the gusts of wind battered his falling form, he closed his eyes and accepted whatever fate the gods had planned for him.

It was unquestionably rash foolishness.

02.

"We don't tell her," Vourden spoke quietly, sitting in a chair looking over the slumbering figure of Lynsia.

"I concur," Kendira replied, running a cool, damp cloth over the forehead of the unconscious girl. "Things are going to be bad enough, without our poor birdy thinking she's to blame for..." the bard's voice trailed off.

"For killing my husband," Ansha commented from where she stood near the door to the small bedroom in the castle. "I don't hold her at fault, but I cannot say I don't have a bit of animosity towards the girl for what happened."

"Which is understandable," Vourden remarked, nodding his agreement with the chestnut-haired woman.

The trio had been in the small bedroom, one usually reserved for guests lacking importance, within Albinasky Keep for a while. Originally, Kendira and Vourden wanted to visit the girl who refused to wake up, but then Ansha stepped in and they had started talking about recent events. It was Vourden's fourth visit in six days to the chamber that held the sleeping Sidhe-Vein, but Kendira often stopped by twice a day, while Ansha kept her distance unless one of the others went in. Vourden had spent nearly two weeks locked in his house until Kendira convinced him to go outside and visit Lynsia the first time. Now, they were all gathered in the room, feeling the weight of the changing world around them, and grasping at the words they spoke in the vain hope it would bring about a solution to their problems.

"Any idea on how to wake her up yet?" Ansha asked, pursing her lips in the hopes of getting a decent answer.

Kendira shook her head slowly, brushing the wet cloth against the sleeping redheaded girl's cheek. "Not yet. She went unconscious right after using her power. She was like this after the darkoyle attack as well; just wanting to sleep, but it wasn't nearly this bad. I think she just has to overcome whatever toll the magic took on her."

"Hopefully she comes out of it soon," Vourden said as his green eyes followed the movements of the bard.

Ansha nodded her agreement. "We have a job to finish. Having her awake is sort of important."

"Are you sure that's what you want to do?" the man inquired, turning his jade gaze to the woman in the scarlet tunic against the wall.

"It's what my husband would want us to do," Ansha answered without hesitation. "We have to complete the task set before us. For Dorho."

"For Dorho," Vourden repeated with an understanding nod.

"For Dorho," Kendira's song-like voice responded, before adding, "for Lynsia, as well."

"Find me when you've finished, Dira," Vourden requested as he finally stood up. "I promised to take Marle to get a bell for her kitten this afternoon, and I wanted to check on the lizard woman now that she's recovered a bit from her injuries."

Ansha dropped her crossed arms to her sides as she moved towards the door ahead of the man. "I'm coming with you. I'd like to see Urna as well. I've been concerned about her."

Bies, the larscot, stood up and shook his fur from where he had curled up next to Ansha's feet. The knee-high, weasel-like creature let out a long yawn and followed diligently behind the woman.

"If I don't find you, dear man," Kendira spoke up, leaning away from the Sidhe-Vein slightly to face the red-haired man, "I'll see you at home for dinner. Don't spoil Marle too much. She won't eat a good dinner if you fill her up with treats from the market."

"I can't help it if I'm a sucker for those big green eyes," Vourden chuckled, his hand opening the door slowly. "I have several years to make up for, anyway."

"Just be in her life," Kendira replied with a warm smile, "and don't remake your past mistakes, dear man."

"You two are getting along rather well," Ansha added, once she was outside the room with Vourden and the door was closed behind them.

Vourden shrugged dismissively and smiled slightly. "You and Dorho were right," he said matter-of-factly, "we needed each other. Plus, I've got my daughter back in my life. I can't complain about that."

"You're doing better from when I saw you at the funeral for Paisley and Dorho," Ansha stated, forcing a small smile to her feline face.

"Not really," Vourden sighed as they walked through the halls of the castle. "I'm just making sure I stay distracted."

Dressed in a pair of trousers the color of burnt silver, a sun-bleached tunic, and a sleeveless black doublet, Vourden moved through the spacious halls of Albinasky Keep next to Ansha. Matching his pale green tabard, a floppy beret decorated the man's head, featuring an ebony star of seven points upon a silver brooch with a polished tiny sapphire in its center. A rapier with a scalloped blade of silvery metal dancing with mint-stained light hung from the belt of the man, while a dark steel gorget shone in the morning sun that crept in through the castle windows.

Vourden nodded a wordless greeting to various servants who tended to the many tasks around the castle halls. Most were busy with repairs and building fortifications since the recent attack by King Borlhauf's men. Things around the keep were still fairly chaotic since the assault, but the spirits of the people hadn't been broken, despite the reckless destruction and loss of life.

"Sheriff," a couple of workers greeted, bowing respectfully to the man as he passed.

"Good morning," he responded, offering a polite gesture from his right hand.

Though he had been up for several hours already, it was indeed still morning for the sheriff of Elgrahm Hold. The sun's brilliance barged into the castle through windows that had been opened to let in the summer breeze. Scents from the sprawling rose gardens that surrounded Albinasky Keep slipped into the halls upon the morning air, giving a sense of life and calm to the building ravaged by the recent battle.

"Greetings, Countess Maizen," a dark-haired healer from the temple spoke up as the two entered the large bedroom where Urna was recovering. "Sheriff Leustren, it is a pleasure to see you as well."

Ansha bowed kindly to the white-clad healer seated next to the bed Urna was resting in. "I just came to check in on my friend."

Urna, the reptilian woman, sat up the best she could in the bed, though a heavy wince crossed her face as she attempted to move. She ended up collapsing back into the pillows behind her with a frustrated sigh.

"Don't move," urged the healer, her young voice calm as the reptilian tried to move.

"Attav'ska!" Urna muttered angrily, turning her dark chartreuse eyes towards Vourden and Ansha while they stood in the doorway. "It's good to see you again. Both of you."

The sheriff was the first to enter, taking a seat near the window along the western wall. Ansha looked over at the slithzerkai woman carefully, and with a concerned expression in her nut-brown eyes, sat on the opposite side of the large bed from the healer. While Urna regained her composure and took several long, steady breaths after her attempts to get up, the others remained quiet, allowing tranquility to settle over the spacious bedroom.

"The word in the castle," Vourden began, letting his green eyes look over the relaxed figure of the lizard woman, "is that you've recovered quite a bit since the attack. Looks like I heard the truth."

"Every day," Urna spoke, her voice a mixture of reptilian hisses and frustrated growls, "it's the same thing. I wake up, they come to do their healing magic, someone brings breakfast, then healing balms and tinctures are brought in, something light for lunch, more healing magic, dinner, someone helps me wash up, and then back to sleep. Same thing. Over and over. Every damn day, but yes, I'm improving. How have you been?"

"Coming to terms with everything that's happened," Ansha answered with utmost honesty. "Many things have changed, most of it for the worst, but it brings me joy to see you awake and talking."

The larscot that accompanied the countess nudged her left leg gently, then flopped down rather unceremoniously. He had stuck by the side of the woman since the loss of Dorho, and she often treated the furry beast like a beloved companion.

"I'm sorry," Urna lowered her head slightly in dismay, "about Dorho. I know how happy you two were together. I enjoyed all the times you both came into my tavern. If the Spire hadn't followed me—."

"Nonsense," Vourden cut her off and waved his hand dismissively. "You shouldn't shoulder the blame for what happened. You had no control over the actions of the Onyx Spire. I, however, would like to ask you about them, and your connection to them, officially if possible. I am the sheriff of this land, after all, and I need to have all my squirrels herded before talking to Lady Eisley, if you understand."

Ansha reached over to the bed and lightly grasped the nearest hand of the lizard woman, offering a kind smile as the sheriff spoke.

"That's understandable," Urna groaned, her eyes moving from the sheriff to the woman holding her hand.

"But that can wait until you are in better health and more comfortable spirits," the sheriff concluded. "The well-being of our friends comes before official investigations and work."

"Great. Gives me time to plot a decent lie," the slithzerkai woman chuckled darkly.

Ansha managed an honest giggle.

"I," Urna tried to move again, but after a pain-filled gasp, fell back into the bed and glanced at the healer. "I have something for you, Ansha. It's in my bag over there on the table, in a small metal box. Can you get it for me?"

Though the healer stood up, it was Vourden who managed to reach the old leather bag first, snatching it from where it rested next to a bottle of brandy. He rifled around in the bag until he found the old metal box and handed it to

Urna, then returned to the table to pour himself a small glass of liquor. As the cherry-scented dark fluid filled the crystal snifter, the reptilian woman opened the twin tiny latches on the box with a dull click.

"I feel you need this more than I do," Urna spoke softly, delicately lifting a small necklace from the container. "It was a gift from my husband, in the hopes that all my wishes and dreams come true. I can think of no one else who needs this more, than you, right now."

A long silver chain was pulled from the box, and connected to it was a pastel cyan diamond shaped like a drop of rain roughly the length of Ansha's thumb. Like threads from a spider's web, golden wire was bound around the gem, encasing it in a protective shell.

"Oh, Urna," Ansha's voice was slow to escape her lips as she admired the beauty of the gem. "I don't think I can accept this. Your husband gave this to you."

"My husband is dead," the lizard spoke with disdain. "Killed by the same people who killed your husband. I want you to take this, and reap revenge from those who wronged us so dearly."

"Urna, I can't," the countess pulled her hands away, shaking her head in disbelief of the offer.

The slithzerkai woman gently took hold of the other woman's left arm, and tenderly placed the necklace in Ansha's palm. "No," Urna said calmly after a deep breath. "My hopes and dreams have been shattered, just like my back. Take it."

"I don't think…" Ansha's words trailed off as she looked over the gem once more. "I think you should keep it."

"Is thats a Wishdrop?" came a raspy, high-pitched, hissing voice from the doorway.

"What's he doing here?" Urna looked to the door, narrowing her bronze gaze upon the kobold. "I said he's too small to have a voice around me."

"I comes looking for the countess," the kobold said sternly, clutching his gnarled staff closely. "Wants to knows when we can leaves this place. I'raha is waitings for us."

"Zakosa," Ansha greeted the kobold, shaking her head at the intrusion of the smaller reptilian creature. "What's a Wishdrop?"

"Powerful magics," the kobold replied quickly, sauntering over towards the countess. "But, it has to be triggered first."

"Yes, you insufferable kobold," Urna grumbled, trying to fall further back into her pillows, "it's a Wishdrop. Extremely rare, extremely powerful, but useless to me now. You keep your slimy hands off it, Short Scale."

"I'm afraid I don't understand," Ansha mentioned, holding the teardrop-shaped cyan gem up to peer at it in the morning light. "What is a Wishdrop?"

Urna cursed through a flash of pain as she tried, and failed, to sit upright once more. Despite the softness of the white robe and the silken sheets covering her black and tan scales, the slithzerkai appeared increasingly uncomfortable, especially with the kobold nearby.

"Short Scale?" Zakosa scoffed, pounding the bottom of his staff against the floor. "You can't even stand up."

"Shut it, kobold," Vourden ordered upon hearing the staff strike the floor. "Behave or be gone."

"Just you wait, Short Scale," Urna grinned, ignoring the pain from her numerous injuries.

"So, what exactly is a Wishdrop?" Ansha asked before the kobold could start his tantrum again.

"They are parts of a meteor that struck Galatiys Peak over three hundred years ago," Urna replied, taking a deep breath to relax her muscles once more. "The rare crystals formed by the meteor are able to hold, and enhance, extremely powerful magical abilities. They are prized by mages, wizards, and necromancers alike; even the divine priests understand their value, but their true worth lies in what happens if they get activated."

The countess shook her head slowly. "I can't do magic. This is useless to me. You really should keep it, Urna."

"If activated," Urna pressed, ignoring the protests of the other woman, "it can grant a single wish, even perform a miracle that would otherwise be unobtainable. Doing so, though, is quite taboo, as it requires a great sacrifice in order to activate the gem's true potential."

"One must be willings to slays a mythic creature," Zakosa added. "Such as a unicorn, dragon, faerie, godling, or an avatar."

"Doing so is no minor feat," Urna continued, "and also considered forbidden to take such a rare life for the sake of personal gain. Unless, of course, you are part of the Onyx Spire."

Vourden set down the snifter and looked about the room for a moment, then turned to the slithzerkai as he spoke. "You say it can grant wishes? Such as bringing back the dead and undoing terrible tragedies?"

Urna nodded slowly. "That would be possible. It's not unheard of. Al'zagur used one to raise the vast majority of his army and gain as much power as he did. Though, he was an avatar, and used his own body as the sacrifice. He basically became a lich through his own greed and lust for power."

"You're going to hold onto it," Vourden appealed, his eyes shifting towards the countess. "We'll find a way to bring back your husband."

Ansha blinked and examined the face of the sheriff for a moment while holding the necklace against her breast. "You think we can do that? Did you not just hear what's required? What about Paisley?"

Vourden sighed and looked at the floor for a moment, before returning the gaze of the countess. "I have Dira, Marle, and Vintru in my life now. I have a family, even if it isn't exactly what I had planned, or who I had planned to be with. You deserve the opportunity to get your husband back, if it's even possible."

"You wills have to kills a mythic creature," Zakosa repeated, stepping closer to the sheriff. "You cans barely fights a darkoyle."

"We're also going to go see a faerie," Vourden said confidently.

"You plans on killing I'raha?" the kobold accused distrustfully.

"No," Ansha answered, pulling the necklace over her head. "We'll ask her to help us get it activated."

Zakosa looked credulously at both the countess and the sheriff. "Then when do we plans on leavings?"

"One week from now," Ansha declared, "even if Lynsia isn't awake. We'll take her with us, either way."

Vourden finished the brandy left in the glass and stood up, glancing out the window he was seated by. "I promised my daughter to get her a bell for her kitten. I should get going. It is good to see you are recovering, Urna."

"Thanks for visiting, Sheriff Leustren," Urna replied with a small smile. "I know we didn't share the same kind of friendship with Dorho, but I see he was truthful when he spoke highly of you."

The sheriff paused near the door to adjust his beret and then threw a knowing grin to the slithzerkai woman over his shoulder. "I will keep your history with the Onyx Spire between us, for now."

Ansha remained by the side of the lizard woman while Zakosa departed the large bedroom with the sheriff. They walked together, past numerous people working to repair the destruction caused by the king's men and the Unnamed Few. Walls had been cracked by arcane magic, even blown open by explosions during the assault, and despite the victory of the defenders, the keep had sustained considerable damage.

It had been a terrible night, almost three weeks before. What was supposed to be a pleasant dinner and warm baths to celebrate Dorho's return with Lynsia, turned into a horror-filled nightmare by the hands of the Onyx Spire and King Borlhauf. The sheriff had just lost his wife, and wasn't in the best of moods, but when the men sent by the tyrant king attacked, everyone was forced to fight. Many lives were lost in the fray, but in the end, Lady Eisley and Elgrahm Hold clutched a decisive victory. Unfortunately, for the defenders, Dorho was slain when a dreadmage pulled him into a blast unleashed by the Sidhe-Vein. To add to the damage done by the invaders, Lynsia had fallen into a coma, Urna's back was smashed, and the throne room was left in crumbling shambles. No one was left unaffected by the attack, and the horrors of that night were still clearly visible around the castle.

Though, not everything was as abysmal as it looked. Losing his wife had been devastating indeed, but the sheriff's son had managed to be saved from her womb. Then there was Kendira and Marle, the woman he had loved years before, and the daughter they had together. They had come back into his life through this damned adventure Vourden found himself dragged into.

As he walked, with the kobold only a few steps behind him, the sheriff found himself wondering what the future would hold.

He didn't consider Kendira his lover, even though they shared a house together now, and they slept in the same bed. Vourden was still trying to process the loss of Paisley, the death of Dorho, the birth of his son, and hadn't put much thought into whatever it was between himself and the bard. Having her around made life easier, and brought a smile to his face, even when grief or stress threatened to conquer his heart. He knew he loved her, but in the same breath, he could just as easily say he didn't. The sheriff knew he would have to figure out his feelings eventually, even if it was just for her sake.

With the attack on the castle, came the declaration of war against King Borlhauf. As the sheriff of Elgrahm Hold, his duties had increased at least tenfold with the official proclamation from Lady Eisley regarding all the king's loyalists still in the region; they had to either support the duchess and her desire for independence, or pack their things and leave hastily. Anyone found waving a red banner with a golden hawk would be detained and questioned. After the brazen assault on Albinasky Keep, an order of "offer no quarter" was given to the soldiers of Elgrahm Hold in regards to anyone found contributing to the king's tyranny.

This all tumbled back onto the quest that had been given to Dorho, and was now being continued by his widow. The sheriff was trying to balance being a family man, on top of his duties to the crown, as well as help with preparations needed to get Lynsia delivered to the faerie in the Faulkendor Mountains. As if the quest wasn't hard enough with being hunted by goons sent by the king, now the Onyx Spire was formally involved, and the land was about to be torn apart in a brutal war for sovereignty.

"We should gets moving soon," Zakosa spoke up, tapping his twisted, skull-capped staff against the stone floor of the castle. "We waits too long already."

For a moment, the sheriff ignored the words of the small, reptilian creature. He wanted nothing more than to get on with the journey himself, but he knew that no one else was prepared to press onward. Everyone needed to grieve and steel themselves for the coming days of war and strife that would curse the lands north of the Free Region.

"I don't—," Zakosa began again.

"Shut it," Vourden snapped, turning on his heels to face the kobold directly as he cut the voice of the smaller creature short. "I have zero reasons to trust you. You conveniently showed up during that fight in the Endless Tomb, and since then, my wife, and my best friend, have both been killed. You did nothing to defend either of them, despite telling us you were sent here to help us. I've seen what your magic could do, and yet, you stood there and did nothing both times. You will respect the wishes and words of Countess Maizen, or may the gods help me that I don't rip your windpipe out with my bare hands. Do I make myself clear?"

The kobold nodded and shrank away from the furious gaze of the sheriff.

"Good," he spat, removing the hand from the hilt of the rapier on his hip. "I don't want to see you in this castle again, kobold."

Without argument, the smaller creature darted down the hall, out of the sight of the sheriff.

After being sure that the kobold had left, Vourden crossed through the wrecked throne room, and headed to the castle's main dining hall. While his feet traced the path Dorho had taken to get back to the dining hall on the night of the attack, the sheriff's mind was plagued with the ghosts of the bodies that had littered the keep's floors from that same night. His hands eventually rested against the heavy wooden doors to the dining chamber, and as he tried to push the horrors of that fateful night from his mind, Vourden shoved his way into the room beyond.

"Daddy!" Marle cheerfully yelled as the sheriff entered the dining hall.

"Is she behaving herself?" Vourden asked, scooping up the small girl as she charged him with a sausage in her right hand.

"As best she can," Lady Eisley responded, a broad smile on her wise face.

The sheriff chuckled and hugged his daughter tightly before setting her down to go finish her breakfast. "Considering who her mother is, I'm shocked she knows how."

Vourden playfully teased the twin tails of his redheaded daughter, and pulled out a chair between the young girl and the blonde noblewoman. Without being asked, one of the castle's servants brought over a plate of grilled sausages, eggs, and buttery biscuits for the sheriff. Using one of the biscuits, the sheriff broke the yolks of his eggs and mixed it into his sausages before taking a hefty bite of the baked bread.

"Since you're joining us for breakfast," Lady Eisley spoke, sipping from a bowl of onyx tea stirred with honey and heavy cream. "We should discuss the plans for the next few days."

03.

Dorho found himself lying in a pool of blackness surrounded by mountains of bones and writhing flesh. Shambling husks that once had been humanoid creatures shuffled among the rolling hills of decaying bodies and lifeless trees. The sky was a lifeless grey hue, like a bored artist had simply slapped a swath of matte silver over the clouds and sun.

Come. Run. Be free. The strange female voice called across the strange land, the words reaching deep into the rogue's mind.

Sitting up, he found that the pain that had swarmed his body for what felt like eons had been nullified. The icy darkness of the shallow pond he woke up in soaked through his ragged clothes easily, sucking away any heat he thought he once had. Feeling uneasy in this unknown, bleak land, Dorho crawled slowly to the edge of the pool, and using one of the many skeletons of the long-dead trees that littered the region, he stood up on shaky knees.

Come. Run. Be free. I've been waiting for you. The whispering voice urged, speaking out from some unseen source in all directions.

"I'm dead," the rogue muttered, looking at his tattered black shirt and blood-stained trousers. "Where am I?"

Come to me. He felt the voice speak within his mind, like it was talking to his very soul.

As he glanced at his reflection in the black water, the rogue shuttered. His skin was battered, torn, and burned horribly. He found his flesh was ghastly pale and the warmth in his body was long gone. Dorho's boots were missing, his beloved wide-brimmed hat was nowhere to be seen, and his rapier had been taken from his waist. In fact, all of his weapons were absent.

The ash-like soil under his feet was firm as he walked, unsure of where to go, as his dark eyes scanned the landscape around the pond. Skulls of countless different creatures littered the ground, along with untold numbers of bones and decaying corpses. One of the stumbling husks of flesh stopped long enough to look over the rogue with empty eyes, opened its mouth as if to scream, then tumbled to the white dirt in a heap.

"Hello?" Dorho found himself asking aloud, not sure who he expected to answer.

Come to me. That same voice, brought up from the deepest parts of the rogue's mind, came once more.

"I don't even know who you are," the man responded, as if he were talking to someone standing next to him.

Come to me, we've danced many times. The whispers commented, the tone taunting the man as he walked.

As if to answer the rogue's unspoken next question, a tower rose in the distance. Built of bones and sinew, it climbed into the emotionless sky like an insult to the gods. Streams of blood formed natural moats around the base of the gigantic structure, while winged, black monstrosities fluttered around the highest peaks. Situated at the highest point of the grisly stronghold, a huge lead coin etched with a jawless skull was embedded in the gore that formed the walls of the terrifying building. From the left socket of the carved lead skull, an enormous red viper wrapped itself around the highest levels of the towering horror.

You know me well. We dance often. Even if we never talk, we have become like lovers. Bound by fate and destined to meet, here you stand in my realm. Come to me. It was as though the voice changed, speaking to Dorho's core from the height of the horrifying spire of bones and entrails.

Despite the uneasiness in his legs, Dorho walked steadily towards the grotesque tower. A bridge made of rotting bodies tied together by their guts floated to the top of the bloodied stream, and after much consideration, the rogue stepped across. Lit by ghostly violet light, a doorway formed from the shifting of bones and lye-stained skin that wrapped around the tower's base.

He hadn't gone far into the tower when the curtain of gore closed behind the rogue, and he found himself standing on a catwalk of massive rib bones and rusted metal bars. No voices called to himself inside the spire, and there was an even greater sense of hopelessness and dread than the land outside. Glowing with a vibrant purple hue, torches mounted into the mouths of various skulls lined the walkway above an enormous well of swirling dark energy.

It was the things at the far end of the catwalk that shocked the rogue most and filled his body with absolute terror like he'd never felt before.

Four pillars of black marble wrapped with rotting muscle climbed into the heights of the tower, and perched atop the pillars was a great dragon. The crimson scales were beyond ancient, while the flesh was decaying to the point that the powerful skeleton of the huge beast was exposed in many places. Vast wings, like clouds of torn leather, moved slowly, creating a steady breeze within the walls of the horrific structure. It was impossibly large, rivaling even the largest trees that Dorho had seen in his travels. Four dead eyes, having long turned white from the lack of life within, pulsed with an enraged red glow briefly upon spotting the rogue.

"Bernard," a woman spoke calmly, sitting upon a throne of skulls under the dragon, "behave yourself. This is an honored guest in my court."

Her hair like bleached ashes, fell like messy silk strands about the woman's shoulders to her waist. Though the left half of her face was covered with a bone-white porcelain mask, the eye the rogue could see was a brilliant shade of red. Lips, painted with the color of rubies, offered a stark contrast to the pale skin of the tall, thin woman. Wings with feathers as black as night folded behind her back as the strange lady gestured for the colossal dragon to calm down. An ebony gown, glittering with specks of what the rogue assumed was amethyst dust, flowed like liquid charcoal over the frail-looking figure of the female upon the gruesome throne.

For a while, Dorho looked at the woman and the dragon he guessed was some kind of pet. The platform, built from what could only be described as a broken iron cage and carpeted with stretched skin, floated at the end of the catwalk in the center of the tower's interior. Below them, in a swirling storm of black clouds and green bolts of lightning, dark energy radiated up to greet the man, making his body feel heavy and tired.

"Kings, prophets, farmers, beggars, thieves, the rich, the poor, the old, the young, men, and even women," the tall woman spoke, her voice calm, deep, and soothing to the ears, "all are welcome and equal in my eyes. Everyone and everything ends up in my Undertow as long as I am patient enough. My only duty is to make sure you are all accounted for in death, just as my sister accounts for you in life."

It wasn't until his dark eyes shifted directly to the woman upon the throne that Dorho spoke up. "Dimorta," he called, his voice almost a whisper. "Goddess of Death, Empress of Decay, Mistress of the Lead Coin, and the Great Equalizer in All Things."

"So," the woman shifted on her throne, then stood up, only a handful of steps from where the rogue stood, "you do know me then?"

"Yes," Dorho sighed, "I've sent numerous souls your way. I don't get it though. I'm dead. I know I'm dead. I felt my body stop. Why am I here? How are we talking?"

"Oh," a dark smile crossed the uncovered half of the woman's young face, "don't think of this as a favor. You've given me plenty of bodies to sort through. You were to be processed into the Undertow just like all the other dead that come my way, but it seems you have potential, and maybe the material world isn't finished with you yet."

"I'm not dead then?" Dorho asked, looking at his ruined body. "Am I dreaming this?"

The goddess laughed and took two steps closer to the rogue. "You are quite dead. Dead and buried. Given your proper funeral rites by a member of my temple, laid to rest, and covered with dirt. You are as dead as the bones that I use to make my throne."

Dorho furrowed his brow in confused frustration, ignoring the fact that a goddess was only a couple steps from him. "I don't understand. Why are we talking? Do you greet everyone?"

As the Goddess of Death drew near, it was clear she was as tall, if not taller, than the rogue himself, and despite her thin appearance, wasn't at all intimidated by his mounting frustration. In fact, the snide grin on her face seemed to only grow wider as she realized the annoyance in the voice of the man standing before her unholy chair.

"I haven't spoken to any of the souls that cross through my realm in almost a thousand years," Dimorta's sultry voice was cool and calm, although the entertained smirk on her face showed her amusement with her guest. "Even Al'zagur failed to be granted a meeting with me, regardless of all his power and prayers. Why are we talking? Because I was asked to keep you here for a while. Your journey on the mortal realm isn't finished yet, but what shape it needs to take has yet to be determined."

"So the gods," Dorho spoke, crossing his arms defensively, "don't know everything? I thought you planned everything out."

"Hardly," Dimorta leaned close, a goblet crafted from a skull and embellished with silver appeared in her right hand out of a cloud of swirling ash. "We gave you creatures free will to see what you would do. We simply rule over the realms beyond your comprehension. It wouldn't be free will if we stepped in and took control in order to make things go as we desire. Although, we do occasionally meddle in the affairs of mortals when we realize things might go badly for your realm as a whole. After all, what good are gods without faithful followers?"

The rogue sighed heavily, and as the pressure of the vile energy from the pit of churning soul-consuming darkness pulled at the weight of his body, he forced himself to remain standing.

"I'm stuck here," Dorho's voice came in a defeated whisper, "in this dead limbo, until you figure out whether or not I'm needed. Am I hearing you correctly?"

Dimorta took a slow drink of the pungent scarlet fluid that filled her goblet as her crimson eye scanned over the figure of the man standing before her. "You're definitely needed. This is that 'meddling in the affairs' I talked about."

"If so, then why me?" Dorho inquired.

The Mistress of the Lead Coin reached out her empty hand, slender pale fingers brushing against Dorho's right cheek with their surprisingly cool, but soft touch. Something in the touch of the goddess made the weight of the pit under her dais release the rogue's body. He no longer felt dismay or revulsion at being in the presence of the deity, nor did he feel upset about being in the realm of the dead. The rogue's body, though shivering slightly at the icy touch of the goddess, no longer felt the heavy pull of the dark energy in the room, and he relaxed considerably.

"It's true," Dimorta commented, leaning her colorless face close to that of the rogue, "I could've kept any of you mortals aside, even your lover, Breja, but the other gods felt that you had the most potential for the quest we are to give you. Let me show you something."

Without warning, the goddess pressed her cold lips to Dorho's in a firm kiss.

The chamber they were in fell away, save for the platform, the throne, and the dragon. Everything became black. In fact, it was blacker than black. The world became so dark around them, that no light escaped beyond the dais. No sound came or went, even when the great dragon shifted its weight upon the mighty pillars of gore.

"This is her realm," Dimorta spoke as she leaned away from the kiss. "This is the Void. Absolute nothing. The end of creation."

"Her realm?" Dorho looked about cautiously, still stunned by the kiss, but not questioning the gesture. "Who's realm?"

"The Forgotten Goddess, Xa'morhu," the Goddess of Death replied. "Some of your scholars know her as the Queen of the Void, the Silent End, or most commonly known as Entropy. She represents the opposite of creation."

The rogue tilted his head, perplexed. "Destruction?"

Dimorta shook her head. "Worse. You can handle destruction. We've seen it. Chaos, destruction, war, other terrible things; you mortals are more than capable of surviving that. The one known as Entropy is simply nothing. When you walk into a room, and forget why you went there, that is but a small fraction of a fraction of her power. She is simply nothing. She erases things from existence. Just as with all things we gods rule over, there must be an opposing force. Us gods, we can create and grant spectacular things. Xa'morhu is the opposite of that. She can rip entire realms asunder with a whim. At least, she can, if she's able to break out of her prison."

"And that's where I come in?" Dorho looked at the face of the goddess. "Why can't you do this yourselves?"

"That is part of the pact we made as gods," she replied. "We created you, gave you free will, and in doing so, we promised to never get directly involved in your realm. If we stepped down to your world, and took care of this problem, your kind would come to rely on it. It would become expected with every problem that came up afterwards. So, we have to put it in your hands to take care of it."

Dorho nodded, not sure he fully understood, but he was grasping the path of the conversation. "So, you need me to do something to stop this goddess from getting out of her prison? I still don't understand why I'm special."

"We could've easily brought back any legendary hero," the goddess responded, letting her gaze explore the bleak nothingness beyond her dais. "That's true. Karthax, Dourmond, Haroad the Blooded; any of them would've worked. So, why you? See, there's the entire task of retrieving a long-dead soul, such as Karthax, giving him a fresh body, and sending him on his way. All I had to do with you, is intercept your soul and prevent you from entering the Undertow for a bit. Your body just needs some help from my livelier sister, and you'll be good to go again. You are already on a legendary quest, with a powerful being gifted with magic that will help you greatly. The tasks you've done, and the things you've survived in your life, are more than proof to us that you are capable of completing this task. That's why we picked you, and by we, I mean me."

"Lynsia?" Dorho asked accusingly. "You would have me use her as a weapon, even after I promised not to let that happen?"

Dimorta paused as she considered the words of the dead mortal standing before her. "The Sidhe-Vein? Yes. Both of them. They have the ability, and the power needed to stop what is coming to your realm."

The rogue blinked. "Both? There's two?"

"Oh, my poor corpse," Dimorta smiled wryly as she turned back towards her throne, "there is much you don't yet understand about the world. Things even you have yet to discover, in spite of your numerous adventures and tales."

When the tall woman took her seat, the nothingness that enveloped the dais faded away, and the gore-filled walls of the tower appeared once more. Though, the spiraling mass of wicked clouds and jade-hued sparks had been replaced with a floor of solid basalt.

"You found love," the goddess spoke, motioning to a spot on the stone floor, and a wraith-like image of Lynsia sleeping appeared.

Soon, another figure appeared next to Lynsia's unconscious body. This one clad in a strange chainmail armor of an unknown reddish-gold metal while the right hand carried a glaive across the man's strong shoulders. Over the armor, a faded orange doublet with a hood was adorned with the crest of a white griffon taking to the sky with a set of golden scales grasped firmly in its talons. Shoulder-length golden hair and honest blue eyes marked the angular face, shaped as though it were chiseled from a mighty stone. From the ghostly image summoned by the goddess, Dorho could guess that the man stood easily several inches taller than himself.

"You need to find temperance," Dimorta added, watching as Dorho carefully studied the image she created.

"Two?" the rogue glanced back to the goddess, still unsure of his feelings in the words of the deity. "I thought they were rare. How can there be two?"

"Clearly, your realm felt it was needed," the lean woman responded. "The last time there were two at the same time, we had to restore your world. Wrath and Pride didn't want to play nicely together."

Dorho sighed and walked around the transparent figures of the two Sidhe-Vein, examining the vision cautiously before he approached the goddess once more.

"You're unsure," Dimorta observed. "You've been plagued by uncertainty throughout your life. Isn't that true?"

"I won't deny it," the rogue answered, feeling no need to hide his thoughts from the goddess. "You are asking me to find a second Sidhe-Vein, and stop the return of Entropy. Which is quite a lot to be asked of someone who is currently dead. I'm lost though, because we've been fighting King Borlhauf and the Onyx Spire. How do they fall into this mess?"

Before the final word could fall from Dorho's lips, the black stone of the floor vanished, replaced by a map of the world, or at least what he suspected was a map. It happened so fast, that the rogue jumped back onto the dais with a start. The images of the two Sidhe-Vein faded from view, as Dorho steadied himself with the great map of the world spread out around the platform. The ominous obelisk known as the Onyx Spire arose from a frosty coastline near the bleached skin entrance to the dreadful tower.

"What do you know of the Onyx Spire?" Dimorta questioned inquisitively. "You've had several chances to learn about them. Surely you must know something."

Dorho nodded, looking at the jagged black spike on the sprawling map. "It's a school, archive, laboratory, and home for evil mages and dark priests. They practice and promote necromancy, destruction, and profane things. They believe in dominating others through fear, pain, and loss. That is what I know of them."

"Considering your level of understanding," Dimorta proclaimed with a knowing smile, "you are correct. Most of the residents of the Spire have placed several of us gods on high, myself included. Those gods that you mortals would consider unholy or vile, are revered as saints and parental figures to many of those that seek out the Onyx Spire. This gives us a special insight into the plots and schemes hatched within those black walls."

"Are you going to share any of that insight with me?" Dorho inquired, his frustration floating to his voice once more.

The goddess shook her head and let out a small giggle. "Not at all. Doing so would be imparting divine knowledge onto you. As I said before, part of the agreement with giving your realm free will, was that we were to stand back and see what you mortals did with it. This is a situation where your realm is in grave danger, but we must keep our distance and let your kind figure out the solution. I am merely giving you a nudge in the right direction."

"That doesn't help me at all," the rogue furrowed his brow. "I don't know where to look for this second Sidhe-Vein, and I'm dead anyway; I don't see where I'm capable of helping much."

The goddess waved her empty hand dismissively at the dead man as she responded. "And I plan on helping with some of that. I've already kept you from falling into the Undertow. Several of us gods have put aside our quarrels to ensure you get set on the right path."

"What about the other gods and goddesses?" Dorho asked, looking over the map that formed the floor of the great chamber. "Why are you the messenger? Did I really have to die to have this talk?"

"Your death was part of that free will thing," Dimorta answered uncaringly. "What happened, happened because you mortals were allowed to act without plans and guidance from us gods. The others would love to talk to you, but you arrived here first. My home isn't exactly their favorite place to visit, so for now, you are stuck dealing with me."

A thick, white mist seemed to rise from the floor to the right of Dorho, causing the man to step away in alarm. Like a spark of lightning, a brilliant white light exploded from the core of the dense column of alabaster clouds. As the rogue's eyes recovered from the bright flash, an orb of soft white light flickered in the center of the fog.

"I guess we're no longer alone, my sweet corpse," Dimorta's relaxed voice called from the throne, letting out a bothersome sigh.

Startling the rogue, the mist was quickly sucked into the glowing orb, and another burst of light flooded the grisly chamber. Standing where the mist once hovered, a tall, curvy woman with golden-blonde hair appeared. Her skin, unlike Dimorta, was warm with life and even slightly tanned, while two eyes colored like opals gazed upon the figure of the rogue. A long dress of white satin, tinted with a hint of pale blue, hung loosely over the voluptuous body of the strange woman. From runes carved into the palms of the woman, blood flowed down her fingers and dripped slowly onto the surface of Dimorta's dais, though any pain this caused was invisible upon the welcoming face framed by long blonde locks.

"Dearest sister Dimorta," the woman's warm voice came like a mother's embrace to the ears of the rogue, "you were supposed to make me aware when the hero arrived."

"I was enjoying the company," Dimorta replied in a cold tone, narrowing her gaze slightly. "Not often I get mortals to talk to. I even got to kiss this one before you steal him from me."

"Typical of you, sister," the blonde woman smiled playfully, "giving away your blessing before I can show up to give mine."

"Atheia?" Dorho asked, glancing from the Goddess of Death to the strange woman near him.

A comforting smile crossed the face of the blonde-haired woman as she bowed slightly. "The Matron Saint of Healing, the Lady of Life, the Holy Mother of the Body, and the Grand Queen of Hope. You mortals have given me many titles, all of which are quite cherished."

"This means that my beloved meeting with you," Dimorta spoke calmly as she offered a small smile to the rogue, "has come to an end. Hopefully it will be many more years before I see your soul cross my realm once more."

"Once more?" Dorho messed up his face in further confusion at the words of the deity. "I thought I was dead. Dead and buried, as you so kindly put it."

"You are," Atheia replied before her sister could form the words. "Quite dead, actually. Thankfully, your body still has traces of my power coursing through it, and a medallion blessed by one of my priestesses around your neck. Know that as I take a soul from my sister, she will one day come for her equivalent exchange."

"You're sending me back?" Dorho inquired, uncertainty and a hint of anxiety in his tone. "An equivalent exchange? What do you plan on taking from me for this?"

Dimorta shrugged and took a long drink from her bony goblet. "I will decide when the time comes. Just do me a favor, stay out of my throne room until then."

Atheia placed a bloodied palm to the wrecked chest of the rogue and a deep warmth welled up from within Dorho's body. While crimson fluid began to spill from his open wounds, the damage to his body began to heal. Horrific burns were turned into healthy flesh, deep cuts sealed themselves as if pulled together by unseen thread, and battered skin returned to the normal sun-weathered color. Dorho felt no pain, only the flowing of heat and kindness through his entire body as the power of the goddess worked to undo all the injuries he had sustained.

"Blessed by divine light," the Goddess of Life chanted softly, "I take what was once death, and return it to life. A soul lost, becomes a soul reborn. From this tower of doom, I send you back to the sun's light once more."

A hot wind ripped through the gore-filled tower, and the eyes of the rogue were filled with a friendly light. He felt his body lift into the air, and in an instant, the touch of Atheia was gone. As soon as her hand left his chest, Dorho tumbled to the ground once more, landing on his rear and collapsing to his back in a twitching heap. He coughed and gagged, his lungs feeling like he had been held underwater for hours, while the glow of the goddess's powers faded from his vision.

Damn. He was kind of cute, too. Dimorta's voice echoed from the depths of the rogue's mind as he struggled to his hands and knees.

Adjusting to his surroundings, Dorho's dark eyes focused finally on the soil under his fingers, while his lungs took a deep breath of the dry air. It was night, wherever he was, though he sensed he wasn't in Ameribelle. His clothes were still tattered, his pants stained with blood, his boots were gone, and his weapons were still missing, but he knew he was alive. He couldn't explain it in his own mind, but he knew he had died and was returned to life. As he was struck by another coughing fit, he felt tears fall from his cheeks, brought on by a mixture of joy, anger, and sorrow. He was happy to be alive, enraged at those who had killed him, and distraught by the knowledge he had let Ansha and Lynsia down. His fingers grabbed at the dark soil under him, as if to make sure it was real, and not just an illusion.

"Oh!" the voice of a young woman reached the ears of the rogue as he clenched his fingers into the dirt under his hands. "I almost didn't see you there."

Dorho turned gingerly and sat up to face the speaker, breathing deeply the warm air that assailed his restored body. Something tumbled from his neck, and he recognized it immediately as the medallion given to him by the healers in Merciapola. The polished metal glinted with an opal-like rainbow of faint colors, though the ribbon that once held it looked as though it had been frayed long ago. He guessed it must've been damaged during the assault of magic in the throne room. Dorho glanced up to the mysterious voice while clutching the loose token in his hands protectively.

"You're..." a young woman said, though her voice trailed off, her blue eyes were only a few inches from Dorho's face as she reached out with concern in her gestures.

The revived rogue blinked, unsure if he was seeing an illusion or something else. "You," he managed to say cautiously. "Have we met before?"

Like a waterfall of gold, her blonde locks fluttered in the movements of the young woman as she stepped away slowly. "I'll get my father, hold still," her voice was gentle, but assertive.

Before Dorho could speak again, she was gone, having dashed away to where an older man was enjoying a beverage on the patio of an old farmhouse. The rogue watched, but was able to hear them, as the two conversed briefly. He tried standing up, but quickly dropped to his seated position once more as the woman darted into the house and the man stood up on the patio.

"Are," the man called over to the rogue, walking slowly to where Dorho sat in the field, "you alright? Where did you come from?"

The rogue took a deep breath, trying to reverse the tears that threatened to spill down his cheeks. "I honestly don't know," he said after some time to think it over.

"What happened?" the older man asked, his attire suggesting he was a farmer or field worker. "You look like you've been dragged through hell."

"I," Dorho finally spoke, wiping the tears from his eyes with the ruined sleeves of his black shirt. "I can't explain. I hardly know myself. I'm just glad to be here."

His dark eyes scanned the landscape, failing to see anything he immediately recognized. Dorho was sitting in a field of grain under a freshly risen summer moon. In the west, aspen trees and cottonwoods lined a river that snaked among the low hills. An expansive farmhouse and barn sat just west of the reincarnated rogue, with two children helping a woman who was tending to evening chores. To the north and east were mountains of granite painted with forests of evergreens. A town sprawled out along the base of the nearest tree-lined behemoth, the white buildings peeking out from between the clusters of pines.

"Talking about here," Dorho looked back at the farmer as he was helped to his feet. "Where am I?"

"Kourinthe, in the kingdom of Anslater," the old farmer responded with a worrisome smile.

Dorho shook his head and let out a small laugh in disbelief. "I must've misheard you. I think you just said that this is the duchy of Kourinthe in the kingdom of Anslater. That's not possible."

The farmer nodded, allowing the rogue to use his shoulder to steady himself. "I don't know where you're from, stranger, but that's Petiora over there," his weathered left hand gestured to the town tucked behind the pine trees. "So, welcome to Kourinthe."

"Considering I started out in Elgrahm Hold," the rogue spoke, rubbing his weary eyes that felt like they were caked with dust, "I would say my carriage driver is a bit lost, but I'm not about to start questioning their logic."

"I didn't see a carriage come by," the older man stated, his tone reflecting his troubled confusion, "but if you came from Elgrahm Hold, you are a long ways from home, stranger. Though, that may be for the best, since King Borlhauf is preparing to wage a vicious war against the fair lady of the region. At least it's distracting him from attacking us outright."

Dorho nodded, wondering how many days, weeks, or even months had passed since he fell into the blackness of death. He found himself wanting to figure out about his wife and child, hoping they were doing well without him since his departure. His mind also thought about his conversation with Dimorta, her words still echoing like faint explosions in his head, and as confused as he was about the location of his resurrection, he knew there was a reason behind it. Even if it took him from his home and family.

He had also been relieved of all his items, other than the mistreated clothing he had woken up with. Including his coin purse.

"That's Petiora, correct?" Dorho asked, finally feeling the full strength returning to his legs as he stretched his calves and knees.

"Yes," answered the farmer quickly, "but you look like you've been beaten and dragged through the very bowels of the Undertow. Why don't you at least clean up? You can borrow the loft in our barn if you need to. Corina should be back soon. She's blessed with a healer's touch. She can make sure you're not injured."

The rogue forced a smile to spread across his frustrated face. "Thank you for the offer of kindness. I would enjoy a quick bath, though I think I've gotten enough rest to last me weeks."

"I only ask that you repay our kindness someday," the older man patted the shoulder of the rogue in a welcoming manner. "I didn't happen to catch your name, stranger."

"It's Dorho," the rogue replied after a moment to look over the farm. "Count Dorho Maizen from Golden Bow Gulch. It looks like I'm a long way from home. I can only assume I was beaten and robbed during my travels."

"It's an honor to meet you, Count Maizen, despite your unfortunate circumstances," the farmer greeted him with a handshake. "Even if your arrival is perplexing and unexpected, I welcome you to stay at my farm until you figure out how to get home. I am Jonsal Knepiri, owner of Knepiri Brewery and Farm."

Dorho shook the man's hand firmly, offering an honest smile despite the confusion and anxiety that stirred in his core. "It's a pleasure to meet you."

"What brings a noble from Elgrahm Hold to dusty little Petiora?" Jonsal inquired, produced a pipe made of brass and antler from his vest pocket.

The rogue watched as the man pulled a mixture of tobacco and herbs from a soft leather pouch to pack the pipe before Jonsal put the brass end between his lips.

"I'm looking for someone," Dorho answered finally, glancing towards the buildings hidden in the distant trees.

04.

Stretching slowly, Vourden woke up quietly, his eyes turning to the figure of Kendira still sleeping with her head on the pillow next to his. He smiled, his green eyes exploring the beauty of her cinnamon-hued face in the dim light of the early morning. Carefully, not wanting to disturb her peaceful slumber, the sheriff brushed his right hand along the warm softness of her cheek.

"It's too early," the bard whispered, her voice low, while her emerald eyes only opened long enough to throw him a fond smile.

It had been four days since his first visit with Urna, and life felt like it was gradually returning to normal around the city of Ameribelle. He had fully returned to his duties as sheriff, and even took on some of the duties of the court arbiter, given the previous one had been murdered by the Onyx Spire. This kept him busy tending to the legal concerns of the people in Elgrahm Hold, which gave him little time to dwell on painful memories. With the declaration of war against the king, most of Vourden's day was spent deciding who was, or wasn't allowed to remain in the region, and who was to be interrogated by court officials.

"I'm sorry," Vourden spoke gently, pressing a swift kiss to the woman's forehead as his fingers danced along her long ebony braids. "I couldn't sleep any longer."

With a small yawn and a sly grin, Kendira curled up against his chest, her arms snaking around his sides firmly. "Then just hold me for a while. At least until the sun comes up," she purred sleepily.

"Or until Marle wakes up," the sheriff joked.

Kendira stifled a small laugh and kissed his bare chest. "Luckily the wet-nurse helps keep an eye on Vintru, or else we'd be waking up whenever he wants to feed."

"Without you," Vourden put his arms around the shoulders of the bard as he spoke, "I don't think I could've kept him at home. I was doing barely enough to care for myself after losing Paisley."

She bit his skin quickly, and rather harshly. "You weren't even taking care of yourself. You were becoming an empty shell of your former self. You would've drank yourself to death if I hadn't decided to check on you."

The sheriff grimaced from the sharp attack to his chest, but let it go. She was right. After the attack on the castle and burying the people he knew, he had retreated to his home to drink and sleep away his sorrow. Vourden had been fine with the idea of simply being forgotten and fading away from the living world, but then Kendira showed up one morning to feed him breakfast. She had dumped out all his booze and brought his daughter to see him in an attempt to pull him out of his bleak depression. He couldn't lie, he was still pretty upset over everything that had happened, but the presence of the bard, their daughter, and their son made things feel lighter on his mind.

She wasn't his actual mother, but the bard had taken to Vintru like she was. Kendira took care of everything that the wet-nurse that lived with them couldn't. Though the boy had to be removed from the womb of the sheriff's dying wife, Kendira still helped bathe the infant, made sure he had a decent bed and ample blankets, she even packed him around in a wrap bound to her chest frequently.

After the loss of Paisley, and the assault on the castle, Vourden had lost the will to keep himself going. He didn't have the energy or ability to care for his newborn son, either. It was the bard that stepped up to help him find himself once more, and became a doting mother to a child not even born from her body. Vourden had never asked her to do so, the woman just did. The bard took it upon herself to help the sheriff heal, while tending to the needs of his son, and for that, Vourden was deeply grateful.

As the emotions swelled up inside his body, and tears of grief and self-loathing formed upon his face, the sheriff pulled the bard firmly against his chest. He had left Kendira and Marle many years ago, wanting to carve more glory and gold for himself from the life he lived. His travels landed him in Ameribelle, where he joined the royal court of Lady Eisley, and eventually got installed as the sheriff over all of Elgrahm Hold. Then Paisley ended up in his life, a brief fling from years prior became his wife, and ultimately fell pregnant with Vintru. He had given up a good woman and a beautiful daughter for selfish desires, and after his world came crashing down around him, Kendira and Marle found him wallowing in a pit of despair.

"I'm sorry," he wept, feeling the bard's warm breath against the skin of his chest. "I should've been a better man to you when you needed it most."

There was no hesitation from the body of the bard as she pressed a loving kiss to Vourden's lips. "I'm sorry you had to lose so much to find your way back home," she spoke with a comforting whisper.

"No," he sighed heavily, looking into the concerned green eyes of Kendira as he spoke, "I honestly don't deserve your kindness. I sure as hell don't deserve your love, or even having you and Marle back in my life."

For a moment, the woman said nothing, letting her body rest against the sheriff's torso. "You're right," she agreed. "You don't deserve it. After abandoning us before, I should be furious with you, but I couldn't sit back and watch you and your son suffer. I'm not like that, and you know that. Deep down, I know you're a good man, and Vintru didn't ask for what happened to his mother. So, here I am, and I brought your daughter back to you. Look at what you have now, and don't make the same mistake again, because my mother thinks I'm insane for returning to your side."

"To be fair and honest, I would completely understand if you left me for someone who was kinder to you."

"Like who?" the bard asked accusingly, narrowing her gaze slightly. "I haven't been with anyone since you left."

Vourden paused and blinked at her words. "What do you mean, surely—."

"No one, not even a drunken fling," Kendira cut him short. "Well, not with a man, at least. I can't forget about Lyn, my sweet birdy who sleeps."

The man sighed and stared at the ceiling over their bed for a short while. "What are you going to tell her, when she wakes up?"

"Tell her what?" Kendira inquired, straddling his waist as she peered into his own green eyes. "That you and I are together? That I love you, just as I love her? That I care for you, just as much as I care for her? I think she will understand."

Gently, Vourden placed his hands upon the hips of the bard as she sat on his thighs. "What does Marle think? Have you told her about Lynsia yet?"

The bard wiggled slightly into the touch of the sheriff as she leaned down to deliver a swift, but fond, kiss to his lips. "She likes having her father back. She's been very excited with you spending time with her. As far as the sweet birdy is concerned when it comes to our daughter, I've explained it the best I can for her young mind. I've taken her to meet Lyn a couple times, and Marle thinks of her as an older sister, and hopes she wakes up soon so they can play."

Her body was lean, but strong and graceful, typical for a woman who sang and danced for a living. Kendira's cinnamon-hued skin and long dark hair were seen as exotic in the lands north of the Free Region, as her family originally hailed from the deserts of Ela Warein, in the furthest south eastern reaches of the Kingdom of Anslater. Her parents were from the Anaro'rihk Tribe, a group of gypsies and merchants who traversed the unforgiving lands mining, foraging, salvaging, and hoarding any precious material they could get their hands on. The bard's father had used the wealth he collected over his travels to buy a house and start a school for entertainers in Gallow-Frau Bay, moving his wife and newborn daughter to the city by the sea once the home and business was secured. It was the history that Vourden knew, either from talking with Kendira herself, or visiting with her family before Marle was born.

She was a skilled bard, and a prized, seductive thespian to those who knew her best. Vourden was familiar with her love of writing fantastic tales and poems, if only to use them as inspiration for her next performance. For as long he had known Kendira, he knew she gained her thrills by being adored by those around her, and enjoyed nothing more than some good music and friendly company. Morally, she was often open to new ideas and exploring new things, but her personal convictions were as solid as stone. She was open and honest with her feelings, and stayed true to who she was, no matter what others might ask of her. It was why Vourden had fallen for her years ago. Her body was worth every ounce of the lust it provoked in others, but her true beauty came from her sincerity and love of life.

Thinking of his history with the bard, Vourden's thoughts turned to his own past, and what brought the dancer into his life.

Vourden had been born in the coastal lands near Port Helmglen. His father was from a long line of carpenters and his mother was the timid daughter of a soldier. Despite the words of his father, Vourden followed the lineage from his mother's side, and sought out a life carrying a sword for king and country. He enlisted in the Thornbror Navy, specifically the defense unit known as the Sunsetter Brigade. They patrolled the waves looking for threats to the harbors of the kingdom.

It was during one of these routine patrols, that his life changed forever. He was serving aboard the Dragonstar, a galleon designed for search and destroy missions. A fisherman, who had seduced the captain's wife, and his crew were working out near the Trestlestorm Archipelago when the captain ordered the sailors to attack. He said the fisherman and the crew had failed to pay harbor entrance fees for a while, and they were to capture the ship as payment. When the soldiers aboard the Dragonstar discovered the truth behind the bloody assault on the fishermen, they mutinied against the abuse of authority. The remaining crew were branded as pirates, and they took the Dragonstar as their home upon the water.

They raided villages and looted ships contracted or owned by the kingdom to keep the larders full and fill their pockets with coins. The pirates of the Dragonstar would hide in Port Del'ago in the Free Region when the naval heat got a little too high on the waves, or when they needed a break from life on the seas. When Captain Parker of the Rockhelm Fleet tracked the Dragonstar down, the fight was brutal and claimed the lives of many. With their galleon sinking and aflame, the last twelve men of the Dragonstar limped the ship to shore and grounded her into the sandy beaches north of Gallow-Frau Bay. While the king's men were quick to pursue them, Vourden and the others fled into the forest and split up. The next few weeks were terrible as his last few friends were captured or killed, and he was forced to head to Kaenaan.

It was in Kaenaan that Vourden would train with the rogues and bandits of the land, honing his skills with a sword to ensure he would be able to defend himself against the king's men in the future. He met Dorho here, trained with the younger man, and even went with him on a number of contracts when the rogue needed an additional sword by his side. It was also where he first met Kendira.

The duo had just finished borrowing some valuables from a noble near Goldenveil who was harassing and abusing several farmers for their grain while refusing to pay them for the resources he took. After breaking the noble's knees, burning his house to the ground, and handing the borrowed treasured to the angry farmers, Vourden and Dorho used a troupe of traveling bards to get back to the Free Region. Among the thespians, there was a gorgeous girl with skin like cinnamon and eyes like emeralds. She danced and swayed with the music every night, and as much as the men cheered and tossed their coins to the girl, she wouldn't even give them the slightest touch. Vourden had seen many lovely women in his life, been with several that were decent in bed, but he knew there was something different about this exotic beauty dancing around the nightly fires.

Kendira wasn't desperate for attention or looking for a quick roll in the bedding of a tent. He had to have her in his life, every inch of his body and soul demanded it. Rather than hoot and holler with the other men, he would make it a point to talk to her during the day. She acted like it was nothing, and it truly was just friendly chatter while Vourden sought to learn about her further. The exotic girl would write things about his stories from living on the sea, while he would absorb tales about her joy of singing and dancing. Eventually, they made it to Kaenaan, and after a night of drinks and good food, Vourden was surprised when Kendira went with him to his bed. From that point onward, Vourden did what he could to spend time with his lover whenever his travels intersected with the bard's travels.

There was no one else in his world, it was just him and the bard, though he wanted to be more than just a sword-for-hire in the Free Region. It was that desire for finding something more that would eventually be the downfall of their relationship. She got pregnant, retired from traveling, and they began living together at her parents' school in Gallow-Frau Bay. After spending his youth on the seas, and his early adult life as a bandit, Vourden found it hard to settle down and just be a family man. It was only a couple months after Marle was born that he departed for Elgrahm Hold on a journey with Dorho. They broke up a bandit camp that was pestering sailors that used the river to reach Ameribelle, which gained the duo the attention of Lady Eisley and her court. Vourden stayed behind, telling the rogue he wanted to do some more work with Lady Eisley before heading home.

Only, he never went home. He made Ameribelle his home. He ended up in a role that allowed him to use his skills as a soldier and knowledge of a pirate to the benefit of others, while gaining fame and wealth on behalf of Elgrahm Hold. He intended to go back to Kendira and Marle, but he found himself busy with the rewarding work he enjoyed.

"I love you," he whispered as the thoughts of his past played in his mind, his hands moving up along the sides of the bard delicately, "and I'm so sorry for all the hurt I caused you. You meant the world to me, and I let myself get distracted from what was right in front of me."

"I'm not letting you go this time," Kendira smiled warmly, putting her hands on his exposed chest.

Vourden sighed and just let his eyes explore the body of the woman sitting on his lap. "You're going to have to," he replied softly. "Lady Eisley won't like it if I skip my duties to stay in bed with you."

"Do you want me to cook you a breakfast before you go?" the bard asked, shifting her weight as she moved to let him sit up.

The sheriff shook his head. "No. Don't worry about it. I will grab something from the market when I get hungry. Get some more rest before the children wake up."

"Only if you're certain," Kendira replied, kissing his cheek before laying back down.

Vourden nodded as he rose from the bed, gathering his clothes that had been discarded upon the floor. A dark green tunic, trousers the color of charred silver, and dark heavy boots all found their way onto his body as the sheriff moved about the room slowly. He fetched the scalloped rapier and his pale green tabard from the armoire, as he did every morning. The sheriff gave himself a quick glance in the old mirror to straighten his clothes and check his mess of short red hair before heading towards the bedroom door.

"Oh, my dear man?" came the seductive voice from the bed.

Vourden turned to Kendira and threw her a curious smile. "Yes?"

"I love you," she added. "Even if I hate what you did to me, I do love you. Don't forget that."

For a moment, Vourden paused by the door, thinking of what to say or do as he watched the bard in the bed. He then crossed the floor between the door and the bed, put his hands on the cheeks of the cinnamon-skinned woman, and kissed her deeply. It felt like hours passed by as he held her in that profoundly passionate embrace, their lips dancing together fondly.

"You should get to work," Kendira finally spoke, taking a deep breath as she broke away from the intense kiss. "Or else I'm going to tear those clothes off you again."

Vourden let a small chuckle escape his lips before he pulled away from the beauty of his lover and left the bedroom. He stepped into the hallway and then approached the very next door along the same wall. The sheriff peeked into the second bedroom, checking on Marle briefly with a warm smile. She was sleeping soundly, wrapped up in her favorite quilt with the tiny orange kitten curled up next to her little legs. Due to his selfishness, he had missed almost six years of her life, and he couldn't believe that she was now in his house in Ameribelle. Vourden was determined to not let her go again.

He slipped from the doorway and down the stairs quietly. His pale green beret awaited him on a hook by the main door to the house, and he snatched it on his way out. While the sheriff adjusted the cap on his head, his feet carried him out into the city of Ameribelle, meanwhile the sun began to peek over the distant hills. A decent number of clouds gathered in the sky overhead, signaling the potential for the day to turn into a wet mess before it ended.

"Horrace," Vourden greeted the shopkeeper as he picked up a trio of peppery fish skewers, "looks like it might rain."

"Good morning, sheriff," the older man replied with a cheerful smile. "Then you best hurry up and eat those fish, they might swim away in wet weather."

The sheriff paid the man with a cluster of small bronze tiles and grinned. "If it gets too wet, don't spend too much time out here. I would hate it if my favorite cook fell ill."

"Just don't tell that dark-haired beauty I'm your favorite," Horrace chuckled.

"She's also much more expensive than you are," Vourden smirked.

From behind Vourden's left side, a hand reached over and yanked two of the fish skewers from his grip. Reacting to the surprise, the sheriff turned instantly on his heels and moved to snatch back his breakfast.

"What? You should be excited to see me," the catfolk spoke with a grin, devouring one of the fish skewers with no hesitation, his expression ignoring the lunge from the sheriff.

"Lor…" Vourden felt a smile cross his face as he tilted his head. "Lorvin? What are you doing here? Aren't you supposed to be in prison?"

The feline man laughed and tapped the remaining skewer against the forehead of the sheriff. "I got bored of sitting and waiting for you to rescue me. Then I heard you were having fun up here without me, so I decided to check out of Artinburg Castle and come see what you were doing."

"I assure you, it's not been fun," Vourden put a hand on the shoulder of the catfolk as he spoke.

"You are stirring up a war with the king," Lorvin commented before taking a hefty bite of the second fish. "Sounds better than resting in a prison cell in Goldenveil."

Vourden placed a few more of the bronze coins on the food stall's counter before taking two more of the roasted fish skewers. He pondered what all to tell the catfolk as they walked away from the market, and almost out of instinct, the sheriff turned towards the graveyard near the temple of Dimorta. The fish was roasted in a salted mixture of onions and garlic, and dusted with fragrant spices, but the food helped wake the man up as he walked through the city.

"It's been a while since we last met, cat," the sheriff admitted, taking a deep breath. "We've dug ourselves into quite a bit of trouble here, north of the Free Region. Lady Eisley has decided to make a bid for Elgrahm Hold's independence from the king's rule. We were attacked by soldiers sent by the king, but they were repelled."

"What aren't you telling me?" Lorvin chuckled, finishing the second fish hungrily. "I can tell when someone isn't being completely honest with me."

The sheriff sighed and stopped at the gate of the cemetery, his green eyes looking at the mixture of black and silver fur of Lorvin's feline face. "Dorho was killed," he confessed. "You didn't exactly come at a great time."

"Dorho?" the catfolk spoke in disbelief. "Like, Dorho, the Lord of Rogues? The man that threatened to sell my fur if I interrupted another fishing trip?"

Vourden nodded, then stepped into the cemetery, following the narrow path of gravel that snaked around the temple's property. With the feline man only a few steps behind him, the sheriff wandered over to an area in the rear of the burial grounds, then abruptly stopped.

As they looked upon the soil where the rogue had been laid to rest, Vourden's eyes narrowed in frustration. Normally, a golden token featuring the sigil of Dimorta was placed at the top of the gravestone, but it was missing. Nothing appeared out of place, but each token was forged unique to each body. Under the jawless skull of the goddess of death, there was an inscription featuring the name, title, and date of passing of the deceased. The temple of Dimorta called it a Passage Penny, and it was supposed to be an offering that the soul of the departed would arrive in the Undertow unmolested.

"So, it's true," Lorvin stepped closer to the vandalized grave, kneeling down to put a hand on the polished white stone. "Dorho is dead and buried. You didn't lie to me."

"I would never lie about such a thing," Vourden commented, "but who took his coin?"

"Someone with a strong dislike of our friend?" Lorvin offered, standing up slowly, brushing his hands over his ragged tunic and pants. "We all had our fair share of enemies."

"We've made some special enemies lately," Vourden stated firmly, turning his gaze from the coinless tombstone, to the escaped prisoner. "You might be best off not getting involved in this adventure, cat."

The feline man snickered ominously. "And do what? Go back to jail? Clearly, if something can attack Ameribelle and kill our brave friend here, you need all the help you can get. I'm staying."

"Since you haven't changed at all," the sheriff sighed finally, "you might as well come with me. I need to ask the temple workers about this."

Before leaving the graveyard, the sheriff stopped by Paisley's tombstone and whispered a soft prayer for the soul of his deceased wife.

"Your wife too?" Lorvin inquired, furrowing his brow as he listened to the prayer of the sheriff. "Did the same enemies do this? I'm so very sorry for your loss, my friend."

Vourden nodded as he stood up from kneeling next to the carved marble marker. "The very same enemies. Many good people lost their lives in the attack. Our friend started out thinking he was on a simple quest, but ended up pulling the wrath of King Borlhauf and the Onyx Spire onto his head. Unfortunately, I, Kendira, and Dorho's wife got involved as well."

The catfolk's face turned grim as he understood the darkness that fell upon his friends. "I am sorry I couldn't come to your aid sooner, Vourden. How is Kendira doing? Last I heard from her, she had a daughter and was living in Gallow-Frau Bay, and she hated you to no end."

"Yes, we have a daughter," the sheriff answered, continuing his path to the temple, "and a son. She still hates me, but we're working through it."

Lorvin managed a small smile as he walked next to the sheriff, his silvery eyes glancing around the graveyard with each step. "A son and a daughter? That is great news, my friend. One should cherish such things. It seems I have missed much since my last visit to your city."

"To be fair," Vourden almost chuckled, "you have been literally living under a rock since you got arrested. Before that, you were a hermit in the woods."

"Indeed," the catfolk grinned. "That is true."

The sheriff opened the black iron doors of the Mortalis Sanctum, the temple dedicated to the goddess Dimorta and her authority over death and the Undertow. Crystals emitting a soft violet glow lined the walls of the dark stone temple, throwing their dim light over the gloomy interior. An altar of white marble sat at the far end of the main chamber, resting at the foot of a tower of obsidian. A red cloth had been draped over the altar, marked with the half skull sigil of the Empress of Decay. Dressed in robes of crimson, violet, and black, priests and priestesses scurried about silently, like wraiths in the dim purple light.

"Sheriff," a young priestess greeted, her face hidden behind a white porcelain mask. "Is there anything you need this morning?"

Vourden gestured in the direction of the graveyard as he spoke, "someone vandalized Dorho Maizen's stone. I was wondering if the temple might know about it."

"One of the markers was vandalized?" the young priestess tilted her head, before glancing at the other temple workers who moved about soundlessly.

"Yes, I was out showing Lorvin where our friend was buried," the sheriff added, "and the Passage Penny has been stolen."

The priestess shook her head and sighed. "The token is gone? Those are only to be removed if the body is removed. I'm sorry. No one has spoken of such things. So, this is the first I have heard of it. Would you like to speak to our Anam Cara? He might know more than I do."

Vourden shook his head and dismissively waved his right hand. "I would not trouble him with such things, but if someone wouldn't mind looking into this matter, that would be appreciated."

From behind the ivory mask, the young woman's voice came with a hint of anxiety. "I will definitely have someone look into this for you. I would hate to think we have such disrespectful people living in this city."

As the young priestess hurried to go talk with one of her superiors, the sheriff departed the temple with Lorvin only a few steps behind him. They strolled back towards the market district while the sun climbed steadily higher into the sky.

"You don't want to stay and investigate?" Lorvin asked, glancing back towards the temple.

"I would prefer to talk to the Anam Cara in person, but alas, I have other work to do today," Vourden admitted. "Especially since a certain naetari came to Ameribelle, and I'm only going to assume he brought Kortyx with him."

The catfolk laughed. "You remember her! My sweet Kortyx has missed you."

"Hopefully you didn't bring her to the city," the sheriff said hopefully.

"How else was I supposed to get here?" Lorvin tilted his head as he replied. "Traveling by wyvern is the best. You should try it."

"I did try it," Vourden shook his head in disbelief. "I still get sick thinking of the experience. So, should I expect to hear about a wyvern eating pets and cattle, or is Kortyx going to behave herself?"

"I left her in the care of the Chaugnah temple," Lorvin smiled confidently as he answered. "So she'll be well cared for until I need to leave."

"Which you should do soon," Vourden spoke, halfway hoping the naetari took him seriously. "Like I said earlier, we're dealing with a joint threat from both the Onyx Spire and King Borlhauf. I don't know if I can promise to keep everyone alive through this. Dorho made that promise, and look what happened to him."

"I terminated my residency in Goldenveil to come help you," Lorvin stated, his voice firm and cool. "You're stuck with me."

For a moment, Vourden said nothing. He pursed his lips in frustration, but none of it was truly aimed at the naetari man. The sheriff wanted to tell Lorvin to simply leave and go be safe, but he knew it would fall on deaf ears. Vourden had known the cat long enough to realize he was far too sane to comprehend the goals of the silver-furred creature, nor was he stubborn enough to get through the iron will of Lorvin's mind.

"You should at least get something better to wear," the sheriff finally commented, glancing over the ragged prison attire of the other man. "I'm guessing you didn't think to pack your wallet when you left, correct?"

Lorvin shook his head and chuckled deeply. "I don't carry money," he answered with a poised smile. "I am a simple monk of the land. Money has no wealth in my life."

"Then," Vourden sighed as his green eyes drifted over the different shops in the market district, "it's up to me to make sure you don't look homeless when we get to the castle. At least you're cheap, when compared to Kendira."

With the naetari behind him, Vourden walked through the market to a broad store with a battered crimson sign over the main entrance. Upon the sign, a golden shield with a black bear was painted, which swayed slightly in the morning breeze off the river. Pushing through the dark oak door, the scent of amaranth and saffron assailed the nose of the sheriff as rows of different racks and shelves containing cloth and trinkets from all over the world. Grains and beans, mostly imported from ships traveling along the river, were held in old barrels along the far wall. Arranged carefully in boxes under the front window, satchels of dried spices and herbs sat, waiting to be bought and taken home to be put into amazing dishes. On hooks and shelves, hung various clothes and hats, some locally made, but most were imported from other areas of the world.

"Bergdan?" Vourden called, stepping over to the shop's counter while Lorvin browsed the different wares. "I brought you a cheap customer."

"You already used your favor with that lovely lady," a fruity voice answered as a tall, slender man wearing glasses stepped into view from a back room. "I might be able to find you a discount or two, though."

"I need to get some clothes for my pet cat," the sheriff gestured to Lorvin as he spoke.

Lorvin stopped exploring and shot an offended glare to the sheriff. "I am no one's pet. Not yet, anyway. Just haven't met the right Naephisi."

"Still hoping to catch one's attention?" Vourden chuckled, before turning back to face Bergdan. "My friend here needs some better clothes, at least something clean, if you don't mind."

"Is that all?" the tall man replied with a small laugh as he adjusted the glasses on his narrow nose.

"I'm a humble man," Lorvin spoke up. "Just a simple monk of the land. A wandering preacher who follows the ways of the elements. So, please, nothing too fancy or extravagant."

"Must've spent a little too long in the woods, I guess?" Bergdan commented, motioning towards the state of Lorvin's current tattered attire. "Don't worry, I've got some stuff over here you might like. Luckily for the sheriff, it won't cost too much, either."

Bergdan stepped from behind the counter and walked over to a rack of robes and pants crafted from sturdy canvas. The naetari followed, running his hands over several of the robes before pausing at one that was dyed a deep shade of slate grey with crimson trim. Without a word, Lorvin pulled the knee-length robe from the rack and slipped his arms into the sleeves that stopped at his elbows. As the catfolk brushed his hands over the chest of the garment, he peered into an old dusty mirror across the room with a slight grin.

"I like this one," Lorvin stated, testing the flexibility in his arms with the robe. "Do you have matching pants, and maybe a shirt?"

Bergdan nodded, moving further down the rack and producing a pair of loose-fitting canvas pants the same color as the robe as he replied, "right here. Might only have tunics, but there should be a few matching shirts on the shelf behind you."

"Very nice," Lorvin said, taking the pants and collecting a shirt from the shelf. "Mind if I put them on before we leave?"

"That's perfectly fine," Bergdan smiled, then walked back to the counter. "You can use that room," he pointed to a closet, "if you want to change out of those rags."

"Here," Vourden offered, setting a small stack of five silver coins on the counter for the shop owner as Lorvin vanished into the closet.

Bergdan's blue eyes studied the coins for a moment before taking the top two and sliding the other three back to the sheriff. "You've been through a considerable amount of trouble, sheriff. Are you doing well, after everything that's happened?"

"I'm staying busy," the sheriff responded with a low tone. "I miss Paisley and Dorho, but I'm making my way forward."

"I'm sorry for your tragedies. That attack," Bergdan remarked as he slid the coins into a drawer under the counter, "was terrible for the city as a whole. Those of us on the outside felt helpless as we watched and listened to the battle on the castle grounds. I can't imagine what it must've been like inside those walls."

"Many good people died," the sheriff answered. "Many of them needlessly because of the greed of a tyrant. I should apologize if the ban on ships arriving from Briargale causes your business any trouble. After that brazen attack, the duchess and I made our ruling regarding people and goods from Borlhauf's lands to protect and prevent future incidents."

"It's made it harder getting certain items," the store owner agreed with an understanding nod, "but I would rather put the security of our city as a priority over a few material goods. I wonder though, what was the king after? Lady Eisley hadn't officially declared her independence, though there were rumors it was coming soon. Was it a preemptive attack? Because it only seemed to stoke the fires of liberty further for Elgrahm Hold."

"I lack the authority to say," Vourden gave the words a thought or two before responding. "I can tell you, though, that what we're doing up here has thrown a burr into the king's plan on taking over Anslater."

"I don't doubt that at all," Bergdan shook his head, then gestured to the closet where Lorvin was getting dressed. "What about the cat? Friend of yours?"

Vourden nodded and snickered lightly. "Unfortunately, yes. He's an old traveling companion. He tends to stick to himself, but he's decided to come help us."

Lorvin stepped out of the closet, clad in his new slate-hued attire. His hands brushed over the clean garments, straightening them out briefly. He tossed the old rags into a trash bin behind Bergdan, then picked up a length of chain that held a weighted brass orb at one end as his eyes caught sight of the weapons.

"A meteor hammer?" the catfolk questioned, holding it up curiously. "Don't often see them this far south."

"Some of the guards dropped off a few weapons left by the attackers," Bergdan confessed, watching the naetari with the chain. "Take it, if you want. If you're here to help our sheriff, I don't see a need in charging you for the means to do so."

"You don't mind?" Lorvin's mouth slowly curled into a sly grin.

Vourden shook his head and stopped himself from laughing. "You just gave a crazy hermit a weapon. Thanks, Bergdan."

Bergdan nodded with a kind smile. "Go ahead, I don't need it. If you're here to help, you're a friend."

"Thank you," the naetari said as he wrapped the chain of the weapon around his waist, letting the brass ball hang next to his right thigh.

"Yes, thank you," Vourden spoke as he stepped towards the door. "I need to get to work."

"Have a great day, both of you," Bergdan waved, then straightened his dark leather vest as the two went back out into the city.

"So," Lorvin glanced to the sheriff as the shop's door closed behind them, "do I get to find out what it is that the king wants so bad, that he's willing to attack Ameribelle? Or are you going to keep me in the dark, friend?"

Vourden remained silent as they walked away from Bergdan's store, his feet carrying him towards the massive inner wall that divided the rest of the city from the hill that housed the castle. They were almost to the blooming courtyard when the sheriff brought them to a halt.

"Lorvin," Vourden called to the other, his voice ripe with stress. "Are you certain you want to be involved with this? We're going up against the tyranny of King Borlhauf, and the cruel darkness of the Onyx Spire. These bastards attacked Kaenaan, assaulted Ameribelle, murdered my wife, killed Dorho, and confronted us at the Moonstone Observatory. These are dangerous times, my friend. I'm giving you a chance to go back to your hut in the woods and save yourself."

Just as the naetari was preparing to answer, Ansha approached from the garden that sprawled over the courtyard. Her brow was glistening with sweat, and her breath was heavy and ragged. It was clear she had just finished her morning training routine with some of the guards. The golden eyes of the countess peered over Lorvin for a moment, then darted back to the sheriff as a slight smile crossed her narrow lips.

"Find a new friend?" the woman asked, then gave a welcoming hug to the sheriff as Bies sauntered out from behind the countess.

Stepping away after the swift embrace, the sheriff motioned to Lorvin with his left hand as he said, "Countess Maizen, this is Lorvin Dendrostone. An escaped convict and hermit from the Calinsahr Duchy."

"Lorvin?" Ansha repeated, her smile broadening faintly. "They told me about you, albeit briefly. Though, I'll be honest, I wasn't expecting a naetari."

"No one ever expects a catfolk," Lorvin grinned proudly. "It is quite a pleasure to meet you. Dorho spoke highly of you the few times he ended up in my company. I am terribly sorry for your loss, your husband was a great friend, and a brave man."

"I'm sorry he couldn't be here to see you show up," Ansha forced a smile as she tried to hide her grief at the mention of her deceased husband.

Vourden looked over the countess and shook his head as he thought about the loss of Dorho. He couldn't help but think that it felt strange having all their friends together in one place, and Dorho wasn't around to see it. Years ago, it had been the rogue, the bard, the naetari, Breja, and himself, but their party was shrinking thanks to murderous plots.

"You came over here," the sheriff shook the dark thoughts from his mind as he spoke. "Did you need something?"

"I was asked to go find you," Ansha replied, slightly turning towards the castle. "She's awake. Lynsia's awake. She's asking for Kendira and Dorho."

Vourden nodded slightly. "I want to go talk to the girl, Ansha. I think she needs to know about Dorho. If you wouldn't mind, Kendira might need to be prodded. She was rather content to stay comfortably in bed this morning."

"Now you've piqued my curiosity," Lorvin spoke with a tilt of his head. "Who is this Lynsia?"

"This is your last chance to not get involved with this, cat," the sheriff stated, watching the countess and the larscot head off to collect Kendira.

The feline chuckled and patted the sheriff on the shoulder cheerfully. "I didn't cancel my reservation at the Artinburg Inn just to come shake hands and leave, my friend."

Vourden sighed and looked at the castle. "Then, I guess you need to find out why we're all in so much danger."

05.

    Nadriah shoved her way into the ritual chamber with force, pushing open the twin irons doors as if they were made of hollow bamboo as she moved. Her long crimson robes, covered by a heavy cloak of black wolf fur, blustered and shifted with each hurried movement of her small body. The violet veil that normally shielded her lean face from view now hung down her back, having been pushed aside in the High Tzar's fury. Like thin bands of oil, tightly braided black hair cascaded down the sides and back of her head. Glistening like pure obsidian upon her youthful face, her eyes scanned the chamber quickly while her indigo-stained lips were clenched in a bothersome expression.

    Other than the ritual area itself, the entire room was designed to mimic the inside of a black gem. The walls were smooth as glass and polished to resemble a tumbled jet. Small specks of rubies, sapphires, diamonds, quartz, chrysolite, and citrine glittered like stars in the glossy darkness. Being as wide as four grown men stretched head to toe, the ritual floor covered the bottom quarter of the sphere that formed the room. Nine silver candelabras, each holding six black candles, had been placed at each point of a crimson enneagram engraved into the floor. Ivory rings and matching runes decorated the three matching triangles that formed the enneagram, connecting all the different vertices and points of intersecting lines.

    Three priests of the Onyx Spire stood around the black marble altar in the center of the enneagram. Each one was dressed in a long black hooded gown and a violet shawl. They were much taller than the young-looking High Tzar, but they were greatly dedicated to the rituals of the Onyx Spire and aiding Nadriah in any way she saw fit. One was a vampire, while the other two were simply his human underlings, but they were decidedly trusted by the High Tzar.

    "Do you have Ennaul?" Nadriah demanded of the first dark priest she met upon entering the sphere-shaped room.

The gaunt face of the vampire glanced over the High Tzar before the figure bowed respectfully and gestured towards a black crystal dodecagon resting on the altar. Moving passed the priest, Nadriah moved to the altar and lifted the fist-sized gem in her hands from the cup of bone used to hold it. Swirling inside, a mist of crimson and red energy could be seen, moving angrily with the discontent of being imprisoned in the piece of quartz.

"I warned it not to fail me," she muttered, clenching the crystal tightly in her hands, her mind playing with the idea of shattering it and extinguishing the last remains of the dreadmage's soul.

"The construct is ready, High Tzar," the vampire spoke, the voice an elegant whisper within the round room.

Four slaves stepped through the door of the ritual chamber, carrying a body crafted from corpses and adamantium metal. The sturdy, dark metal had been used to fuse the different parts together, as well as provide a skeleton in places where bones were missing. Put together, the construct was almost as tall as the vampire, but was stout and wide like it had lived the life of a lumberjack. Over the multiple different patches of flesh, runes had been carved, and several arcane inscriptions had been engraved as well. A dome of the heavy metal covered the top of the construct's skull, while a similar plate protected the chest. It was a gruesome creature, but impressive as well.

With only hand gestures, the vampire directed the slaves to drop the body upon the altar and leave. They rushed from the room, eager to be out of the sight of the furious High Tzar and her mysterious priests.

For a moment, the High Tzar looked over the priests gathered in the room with her, then to the crystal sitting in her hands. She debated whether or not Ennaul even deserved being brought back. It had failed to return with the Sidhe-Vein, though the monster had killed the rogue that had been making things hard. She smirked eventually, settling on the idea of punishing the former creature for its failures.

"Let us begin," Nadriah spoke calmly after resolving her decision mentally.

The vampire produced a knife with a long, curved, black blade, cut under the plate that protected the construct's chest, and held the wound open. Ignoring the gory mess assembled within the body of the construct, the High Tzar took the crystal orb and jammed it into the chest cavity, roughly where a heart would belong. As their leader's magic pulsed with an eerie green and indigo energy, the priests began to chant ominously.

Their voices rose and fell as if propelled by unheard instruments. The words a mixture of magic and prayer, filling the circular room with power that the High Tzar channeled into the crystal she held in the construct's chest. Slowly, it transitioned from words and song to growls and cries moved by the dark desires of the magic they summoned into the ritual chamber.

A blast of cerulean light tore through the construct's body, pulsing over the flesh and metal like insects made of lightning. The fingers began to move, and the toes started to flex. Deep from within the throat, a furious snarl escaped, followed by a mournful moan. Another rush of sapphire light flickered within the body of the construct, and the eyes shot open, revealing twin milky green orbs that appeared equally afraid and angry.

"Return to me, Ennaul," Nadriah commanded, removing her hand from the crystal held within the body's chest cavity. "Rise and resist the call of the Undertow. Death is but a blessing, and I refuse to grant it."

Like it was struck with absolute terror, the flesh construct sat up abruptly, screaming into the air of the ritual room. The voice came out as a vile echo of several voices combined, neither entirely male nor female, as it wailed into the dark room.

"Be quiet, my childe," Nadriah ordered, wiping the viscera from the chest cavity on a damp rag offered by the vampire.

The howls from the construct silenced quickly upon the words of the High Tzar. As the eyes of the monster turned from their milky green color to a brilliant shade of violet, it looked upon The Voidling with a startled expression. It flexed and moved its fingers and toes, then bent and stretched its arms and legs slowly.

"I," it began to speak, the words coming out as a hollow growl, "I'm alive?"

"Not really," the High Tzar admitted coldly. "You definitely died. Killed by the very Sidhe-Vein you were supposed to bring me."

"I failed," the construct muttered, the terror in its eyes turning to horrified guilt. "The man. He stabbed me. I couldn't move. She screamed, and the magic hit us."

Nadriah nodded as she paced about the altar that held the construct. "Good. I see you remember and understand. I was worried your memories would be broken. It's not as fun to punish someone if they don't even remember what they did."

"You brought me back?" the flesh creature visually explored its animated body as it spoke.

The leader of the Onyx Spire continued to slowly walk around the altar as she replied, "of course. I told you, if you failed me, I wouldn't allow you the peace offered by death."

As the chanting from the priests faded into nothingness, and the animated monster moved to sit upon the edge of the altar, the High Tzar picked up a silver goblet resting upon a small table near the room's door. She carried the goblet around the room, black eyes scanning the gems that sparkled and flickered within the smooth black walls. After walking thrice around the room, Nadriah approached the vampire and held up her wrist close to the priest's lips. Without hesitation, the undead clamped down upon the pale flesh of the offered arm, fangs puncturing deeply until the ebony blood of the High Tzar flowed freely. Letting her midnight blood drain into the silver vessel, the small figure of the Spire's leader slowly returned to the altar.

"Drink this," she ordered, "and share my power. Share my vision. Be reborn anew through this connection of blood."

Without questioning the command, the creature took hold of the goblet. It looked over the offering of blood, then examined the face of the High Tzar for only a moment before drinking deeply of the ink-like liquid. From the areas where metal was joined to flesh, the thick, dark fluid dripped from the body of the construct, splattering upon the altar. The stitched-together figure went rigid briefly, dropped the polished goblet, and then a low hiss escaped from the assembled construct.

"Good, childe," the High Tzar spoke softly, watching the creature be overcome by the magic in her blood. "Embrace that feeling. Do not resist it."

"What is this?" the creature called, clenching its fists as if it were struggling in pain.

The Voidling picked up the dropped goblet, running her fingers over the polished rim of the vessel as she walked around the altar one more time. The dead veins of the created monster filled with the black ichor, and gave the assembled flesh an unholy, shadowy tint.

"That is my blood," Nadriah's words came sternly. "The blood of one blessed by the goddess Xa'morhu. The blood of her chosen disciple and scion. With this, I grant you a small taste of my power."

"Why?" the monster asked, still clearly struggling with the influx of arcane power. "Why would you give me such a thing?"

The High Tzar smiled dangerously, "I need you to be stronger than you were before, if you are to continue to serve me. Even a mangy mutt needs a little food once in a while."

"Then," the constructed monstrosity growled as it stood up, testing its feet gingerly, "how may I serve you, High Tzar?"

Despite the creature towering over her small figure, The Voidling refused to step back, unafraid of the thing she had brought into the world. Midnight blood, still flowing from the wound in her wrist, dripped like black tendrils down her fingers. She took the ichor from her fingers, and created a handprint upon the left pectoral of the monster, a light touch of her magic burning the design into the creature's chest.

"I will no longer call you Ennaul, for he died as a failure in Ameribelle, defeated by a girl and her keeper," spoke the High Tzar. "From this moment forward, I mark you as my property, and you shall be known as Revenant."

For only a brief moment, the creature paused, then nodded in understanding. "I am Revenant, property of the High Tzar. What is my task?"

"You failed to retrieve the Sidhe-Vein," Nadriah reminded the flesh construct, "but I cannot ignore your success in fetching the Tome of Entropy. So, with that in mind, I want you to seek the Seal of Ourixys in the Galensteil Wastes. Both the Tome and the notes of the Black Rose suggest it is there. You are going to join the forces of King Borlhauf on the border of Anslater, and lead the units from the Onyx Spire as we push into the eastern kingdom."

"As you wish, High Tzar," the monster spoke respectfully. "Is there any clues where one should look in the Wastes?"

"It was entrusted to a world of glass before the Fall of Atlantis," The Voidling answered, "according to the Tome of Entropy. I can only guess it is some kind of long-forgotten reliquary buried beneath the dirt. As you can imagine, no one was supposed to find these things. The Forgotten Goddess was not supposed to be remembered, much less, actually found and freed from her prison."

And such was the truth of her words. A former High Tzar known to the world as the Black Rose had assembled the Slate of Nullification, starting with a shard she retrieved from the lair of Atra'oxya. The Black Rose figured out some of the power of the Slate, but never truly unleashed its deepest secrets, so it was locked in an artifact storeroom deep under the Onyx Spire. Like all the High Tzars, the Black Rose kept a library of personal notes, research, and discoveries, but when she betrayed the Spire, many of her records were destroyed out of spite.

Well over a thousand years had passed, nations were born and fell, nobles were crowned and slain, and with the flow of time, the Slate of Nullification became forgotten. Then an aspiring young student, driven by curiosity, found the Slate tucked away, dusty and dull with misuse. She slipped the round slate, which looked like nothing more than a black hole with a rim of gold and jet, into her robes and dashed back to her room. When her studies were done and tasks were finished, the girl would spend her free time seated before the Slate, trying to figure it out. The empty, bleak, infinite blackness of the relic intrigued the student, and for many months she tried to figure out its secrets.

The student tried using magic on the Slate, and it appeared to absorb the energy effortlessly. It refused to burn when assaulted by fire, resisted the deathly chill of ice, and seemed to completely ignore being struck by lightning. Nothing worked, and nothing appeared to solicit a response from the deep darkness held within the gold and jet band around the edges. Frustrated, but unwilling to give up, the small student simply put aside the Slate until her interest got piqued once more.

While cleaning the Spire's archives, the student stumbled upon an old, leather-bound notebook stashed in a gap between the rock slabs of the wall behind a towering bookcase. Anyone of thicker stature wouldn't have been able to reach it, making the girl feel like she was destined to find it. A quick glance through the ancient pages, seeing the author had written about their own experiences with the Slate, was all the student had to see before sneaking it into her robes. Whether it had been placed there by someone wanting to preserve the knowledge, or by someone wanting to hide it from view, was of no consequence to the student. The only thing that mattered, was that she had found it.

With the old notes in her hand, she returned to studying the Slate of Nullification. It wasn't until several months later, and after several frustrating experiments, that the student came to a serious realization: the Slate was nothing. It wasn't just nothing, it represented the opposite of creation. Magic was absorbed into it. Small animals subjected to the limited powers of the Slate weren't just killed, they were removed completely from existence. Rather than scratch the seemingly infinitely deep surface, tools simply vanished when forced into the Slate. After assuming the Slate was just an interesting minor trinket, she came to understand what it truly was.

She took the relic to an empty room one night shortly after the moon had peaked in the sky. Devoid of furniture, tapestries, and lacking even a window, the room became the darkest hole in the world once the student shut the door and blew out her candle. For several minutes, the girl considered how to proceed as she held the Slate in the blackness of the tiny chamber. Then, she cleared her mind of everything. Not a single thought was allowed to cross her mind, and instead she simply focused on the concept of nothing. She sat in the darkness, with the Slate of Nullification, the beat of her young heart matching the sound of her brain trying to envision what nothing would truly look like.

A voice called to her from the Slate. It was a harsh whisper, sounding ragged and dry, but a voice nonetheless. Through the connection, a small part of the goddess' power reached through the Slate, wrapped the student in its grasp, and turned her into the being that would become the next High Tzar.

"Go get some clothes," Nadriah said as she came back from her memories. "Then prepare to depart for your new position as a general in my army."

"As you wish," Revenant replied, bowing respectfully before stepping out of the ritual chamber.

After watching the large, artificial man leave the chamber, The Voidling turned to face the vampire as she pondered things in her mind. She felt that sending Revenant to find the Seal was a perfect way for the monster to regain her trust, but she still needed to deal with the missing Sidhe-Vein. What she wanted was someone loyal to her, but unexpected by the enemy. Someone dangerous, but subtle.

Someone who could tell you a lie so beautiful that the truth would seem absurd.

"Does Caynderia Seele still lead the Whisper Troupe?" the High Tzar asked, hoping she hadn't removed them during her rise to the throne.

"Indeed, High Tzar," answered the vampire, giving a submissive nod as it addressed the leader of the Onyx Spire.

"Have her come to the Unhallowed Sepulcher before the moon rises tonight," Nadriah ordered, "and bring some of her shadowy friends with her. I have a job for them."

As all three priests bowed respectfully, the vampire conveyed a simple, "As you wish, High Tzar," while Nadriah prepared to depart the circular room.

06.

"I'm sorry, Lyn," Kendira spoke softly, sitting on the side of the girl's bed in Albinasky Keep. "He died protecting you, just like he promised to do."

Vourden nodded in agreement, leaning against the window casement as his green eyes watched over the others in the room. "We all want him here with us, but like so many others that night, he was killed by the enemies that attacked us."

"None of us would be here right now," Ansha added from a seat next to Vourden, taking a deep breath to steady her emotions, "if he hadn't stopped that monster in the throne room."

Lynsia put her slender arms around Kendira's shoulders and buried her sapphire eyes in the blouse of the cinnamon-skinned woman. "This is all my fault, isn't it?" she wept. "I didn't want anyone to die because of me."

"No, not at all," Vourden offered, looking on as the bard ran her hands comfortingly through the crimson hair of the younger girl. "None of us wanted this, but this isn't your fault. I don't know what the Onyx Spire and the Thornbror Kingdom have in mind for you, but it is our objective to keep you safe from them, lest we ever find out."

"Once we get you to I'raha in the northern mountains, we will know more, I am certain," Ansha spoke as her fingers delicately petted the soft fur of the larscot leaning against her right leg. "We'll be leaving in a few days, so I hope you are ready to meet the faerie that made you."

"And then we can get our revenge," Kendira commented softly as she held the sobbing Sidhe-Vein. "For you. For Dorho. For Paisley. For everyone we've loved and lost along the way. Their cruel deeds will not go unpunished, my sweet little birdy."

"I," Lyn took a deep breath between sobs. "I just wanted to be safe and happy. I just want everyone to be safe and happy. I didn't want to be taken from my family. Now that family is gone."

Ansha's mouth was already opened in response when a soft knock to the small room's door resounded along the white stone walls. She started to move, but it was Vourden who reached the door first, cracking it slowly open, before pulling it the rest of the way. Holding herself upright with the aid of a crutch under her left shoulder, Urna hobbled into the Sidhe-Vein's room. She made her way to an empty chair at a small square table where Lorvin sat, and dropped painfully into the seat, forcing a grin across her reptilian face.

"It's good to see you awake, girl," the slithzerkai greeted, adjusting her weight to get comfortable the best she could. "I heard you were up and talking finally, and managed to get a break from the healers."

"You're looking almost decent, lizard," Lorvin teased, putting his feet up on the table as he leaned back in the chair.

Urna laughed darkly and lifted the crutch for emphasis as she replied, "those damned healers are persistent, but they're working miracles with this old body of mine."

"Miss Pa'kithka," Lynsia glanced over the shoulder of the bard to the lizard woman, "I'm sorry for Jarlen and what happened to you. This was all my—."

"Hush, girl," Urna waved her hand dismissively, silencing the girl's words. "This was all the work of the Onyx Spire. When I lived there. Yes, I was a member of the Spire. When I lived there, a new High Tzar rose through the ranks quickly. Quicker than anyone had ever done before, it was as if no one could react with the speed at which she climbed the ladder. We called her Nadriah, or The Voidling, depending on how you knew her. I would almost be certain that all of these troubles we've been through is her doing."

"I was going to talk to you about that tomorrow," Vourden smiled slightly, returning to his place by the window. "I'm not going to complain about your openness though."

"You," Lynsia paused for a moment to process the words of the reptilian woman, "lived there? You were a part of the Onyx Spire?"

The slithzerkai nodded and sighed heavily as she thought about her own past. "I did. I was drawn in by the allure of dominating, controlling, and gaining power from others, but after enduring more than my share of abuse and violence, as well as realizing the harm I was doing to others, I left. It is a place that embraces the darker truths of our reality, and seeks to spread their corruption until the rest of the world bends a knee to their brutal ways."

Ansha scratched Bies behind his ears as she listened, and finally responded. "So it's a bid for world domination? Such a simple-minded goal."

"I doubt it," Urna continued, shaking her head a bit. "It's never that simple with the Onyx Spire. There's something more to it. They teach how to embrace the Nine Unhallowed Sins of wrath, lust, greed, pride, treason, gluttony, envy, apathy, and corruption in ways that would make any sane person cringe in horror. They want the rest of the world to understand what it's like to let go of moral and ethical standards, and live to the fullest extent that your body, heart, and mind will endure. So, it's never as simple as world domination, even if that's what it appears to be from the outside."

"The way you say it," Vourden said as he pulled a thin cigar from the pocket on his tunic, "sounds almost beautiful."

"It always sounds that way," Urna admitted, "until you see it for yourself. It's wild experiments performed without any regard for ethical standards or social morality. It's gaining pleasure and excitement from the suffering and pain of others. It's crushing perceived enemies in such a manner that their allies are hesitant to endure the same anger. It's untamed arrogance and blatant brutality paraded around as glory and authority."

"And they want our sweet birdy?" Kendira asked, pressing a swift peck to Lyn's cheek.

"For some reason, yes," the reptilian nodded. "I doubt King Borlhauf has any idea what he's gotten involved in, but I highly suspect this was an Onyx Spire scheme from the very beginning. Knowing the Spire the way I do, and with my understanding of Nadriah, I would be willing to bet gold that the king of Thornbror is just being used as a tool. Not that he doesn't deserve it, honestly. I just wish I knew more about what they wanted with you, Lynsia."

Lorvin picked at his teeth for a moment with one of the claws from his left hand, silvery eyes scanning the slithzerkai quietly as he digested the words she spoke. "Sounds like a good reason to get the girl stronger and able to control her powers. If they want her so badly, it might do well to give her the tools to bring them down as well."

"She's not a weapon," Kendira blurted.

"I never said she was," the cat argued, "but if what you said earlier is right, that girl killed a darkoyle and a dreadmage with her magic. That makes her stronger, by far, than anyone else in this room. She's the best chance we've got in defending against whatever sick plot the Onyx Spire has."

"I'm not a weapon," Lynsia protested as well.

"What would your husband say, Ansha?" Lorvin turned his silver gaze to the countess as he continued to pick at his teeth. "If he were here in this room, listening to the information from the lizard. What would he say?"

For a moment, Ansha said nothing. She merely closed her eyes and focused on running her fingers through the soft, dark tan fur of the larscot. When her golden eyes opened once more, a sigh, devoid of confidence, but filled with hope and sadness combined, escaped her lips.

"Dorho," she breathed the name slowly, "would want us to take her to the faerie up north. He would want us to get to the bottom of this mystery and finish the job he started. He didn't care about getting tangled in the affairs of nobles or cults, unless he could get paid and leave it behind him when he was finished. I believe he would do the same here."

"I agree," Vourden said after using a candle to light the cigar between his lips. "Dorho was a good man, and wouldn't let the pests from the king or the Spire bother him. He'd press on with his original duty just to spite them. We should do the same. If anything, to honor him."

"I'm going with you," Urna suddenly added, a slightly twisted smirk on her face. "You can thank the Onyx Spire, but I have my own goals in seeing this journey to its end now."

Ansha blinked as she looked over to the injured slithzerkai. "Are you sure? You aren't even fully healed yet. Not even close. I'm honestly surprised they let you out of bed to come down here."

"You lost your husband, poor woman," the reptilian said. "The least I could do is offer to go along on the journey I originally tasked him with. Plus, without Jarlen and the Rock Chaser, what else do I have to do?"

"I don't exactly want to go back to the grand hotel I was at in Goldenveil," Lorvin sighed, glancing from the countess to the Sidhe-Vein before looking at Vourden. "So, I guess you're stuck with me as well."

"Breaking out of jail, just to sign up to butt heads with the Onyx Spire," Kendira laughed a little at the feline man, "is exactly something you would do."

"Well," he gestured to Urna and chuckled, "you'll need at least one able-bodied person to make up for her being crippled."

Ansha wiped her eyes and tried to hide her tears as she pulled the large weasel into her lap.

"What's wrong?" Kendira questioned, tilting her head in concern for the countess.

Shaking her head sorrowfully, the countess spoke softly. "Just thinking about Dorho. All those years he and I shared, listening to him talk about his adventures with all of you, I finally get to meet you all, and he's taken from us. I know he would be excited to see you all together, going on a final adventure, and willing to finish what he started. It makes me miss him. I miss him so much."

Vourden put a gentle hand on the shoulder of the countess, listening to her voice break with emotion as she talked.

"Of course we wouldn't give up," Kendira smiled warmly, brushing her right hand down the back of the grieving girl in her arms. "Dorho wouldn't let us. Anyways, you're his wife, that makes you part of our family too."

"Talking about family," Urna interrupted, wincing as she shifted her weight slightly from one leg to the other. "Are you certain, being pregnant, that you should be going on this adventure with us?"

Ansha shrugged slightly and wiped her eyes again. "I figure I've got a few months before I need to seriously consider settling down to prepare for our daughter. I'll be fine."

"As long as you are certain," Kendira added with a kind expression. "No need to be putting yourself, or your child, in unnecessary danger."

"What do you say, Ansha," Vourden said, looking from the Sidhe-Vein to the countess, "if we prepare to leave in five days? Should give the girl and lizard ample of time to heal up a bit. We won't have to rush for supplies, either."

Countess Maizen nodded. "Sounds like a decent plan. Kendira? Lorvin? You've done this more than I have. Does that work?"

Both of them nodded in agreement.

"I'll have to give Kortyx some exercise," Lorvin added, throwing a mischievous glance to the sheriff, "but I can linger around town for a few days."

"Actually," Vourden rubbed his chin as he stepped towards the bedroom door, looking at the impish grin of the cat. "Thanks for bringing up the wyvern. I have a job for you that will make things for us go smoother and easier."

"Oh? My own job?" Lorvin chuckled roguishly. "You really have missed me, if you're willing to give me a job."

The sheriff nodded. "Scary, I know. Asking you, of all creatures, to be responsible. The thought terrifies me as well."

"This is like asking Marle to not bring home stray cats," Kendira laughed.

Holding back his own laughter, Vourden grinned. "We've got a little druid running around with us. A kobold named Zakosa. He says he knows where the druids of Red Aspen Grove are. You can move much faster with Kortyx than we can with horses or on foot. I want you to take our little friend, and see if you can find the grove ahead of us. That way, we won't be wasting time once we're done visiting the faerie up north. The druids will be waiting for us, and we can quickly arrange transportation if needed. Can you do that?"

Lorvin furrowed his brow, thinking over the request. "You want me to take some smelly kobold to look for a grove of druids?"

Urna giggled at the words of the cat. "And not eat the poor little coward, either."

"Listen," Vourden's voice suddenly lost the playful tone as he glanced around the room. "We're all aware that there was a spy among us after leaving Merciapola. Garneil showing up in Dracamori wasn't a fluke. He knew we were headed there. He knew to find us there. We went that route specifically to avoid him, and yet he still caught up to us. Paisley died because someone told him where we were."

"You think it was the kobold?" Kendira tilted her head, curious. "I do agree, him showing up in the middle of that fight with the troll was a bit convenient, but he also knew about the faerie and where we needed to go."

"He helped us get rid of the monsters in the Endless Tomb," Ansha spoke up.

"And then he hid during the battle in Dracamori, and stayed behind a pillar when Albinasky Keep was attacked," the sheriff continued, his voice a damning tone in the small chamber. "He basically watched as our friends and loved ones were murdered around us."

Lorvin nodded and smiled a bit. "I see. You want me to distract the tiny druid. Lead him away from you to see if your theory is correct. Is that right?"

"You catch on quickly, cat," Vourden smiled slightly.

"I'll be your carrot on the stick," the monk replied with a grin. "Sounds fun."

"Much appreciated, friend," the sheriff bowed slightly before turning back to the door. "I will advise the duchess of our plan to leave in a few days. Maybe she can help procure some supplies for us."

"I will see if I can find us some way to communicate over long distances," Urna stated as she used the crutch to push herself up from the chair. "The Onyx Spire used to use saystones, which were crystals with some minor magic infused into them. Would be rather helpful in this situation."

"Wait," Kendira almost jumped to her feet as she called out to the sheriff and reptilian. "Dorho always told us to never split up the party. We might need Lorvin or the druid if we encounter a problem heading north."

"Never split up the party," Vourden took a slow breath as he repeated the words in agreement. "He hated dividing us up, and refused to do it. I think, for once, this calls for such a tactic. Test my theory about the kobold, locate the Red Aspen Grove, all while dealing with I'raha. We can move faster this way."

"I agree," Ansha injected. "I like Vourden's idea. By the time we finish with the faerie, we'll already know where the druids are, and they'll be waiting for us."

"Then," the sheriff glanced around the room as he opened the door, "it's settled. We leave in five days, except for Lorvin. I want you to find our little lizard friend, and take to the skies as soon as you are able."

"Consider it done, boss," the cat smirked, dropping his feet off the table.

Without adding another word to the bedroom's air, the sheriff stepped into the hallway beyond the door. Just as any other day, maids and workers tended to the demands of the castle. They bustled about like bees looking for fresh flowers while Vourden traversed from one hall to another. His feet took him through some fresh repairs to the white stone of the great keep as his eyes scanned the courtyard beyond the broad windows. He found that his thoughts turned to the days ahead as he walked, drawing a slow breath from his lungs as he watched the sway of the garden through the windows.

They were well into the summer months, and life had almost returned to normal. As normal as he could have hoped for, considering everything that had happened. Though he had lost Paisley, he had gained a son, and his daughter had been returned to him. He had a good woman in his life who pushed to see his life improve from the losses he had endured. Life was just beginning to settle a bit under the heated light of the summer sun.

Now, they were planning on tossing it all to the wind to continue the journey they had started with Dorho. They needed to take Lynsia north to meet with the faerie that had created her, and then find the druids of the Red Aspen Grove to train the girl to control her powers. Though the person originally tasked with these goals was gone, his friends were going to risk life and limb to see it finished.

No, it wasn't Dorho's family finishing his adventure. They were his family. Ansha, Kendira, Lorvin, Urna, himself, and even the young Sidhe-Vein. They all shared a bond that was more than meager friendship.

"What's on your mind?" came Lorvin's rumbling voice as he stepped up to the window next to Vourden.

"Hmm?" Vourden turned slightly away from the view from the window as he noticed the naetari man.

"This isn't like previous adventures," Lorvin stated calmly as he examined the gardens in the courtyard. "This isn't hunting some trinket for a noble, nor is it removing a troublesome band of thieves from some nearby cave. We've fought gremlins, plundered crypts, and snatched gold from government officials. This is nothing like that. We've got a Sidhe-Vein we're protecting from the Onyx Spire, while the region is being torn apart by war because of a tyrannical king."

The sheriff nodded and sighed. "This is more than just pride, fame, and fortune. You're right about that, Lorvin. This job we've been shouldering, it goes deeper than anything we've ever done before. I get the feeling that what we're doing will vastly affect the world as a whole. We can't fail."

"I'm going to be honest," the monk looked over at the sheriff slowly, "for once in my life. When the prison guards were talking about the attack up here, I decided I couldn't just sit around any longer. I had to know how you all were doing. I had to do what I could for the few people that showed me kindness in my life. I only wish I had made it sooner."

Vourden shook his head and put a hand on the shoulder of the feline man. "You have no idea how relieved I was to see you arrive this morning. I wasn't expecting it, but you are a pleasant sight for weary eyes, my friend. No, my brother."

"We'll meet again at the druids' hidden grove, my brother," Lorvin let a warm smile crack his face. "Just focus on what needs to be done, because this is nothing like we've faced before."

The sheriff turned to the window momentarily, before continuing his walk down the hall. "When this is all over, we'll have a great feast so we can relax. You best get going; I suspect the kobold is at the stables with the wagon. I need to talk to Lady Eisley, let her know what our plan is."

The naetari nodded and smiled before the sheriff wandered away. When Vourden turned about, wanting to thank the cat for joining their effort, he found that the monk was already gone. He never heard the strange cat leave, but it was like the monk had simply vanished.

Such was expected when dealing with Lorvin, the sheriff thought, almost chuckling.

Shaking his head at the oddness of the feline man, Vourden continued, wandering the halls in search of the castle's primary resident. It didn't take long for the sheriff to locate Lady Eisley, who was meeting with her military leaders in the main library over a spread of maps and tomes dedicated to history and tactics.

Her long, blonde hair was tied into a trio of tails with emerald-hued ribbons, while her blue eyes, like orbs reflecting the sky, scanned over the documents spread out over the heavy oak table. She was tall, and despite her thin frame, she stood with dignity, authority, and strength, even surrounded by the men leading her forces in the war for independence. On top of her head rested a thin band of gold beads and sapphires, the golden strands clutching at a single, large ruby above the woman's brow. An ankle-length dress of deep shades of green featuring a swirling floral pattern adorned her slender body, while a cloak of silver silk draped down her figure like a waterfall of polished metal.

"Lady Eisley?" Vourden spoke up as he drew near the table, glancing over the six others gathered around the maps.

She looked up, though her hand never left the spot where Stonewalker Gate was marked on the map she was working with. "Sheriff Vourden? I hope you have good news for me. I heard the girl finally woke up from her condition."

"Indeed, she has," the sheriff commented. "Countess Maizen wants to leave for the Faulkendor Mountains and Euthrox in five days. We will be taking the slithzerkai and," he paused, thinking about Lorvin, "a monk with us."

"Us?" Lady Eisley stood upright, tilting her head as she examined the sheriff.

"Yes," Vourden missed the tone in the woman's voice. "We'll be leaving in five days' time."

"No," Lady Eisley shook her head abruptly. "You will be staying here. They will be going without you."

The sheriff blinked as a perplexed expression shone on his face. "But, Countess Maizen and the others are expecting me to—."

"I don't care," the noblewoman narrowed her eyes, shaking her head again. "I mean, I do care. It's just that with the death of my court arbiter, the law and justice of the land rests solely in your hands for the time being. In fact, I'm making you the hold's justiciar. I hate to ask more of you than you've already done, but I need you to take over Jeresal's work as well as your own. You are the chief arbiter of Elgrahm Hold, as well as my trusted sheriff. At least, until I find someone else to replace Jeresal. So, I'm sorry, I cannot permit you to go with the countess."

Vourden took a deep breath, speaking as he stepped closer to the noblewoman. "I cannot allow them to carry this task on their own. It is just as much my duty as it is Countess Maizen's."

"No, it isn't," the woman refused to back down as she crossed her arms over her chest. "I only tasked you with helping them get the girl from the Moonstone Observatory. That was before the Onyx Spire attacked and killed Jeresal. Now, I need you here in the castle to help me. I need you to help Elgrahm Hold. Your duty is here to me, and my people."

"Then, how am I to assure their safety?" Vourden fought to not show his annoyance with the noble's orders.

Lady Eisley shrugged nonchalantly. "Find someone else. Your responsibility is in this castle. Send someone else in your stead."

Vourden could tell that she was settled in her decision to force him to stay. In front of her generals, it would be improper to argue with the noble, and the sheriff knew it. When all was said and done, Lady Eisley was his superior, the duchess of Elgrahm Hold, and he was simply employed as her sheriff. To protest her words, would be distasteful and seen as insubordination, especially to witnesses.

"Of course, Lady Eisley," he replied, bowing respectfully. "How might I be of service to you and Elgrahm Hold?"

There was a delicate pause to the noblewoman's voice as she looked over the suddenly submissive man. "Go, enjoy an evening with your friends. Return to me in the morning, prepared to assume your new position, Justiciar Leustren."

"Very well," Vourden sighed in an effort to hide his true feelings, "I shall see you in the morning."

There was nothing more to say, nothing more to argue, Vourden thought as he left the room. At least, not with her generals standing around. He stepped away from the castle's library, taking a few deep breaths to keep himself from stomping back in and raising his voice at the noblewoman.

"Find someone to go in my stead?" the justiciar said as he found himself looking out into the garden once more from the windows.

He was preparing to head home when he turned to see Ansha looking at him from several steps away. The larscot was waiting next to her left heel, keeping an eye on things going on around the countess. For a moment, the new justiciar considered telling her what had transpired with Lady Eisley, but he shook his head at the thought.

"Headed home?" Ansha asked, her voice soft and kind.

Vourden paused, thinking of how to explain that he wouldn't be going with them. They had traveled together through Mulman's Hollow, killed a bandit lord, retrieved the Sidhe-Vein, put monster and man to the sword, endured hardships he wouldn't wish upon anyone, and now he was being forced to leave them on their own.

"No," Vourden admitted, suddenly thinking about the trip through Golden Bow Gulch. "I'm going to visit the Den of Red Venom's camp outside the city's walls. I want to have a word with Orota. I'll meet you all for dinner at the Swayed Lamb. Please let Kendira and the others know."

07.

    Dorho left his horse with the livery outside of Petiora's southern gate. He was rested and bathed, and had spent the last three days helping Jonsal with duties around the farm to thank the family for putting him up. Luckily, he had borrowed some old plain clothes from the farmer, and though the beige tunic and sun-bleached brown trousers weren't his usual attire, they were better than the tattered remnants he had shown up with. The rogue still didn't understand completely what had transpired to bring him to the kingdom of Anslater, but he was getting used to telling folks that he had been beaten and robbed. He still had no weapons, and his old, dark hat was still missing.

    Jonsal had given him a handful of silver tiles to pay for his work around the farm, though Count Maizen had initially refused to be paid. The rogue eventually admitted that he needed to replace some of his lost goods. After working hard all day with the men of the farm, the rogue borrowed a good horse and made his way to the nearby town of Petiora, hoping to catch at least a couple shops still open as the sun was beginning to set.

    A dark, wide-brimmed hat formed from softened reptilian leather caught the rogue's eye as he wandered the streets between the white stucco buildings of the town. Without even questioning the decision, Dorho tossed the haberdasher four of the silver tiles from the pouch tied to his belt. From the same shopkeeper's wife, Count Maizen was able to purchase a studded vest made from the same leather, as well as a hooded cape dyed with a dark, wine-like red stain. As he left the family-owned cluster of apparel shops, the rogue finally felt somewhat normal in the new attire.

    Though the blacksmith was in the process of cooling his forge and closing the shutters to his shop filled with weapons, armor, and tools, the old man agreed to sell the count a pair of twin katiss swords. Curved slightly like a cat's claw, the blades of the short swords were only somewhat longer than the rogue's forearms, but they would do well to replace the rapier and other tools he had lost. All the other items in the stall were standard long swords, axes, or related to the trades around the town, nothing that would have benefited the castaway count. Dorho thanked the old man and departed with only two silver and three bronze tiles left in his pouch.

Dorho's dark eyes scanned the street as the sun finally dipped below the hills around the town of Petiora. It was definitely summer, as the quiet aromas of stews and warm hearths found in the colder months was only a memory, replaced by neighbors talking and the scent of grilled fowl flowing on the gentle breeze. The roads of Petiora were paved with dark cobblestones hewn from granite, while the white stucco of the buildings rose among the pines like ghosts.

"Lookin' fer a drink, traveler?" came a sultry voice from the patio of the tavern, calling to the rogue as he walked through the darkening town.

"Perhaps," Dorho answered with a kind smile, his eyes examining the lone, red-haired woman leaning against the patio railing.

"Perhaps?" the woman giggled. "Perhaps ya'd like ta get a decent meal and put those boots up fer a bit?"

Dorho turned towards the tavern and took a few steps closer to the young woman. "Depends," he said.

The woman brushed a bit of the long, crimson locks from her face and grinned. "Depends on what?"

"I'm looking for someone," Dorho spoke with a smile. "If you can help me find him, I'd be obligated to join you for a drink and a bite to eat."

"Oh, well then," a sly smile crossed the tall woman's face. "What does he look like? Being a tavern, many faces, and even more stories pass through these doors."

Dorho chuckled, wondering for a moment if the barmaid was related to Kendira. "Muscular fellow. He wears a very unique set of armor, with a crest of a white griffon. Probably carrying a glaive with him. Have you seen him?"

"Is that so?" the barmaid lofted her brow, then grinned. "C'mon in, I know who yer lookin' for. Are ya a friend of his?"

Without protest, the rogue followed the woman into the tavern and was seated in a corner between the kitchen and the entrance. She didn't permit him a chance to reply before she vanished briefly, only to return with a tall mug of frothy ale. It smelled of amaranth, rice, and wheat, with a pleasant citrus note tucked into the fragrance of the brew. Before the count could argue, the tall redhead took a seat to the left of the rogue.

"So," she continued to grin, "are ya a friend of the prince?"

Dorho took a sip of the beer, then a slightly longer drink as he found the taste pleasant. "Something like that. We met before, but it's been a long time since then." His words were nothing but lies, but the truth would sound insane. "Sorry, it's been a long few days. My carriage was attacked, and I was mugged before being left in the Knepiri fields. I guess my mind isn't completely recovered yet."

"Mugged?" the barmaid shook her head woefully. "That's just terrible. Do ya have a name, stranger? I'm Peira, oldest daughter of the tavern's owner."

"Count Dorho Maizen," the rogue stated calmly, lifting the mug in a gesture of greeting.

"Oh," the woman wiggled slightly. "Count Maizen? So yer a noble? Are ya visitin' for the weddin'? Is that why yer askin' about the prince?"

Dorho sipped more from the mug and smiled, falling back on his training in Kaenaan to read the information he was given. "Yes, I've come to see the wedding and congratulate the prince. He might not remember me, but I remember the kindness he showed me upon our last visit."

"That's wonderful," Peira smiled warmly. "I'm sure Jolson will be glad to see ya. I guess that means ya'll be stayin' the night before headin' to Vansenhul on the morrow? It's almost four days ta the capital from here, and the weddin' is a week away."

"Who's the lucky lady?" Dorho pressed with a kind expression between drinks. "I missed the opportunity to meet anyone else during my previous visit."

Peira sighed happily as she thought about the answer. "Cerulla Cloudrain. She's some kind of sage that's been workin' fer the royal family fer some time. Us normal girls would've gone ta war fer a chance with the handsome prince, but he chose the so-called Faerie Queen of Anslater. I've heard they've had some kind of deep connection fer a while, but now they're makin' it official. She'll be the new Princess Galheam, and eventually the true queen of the land and people. I'm thankful, though. She's a good soul. I met her once, when they came through the town on a vacation a couple years ago. Very kind and thoughtful."

"Great to hear," the rogue replied. "I'll be looking forward to meeting her officially."

"Would ya like," the woman paused, glancing over the count momentarily. "Would ya like some company ta the weddin'? A man of nobility shouldn't be going ta this kind of event on his own."

For a while, Dorho considered the words of the woman. He knew what her end goal was by the way she sat close and moved upon hearing his title. It would be easy enough to tell her that he's married with a child on the way. Though, he could benefit from having a guide in this strange kingdom. Part of him wanted to shoo the woman away, but then part of him felt she could prove useful in the coming days.

"Mind if I ask for a plate of hot food while I think your offer over?" Count Maizen responded, being honest with the woman for once, as he needed to consider taking her with him.

"Of course, Count Maizen," Peira spoke as she stood up and headed to the kitchen, leaving the rogue to finish the beer in peace.

He had met this type of woman before in his travels. Eager to find a man of wealth who will take her out of her small town. They were women with lazy dreams of grandeur that they didn't have to work for. Each one was always the same, and each one was always insufferable and clingy. These types always made Dorho glad he had Ansha, and a reason to back away from such terrible situations.

Though he was in Anslater, a kingdom unfamiliar to him. He barely knew the road from the farm to the town of Petiora. Having someone to help show him around would be useful, even if it only made him less conspicuous as a guest in a foreign land.

There was also the matter of Ansha. His wife. Though he wasn't sure how she would handle his return from death, he still loved her dearly and wanted to be reunited with her soon. They were expecting a child, and had a home ready for them in Golden Bow Gulch. He didn't want to ruin that. Dorho had to remain faithful to her, as she would be faithful to him until they met again.

"Roasted chicken with seasoned rice and beans," Peira called as she dropped into the seat next to Dorho once more, pushing the plate in front of him. "I brought you two fluffy rolls as well, and a bowl of local blueberry jam."

She was tall, but Dorho wouldn't dare call her slender, nor fat. She was well-built, even if a bit curvy in the right places. One could tell she was a woman who didn't shy from a good meal or hard labor. Her long, red hair was pulled back into a single tail that crept down to the middle of her back, tied up with a short length of black silk. Peira's teal eyes were kind, though a hint of mischief seemed to lurk just beyond the turquoise orbs. A short-sleeved, jade-hued tunic and a navy blue skirt covered most of her tanned skin, with a standard barmaid's apron worn over everything else. She was plain to Dorho, though he supposed anyone else might find her attractive.

She was definitely not Countess Ansha Maizen.

"Sorry," Dorho finally spoke up, slathering half of one roll with the jam. "I really don't need the company on this trip. I appreciate your offer, though. This is something I need to do alone, but you're more than welcome to keep me company while I eat."

"I don't mind talkin' to ya," Peira replied, managing a small smile through her disappointment. "Maybe we can meet up on yer way back through?"

"Perhaps," Dorho smiled a bit, shoving the roll into his mouth.

Through the rest of the evening, the two shared a light conversation, mostly regarding the contrasts of Elgrahm Hold versus the Kingdom of Anslater. Dorho spoke of his new home in Golden Bow Gulch, life in the Free Region, and what he knew about the conflict between Lady Eisley and King Borlhauf. Though, during the conversation, he removed Lynsia, her journey, and his part in the rift between the duchess and the king. The meal was delicious, and the beer was some of the best Dorho had ever consumed. After several tangents in the discussion between the rogue and Peira, the count felt like it was time to get some rest, especially after he counted his third yawn of the night.

Despite the sadness in the woman's voice, Dorho departed the tavern while the moon lifted high overhead in the star-filled sky. His coin purse was empty, but his belly was full, and he had great hopes for the rest of his journey to locate the second Sidhe-Vein. He gathered his horse and returned hastily to the barn loft that Jonsal allowed him to use as a bedroom. The rogue barely got his new hat and boots off before the desire for sleep overtook him, and he found himself wrapped in the warm embrace of a midsummer slumber.

As his body rested, his mind dreamt of an endless field of green grass, like an ocean of swaying emerald strands. He was standing in the middle of it, with no roads or houses to be seen. Swathes of clouds spread out over the clear blue sky, blocking the sunlight from burning the rogue's skin as he looked around the vacant field of green.

"Dorho..." the goddess called through the veil of Dorho's dreams.

"Di..." the rogue answered, his dark eyes scanning the field once more. "Dimorta?"

Tearing through the soil only a few steps from where the rogue stood, a coffin of blackened iron and obsidian rose to greet the confused count. Locks clicked loudly as the dark sarcophagus twisted and turned until it was standing on its end, the jawless skull motif of the goddess marking the heavy stone lid. Dorho instinctively stepped back, not sure what to expect from this sudden intrusion into his dream.

"Dorho," the voice of death called once more, as the lid of the casket fell away, striking the ground firmly.

As though she were stepping from a simple door, Dimorta walked out of the upright coffin. Like a messy cascade of white ashes, her long hair fell about her shoulders to her waist, swaying with each movement of the deity's body. Just as before, the left side of her face was covered by an unpainted ivory mask, while the other eye, a startling shade of crimson, peered at the rogue while the ruby-stained lips curled into a slight smile. She was tall and thin, which was easy to tell under the long, onyx-colored gown that flickered with something akin to amethyst dust. As though it were a cape made from the midnight sky, massive black wings stretched outward briefly before being folded behind the goddess.

"I come to ask a favor," Dimorta spoke, her tone hushed as she approached the rogue slowly.

"Another one?" Dorho sighed.

"A soul was taken from me," the goddess stated, ignoring the clear protest from the man. "A soul that has evaded me for many years. It was in my grasp, and it was yanked away."

"You mean, besides mine?" Count Maizen smirked slightly. "I'm sure I've sent many to you that you weren't expecting yet. So what if one gets taken from you?"

Dimorta stood only two steps away from the figure of the rogue when she stopped walking. It was then that Dorho realized the kindness in her eyes and warm smile on her face had been replaced with frustration and rage.

"You want me to find a soul for you, on top of stopping Xa'morhu from being reborn?" Dorho finally asked, narrowing his gaze, unable to hide his displeasure.

Dimorta nodded. "You've encountered this soul once before. You were there when it was finally sent my way. Then the Onyx Spire ripped it out of the Undertow and took it from my domain."

"You're not a fan of necromancers then, are you?" Count Maizen quipped before letting out a mildly defeated sigh. "Fine, I'll play fetch. Is there anything I need to know?"

"The soul has become a monster," the goddess said sternly. "More so than before. Imbued with power from Xa'morhu's scion. You will know it when you see it."

Dorho looked about the field of grass, noticing that it was slowly withering away the longer the goddess stood before him. "And just how am I to make sure this soul gets back to you? Obviously killing it before didn't work."

"You won't," Dimorta stepped forward and blatantly, but suddenly, grabbed the right arm of the rogue. "You're going to obliterate it for me."

Pain ripped through the arm of the count as violet flames shot out from the grip of the goddess. Driven to his knees by the agony that washed over his body, Dorho could only look on as the skin along his arm was burned and marked by the lethal power of the goddess. A scream flew from his lips, falling upon the uncaring ears of the tall woman as her grip tightened upon his forearm. He struggled, pulled, and tried to yank himself free from her grasp, but when her left palm was pressed to his forehead, a vicious bolt of amethyst lightning ripped through the vision of the rogue, sending him to the ground in a heap.

Coughing and wheezing, Dorho sprawled out on the dying grass of his dream. Blood dripped from his mouth and nose, and his breath came harsh and ragged. Dimorta stood over him, like a hunter inspecting a fresh kill. Her eyes peered into his soul, judging the pain on his face as he fought to get back to his knees at least.

"Your arm," the goddess spoke coldly, "it now bears a scripture from my Withering Bible, and within the words, burns my powers over death."

Slowly, his body feeling like it had just been crushed and set aflame by giants, Dorho lifted his arm into his view. Runes colored with dark violet stains appeared carved into his sun-beaten skin. Other patterns, similar to summoning circles and magic charts, were marked in deep, coal-like hues. On the back of his hand, seemingly engraved in a red that would make any rose jealous, sat the jawless skull sigil of the goddess.

"It was time to level the playing field," Dimorta called as Dorho struggled to his feet, fighting through the pain in his body. "A scion of death to battle the scion of entropy."

"Why?" Dorho asked, spitting blood onto the ground at his feet. "Why are you doing this?"

Dimorta reached out, wiping a bit of the scarlet fluid from the man's chin as she answered. "I am the goddess of death. I am the ultimate force of equality. No one is rich or poor, or good or evil in my eyes. You are all mortals. You will all die. I do not care who, how, when, where, or why. Only that your souls end up in my Undertow. Xa'morhu appointed a scion, who took a soul from me. It's one thing when a necromancer transfers a soul to a new body, or when they simply animate the dead with a bit of magic. It becomes an insult when the soul itself is yanked from my domain and shoved into a monster. I have to leave you mortals with your free will, but that doesn't mean I can't level the odds a bit."

She sucked the blood from her fingers as she examined the rogue and his modified arm.

"And this is supposed to help me?" Dorho held his arm up, growling through the agony.

"Jakhyru, Solarea, and Atheia wanted to make you their scions," the goddess confessed with a slight smile as she tasted the blood on her tongue. "I already gave you my blessing, and after this new insult to my domain, it was decided that you would become my scion instead. You will become a messenger of death to those who oppose us."

"About that," Dorho clutched his pained arm protectively. "Your blessing. You mentioned that before. What does that mean?"

"We're talking, aren't we?" Dimorta replied. "It allows me to reach you easier. It also means that if you die again, you'll end up in my tower, rather than the Undertow. So I would suggest against it, unless you don't mind entertaining me for a long time."

Count Maizen grumbled as he backed away from the goddess, his dark eyes scanning the decaying grass of the empty field. "So, is this real? I'm not just dreaming this?"

Dimorta snapped her fingers, and suddenly they were standing in the loft of Jonsal's barn. The smell of drying grain and old wood assaulted the nostrils of the rogue as he spit up more blood with a few more coughs. Without the burning sun, the summer air had turned cool against his skin, and the white light of the moon crept in through cracks in the old walls of the barn. Wooden floors creaked and groaned under the weight of the rogue as he glanced about the barn cautiously.

"Take care of yourself, Dorho," Dimorta said softly, taking a few steps away from the count. "Don't worry about your daughter. I won't let any harm come to my future disciple."

"Wait," Dorho begged, walking after the goddess. "My daughter? Your disciple? My arm. Your power. How am I supposed to—."

She turned quickly, placing her right palm to the man's forehead before he could finish the thought. Violet light flashed brilliantly through the eyes and mind of the rogue, and just as quickly, the world fell silent and dark. Dorho fell into a deep, unplanned slumber before he even hit the floor.

"All will be revealed to your mortal eyes soon enough," the words of the goddess called, barely reaching the ears of the rogue in his sleep.

After what felt like several hours, the rogue came to. His body ached, and his arm still burned, but he otherwise felt quite rested. The sun was just beginning to seep through the gaps in the barn's walls, bringing heat to the chill in the air. As he expected, Dimorta was gone, and if it wasn't for the marks on his right arm, he would've brushed her visit off as a side effect from the beer.

He sat up slowly, feeling the sting shoot from his shoulder to his fingers and back again. As his eyes adjusted to the faint morning light, he spied the clothes neatly folded over the loft railing. A pair of dark amethyst trousers and a matching soft cotton short-sleeved tunic rested next to a black leather vest of brigandine armor featuring silver skulls for buttons and prismatic onyx studs. The wine-colored cloak remained, though a jawless skull now adorned the rear of the fabric, while the trim took the design of a slithering snake. Luckily, the reptilian leather hat was unmolested, sitting on the floor next to a pair of soft, fur-lined boots the color of fresh charcoal.

"Thanks," Dorho muttered as he examined the clothes from the bedroll. "I guess I spent that money for nothing."

The scion of death stood up sluggishly, checking the new markings on his right arm. Seeming like nothing more than a very intricate tattoo now, the design ran from his fingers to his shoulder, though his skin still felt the burn of Dimorta's magic. Runes, writing, sigils, arcane diagrams, and occult circles covered his flesh in a way that looked like someone had simply wrapped his arm in the pages of an unholy tome. It didn't feel like his own arm anymore. He couldn't explain the sensation, but he didn't want to believe it was still his skin. It looked repulsive, demonic, and profane.

"I just wanted to take that girl to Euthrox and retire to a quiet house with my wife," the rogue sighed, before getting dressed and rolling up the bedroll he had been borrowing.

Dorho put the twin curved swords on his hips, donned the new, dark hat, ran his fingers over his facial hair and tested the feel of the gifted attire. Everything fit perfectly, and he found it surprisingly easy to move in. Even the boots, though lined with soft fur, weren't too warm and still allowed him to walk unhindered. For only a moment, he wished he had a mirror.

"Scion of death, huh?" Dorho whispered to himself as he glanced around the loft. "We'll see about that."

Leaping from the loft, rather than using the ladder, Dorho dropped onto a stack of bagged grain, then slid down to the floor of the barn. Despite the ache in his arm, and the strange events in his slumber, the rogue felt lively and eager to start his day. He sauntered from the barn and into the light of the morning sun, making his way towards the house where Jonsal and his family resided.

The house itself sat upon a small rise in the middle of the field of grain with the barn only a short distance to the north. A corral connected to the rear of the barn contained the farm's five horses, while a flock of chickens roamed a pen along the side of the main house. Made of clay, dark granite, and pine timbers, the house itself looked as though it was pulled from the very soil itself. Wheat grew to the south and west of the house, while sorghum and amaranth grew on the remaining land. It was a rather charming plot of land, and the people who owned it were just as pleasant.

"New clothes?" the old farmer asked, stepping out of the house and almost running into the rogue.

Dorho tipped the hat in greeting and smiled warmly, though he hid his right arm under the fabric of the cloak. "Indeed, thanks for the coin. I feel like a proper count again."

"It looks," the old man looked over the silver skulls and all the dark colors, "appropriate for you. Suits you well."

"Thank you for your kindness," Count Maizen replied. "I hate to leave on such short notice, but I need to get to Vansenhul."

"Found that man you were looking for?" Jonsal inquired. "How do you plan on getting there?"

Dorho nodded confidently. "The man I'm looking for lives in the capital city. As far as getting there? I was hoping I could borrow one of your horses."

For a moment, the old man rubbed his chin, then vanished into the house, leaving Dorho on the wooden porch.

When he returned, Jonsal was joined by his eldest daughter. She was shorter than Dorho, but not by much, and her slender figure masked the fact that she lived and worked on a farm. Her face was fair, yet pretty, and framed by long, blonde hair, while eyes of the bluest skies peered over the rogue cautiously. The girl was easily one of the strongest members of the family, something Dorho had witnessed several times during his stay on the farm. She was also the first person he had met after being revived.

"Corina?" Dorho called her name as he tilted his head in confusion.

"You're a visitor from another kingdom, a stranger in this region," Jonsal said. "I wouldn't want you getting lost or mugged again, so my girl will be going with you. She'll also make sure you bring back my horse. Might also do her some good to get out of this dusty little town and see the big city for a bit."

"I would tell you to keep her here," Dorho responded, "but I know better than to argue with you. You've already been beyond welcoming with me."

Dorho really didn't want to involve the girl in his quest, especially after everything the family had already done for him. He could find the capital of Anslater easily enough, if he wanted to do it on his own, but he also had nothing to trade or pay with for the use of the horse. For many of the same reasons he refused to take Peira, he wanted to tell Jonsal to keep his daughter at home, but Dorho needed a horse if he wanted to reach Vansenhul in a timely manner.

"You proved to be a man of your word," the farmer said wholeheartedly. "You worked your ass off to cover your stay. In fact, you worked far harder than we ever expected you to. Most nobles I've met were useless sacks of skin. You're different. My daughter will make sure you don't get lost on the road. She'll also make sure the horses get back to me. Just do me a favor, Dorho?"

Count Maizen smiled a bit at the words of the old farmer. "And what would that be?"

"Show her a good time," Jonsal requested. "She's been on this farm her whole life. Let her enjoy the trip to the big city. That's all I ask."

"Are you certain, Jonsal?" Dorho let his eyes glance over the girl next to her father. "It's four days to the city, and I'll probably be there a week or so. She'll be gone for almost three weeks, most likely. I'd hate to worry or inconvenience you and your family with her absence."

"Count Maizen," the old farmer sighed heavily. "Listen, the war being waged by King Borlhauf, it takes a toll, even out here on a dusty old grain farm. Our trade routes have been impacted, traders from Thornbror don't come this way anymore. King Vimor requires that we allocate a certain percentage of our production for the war effort, which hurts our ability to brew our beer and trade with locals. The younger children may not see it as much as the adults do, but I know Corina sees it. It wears on her just like it wears on myself and my wife. Let her enjoy a break from her duties on the farm. She's earned it."

For a moment, Dorho considered ways to turn down the offer of the old farmer, but he ultimately nodded. "If that is what Corina wants, then she can come with me. Besides, it might be nice to have someone to talk to."

"Corina?" Jonsal put a hand on his daughter's shoulder. "Help Count Maizen get a couple horses ready, I'll help your mother pack you both some food and goods for the journey."

The daughter's deep blue eyes lit up with excitement as she spoke, "of course, father. Thank you!"

Turning to the door of the house, Jonsal paused to throw a glance over his shoulder towards the rogue. "Keep her safe. You have a good reputation with us."

08.

Soaring over the land on the back of the powerful wyvern, Lorvin brushed his fingers over the rough scales of the massive beast. They had left Ameribelle two days ago, and were already deep into the Needlebreak Mountains east of Stonewalker Gate. Pine and spruce trees rose from the crags below as the mighty reptile moved among the clouds at an amazing pace.

Kortyx made the act of flight seem like an effortless endeavor, her great wings pushing them through the sky as though it were just a leisurely swim. Her scales, like a colorful mix between copper patina and desert sandstone, glistened lightly in the afternoon sun during breaks in the scattered clouds. Though Zakosa clung tightly to the cluster of horns protruding from the top of the wyvern's head, Lorvin sat relaxed upon her back between the vast spread of the graceful wings. From the tip of her angular snout to the venomous spine at the end of her tail, Kortyx was easily three and a half times as long as Lorvin was tall. Her long body pulsed and swayed with the strength and agility of her lean muscles with each movement, appearing like a winged serpent in the sky. Though Kortyx was like a fish in water when it came to flight, two stout legs allowed the great creature to grab prey and carry things if needed. Despite the size and strength of the great beast, the monk felt no fear, being more at peace upon the back of the wyvern than he could ever be in a city.

Not only was Kortyx a great method for traveling, but she was a trusted companion for the naetari. He had found her as a hatchling after trophy hunters killed her parents in the canyon west of Uhmberholdt. They were hunting rare animals for a greedy noble with more money than common sense, and after dispersing the hunters from the region, Lorvin found a frightened hatchling hiding in the back of the nest cave. Unwilling to leave the baby to face its fate alone, Lorvin raised the wyvern with the intent on releasing her back to nature, but after almost two years, the growing reptile refused to leave the naetari, preferring to follow the feline wherever he traveled. Alpenglow supplied books and knowledge to the naetari, giving Lorvin the ability to confidently raise and bond with the growing beast. Fifteen years ago, he gifted the wyvern fledgling the name Kortyx, and they became family to one another.

    Despite almost two days of flight, the kobold still was very uneasy around the much larger, much more powerful reptile. Even more so when it came to flight. Lorvin laughed at the small kobold keeping a firm grip on the spikes on the back of Kortyx's head, and playfully ignored any complaints from the druid whenever they prepared to take to the skies once more. There was no saddle, as one might expect with a mount like a horse or skathya, just a heavy wool blanket held down with a leather harness. For Lorvin, he was comfortable on the back of the wyvern high over the world below, in fact, he cherished the feeling. For those that had the pleasure of flying with Lorvin and Kortyx, the naetari found their reactions amusing and exciting.

    The sun was well on its way down behind the western horizon when Lorvin finally pointed to a small lake in a valley between two great stony mountains. A quick command was barked from the lips of the naetari, and immediately, the powerful wyvern started downward. Lorvin howled with excitement as he felt the rush of the early evening air through his fur, and Kortyx let out a sound that seemed like a cross between a shriek and a growl. Zakosa closed his eyes, clinging tightly to the horns of the mighty beast. The howl of the wind as it whipped by the plummeting wyvern was nearly deafening, drowning out the whimpers of terror from the kobold as the great reptile dropped between the mountains.

    Great wings went wide above the lake, slowing the descent of the wyvern before Lorvin's trusted companion settled down upon a rocky shore shielded by junipers and spruce trees. With the setting of the sun, the valley was already blanketed with shadow, shielding the travelers from the heat offered by the summer light.

"Thanks to the gods that's over," Zakosa snarled as he slid from the neck of Kortyx.

"What," Lorvin laughed, rubbing the back of the wyvern's head firmly, "you still don't like traveling this way?"

"No!" the druid yapped. "We should nots even be here. I was supposed to helps guide the Sidhe-Vein to the faerie. Thats was my duty."

"I think this is fine," the naetari stated with a grin as he looked for a place to set their camp. "We go find the druids, let them know who's coming, and then Vourden and the others won't have to waste time coming down here. This way, they already know where they're headed next."

"This was nots the plans from I'raha," Zakosa argued.

Lorvin scratched his chin mockingly and shook his head dismissively. "I've never met this I'raha you speak so fondly of, and I only met you just the other day. Meanwhile, I've known Vourden, Dorho, and Kendira for years. I'll let you guess who I respect more."

"That's reckless," the druid narrowed his amber eyes in defiance.

"Reckless is you throwing a fit instead of helping get our camp set up," the monk replied, untying the packs of supplies from the back of Kortyx's harness before dropping to the ground himself.

Lorvin unfolded his hammock and strung it up between two tall pines just a few steps from the edge of the lake's clear water. While the druid scoffed and planted himself on a stump like a petulant child, the monk began gathering wood and bark to build a fire. He ignored the behavior of the sulking kobold while focusing on building a small fire against a cluster of rocks to protect the flame from the breeze of the evening. Honestly, the naetari didn't need the kobold's help, as he had done this countless times in his travels, but having the small druid sulk was going to kill the pleasant mood.

"If you won't help with the camp, why don't you find us something to eat?" Lorvin asked, digging through the pack of rations he had set up before departing Ameribelle. "Unless you enjoy preserved meats and hard bread."

Without a word of complaint, the kobold hopped down from the stump and fetched his gnarled staff from the pack he had fastened it to. He sneered silently, but wandered off into the cluster of pines among the shattered rocks that formed the shore of the mountain lake.

"It would be faster if you just took Kortyx with you," Lorvin spoke, though he was trying to hide his laughter at the antics of the small reptilian.

"Well," the catfolk grinned, looking to the wyvern who was watching him patiently from where she had landed, "at least he's gone for a bit. Kortyx, hunt," Lorvin commanded with a smile as he gestured to the sky.

The giant reptile howled and with a push from the mighty wings, took to the sky in a single leap. Lorvin watched as his trusted companion flew high and began to circle about, slowly widening the path of her flight. He preferred that she be allowed to hunt for her own food, to preserve her own natural instincts. Though, around cattle farms and cities, he would feed her things he could catch or trade for, to prevent unwanted accidents from occurring. After a few minutes of watching the wyvern hunt, the powerful beast vanished behind the western peaks, leaving Lorvin alone by the lake.

His hammock was hung, a fire was crackling in a cluster of broken stones, and the cold water of the mountain lake gave them plenty to drink. For a moment, the naetari glanced about, then stepped over to a spruce tree, its trunk nearly as thick as the catfolk's thigh. Lorvin, after scanning the terrain once more for the kobold or the wyvern, tossed his shirt and meteor hammer to the ground next to his hammock.

He offered a silent prayer to the gods of the earth, plants, rocks, and sky, then drove his right palm into the bark of the tree. Without pause, he shifted his weight from his right foot to his left, took half a step, and immediately struck the tree with his left elbow. Then his left knee, followed by his right foot. Each strike was intentional, with the whole of his strength behind each blow, and with each hit he moved slightly quicker. It only took a minute or two before he was pummeling the trunk of the tree with a fierce, steady, rapid rhythm of punches, elbows, knees, and kicks. Though the bark of the spruce bit into his skin with each hit, he kept going, pushing his thoughts to places far away from the camp by the lake.

Lorvin was used to it, having trained for years with the monks of the Chaydenhall Monastery. Like druids, the monks were worshippers of the land, defenders of nature, and kept a natural way of life. Unlike druids, the monks of Chaydenhall didn't form groves, wouldn't rely heavily on magic, and gave more praise to the deities related to nature, whereas the druids put heavier emphasis on the energy and power of nature. The Chaydenhall monks were closer related to priests and nuns, while the druids tended to be closer in kinship with faeries and forest sprites. For a moment, he thought of how similar his path was with that of the kobold, and yet, how different they both were.

Like Kortyx, Lorvin was an orphan. Before his fifth summer, his parents were slain during a feud between naetari clans when the rival clan's warriors ambushed their village during the dark of night. Anyone caught fleeing from the battle were struck down by a rain of arrows and darts. His mother and father had been some of those who tried to escape and paid the price. Traders roving through the valley that held the remains of the village found Lorvin looking for food among the destruction and corpses. They left the young catfolk boy with the residents of Chaydenhall after gathering supplies from the monastery and trading with the monks. Here, the young naetari would train his mind, hone his body, and focus his spirit into a tool that could be used to protect, endure, and teach the things nature had to offer.

He learned the runes and prayers needed to channel the divine power of the deities of nature. The understanding of Chay Ta Freu, the monks' martial arts, was literally beaten into the body of the naetari. Knowledge from books about wilderness survival, plants, animals, and various other nature-related topics was taught to Lorvin as he grew in the ways of the monks. On multiple occasions, the students of the monastery were left in the wilderness without food, water, or even sleeping rolls. They used these moments to embrace the flow of the natural world, and appreciate the things truly given to them by the gods that oversaw the beauty of nature. It was a harsh way to grow up, but being so young, Lorvin adapted to the training and way of life quickly.

    Despite his thoughts on the past and distant places, Lorvin heard the kobold approaching long before he saw the small reptile. The druid carried a cloth full of edible morels, a single decapitated grouse, and a satchel of wild rose mixed with elderflower. Like a disgruntled child, Zakosa dropped everything between the monk and the fire, then returned to his stump without saying anything.

    Lorvin scoffed at the attitude of the druid before turning his attention to the edible things brought into the camp by the kobold. He mixed the morels, after cleaning them, with some rice given to them by Kendira and placed them in a pan over the flames. With a small knife, the naetari made quick work of the dead bird, removing the feathers and innards quickly before splitting it open and setting it on a rack over the shielded fire. Combining rooibos tea leaves with the roses and elderflower, the monk filled a kettle with fresh water from the lake and set it to brew next to the grouse. With their dinner cooking and the sun's light fading from the sky, Lorvin crossed his legs and sat on the ground where he could tend to the meal as it simmered.

    "You haves scars," Zakosa finally spoke up, the reptile's voice a low hiss in the darkening world as he gestured to Lorvin's chest. "You didn't lies about being a monk."

    The naetari looked down at the three runes carved across his chest. One represented his vow to protect nature, the middle one was his vow to never take a life, and the mark on his left pectoral was his vow to always be loyal to those who he considered family.

"Just a reminder to always be who I truly am," Lorvin smiled a bit. "Although, I'll be honest, no one is quite sure if the same could be said about you."

"What does that mean?" the kobold tilted his narrow face.

"Vourden told me everything," Lorvin said as he stirred the rice mixture. "You came out of nowhere, claiming to be sent by a faerie. Then, you hid like a coward while his wife and our friend was killed. I also find you a bit suspicious. You claim to be a druid of the Red Aspen Grove, but I've yet to see your plaque."

"Is that whys we are outs here?" Zakosa spat accusingly. "That sheriff doesn't trusts me, does he?"

"I've met druids from the Red Aspen Grove," the naetari mentioned without pause. "They all carry a plaque made of aspen wood, marked with the sigil of their rank and name. Yet, you don't display one. You dress like a druid, act like a druid, but there's nothing to say you aren't working on behalf of the Onyx Spire."

The druid growled and stamped the bottom of his staff into the ground firmly. "I am nots the enemy."

"Whether you are or not," Lorvin shrugged, "matters nothing to me. I don't even know you. I was asked to keep you away from Lynsia and the others as a precaution to prevent you from spying on them. They are avoiding a repeat of Dracamori."

Grumbling loudly, the druid fumbled around, reaching into his fur robes before producing a palm-sized disc of aspen wood. Upon the round chunk of wood, the symbols for spines and tails had been carved, suggesting the name given to the kobold during his training at the grove. Under the symbols were three red circles, suggesting the reptile was at least a third-tier druid, and a series of eleven black dots, one for each year of service Zakosa gave to the Red Aspen Grove after finishing his apprenticeship.

From what Lorvin knew of the druids of Red Aspen Grove, he understood a little of their culture and the significance of the designs on the plaque. Being third-tier, the kobold was only two steps under the Grand Ovate. Starting out, they were called a low apprentice, then promoted to a high apprentice. Once they graduated from the apprentice stage, they became a first-tier druid, and could undertake duties outside the grove without supervision. A second-tier druid would be expected to take at least one low apprentice with them on trips outside the grove. They were like teachers, preaching the basic principles and getting new students acclimated to life within the group. A third-tier druid was similar to a college professor or librarian, building on the foundations of those new students once they became high apprentices.

Above these teachers sat the Four Orders, which acted like senate or council members. The Winter Order saw to the darker rites and rituals of the grove, such as funerals and forcefully removing disorderly creatures from the area. Opposite of this, was the Spring Order, who oversaw the livelier festivals and events, such as weddings and births. The Autumn Order took care of trades, farming, and cultivation needs for the grove. Finally, the Summer Order dictated recruiting, education, and giving out judgments not fitting of the Winter Order. Each of the Four Orders contained five members, which were some of the strongest druids living in the Red Aspen Grove.

At the head of the Red Aspen Grove, seated on the Canopy Throne, was the Grand Ovate. Though the Four Orders ran the grove like a senate, it was the Grand Ovate who had the final say if it was needed. They were an elected position, chosen from the most powerful of the druids, and then the Grand Ovate would serve until death. It was expected that they would allow the Four Orders to run things, reserving the ultimate authority of the Grand Ovate for only the most dire of situations.

He understood a little, as his own beliefs and travels had put him in contact with several members of the Red Aspen Grove over the years, but Lorvin had never officially visited the home of the druids. He respected them, even if they didn't fully align with his own beliefs or lifestyle.

"A third-tier?" Lorvin inquired, examining the plaque carefully as the kobold held it out. "I've honestly never heard of the Red Aspen Grove accepting kobolds, but we'll see if your story checks out once we get there."

Zakosa tucked the disc back into place under his fur robes, then shook his head. "Believes me or nots, I am not the spy. I works for I'raha."

"We're headed to Anslater, correct?" Lorvin asked, turning the grouse over carefully.

The kobold nodded in agreement. "Yes. The grove is about two days southwest by horse from Vansenhul."

Lorvin produced a pair of tin cups and matching plates from one of the sacks of supplies they had been given. Into the cups, he poured equal amounts of the hot tea, and added a scoop of honey to both mugs. He placed one of the cups of tea next to the kobold on a flat rock, then returned to where he was seated to continue working the meal over the fire.

"We'll start moving through the Calinsahr Duchy tomorrow afternoon once we cross the Helmstad River," Lorvin stated before taking a slow drink from the steaming tea. "Once we drop into the Phavora Lowlands, and fly over the Goldenveil Bay, we can follow the coast down to Vansenhul. Shouldn't take us but maybe a week to get there. We can cover far more distance in the air with Kortyx than we can on the ground with a horse."

"So," Zakosa set his skull-topped staff down to pick up the offered mug of tea, "you won't considers turning back?"

The monk smiled as he took another drink from the cup. "Not at all. I was given a task by a good friend. We're going to find the druids, and I'm going to determine whether or not you're the spy who got Paisley killed."

"I can assures you, I am nots the spy," the druid protested defiantly.

"We'll see," Lorvin glanced at the kobold from over the rim of the mug. "I hope for your sake, you're being honest with me. I'd hate to have to find out which one of us is stronger."

Before the druid could argue further, the wyvern returned, dropping a red elk stag on the rocks behind Zakosa. Swiftly, Kortyx landed, staring over the kobold for a moment before tearing into the dead elk with her large fangs. Teeth pulled at the flesh of the carcass as bones were crushed between the massive jaws of the wyvern. By the time the rice and spatchcock grouse was finished, the elk had vanished down the throat of the great reptile.

"I made a vow to never end a life that was not for me to eat," Lorvin stated as he put a quarter of the grouse on each plate, with a generous helping of the morels and rice. "I would hate to find out you're the reason Paisley and Dorho died, because Kortyx never made that same vow."

"I assures you, I am nots the spy," Zakosa insisted, before taking a large bite of the grouse meat. "Maybe you should looks to those you trusts the most."

Focused solely on eating, the monk never replied. Though, he did hear the words of the druid.

It had been a long day of flying, and despite how relaxing it was to explore the world from the air, it made Lorvin hungry. Using a piece of hardtack to shovel up the mixture of rice and morels, the naetari made quick work of his first plate of food, and swiftly grabbed another quarter of the grilled bird and another helping of the rice. Other than a little crushed chili pepper and salt he had dusted it all with while it cooked, the food was rather unseasoned, but it filled the hole created by the day's flight.

"Don't you worries about predators when outs here?" Zakosa asked after a long moment of silence between the two as they ate.

Lorvin glanced over the rim of his tea mug and then gestured towards Kortyx. "Why would I worry? My traveling companion is one of the largest flying predators the world has ever seen."

"Poachers?" the druid questioned. "What abouts hunters of the legendary, rare, and valuable creatures?

"We usually end up hunting them," the monk replied. "Ever since the fall of Atlantis, the creatures of the

Enlightened Aeon have been persecuted relentlessly. I want to preserve them, all of them. Dragons, hydras, wyverns, dryads, centaurs, and so many others. I really don't care how dangerous or insane it sounds, but allowing these magnificent creatures to be wiped out for power, wealth, or glory is just wrong. Tell me, kobold. If you aren't the spy responsible for killing my friends, then what destiny put you on this quest? What is your goal in all this?"

"I wants to restore the swamps back to a good home for us in the Endless Tomb," Zakosa answered proudly. "Al'zagur poisons our home. Monsters take over. I'raha offer to helps me restore the swamps and get rids of the monsters."

"If you are indeed a friend," Lorvin spoke between bites of the grouse meat, "I hope you are able to reach your goal. Evil should not be allowed to flourish unchecked."

"I haves my own suspicions on who the spy is," Zakosa said coldly after taking a long drink from the tea, "but I assures you, it is not me."

"Oh? Do tell," Lorvin requested, setting his cleared plate aside and moving to stretch out in his hammock.

"Someone who wants to do great harms to a mutual friend," the druid replied, taking the last leg of the grouse greedily. "Though, I haves my doubts that this mutual friend sees me as such."

"Talking about Vourden?" the catfolk lifted his brow in curiosity as he relaxed. "Sure, he's a little rough around the edges, but the man just lost his wife. He's an honest fellow, though. Far more honest than the likes of Dorho or Kendira, though for different reasons, I suppose. Since meeting you, two important people have died in his life, and so, he doesn't trust you, but that's between you and him. Though, I can't say I trust you, either."

"Whats do you suggests?" the kobold asked, chewing on a bite of the meat.

"Me?" Lorvin shrugged as he rolled over, his eyes away from the fire. "Get some sleep. Wake up with the intent to prove him wrong. Prove us all wrong."

Lorvin let his thoughts wander to other times and places until he was fast asleep, which didn't take long. After a long day in the air, a heavy meal, and good tea, it didn't take much effort to find sleep. His last thought was simple, he hoped they were all wrong about the kobold, but he hoped the suspicions of the small reptilian man wouldn't be proven true.

09.

Dorho and Corina had been on the road for a day and half when they reached Wayfarer's Folly, a cluster of buildings on the plains that served as an inn, tavern, temple, and courier office for travelers. An outpost for the Anslater army was also constructed on the edge of the group of buildings, but even that equaled nothing more than a small barracks, stable, and office. It wasn't an official town, but it was an important spot along the road if you were traveling through the expansive plains of Kourinthe. From the center of Wayfarer's Folly, a road stretched southward, eventually leading to the Stragent Region, and from there it continued to the Galensteil Wastes. Continuing to follow the main highway east would put a person in Vansenhul within two days. Traders were set up with their wagons of wares on the roads leading in and out of the cluster of stone structures. It was quaint, charming, but provided a much-needed break from the road for weary travelers.

"We have some time to spare," Corina mentioned as she finished explaining the area to Count Maizen. "From here, it will take about two days to reach the capitol. The wedding is five days away still, right? It wouldn't hurt if we stayed here for the night. Maybe we should relax with some hot food and good drink before continuing onward?"

Dorho nodded and offered an approving glance from under the dark hat. "Sounds pleasant. I'm sure the horses would appreciate the break as well."

The farmer's daughter guided them to the public livery on the eastern edge of the way station. For a trio of bronze tiles, the horses would be kept fed, groomed, and safe while the pair enjoyed a respite from the road.

Dorho removed the twin katiss swords from the saddle of his horse, and secured them to his waist as he moved towards the entrance of the livery. He could feel the eyes of several others on him as he walked. The silver skulls and markings on his right arm weren't exactly normal, especially to country folk traveling through Wayfarer's Folly, so he understood the glances of suspicion. The sigil of Dimorta on the back of his cloak would've drawn even more attention, but he had folded it up and stashed it in one of his travel bags due to the hot weather. He had debated wrapping his arm to hide the markings the goddess had burned into his skin, but for the same reason he put away the cloak, he decided against it.

"Hey," Corina called, jogging up to the rogue after securing her horse. "Don't go too far without me. I'm your guide, remember?"

"I remember," he responded, offering a small smile while he glanced at the young woman.

They had spent the last day and a half with just each other for company, and Dorho talked often with the young woman in his care. She was smarter than most people gave her credit for, and harbored a naturally caring personality inside that shell of a rural farmer's daughter. Even though they had met a few times while Dorho was helping around the farm, it wasn't until the previous night that Dorho realized how much he enjoyed her companionship. He found that she possessed a wonderful sense of humor, a quick wit, and had no problem being brash or bold in situations other women her age might shy away from. As much as he had protested bringing her with him, he had warmed up to the idea of having her accompany him to the capitol.

She wore cloth breeches the color of sandstone, and charcoal-hued leather boots that rose almost to her knees. A leather vest made from the same leather as the boots covered her short-sleeved sky-blue blouse. Corina never braided her blonde hair, nor did she pull it back in a tail, it fell naturally just beyond her shoulders like a cascade of sun-bleached wheat. Being nearly as tall as the rogue, she had no problems meeting his dark gaze with her twin sapphire eyes, which highlighted her gracefully angular face. She was slender, but just as strong as one would expect from a farmer's child. Shiny earrings hung from a thin gold band on each ear, displaying a small emerald at the end of the thumb-length silver chain. Corina was a mere farmer's daughter, but she held a strength and beauty in her figure that many lacked.

"Come on," she urged, "we can check out some of the trader wagons before we go get dinner at the tavern."

Dorho nodded in agreement, casting a precautionary glance up and down the road through Wayfarer's Folly. "Sounds fun. Though, I'm just enjoying a break from riding."

"Oh!" she exclaimed, dashing off to a cart full of bright textiles and ornate clothing. "Look! I could wear something other than my farm clothes."

"What's wrong with what you're wearing?" Dorho inquired, his dark eyes scanning the young woman momentarily.

"I'm the company for a visiting noble," Corina stated with a wry smile, "and we're headed to the prince's wedding. I look plain, standing next to you."

"You should be careful with the coin your father gave you," Dorho insisted, turning his eyes to the many different fabrics and colors offered by the wagon's owner. "You don't want to end up in Vansenhul a coinless pauper, do you?"

As if she hadn't heard him, Corina's left hand brushed over the sheer cloth of a dress colored like pale jade. White silk cord wound through silver hooks, closing up the back of the dress in a rather elegant fashion. The edges of the dress were graced with bands of dark blue cloth with a golden swirl pattern woven in. Even Dorho had to agree, it would look nice on her, though he had someone else in mind as he gazed over the garment.

Despite the elegance of the dress, a design on the wagon itself caught the eye of the rogue. It was small, almost too small to be noticed. An upside-down arch with a line passing through the middle, bridging both sides of the arc. Under the connecting line, three dots were placed in red ink. It was the symbol of a trader from the Free Region.

"Look at it!" the young woman spoke excitedly. "It's beautiful."

"I can custom tailor it," the female shopkeeper spoke up, holding up a thread and needle as she hunched behind a workbench. "If it's needed, of course."

"What would it cost?" Corina pressed, ignoring the rogue's distracted gaze.

"For you?" the shopkeeper smiled warmly before answering. "Twenty gold, if your husband approves, of course."

"I'm not her husband," Dorho's dark eyes shifted to the older woman quickly, "Though, I do wonder, when the robin's song is the sweetest?"

For only a brief moment, the shopkeeper paused, then a broad grin crossed her face. "The robin's song is sweetest in the morning, but those who listen hear the true beauty at dusk."

Dorho nodded and allowed a slight smirk to show on his own lips. "So, I guess you and Myrda are friends?"

"Myrda?" the older woman laughed. "That's my sister! She told me what's going on in Kaenaan. Such terrible news. Unfortunately, the border is closed at the moment, so I can't get home to see her."

Corina looked at them both, tilting her head in confusion. "I... I'm afraid I don't understand what's going on."

"Her sister, Myrda," Dorho motioned towards the older woman behind the workbench, "helped keep my clothes in order whenever I found myself in Kaenaan. She's a good friend of mine."

"Yes, but what about robins?" Corina probed, still perplexed.

"Guild codes, m'lady," the shopkeeper answered. "Contractors, rogues, and such who are part of the guilds in the Free Region have codes and phrases to identify one another."

"Then, Count Maizen, you are..." the farmer's daughter began, looking accusingly at the man.

"The Lord of Rogues," Dorho bowed deeply, "at your service. Contractor of Kaenaan, head of Golden Bow Gulch, and currently on my way to go visit a prince for his wedding."

"I've heard rumors about you," the wagon owner spoke, throwing a knowing smile to the rogue as she pointed with the needle in her hand. "Anyone who's gone to Kaenaan has heard about you, but I won't ask what business you have with the prince and his wedding."

"So," Dorho looked from the shopkeeper, to the dress, then to Corina, before his eyes went back to the lady with the needle. "Are you sure that dress is worth twenty gold? My companion here would look rather lovely in it, don't you think? Wouldn't want your sister to find out you sent her to the wedding looking like a commoner, would you? You'd be doing the guild a favor, honestly."

The older woman nodded eagerly. "If I can just take her measurements, I can have it ready to go by the morning. If you don't mind waiting, of course," she offered. "If you'd put in a good word for me at the guild, I can ignore the cost for this piece. Would that be acceptable, Count Maizen?"

Dorho turned to Corina and smiled smugly. "What do you think? Let the lady take your measurements, and we can go find something to eat."

Corina paused, still trying to process everything she just discovered. "No charge? Are you certain that's okay?"

"Count Maizen is a highly ranked member of the guild, m'lady," the shopkeeper responded, "it would be wrong to charge him, or you, after all the deeds he's done for those of us who rely on the guild to make a living."

"Go on, Corina," Dorho urged, "it's fine. Consider it my gift to you for guiding me to the capitol."

"Well, if you're certain," the farmer's daughter replied, her voice bothered by a hint of concern.

The rogue took a seat near the workbench as the older woman and Corina stepped behind a curtain and away from the prying eyes of others. He chuckled quietly, wondering if it was luck, fate, or sheer coincidence that they'd bump into someone from the Free Region in Anslater. It made him feel more at ease, knowing he had allies from the guild, even so far from his home in Kaenaan. He hoped it would continue to go this well until they could meet with Prince Jolson in Vansenhul.

After only a few moments, the women returned to the workbench next to the wagon. Corina straightened her blouse and vest before thanking the older woman and standing next to the seated rogue.

"Still hungry?" the farmer's daughter asked, waiting for Dorho to get to his feet.

"Might I suggest the wagon over there?" the shopkeeper pointed to a stall across the road next to the tavern. "He's got some amazing skewers and croquettes."

Dorho stood up slowly and smiled kindly. "Thank you. We'll go try it."

With Corina to his left, Dorho departed the textile shop and began crossing the cobblestone road. Two men, both dressed in dark red gambesons and hooded black tunics approached the pair from the west. Two more men, dressed similar to the others, moved in from the east. Dorho's eyes scanned the four men carefully as he kept walking towards the food stall. They were easier to read than any book he had ever been presented with.

"Stay close to me, Corina," he whispered, grasping the woman's wrist and pulling her against his side. "Do you understand?"

"Is something wrong?" she mouthed, her words nearly silent as she followed the gaze of the count.

A fifth man, dressed the same as the other four, ran up from behind and latched onto the free arm of the farmer's daughter. As soon as he began to pull the woman away, Dorho spun about, unsheathing a katiss in his right hand as he moved. The steel of the blade flashed in the afternoon sun, blood sprayed across the cobblestone, and the man howled as he backed away hurriedly. While Count Maizen pulled Corina behind him, the other man's hand fell to the ground, freed from the flesh of his arm. Witnesses screamed and fled the street, putting as much distance as they could between themselves and the scene in the middle of the road.

"Count Maizen, from Elgrahm Hold?" A sixth man spoke up, stepping up next to the men on Dorho's left.

"Depends on who's looking for me," the rogue barked dangerously, putting the blade of the katiss between himself and the speaker.

"A barmaid in Petiora said we could find you here," the man spoke, tapping his hand against a broadsword on his hip.

"Peira?" Dorho narrowed his gaze as he spoke the name as though it were a curse. "So, what do you want?"

"Oh, nothing," the man laughed darkly. "Just was told that a noble from the Thornbror Kingdom had turned down that poor barmaid, and was on his way to the prince's wedding. Now, normally we wouldn't raise a fuss, but seeing as Anslater and Thornbror are at war, and you're dressed like those thugs who raided the capitol a while back, we seem to have a problem."

"I would suggest you go back to your homes," Dorho pulled the other katiss free as he spoke, keeping himself between Corina and the bandits. "This is not a fight you want, nor is it one I desire."

"You're even using the same weapons as those who attacked the Sages Arcanum," the man continued, still drumming his fingers against the hilt of the broadsword. "I'm willing to bet there would be a handsome reward for turning you over to the army."

"And I'm willing to bet you know nothing about me," Dorho insisted. "I'm from Elgrahm Hold, we're at war with King Borlhauf as well."

"Maybe so, but that's still a territory of the Thornbror Kingdom, which makes you an enemy noble," the man argued. "An enemy noble just wandering free through our peaceful kingdom, wearing black and skulls like those Onyx Spire bastards. Sounds suspicious to me."

"He cut off my damn hand, boss!" the other man bellowed, clutching his right arm as two of the other bandits applied a tourniquet.

"And you assaulted my comrade," the bandit leader stated with a sly grin. "You need to be apprehended for the safety of the people of Anslater. I, Kandath, leader of the Black Wing Brigade, will gladly accept your surrender."

"Count Maizen?" Corina whimpered from behind the rogue.

"Don't worry, they won't hurt you," Dorho spoke confidently, his dark eyes watching the movement of the five unharmed men.

Kandath drew his broadsword. "If you surrender and agree to come with us, no harm will come to the peasant girl."

While two finished treating the severed limb of their ally, the remaining bandits unsheathed their own swords. Dorho played with the thought of throwing down his blades and giving up against being outnumbered, but he remembered Kreeve capturing Ansha in Mulman's Hollow. He refused to let that happen again. He had made Jonsal a promise to protect his daughter, and he intended to keep it.

"I'm sorry," Dorho spoke coldly as he glanced back to Corina, then to the bandit leader once more, "I just can't surrender. I don't know how."

Kandath shook his head and sighed deeply. "Such a pity."

The man on the right attacked first, coming at Dorho with a massive overhead swing of his heavy sword. Leaping to the right, Dorho saw the obvious attack incoming and used his left katiss to knock the other blade aside. Resounding through the street, the clash of metal on metal rang like an alarm as the right hand of the rogue brought the other katiss up in a wide arc, driving the claw-like steel through the gut of the unskilled bandit. In a fluid motion, Dorho slammed his foot into the chest of the wounded man as he yanked his blade free from the torn flesh, sending the bandit to the ground several paces away.

With no time to recover, Kandath came at Dorho while the others went after Corina. The bandit swung low, from left to right, hoping to catch the rogue's waist as he turned from the man he kicked to the ground. With no time to back away from the swing, Dorho hurled his right katiss at the chest of the charging man, forcing Kandath to halt his movements and roll away from the flying blade. Using the curved blade in his left hand, Count Maizen pushed aside the broadsword harmlessly as he stepped into the rolling movements of the bandit leader. Like a brick, Dorho smashed his empty fist into Kandath's temple, then with a heavy push from his boot, shoved the man away.

As one of the men grabbed onto Corina's blouse, Dorho flew into him with the remaining katiss aimed at the man's throat. As though he were wielding a spike, the rogue plunged the curved blade of the sword through the neck of the bandit, freeing Corina from his grip before letting the man bleed out on the cobblestone road.

"Come on," Dorho pleaded, looking on as Kandath got back to his feet, rubbing his head, "I've already taken out three of your men. There's no need to continue this madness."

"You're still outnumbered, fool," Kandath growled, putting his right foot forward and aiming his broadsword at Dorho's chest.

Count Maizen flexed the fingers and hand of his right arm, took a deep breath to steady his movements, and put himself between the bandits and Corina once more. His dark eyes locked upon Kandath with a dangerous expression, while he began to feel something burning deep inside his body. It was like an eerie flame was leaking into his muscles, and any weariness he felt was suddenly gone. Dorho's skin tingled, and the markings from Dimorta stung, but for the rogue it felt good. It was a welcomed sensation. It made him feel stronger and capable of pushing through anything. The energy was dark and mysterious, but it filled him with confidence and rejuvenated his body almost instantly.

"Surrender, or be prepared to die," Kandath snarled furiously. "You are an enemy of the people of Anslater."

"Then you leave me no choice, but to send you to the Undertow," Dorho concluded out of frustration.

Again, Kandath attacked. His sword dropped low, then was brought upwards in a vicious swing that targeted

Dorho's left flank. The rogue put his left foot forward, striking against the broadsword with a quick parry from the katiss, then spun to the right, pushing the enemy's blade away in front of him. In the blink of an eye, Dorho's right hand was clenched around the throat of the bandit leader's throat, while the scriptures on his arm pulsed with vile energy.

He could've let Kandath go, but at the moment, there was no such desire in Dorho's heart. That dark energy that flowed into his entire body fueled his thoughts, and he could only think of sending the bandit leader straight to Dimorta's realm. Feeling the strength of the eerie energy coursing through his veins, Count Maizen tightened his grip on the throat of the man, even lifting him into the air until his feet no longer touched the street.

"Let me," Kandath struggled to breathe and talk through the fierce grip. "Let me go."

The bandit swung with his sword, despite the strength being sapped from his body in a rush. With cat-like reflexes, Dorho brought his katiss up and jammed the curved blade into the forearm holding the broadsword. Rendered useless with a twist of the rogue's sword, Kandath's hand went limp and dropped the blade at Dorho's feet with a loud clank.

With a vibrant burst, violet light ripped through the markings on Dorho's arm in a brilliant flash that even made the afternoon sun seem dark. Held fast in the powerful hand of the rogue, Kandath's body went limp, his skin turned dull and pale, while his eyes faded into colorless white orbs. From the nose, mouth, and open wounds of the man, darkened indigo energy escaped the body of Kandath, absorbed by the runes and designs on the rogue's right arm. It was a horrendous scene, even for the rogue, but the power that swelled up inside of him drove Dorho to endure it.

When the last of the strange indigo mist left the body of the bandit leader, Dorho abruptly let go. Like a sack of rocks, Kandath fell to the stones of the road, his body breaking apart and turning to ash as it hit the ground. The eastward breeze scattered the dust-like remains of the man's corpse, leaving just his sword and clothes laying upon the highway in Wayfarer's Folly.

Clenching his right hand into a tight fist, feeling the churning heat of Dimorta's deathly magic pulsing through his skin, Dorho turned his eyes to the remaining bandits. Without a word, they dropped their weapons and left, grabbing the one who had lost his hand during their escape.

"Hey!" Dorho heard a guard shouting. "What's going on here?"

"These men," Corina moved suddenly, stepping between the three guards and the count, "they attacked me. My friend was only trying to defend me."

"It's true, I saw it," came the voice of the textile trader. "They had just bought a nice dress from me, when these ruffians assailed them."

The pain in his arm flooded through his body, forcing Dorho to his knees as he cradled his right arm protectively, having dropped his remaining katiss. He had felt amazingly powerful only moments before, and now it was like he was being eaten from the inside out. Tears welled up in his eyes as he took deep, steady breaths to try and calm his body down from whatever it was he had just experienced.

"Is he alright?" one of the guards asked, motioning towards Dorho.

Corina nodded. "He's fine. He just needs some rest and food. He'll be just as new by morning."

"This is a terrible mess," another guard spoke up. "You're lucky to have such a good friend with you, miss."

"The Black Wing Brigade are a nasty sort," the third guard added. "They've been hustling travelers for weeks. Especially people from Thornbror who can't go home due to the closed borders."

Again, the shopkeeper piped in, "If she can get him to the inn, I'll pay for their stay. Consider it my gratitude for dealing with those thugs."

"Indeed," the first guard rubbed his bearded chin, "most people don't have the skill to handle Kandath and his men like that. We should be thanking you."

"Come on," the second guard leaned down to help Dorho up, "the inn isn't that far. You did us a huge service by teaching those bastards a lesson. We've got enough on our plate, with the war and all that, without having to deal with bandit clans as well."

"I'm," Dorho finally managed, catching his breath as he tried to relax. "I'm fine. I think."

Before he could resist, Corina put her arm under Dorho's shoulders and helped guide him into the inn. One of the three guards pulled the innkeeper aside and spoke to the short, old man, while the other two ushered the exhausted, aching rogue to a bedroom down a long hall. Everything was a blur to Count Maizen, as most of his attention was on the pain that burned deep under his skin. His knees were weak, and he felt like he was forcing himself to keep breathing. As if he were just a bag of potatoes, Corina dropped the rogue onto the bed in the small chamber, after tossing his hat onto a table under the window. Once the guards had vanished, the innkeeper entered with a bowl of cool water and a clean rag. Hushed words were exchanged between the farmer's daughter and the innkeeper, then the door was closed with a soft click, and Dorho found himself alone with the strong daughter of Jonsal.

"You going to tell me what that was?" Corina ordered softly, her fingers deftly working the buttons on Dorho's vest. "That thing you did to that man. You killed him just by touching him. What was that?"

With the pain pulsing through his veins, the rogue couldn't fight back as the young woman began taking his vest and shirt off. Soon, she was massaging his chest with the damp cloth soaked in the cold water. She brushed it over his forehead and down his cheeks as well before dipping it back into the bowl.

"Di..." Dorho struggled, taking several deep breaths as he flexed his right hand a few more times. "Dimorta's power. I'm sorry you had to see that."

"No," Corina shook her head, "don't apologize. I'm safe because of you."

Before anything else could be said, the innkeeper returned with two mugs of sweet-smelling, spiced liquid. He set the tray on the table next to Dorho's hat, and left just as quietly as he had entered. After running the cool, damp cloth over Dorho's skin once more, Corina fetched one of the mugs and sat upon the edge of the bed closest to the rogue's right side. When she tipped the mug to his lips, he could taste the apples and elderberries in the drink, as well as something that was uniquely spicy and earthy at the same time. It hit his tongue like a sweet, but pleasant rum-infused beverage, but there was something deeper to it. Something earthly, bitter, and dark to the flavor. Whatever it was, it wasn't bitter to the point of being unpleasant, just bewildering. It was something Dorho knew, but with his mind focused on the pain in his body, he couldn't process what it was.

"Luckily for you," Corina said finally, after getting Dorho to drink nearly half the mug before setting it aside, "I'm a practitioner of the Atheian Way. It's useful with all the accidents that can happen on a farm. Just try and relax, Count Maizen."

Her right hand touched his chest, and the young woman closed her eyes. Corina's lips moved as though she were speaking to someone, but no words could be heard from her mouth. Like glittering emerald dust, faint traces of magic began dancing over Dorho's chest, emitted from the hand against his skin. As the flickering green energy flowed over his body, the agonizing pain that had flooded his veins felt as though it were being chased away. Replacing his agony was a sensation of comfort and warmth, like being embraced by a long-lost lover. Even the sensation in his right arm faded into a lovely heat that caused his breathing to become steady and calm.

He knew about the Atheian Way. The practitioners were sometimes called white mages. Those that followed the Atheian Way were regarded as the best healers in the entire world. They could channel far more healing energy than most other healers, thus allowing their patients to recover far faster from even the most severe injuries. In exchange, their access to other forms of magic was highly restricted, but no one understood why.

As his body relaxed into the pleasing warmth of the healing energy from the young woman, sounds in the room seemed to blend together. Colors and lights all over the small chamber pulsed and flickered with the beat of the rogue's heart, creating a magnificent display that amazed the comfortable rogue. Eventually he realized that he was so tranquil, that he could barely move his arms or legs without putting a decent amount of thought and effort into it. His mind drifted away from the events of the day, focusing on the pleasurable sensations flooding his body. The faint rustle of the wind outside the window, stirred together into a charming song with the murmurs of inn patrons far away from where he lay. By the time he realized what was happening, he felt like his body was sinking into the bed itself.

"Coor..." Dorho tried to speak, but his mind was falling into the void of mush that was a feeling of extremely lethargic relaxation. "Coor'rum?"

"You needed to relax," Corina's voice came softly, mixing with the other sounds of the room. "Afterall, you saved me today."

There was nothing Dorho could do. He couldn't fight back. His body was unresponsive, and his mind was drifting through incoherent thoughts. Corina pressed her lips to his own, caressing his chin in her gentle touch. For only a moment, he wanted to resist and yell, but he couldn't. His mind and body went with it, instead. The effects of the coor'rum made her touch feel euphoric against his skin. Each breath against his neck felt like a lover's full embrace, and her soft whispers like a song to his ears.

Gone was the searing pain of Dimorta's magic burning through his flesh. Now, all he felt was the exhilarating sensation of the woman's body against his own. Every time he considered telling her to stop, his mind would fade into oblivion as her lips would find a new spot to capture on his body. Her healing magic had pushed away the wretched pain in his flesh, and the coor'rum had drowned out his logic and reasoning. He was lost in a euphoric, psychedelic, pleasure-driven experience, and his body and mind were unwilling to tell him to stop.

Somewhere between the hallucinations, exciting embraces, and the relaxing warmth of the Atheian Way, Corina's clothing had been left on the floor along with Dorho's pants and boots. Fully captured by the mental and physical effects of the coor'rum, Dorho pinned the farmer's daughter to the bed and took pleasure in everything she offered to him. She was completely submissive to his drug-induced desires, and denied him nothing.

Run, or be reborn, a familiar whisper echoed deep within Dorho's mind just before he fell unconscious next to the naked form of the farmer's daughter.

When he woke up again, the sun was well below the horizon, but a faint red glow remained in the sky. He found himself alone in the bed, with his clothes neatly folded on the table under the window. An oil lamp hanging next to the bed threw its soft amber light around the room in a pleasing manner. It was a rather nice evening, and Wayfarer's Folly had turned quiet as people were beginning to retire for the night.

Count Maizen rubbed his head, unsure if he knew exactly what had happened earlier in the day. He remembered getting into a quarrel with Kandath and his men, even remembering killing a few of them, but after that, things became a confusing blur. Deep in mind, there were whispers and visions of Corina tending to him with a cool cloth, but it was all foggy and unreliable. Though his memory was filled with holes he couldn't fill, his body felt great, despite the fight he had been in earlier.

Without spending too much time trying to figure out what had happened, he put his clothes on. He picked up the dark hat and smiled, placing it on his head before stepping from the small sleeping chamber. His feet had nearly carried him to the end of the hall when the short, old innkeeper nearly bumped into him.

"Count Maizen!" the small man exclaimed happily. "So glad to see you awake! Your lady friend said she was going to the tavern to get a hot meal. Did you get enough rest?"

"Yes, I feel great now," Dorho stated, "thanks for asking. I'll go see if I can find her. I should probably get food in my belly as well."

The short man smiled. "I suggest the pork cutlet. It's my favorite thing they serve. Almost as good as the wife's cooking."

"Don't let her hear you say that," Dorho chuckled, heading towards the door.

The Lord of Rogues slipped out of the inn and down the steps to the street. With as few buildings Wayfarer's Folly had, finding the tavern wasn't a problem. The front door of the tavern was only a couple dozen steps from the inn, and being that the cluster of buildings was a way station for weary travelers, it appeared to be rather busy. Momentarily, he tried to recall what had happened after the fight in the street, but then he shook his foggy head and climbed the stairs to the patio.

"Count Maizen," Corina called, waving to the man from her seat on the patio.

She was sitting alone at a crude table with an oil lamp. A plate that had once held food sat in front of the young woman, while her left hand held onto a mug of onyx tea. As the rogue stepped closer, she untied a cloth pouch from her belt and tossed it to the man.

"The guards dropped this off for you," the farmer's daughter stated with a smile. "It's payment for removing Kandath from their list of local problems."

Dorho took a seat across the table from the young woman, throwing her a warm grin as he set the sack of coins down. Something lingered in his mind, it was hiding in that wall of fog left after the fight with Kandath, but he knew there was something there. It was like having an itch he couldn't scratch. After counting the payment from the guards, and unable to push away the fog, Dorho decided to just ignore the sensation for the moment.

"Ten gold coins, ten silver tiles, and a bronze bar," Count Maizen stated as he tucked the pouch into his vest securely. "Not bad for taking out some garbage."

"You seem to be doing much better now," Corina spoke warmly. "I was honestly a little worried that the Atheian Way wouldn't work on you after you mentioned Dimorta's power, but now I'm relieved."

Dorho sighed and leaned back in his chair, pushing the rear of the seat against the wall of the tavern. "I should thank you then. Because I don't remember much after killing Kandath. The world between then and now is a blurry unfinished canvas in my mind. It was like Dimorta's power took over and the rest of me faded away."

The young woman tilted her head slightly and the edge of her mouth lifted in a curious grin. "Really? You don't remember anything?"

"Not particularly," Dorho rubbed his forehead after thinking over her words carefully, then dropped his hat onto the table.

"That's a pity," Corina giggled, before taking a sip of her dark drink.

"Why?" Now Dorho was intrigued.

"Maybe I'll have to refresh your memory," she teased, "but after you get something to eat."

Corina waved politely to one of the servers to catch the girl's attention. Promptly, the rogue requested the suggested pork cutlet and a mug of onyx tea. Though, he asked for the onyx tea to be served in the evening style, with a mixture of butter and sweet wine, as he planned on going back to bed after the meal was finished.

"I was thinking of visiting the bathhouse after we eat," Corina spoke up as the server vanished back inside the tavern. "If you don't mind, you could honestly use a shave and a haircut before the wedding. I wouldn't mind doing that for you. You might get off looking haggard in Elgrahm Hold, but for a wedding, especially the prince's, you might want to improve the look a bit. Just a thought."

Dorho rubbed his chin, then ran his fingers through his dark hair. She was right, it had been weeks, probably months, since his last trim. Though, he never intended to deliberately show up for the wedding. The rogue just wanted to meet this prince, to see if he was indeed the second Sidhe-Vein. He could care less about royal weddings and formalities.

"I should at least look like I belong," Count Maizen said finally, just as the server dropped off the mug of fresh onyx tea stirred with honey and wine. "Do you even know how to shave a man?"

"Please, Count Maizen," Corina shot him a dubious gaze from her deep blue eyes. "I may be just a farmer's daughter, but being raised on a farm with my father and two older brothers, not to mention the various seasonal workers, there are some skills I picked up on quickly. How to make a man look presentable when he steps off the farm, is just one of my many talents."

"True enough, I suppose," Dorho agreed as he sipped the warm beverage. "You're also an impressive healer. I do wonder though, isn't the Atheian Way passed down through a bloodline?"

"My mother, Scisera," the young woman confessed, turning her gaze away from the rogue to hide the hint of sorrow that soon found her words, "was my father's first wife. Launa is his second wife, mother of my younger siblings. My father was terribly injured five years after my birth. He was bleeding out, crushed by the collapsing wall of the old silo, and my mother used the Atheian Way to trade her life for his. She died so that he could live. I inherited her bloodline, and her powers."

"So," Count Maizen paused, then blinked as he looked over at the young woman, who was clutching tightly at her mug. "When you healed me?"

"I was transferring some of your pain to myself," Corina's voice had weakened. "That's the curse of the Atheian Way. Unlike other healing magic, the Atheian Way requires a sacrifice or trade, often resulting in the white mage taking on some of the injuries of the wounded. I'm not sure what you are doing wielding the powers of death like that, but they were tearing you apart on the inside. Anyway, you protected me, so I felt responsible. I had to do something."

For a while, Dorho only watched as the farmer's daughter struggled with her emotions. He was trying to figure her out. She had been the second one to greet him after waking up on the Knepiri Farm, helping him get back to feeling normal. He had never considered that she was actually a healer hiding under the façade of being a farmer's determined daughter. She had brought him his first meal, kept him company when he struggled being so far from home, and even helped him wash up as he recovered from his visit with Dimorta. She was a mystery to the rogue, but her layers were beginning to unravel in front of his dark eyes.

"You weren't left on our property by bandits," Corina accused abruptly, her blue eyes looking at the katiss blades strapped to the waist of the count. "I had my suspicions after I used the Atheian Way on you that first night. I was checking you for injuries, but there was something lingering in your spiritual energy, deep in your veins. Then today, the way you handled those men. There's no way someone like you would simply be kidnapped, beaten, and robbed, even without death magic to aid you. So, who are you? What are you?"

Dorho sighed, realizing that her sapphire orbs were peering right through his wall of lies. "You're right," he declared, setting the mug down lightly. "I'm not the person I told your father about. While true, I am the Lord of Rogues, and Count Maizen from Elgrahm Hold, there's more than that. Some of it I don't even understand yet, not completely anyway. How do I even explain what has happened to me in the last few weeks? I hardly feel like any of it was real myself."

"Why don't you start with those strange tattoos?" Corina pointed to his right arm. "You didn't have them when we first met."

Straight to the point, Dorho thought. He wondered if she had told anyone else about her concerns regarding his appearance on the farm. If she had, no one had mentioned it to him, or treated him any differently after first meeting Jonsal. He considered telling her everything. His mind played with the idea of unleashing every detail, but he didn't want to drag her into the mess with the Onyx Spire. Dorho just wanted to get to Vansenhul, meet the second Sidhe-Vein, and send her home.

Then he thought about his own home and Ansha. His wife and unborn child. So far away from him, who most likely thought he was still dead. He wondered how the others were all doing. Were they still pursuing his original quest? Had they given up? He had been taken from them and sent on a different path, in more ways than one. Dorho had been tasked with taking Lynsia home, found himself fighting against the forces of King Borlhauf, but was now seeking another Sidhe-Vein and facing off against the damning darkness of the Onyx Spire. For a moment, he wondered if he would ever see his home, or Ansha, ever again.

Run, or be reborn, that voice, deep within his mind, echoed once more.

"These," Dorho looked over his right arm and paused, "markings were a gift from Dimorta. She's marked me, you could say. How do I say this, without sounding crazy? I was killed by the Onyx Spire and resurrected on your farm, I'm not sure why I was brought back, though. I was told to seek out the prince of your land, that he may know someone who can help me figure out why I'm still here."

Again, he sprinkled the truth over a log of lies. He didn't want the young woman involved with his quest. Dorho had made a promise to keep her safe and let her enjoy a trip to the capital.

"See," Corina leaned closer, her voice quieter, though her condemning tone hadn't left, "I knew something was off about you. That first time I used the Atheian Way on you, your energy reeked of death, like you were a dug-up corpse. You don't sound crazy, by the way. Remember, my mother gave her life so my father could live. Though if you're looking for the prince, you're probably actually looking for the sage of Anslater, Cerulla. She's the warden of the land itself, and very wise in the ways of the world."

"A sage?" the rogue rubbed his chin as he reflected on her words. "She might know something, perhaps."

Despite the strength he knew her slender body possessed, when Corina grasped his hand in her own, the touch was delicate, but deliberate. A warmth flowed from her fingers, like a loving hug from a concerned mother, pouring through his veins and pushing away his worries.

"Do..." she began, but then turned her face away again abruptly.

"What?" Dorho asked, clutching her hand as he felt his mind at ease with the connection.

Despite the lack of bright light, the blush on Corina's cheeks was undeniable. The young woman took a deep breath and shook her head, as if she were trying to fling cobwebs from the depths of her mind.

"It's nothing," she spoke eventually, letting go of his hand slowly. "Just, don't lie to me again, Count Maizen."

"Now you're the one lying to me," the rogue stated, his lips curling into a kind grin. "What's really bothering you?"

Without saying anything, Corina slid her chair next to Dorho's, then placed her head on his shoulder as her arms found their way around his torso. At first, the count thought of Ansha, and pondered pushing the young woman away, but he relented when he saw her face struggling to contain the emotions hidden behind those deep blue eyes. Like a protective older brother, he put his right arm around the shoulders of the farmer's daughter and pulled her close and tight.

"You say you died and were brought back on our farm?" Corina eventually spoke after the server delivered a plate of pork cutlet, rice, and carrots smothered in a rich brown gravy.

"Yes, that's true," Dorho admitted again. "Dimorta said I wasn't done here. That I needed to find that prince to figure out my purpose. She gave me these markings to remind me of my destiny."

"So, do you believe in fate?" she asked softly.

Count Maizen scratched the hair on his chin and thought over her words. "I guess I do, in a strange way. I believe we are all allowed to live our lives as we see fit, to dig our own graves, or build our own castles. I also believe that the choices we make determine the final outcome, but I also believe sometimes that other forces push us in certain directions. So, does that count as a yes, or a no?"

Corina shrugged slightly, moving her right hand to brush her fingers over the ones Dorho used to tease his goatee. The touch was subtle, but the message was clear as her fingers entwined with his own, pulling his hand against her chest. Again, Dorho's thoughts turned to Ansha, and he wanted to shove the young woman aside, but he didn't. There was something in her touch that his body craved, but he couldn't explain the sensation. Was it longing? Familiarity? He didn't know, but he allowed the farmer's daughter to keep holding onto his hand. She was a strong woman, but in that moment, there was a child-like weakness in her figure that made the rogue unable to turn her away.

"As a practitioner of the Atheian Way," Corina whispered against his shoulder, "I'm a path for Atheia to bring her healing power into the world. You're marked by Dimorta. Do you understand?"

"Maybe?" he responded, remembering his visit to Dimorta's tower. "But, not completely."

The young woman sighed. "They're opposites, but sisters. One is the bringer of life, the queen of healers, and mother of charity, while the other is the empress of death, the ruler of the Undertow, and the authority over equality."

"No need to remind me," Dorho almost laughed, thinking of the banter between the sisters he witnessed.

"For years, I've had a dream," the healer spoke after a steadying breath. "The same dream. Over and over. In it, Petiora and Kourinthe as a whole were being destroyed by a terrible monster. Something massive and faceless, but purely evil. It has no name, and only hungers for devastation. When it reaches the farm, I can hear Atheia speaking to me. Her voice is soft and kind, and she tells me to embrace death as others embrace life. As the monster begins to tear through the house to reach me, I scream, and an explosion of green light rips through the room. Just before I wake up, every time, a man appears cloaked in a pale violet aura between myself and the monster."

"You believe that was me?" Dorho replied as his eyes drifted from the young woman to his plate of warm food. "You think this was fate?"

She shook her head slowly. "The sage from Ostenfel Castle told me that a great darkness was coming to our world, and on the heels of death, an age of great tranquility would rise. I was able to talk to her during one of her few visits to the farm to check on our harvest and soil preservation methods. She's a very wise woman, so I felt like she might have some insight on my visions. I never understood what she had said, but now…"

He wasn't sure if it was instinct, or something else, but Dorho hugged the young woman tightly as her voice trailed off. "A monster is coming. Darkness is looking to swallow everything we love. This is why I need to speak to the prince, and maybe this sage as well, to figure out what my role in all this is. I need to know what was so important that I was returned from death."

"You know about the monster as well?" Corina's eyes looked over Dorho's face as she spoke. "Then we both know what's coming?"

For a moment, Dorho considered what to tell her, then he sighed in acceptance. "When I died, but before Dimorta sent me back, she told me that a terrible fate was looming over the world. A great evil long forgotten by most. It seeks to undo everything with a cloud of chaos and desolation."

Dorho thought more about his visit with Dimorta at her gore-filled tower. It had been Atheia that had returned him to the living world, so he wondered if it was her decision to leave him at the Knepiri Farm. If so, then the meeting between Corina and the rogue wasn't just pure coincidence. Dimorta mentioned giving him a nudge in the right direction, but this felt like it was planned with intention.

Detaching her hand from his, Corina picked up the fork offered with the plate, broke off a piece of the pork cutlet with a bit of the rice, and held it up to Dorho's lips.

"You should eat," her words came with a sorrow-filled weight that struck the man to the core.

Without complaint, he accepted the offered bite of food. It was delicious. Even though the meat was tender and juicy, it was covered in a light, but crispy breading that was filled with hints of rosemary, sage, and dried cheeses. The gravy, clearly made from a combination of beef, venison, and pork stock, was seasoned lightly with onions, garlic, and herbs. Then the rice was the perfect mixture of flaky and creamy infused into the thick gravy that had been poured over the dish. It really was amazing, just as the rumors said.

"You're avoiding something," Dorho stated after swallowing the pleasurable bite.

She nodded, breaking off another piece of the pork cutlet just as she had done before, and held it up. "I am. Very much so, but so are you. We're both keeping secrets. I can see it in your slight hesitation to be close to me. What's her name?"

Count Maizen paused his chewing, wondering how she saw through him that well. The question was blunt, direct, and shocked the rogue. Ansha hadn't even been able to see through his veil of secrets that well. Either he had gotten easier to read, or this woman knew him better than anyone else, despite only knowing him for a handful of days.

"Well?" Corina asked, sitting upright slowly as she scooped up some of the rice and carrots with the fork. "Time for you to tell me a bit more about yourself, Count Maizen. Who is she?"

"Countess Ansha Maizen," Dorho spoke after a moment to consider his options. "We've been together five years, and have a daughter on the way. Well, that was before

I was killed. I don't know how they're doing now. They don't even know I'm alive here."

"You're married?" Corina sighed while holding the fork up for Dorho. "Figures. She thinks you're dead, though, right?"

"I don't even know how long it's been," Dorho nodded his answer. "Weeks? Months? I know it hasn't been years, yet. I don't want her to move on, but as long as she knows I'm dead, there's nothing stopping her. I suppose my death would annul the marriage, though. I don't know if I'll ever see her again. I don't even know if I'll ever meet our daughter. I miss them dearly."

He accepted the bite of food, but the knot of emotions that curled up in his chest killed his ability to taste it. Now he was just eating because he was hungry, and not because he wanted to. A couple heavy breaths escaped his throat as he fought to keep the tears from his eyes as he thought about everything he was going to miss as long as he was unable to reach Elgrahm Hold. He could have accepted being dead, as long as he knew Ansha was safe, but now he was alive and far from his home and those he loved. To top it off, between the war closing off the borders, and the tasks given to him by Dimorta, he wasn't able to send a courier or contact anyone in Elgrahm Hold. The thought of it all tore him apart inside.

"I'm," Corina spoke tenderly before pressing a soft kiss to his lips. "I'm sorry."

Abruptly, she stood up from her seat and began to step away as her hands wiped the tears from her eyes. Dorho almost let her walk away, but something deep down in his core forced him to grab her wrist. She was strong, and despite her attempts to yank herself away, the rogue held fast and pulled her back. Corina landed roughly in the lap of the count, and his arms folded about her slender sides in an instant.

"No," Dorho shook his head lightly as he held her tightly to his chest, "I'm the one that should be sorry. My life is a horrific mess, and somehow you've been dragged into it. I should've been honest with you and your father. You deserved that much, but I'm trying to protect more than just myself now."

Run, or be reborn, came that familiar voice, once more lingering in the back of Dorho's mind.

"You shouldn't even be here," Dorho concluded, and after a long pause to fight through his emotions, pressed a kiss to the forehead of the young woman. "If you want to go back home, I won't stop you."

"I don't want to go home," she blurted, her soft tone dripping with frustration as she leaned back enough to slap the rogue's face harshly. "I want to stay with you. I've been dreaming of this person marked by death for years. Wondering who they were, but when I finally meet you, you're... you're amazing. Brave, courteous, fun to be around, protective, yet comfortably domineering. You're everything I had hoped for, and yet far more. I knew you were special when I first met you, even though I knew we would meet eventually. Now, here you are, my—."

Dorho kissed her, and not gently, either. His mind raced with thoughts of Ansha and the others, but right in front of him was this poor woman spilling out her emotions, and he couldn't force himself to hold back. There was something so familiar about her, he couldn't take his hands or gaze off of her. Had they met before? Although he didn't think so, he still craved being close to her. Having Corina close was like mixing wind with fire, but a bit like lodestone and steel as well. While his face stung from the slap from the farmer's daughter, his hands cupped her cheeks roughly while the sudden shock in her deep blue eyes faded into the intense embrace.

Run, or be reborn, that deep voice called once more, like a whisper through the thoughts racing in his mind.

"You saw a man of death in your dreams," Count Maizen spoke as their lips parted slightly. "The gods sent me to you for a reason. Yes, I miss the countess, and everyone else I was taken from in Elgrah Hold, but," his dark eyes peered into hers while his hands brushed through her golden hair.

"But what?" she breathed as fresh tears formed at the edges of her eyes.

Dorho kissed her again, softer this time, then smiled fondly. "I can't take my hands off of you. I can't explain it. I feel like I've known you longer than we've been together. Something keeps pushing my hands towards yours."

"You're death," Corina sighed happily, grasping the shoulders of his vest with her hands tightly.

"And you're life," he stated calmly. "Opposites working in tandem. You asked if I believed in fate. I do believe that we were destined to meet, perhaps we've met in previous lives too, but our meeting was unexpected even if we knew it was coming."

"Dorho?" She called out to him quietly, daring to use his first name.

"I've been reborn," Dorho grinned, ignoring her voice as he continued. "I've been reborn and given a second chance. In doing so, I was put within your reach. Do I believe in fate?"

Her hands reached up and her fingers grazed along his jawline. "Dorho?" she repeated.

Dorho kissed her one more time, wrapping one arm around her waist while the other coiled around her shoulders. "Yes, when it comes to you. Yes, I believe we were supposed to meet."

"Dorho?" Corina called again, her voice slightly more urgent as she took a deep breath.

"Yes?" he smiled warmly.

She leaned heavily into his embrace and closed her eyes as Corina put her head on his right shoulder. "I love you. Call it fate, but I always knew I would."

"Now I know who has been invading my dreams," Dorho stated, hugging the young woman tightly in his arms.

10.

Ansha stirred from her thoughts as she sat in the vardo, which was a significant upgrade from the wagon they had been using since leaving Kaenaan. They were half a day north of Dracamori as the horses pulled the luxurious caravan slowly closer to their destination in Euthrox. Orota and her gang allowed the countess and the Sidhe-Vein to use one of their living wagons for the trip, which was greatly appreciated.

"Something amiss?" Urna asked, turning from the window she was gazing from.

"No," Ansha said, then sighed longingly and shook her head. "Yes. Yes, there is. Dorho should be here, but he was taken from us. It's been weeks, and I keep expecting him to suddenly show up like he always did, but in the end, I know he's gone. Does this ever get easier?"

Urna shook her head as well, then enveloped the countess in a kind hug. "No. It never gets easier, but eventually you heal, and you find things that bring you joy again. Like that little girl you're carrying. She's going to light up your world like you never imagined."

"Plus, there's the Wishstone," Lynsia added from her bunk at the front of the wagon.

"We'll have to find a way to get it activated, first," Urna commented with a nod, "but yes, there's always a chance we can get him back."

"Here," Kendira unwrapped a loaf of brown bread, cut off a wedge and handed it to Ansha. "You and the little one need to eat."

"Thank you," Countess Maizen responded politely as she took the offered wedge from the bard. "Are you going to survive being away from Vourden?"

Kendira laughed and brushed a bit of her black hair behind her left shoulder. "I'll be fine. I worry about him being left alone with two kids in the house."

"She's got me with her," Lyn called out proudly with a giggle.

"You two are too adorable," Urna smiled, taking a wedge of the bread as well from the bard.

"She's my sweet little birdy," the bard replied with a fond smile.

"So, have you settled on a name yet?" Lynsia inquired, peering at Ansha through sky-blue eyes.

Countess Maizen smiled warmly and ran her empty hand over her abdomen. "I'm going to name her after my mother, Tuttala. Tuttala Maizen."

Kendira grinned as she spoke, "seems like a fitting name for Vintru's future wife."

"She's not even born yet," Ansha protested with a snicker.

"Maybe so," the bard insisted, "but you are going to have to stay close to Vourden and myself. No becoming distant once this mess is over and settled. We're raising our families together. I want our kids to be friends and play together in the future."

Ansha leaned across the wagon to plant a quick, friendly kiss on the cheek of the bard. "No way. You've become a great friend to me. You're stuck with me. I'm sad that I've lost my husband and my father, but I've gained an amazing new family here."

"I don't think anyone here hasn't lost someone important to them," Urna added between bites of the sweet bread. "Paisley was taken from Vourden. Ansha had Dorho taken from her. The girl's family was murdered by the king's men. I lost Jarlen in a fight against a dreadmage. Orota had to step up as leader of the Den after both her previous leaders were slain."

"Kendira gained a birdy," Lynsia spoke as she hung her head off the edge of the bunk, "and her sheriff returned to her."

"True," Ansha smiled slightly. "Kendira seems to be the lucky one."

The bard shook her head as she swallowed a bite of the dark bread. "I would definitely not call myself lucky. I watched people get their hearts broken, watched a dear friend get killed, toiled over a sleeping beauty, and had to help a wayward man find his spirit to live."

"You've been like a pillar these last few weeks, Kendira," Ansha admitted, hugging her friend. "Giving the rest of us support when we needed it most. I don't know what we would've done without you, honestly. You rescued Vourden, comforted me, and tended to Lynsia, all while running the sheriff's house and helping with his two kids."

"Because when I needed someone most," Kendira spoke softly, "he walked away to seek fame and fortune."

Urna shook her head as she replied. "But in the end, you even got him to see what he had lost. You truly are an amazing woman."

"I try," Kendira sheepishly said.

The countess leaned back on the bench she had been seated on and glanced out the window as the conversation died down, other than Lynsia and Kendira speaking with one another. She broke off small bits of the bread and ate it slowly, savoring the sweetness of the molasses and wheat in the crumbly wedge, while her hazel eyes watched the birch trees from the moving wagon.

Summer was well underway, but the threat of a storm loomed overhead as a breeze rustled the leaves and grasses around the vardo. They had entered the forested hills north of Dracamori late in the morning, and from where the countess sat, she could see no end in the terrain. So far, their travels had been quiet and uneventful. They had stopped in Dracamori to get some fresh bread and rest for the night, though they were uneasy, considering the recent events that unfolded in that town. The blood of the fallen still stained the streets during their visit, giving a horrid reminder of the cruelty they were facing.

They could've stayed at the inn, but all of them chose to remain in the caravan. It featured a trio of bunks in the front which were shaped like a U, a padded bench that could be unfolded into a bed, and enough floor space for a few extra bedrolls. Orota promised that five or six adults could live comfortably in it for several days, but after spending some time in the wagon, Ansha was certain it could fit eight or nine if they didn't mind the company.

Near the rear of the caravan was a small stove of iron and clay that provided heat, as well as a cooking surface if needed. A square table and two stump-like chairs served as a dining table. Rugs made of various furs lined the wooden floors, adding a touch of domestication and warmth to the mixture of greens, blues, and beige used to color the interior. A pair of small, circular windows let in natural light from the outside, one over the folding bench, and the other next to the dining area. Through a canvas panel behind the middle bunk, one could access the wagon's driver and a small patio, while an amalgamation of brass and oak formed the main entry at the rear of the caravan. Overhead, the tight canvas roof fluttered with the motion of the wheels, and twitched with the breeze of the coming storm. It was quaint, but lovely, the countess thought, and far more comfortable than their first wagon.

Seemingly completely healed from whatever injuries left her sleeping for so long, Lynsia had been swift in picking the center bunk against the front wall, furthest from the door. Urna and Kendira took over the other two bunks, while the countess had been given the bench that could be unfolded into a decent bed. Orota, who was driving the wagon at the moment, opted to sleep on the floor, considering her larger size made the beds look like they were built for children. Bies, true to his loyal nature, could often be found curled up against the back of Ansha's legs after she went to bed.

She ran her left hand through the soft fur of the larscot, who was stretched out on the bench with her, his head resting in her lap. Ever since the passing of her husband, the weasel-like creature had become a blessed companion by her side. Her hazel eyes shifted to the scalloped blade of the rapier leaning against Urna's bunk. Like the other gifts from the faerie they were going to see, the larscot had fallen into her care.

The rain had started to pelt the sides and roof of the vardo when a structure, then another appeared in the distance along a silvery band of water. Ansha slowly stood up, making her way towards Lynsia's bunk carefully so as to not tumble with the motion of the moving wagon. Opening the canvas hatch to where Orota sat was a matter of leaning over the bed and undoing a large brass buckle.

"Where are we?" Ansha asked, crawling through the opening in the canvas to sit next to the burly woman.

"Pershing's Ferry," the muscular driver responded.

The countess nodded a bit, then glanced back to the others inside the caravan before looking at the weather again. "Looks like it plans on getting worse outside. If you want, we can stop to rest here. What do you think?"

The chartreuse eyes of the large woman gave a warm glance to the countess. "We can do that. I'd rather not force myself, or the horses, to spend too much time in this rain."

"I'll let the others know the plan," Ansha spoke before slipping back through the hatch.

After closing the hatch and sliding off the Sidhe-Vein's bed, Ansha smiled warmly. "We're going to be stopping in Pershing's Ferry soon. I know we haven't gone far today, but the weather is turning sour, and looks like it will be getting worse soon."

"That bread is pretty good," Urna smiled as she finished her last bite, "but this weather calls for a hearty bowl of stew."

"It's my mother's recipe," Kendira grinned, "but I agree with the bowl of stew."

"Vourden's lucky," Ansha added, sitting next to Kendira as she listened to the rain slapping the canvas roof. "Kendira is a rather skilled cook. I feel like I've been spoiled every time I have a meal in their house."

"She can sing, dance, throw fire, and cook?" Urna responded dubiously, but snickered softly. "Surely she must be the envy of every man she meets."

"But," Lynsia grinned, rolling onto her stomach and flinging her arms around the waist of the bard, "they can't have her. She's mine."

Kendira laughed, stealing a kiss from the Sidhe-Vein's lips. "Very much so, and you don't have to share me with Vourden until we get back to Ameribelle."

"How is that going, by the way?" Urna inquired, lifting one of her brows in interest.

"It's going well," Kendira grinned wryly. "Vourden gets his time, Lyn gets hers, and luckily our bed is big enough for all of us."

"She gets spoiled," Lynsia blurted with a giggle.

Ansha smiled warmly as she replied. "As she should be. Look at how much she does for you and Vourden."

"Thank you, Ansha," the bard spoke up as she wrapped up the rest of the sweet, dark bread.

"For what?" the countess briefly looked confused. "I'm just being honest."

"You're the one that suggested I go check in on Vourden after the attack," Kendira continued, sighing softly. "I was fine with watching him suffer, but you were right. I couldn't just sit there and watch him and his son go through that alone. Your push made me realize what he and I both needed. So, thank you."

"He needed help," Ansha shrugged, watching the small town of Pershing's Ferry drawing closer. "I wasn't exactly in the best place to help him myself. I had my own things to take care of."

Without warning, Kendira gave the countess a firm, but friendly hug. "We'll make everyone who wronged us pay for what they did."

Ansha smiled, returning the hug with one of her own.

Just as the first wave of thunder cracked through the clouds above, the comfortable wagon pulled up to the livery. The river north of the town churned and boiled with the wind and rain, pulsing like a furious serpent in the distance while Orota and two of the stable workers found space for the four horses after parking the wagon behind the structure. From a pleasant, but overcast day, to pure misery, the weather reminded Ansha of how her life had gone since Dorho first talked to her father about this quest.

Kendira, Urna, and Lynsia departed the wagon and dashed for the covered porch of the building that housed both the inn and tavern. Ansha paused, glancing over the rapier and the old dark hat with the wide brim that she had brought with her. Her fingers quickly brushed over the hat, but before she really put much thought into it, she snatched it up and put it on her head. The old, beaten, shabby hat was a bit too large for the woman, but she smiled as it settled over her chestnut-hued hair.

She had returned to a bleached white tunic and a lightly-tanned leather vest, similar to the attire she left Kaenaan with. Although things were beginning to fit a little tighter, her chocolate-colored breeches and tailored boots made from elk leather contrasted well with the light tones of her upper body garments. Ansha had cut her hair shorter before leaving Ameribelle, to just below her ears, but it was still naturally wavy and soft to the touch, though now it was mostly hidden under her late husband's abused hat. Her hand reached for the rapier, securing the enchanted blade to her left waist before stepping out of the vardo. She had considered taking her jian, but the hat and rapier both belonged to someone who was still very important to her, so they had to be worn together, she believed.

"Stay," Ansha ordered, looking at Bies, who was following her closely.

A soft whine escaped the throat of the large weasel-like creature, but it wasn't until the countess snapped her fingers and pointed to the bunks that he moved away. Hopping onto Lynsia's bed, the larscot's beady dark eyes watched the woman shut the wagon's door.

With Orota only a few steps behind her, Ansha made her way to where the others had gathered under the roof of the tavern's porch. Afternoon hadn't quite surrendered to the evening yet, but the darkness offered by the clouds made the hour feel later than it really was. From what she could see, Ansha guessed most of the residents and travelers in the small town had already sought cover from the fierce storm, as the streets seemed empty, except for a couple of people running to one building or another.

"Seeing that hat and sword in this weather," Kendira spoke up, her green eyes gazing over the countess carefully, "it's like seeing a ghost step out of the fog."

"Feels strange, wearing them," Ansha admitted with a small smile, "but it feels right. Feels like this is what he would want."

"Why are we standing around out here?" Orota bellowed with a grin. "I'm hungry, wet, and sober."

The interior of the large tavern was lively, as people ate, drank, talked, and gambled with one another. By the crackling flames of the hearth, a lone minstrel played a lute, drawing the attention of Kendira almost immediately. Scents of baking bread, stale beer, and grilled meat filled the air, mixing with the unmistakable odor of people who were exhausted but hiding from the weather. Simple oil lamps offered their warm glow to the gloomy day, the brilliant flames flickering and dancing with the energy of the room. A doorway on the opposite wall and a wide staircase separated the tavern from the inn, giving weary travelers a place to rest once they had consumed their fill of food and drink. It was a raucous place, but still managed to embrace its own rural charm within the forested hills along the river.

As a group, and pulling Kendira with them despite her desire to join the music, the women found an empty table between the bar counter and the door leading to the inn. Orota propped her great hammer against the wall as she leaned back in her chair, positioning herself to keep an eye on the room from her seat. Dressed in dark robes fitting a mage of her caliber, Urna slipped into a seat between the Jotunblöd and the countess. Kendira and the Sidhe-Vein took the next two chairs, leaving the one between Lyn and Orota empty.

"His lute is out of tune," Kendira muttered, after requesting a mug of cider.

"It's busy," Ansha stated, before asking for a tea sweetened with honey, "it would be best to not get split up in here."

"Get some food in you first," Orota smirked, "then take your birdy and go teach that bard a thing or two."

Urna nodded, her gimlet eyes gazing over the many faces in the tavern. "The countess is right, we shouldn't be getting divided. Not with the Onyx Spire likely looking for us."

Despite the crowd that had gathered out of the reach of the storm, it didn't take long for the server to gather the requested drinks. Ciders for the bard and reptilian, wine for the red-headed Sidhe-Vein, tea for the countess, and a tall flagon of mead for the burly wagon driver. Bowls of stew, bread with dishes of sweetened butter, and skewers of grilled fowl were brought out without delay, distracting even the bard from the noise and chaos of the busy tavern.

"Does this improve things, Orota?" Ansha chuckled, pulling a bite of meat from the skewer in her hand.

"Definitely," the Jotunblöd answered.

"Not nearly as good as my bard's cooking," Lyn gleefully expressed, "but it's still pretty decent."

Kendira slurped down the rest of the broth from her stew and grinned. "I need to go fix that lute," she said before planting a kiss on Lyn's cheek. "Come, my sweet birdy, I need you to sing for me."

"You two are chaos personified," Ansha muttered with a grin, watching Lynsia mop up the remains of her stew with a piece of bread.

After finishing her own meal, Lynsia laughed and grabbed onto Kendira's wrist as they meandered through the crowd towards the minstrel. Cheers from several men could be heard as the two almost vanished behind the many others gathered in the tavern. It didn't take long for the lute to stop playing, followed soon by a set of panpipes calling out over the voices of the people hiding from the weather. A moment later and the lute, slightly tuned differently, began to harmonize with the song emitted from the bard's pipes. Lynsia's voice rose up with the hum of the lute, weaving a tale about a thief taunting a noble. Other conversations slowly died down as the melody of the Sidhe-Vein's voice pulled at the ears, hearts, and minds of those seeking to stay out of the rain.

"They're a good pair, though," Urna spoke softly, sipping from her mug of cider.

"Hopefully they get to stay together through all of this mess," Ansha replied, taking a moment to chew on a bit of bread smeared with the sweetened butter. "Honestly, I hope we all can stay together, even as friends, after all this is over."

The lamps flickered, then flickered again, and died. Not just one or two, but every source of light in the tavern was snuffed out all at once. Even the fire crackling in the hearth was extinguished. Darkness, and an eerie chill flooded the room in an instant. The light-hearted mood of people just trying to stay out of the storm was quickly consumed by a hushed panic that rushed into the tavern like a wind of whispers.

As all the lamps, and even the hearth, ignited once again just as swiftly as they had gone out, Lynsia shrieked. The sound pierced through the hushed murmurs in the relit tavern like a hot knife through pig fat. Rushed footsteps could be heard stomping in the direction of the building's entrance, though the clusters of stunned patrons made it nearly impossible to see what was happening.

Ansha, Urna, and Orota leapt from their seats, preparing to charge for the door, when an explosion of blackness ripped through the air right in front of them. Kendira, her face wet with blood from several deep wounds to her forehead, was thrown from the burst of shadowy magic, and like a cloth doll, slammed down onto the table they had their meal at. The bard snarled angrily and tried to get to her feet, but collapsed into the mess of soiled dishes and spilled drinks.

"I've got her," Orota ordered, pointing towards the door. "Go get the girl!"

Ansha paused, wanting to check on her injured friend, but a tug from Urna pulled the countess' attention to what needed to be done.

"I don't like this," Urna hissed as she headed for the door.

Pushing through the crowd, and then rushing out onto the porch, Ansha already had the rapier drawn as she stepped out into the rain. She was only a step or two behind Urna, but they were already a considerable distance from the men carrying the Sidhe-Vein towards the bridge over the river swollen with rain. Almost out of pure instinct, the countess took off running, wishing she had her bow instead of a sword.

She had nearly passed Urna when she saw the reptilian hand holding up a small red gem. The slithzerkai spoke a swift chant, words unfamiliar to the countess, and the gem flared to life with a bright burst of crimson light. Fire and lightning ripped through the wet air, crackling and burning through the heavy rain in a heartbeat before smashing into the cobblestone road under the feet of the running men. Rocks, soil, and mud were thrown into the storm, while the four men screamed and tumbled to the ground in a heap. As the men attempted to stagger back to their feet, Ansha closed the distance with them, silently hoping to find Lynsia unharmed from the blast.

The man that had been carrying the Sidhe-Vein clutched at the mangled mess of gore that had been his right leg, while two others groaned in pain and rolled in the wreckage of the blasted road. Crawling away and dragging an unconscious Lynsia with him, the fourth man glanced at the countess with a panicked expression as she caught up to the girl's captors.

"Let her go!" Ansha demanded, pointing the tip of her dead husband's sword at the man.

"They'll kill us!" The man begged.

"If you don't," Urna stepped up beside the countess, the red stone glowing fiercely, "I'll kill you."

"I was told," a whisper lifted up from the wind that strolled through the town, "there was a traitor."

"She's here!" the man cried with fright, trying to run with the girl, though his clearly broken left leg wouldn't allow it.

Though rain hammered down from the dark clouds above, the group of black-robed figures standing on the bridge appeared as though they had stepped out of a nightmare. Ansha swore they hadn't been there just a moment before, as her eyes scanned the three tall, hooded creatures walking towards her from the bridge.

"She's a vellorean," Urna spoke dangerously, gesturing towards the hooded beings approaching them.

The whisper that rode in on the wind rose up once more. "Not them," it hissed with a deep, feminine sound, "but I am."

In less time than it took to blink, a black cloud swirled up from the ground behind Urna, and a tall, thin woman materialized from the shadowy mist as though she had been standing there the entire day. Robes the color of a cloudy midnight sky covered the ash-white cloth dress of the woman while a dark, blackberry-hued hooded cloak kept the weather off her slender figure. The skin of her face, the same color as sun-bleached undyed cotton, was a stark contrast to the inky blackness of her long, braided hair and eyes. Lips, looking as though they were stained with mulberry juice, conveyed only contempt as she looked upon the reptilian woman.

Without warning, ebony flames were thrown like a lance from the deft hands of the strange, pale-skinned woman. The burning spear of darkness slammed into Urna with unrelenting force and fury, throwing the slithzerkai to the ground at the feet of the three figures stepping off the bridge. Gasping for air and writhing in pain, Urna was blasted again with another spear of flaming shadows, then a third strike, all delivered in less than a single heartbeat.

Ansha was already lunging with the scalloped blade of the rapier, aiming for the pale woman's chest, as the third blast of magic struck the slithzerkai. A snake-like stream of black mist rushed forward from the right hand of the vile woman as she spun on her right heel to meet the charge of the countess. As though it were the tendrils of a whip, the shadows slapped against the hand holding the rapier, instantly coiling around the pommel and Ansha's wrist. The tall, dark-robed woman stepped backwards, pulling the cord of darkness in her hand as she moved away from the attack of the countess, yanking the pregnant woman forward and off balance. Spinning on her left foot, the wicked woman crashed the back of her left hand into the face of the stumbling countess. Ansha would've reeled away from the blow, but the woman yanked fiercely upon the blackness coiled around her forearm and sword, striking her face yet again, dropping the countess to her knees in agony.

"Do not toy with me," the words like a whisper in the storm, emanated from the lips of the tall, pale woman as the black vines around Ansha's wrist turned to a rope made from thorny briars.

There was zero emotion in the voice of the mysterious woman, though her eyes, despite being completely black like polished orbs of coal, looked upon the countess with utter disdain. While the thorns of the briars ripped at her arm, Ansha tried to climb back to her feet, but the other woman backhanded her so hard, the countess was certain bones had been broken in her cheek. Her nose and lips leaked with warm crimson, she could feel the blood against her skin, in spite of the splattering of rain against her face.

"Cay..." Urna coughed as she managed to at least get up on her hands and knees. "Caynderia. It's been a long... long damn time."

"The traitor can still speak?" the tall woman's whisper-like voice called out over the wind and rain. "You're more resilient than I gave you credit for."

From somewhere behind Ansha, a furious red glow grew and hellish fire burned like a crossbow bolt through the air. Exploding into a brilliant flash of flame and thunder, the burning lance was intercepted by the pale woman's right hand, which had conjured up a barrier of scarlet energy. Before the woman could respond with magic of her own, several more of the flaming arrows of bright ruby light exploded into the three hooded figures by the bridge. Out of the storm, Kendira appeared in a rush next to the countess, as Caynderia wheeled away defensively, letting go of the briars that held fast to Ansha's wrist.

While her minions growled and rolled on the street from their burns and broken bones, Caynderia examined the bard with a dangerous expression. "Foolish human," she muttered.

"Are you okay?" Ansha asked, getting back to her feet as the briars around her forearm faded into black dust, leaving their deep puncture wounds behind.

"No," the bard replied, never letting her emerald eyes leave the pale woman, "but I couldn't just stand back while one of my lovers is attacked."

"We have to get Lyn," the countess insisted, as she shifted the rapier to her good hand.

The man clinging to Lynsia let go of the Sidhe-Vein and attempted to run away, though his shattered limb prevented him from going far. The mighty hammer of Orota struck the man from the darkness and rain, slamming into the middle of his back with a deafening crack, while a second blow to the man's head stopped his movements. Scooping the knocked-out girl up like she was weightless, the burly woman made her way closer to the countess and bard, keeping Caynderia in her sight as she walked.

"We'll be taking her back," Kendira snarled, letting loose with another barrage of flaming bolts.

With a swath of red magic, the dark-robed woman nullified the assault effortlessly, letting the arrows of fire detonate against her crimson barrier. As though she were throwing down a glass to shatter it, the pale woman summoned an orb of crimson energy enveloped in her black flames, and sent it into the ground furiously. Immediately, the cobblestone of the street began exploding under the feet of Ansha and the others while blasts of black and red fire erupted from the soil. Chunks of stone became shrapnel that battered and slashed at the flesh of the group, while arcane fire burned at everything it touched. Orota grabbed onto the bard and forced her backwards as they fell with the force of one of the many bursts of magic from the ground. They collapsed onto the porch of one of the few stores lining the street in Pershing's Ferry, as the explosions and fire finally came to an end, leaving the group out of breath and clutching their many wounds.

Ansha rolled onto her back, having buckled after a chunk of the street's cobblestone left a deep gash along the right side of her face, cutting through her ear and leaving her a bloodied mess. She was certain that at least one of her legs was broken, if not, it was badly sprained. The blow to her head left her dizzy and unsure of her surroundings, but she was well aware of the pain echoing through her body from her left shoulder.

"Fine," came the whispered voice of the vellorean as the pale woman moved to where she stood over the injured countess, "keep the girl. For now."

The right arm of Ansha went for the rapier that had been dropped, but the left foot of the pale woman came crashing down against her elbow. Something snapped under the assault of the wicked woman's foot, bringing a deafening scream from the lips of the countess.

"You, however," Caynderia spoke, her voice vacant of any emotion, before slamming her right heel into Ansha's head.

"No!" Urna's voice bellowed, as another heavy blow from the vile woman's right foot struck the left temple of the countess.

The world went black and silent, as horrific amounts of pain took over Ansha's body.

11.

"They've got her!" Urna's desperate voice cried through the connection between the saystones.

Lorvin paced in the clearing, holding the blue gem in his left hand as he listened to the reptilian woman's depiction of the attack in Pershing's Ferry. He had just laid down in his hammock, his belly full of venison and rice, when the small gem began to glow and hum. Zakosa and Kortyx sat anxiously near the fire on the riverbank, watching the feline man pace in the distance.

"They took Ansha!" the woman's voice howled, the voice like an echo through a valley as it flowed in from the minor magic of the stone.

"We couldn't stop them," Kendira's voice came harsh and cold after a brief pause, apparently while the stone changed hands. "They came after Lynsia, but they took Ansha instead. What are we supposed to do now? We're barely alive ourselves."

For a moment, Lorvin simply walked about, his feet traveling up and down his randomly chosen path. He had no answer to give them. Well, he did, but he knew the women wouldn't appreciate his words.

"What do you think Dorho would do?" Kendira's voice called through the connection.

Lorvin stopped his feet and looked up at the late night sky, which was clear and full of beautiful stars. "If you go after Ansha," he spoke finally and honestly, his tone cold, though he never intended to sound uncaring, "you might as well tie Lynsia up in a bow when you hand-deliver her to the Onyx Spire. You have to continue and press forward, take her to the faerie. I know this is going to hurt to hear, but you have to ignore Ansha and let her go for now, we all do. We don't even know if they're keeping her alive or not."

"But," Kendira hesitated, "Dorho…"

"He's dead," Lorvin stated quickly as the woman's voice trailed off over the connection. "This is no longer about him, and we all need to realize that and get used to it.

Everyone involved needs to think about that girl, and keep her from the reach of the Onyx Spire. If we fail at doing that, then yes, we have failed the memory and honor of our fallen friend. We need to keep moving forward, regardless of our personal feelings."

"Lorvin," the woman's voice, though an echo through the stone, was clearly upset at his words, "how can you speak so coldly about Dorho and Ansha? How would he react to hearing you say that about his wife?"

"It's not cold, it's truth," Lorvin explained. "They're good people, but we can't just go handing Lynsia over to the Onyx Spire. If Dorho were still alive, he would urge you to keep going, to keep the girl safe. Right now, that girl is in danger, and needs to get to that faerie up north. Keep going, Kendira, do it for that girl you love so much."

"And," her voice broke, even through the echoed connection of the stone's magic, Lorvin could hear the tears falling from her cheeks, "what about Ansha?"

Lorvin sighed and shook his head as he considered how to answer. "Once we have Lynsia settled, we'll figure out how to rescue Ansha. We're a handful of women, a cat, and a pair of lizards, so I don't think we stand a chance against the entire Onyx Spire on our own. We'll need an army behind us, or someone much smarter than we are when it comes to sneaking into places."

"We need Dorho," the woman's voice cried through the bond between the saystones.

"Yes," Lorvin's eyes turned to the ground as he took a long, saddened breath, "we do."

The stone went dark and the connection was severed. For a while, Lorvin dropped down to sit on his haunches, staring at the small blue stone in his right hand. He wondered if breaking out of jail to join his friends had changed anything, if he was honestly making any difference for them. With Kortyx, he could fly to the Onyx Spire in a matter of weeks, but he would be vastly outnumbered and far overwhelmed upon reaching that forsaken place. He suddenly felt helpless, like an ant under a man's boot.

"What's the plan?" Zakosa's hiss-like voice called from the small camp near the river. "Are we going back to help?"

Lorvin stood up and took a long, steadying breath as he examined the woods around them. "No, we keep going. We were given a job to do, and we'll finish it. We'll reach the coast tomorrow evening, from there, it's a short flight down to the capital of Anslater. We'll rest there and gather some supplies. Maybe seek guidance from one of the temples. Once we reach the druids, I will take Kortyx and go back for the women. Hopefully they'll be fine until then."

"We should—," the kobold began, rising to his feet angrily.

"We keep going!" Lorvin yelled, cutting off the argument off the small reptilian druid. "T'raha could've found a less problematic druid to summon. What have you even done for this quest, and my friends? Nothing. Vourden lost his wife, Ansha lost her husband, and now she's been captured as well. How many more have to die? How much longer are you going to stand by and do nothing? You stand around, waving that stick of yours, but to what end? You've done nothing. Face it, you're a pathetic excuse for a druid. Now, I'm stuck out here in the woods with you, and you won't stop whining long enough to help me find the Red Aspen Grove."

"I just think..." The druid stepped back slightly, putting the gnarled staff between himself and the monk as his voice trailed off into the night.

"You think we should go back?" Lorvin narrowed his gaze.

Zakosa nodded eagerly, taking another step back from the irate naetari.

"Then go," Lorvin pointed into the darkness. "Go. Take your useless self and just go back, but go with the knowledge that no one trusts you, and we all think you're utterly worthless to this journey. No wonder you can't keep the monsters out of your homeland. You need that faerie to help you, because you don't have the initiative to do it yourself. Just admit it, you're weak, and that's why your swamp will always belong to the goblins, trolls, and ogres. Admit it and leave. I will find the grove on my own."

For a moment, the two stared at each other. The kobold's eyes were filled with restraint and distress, while the naetari watched the druid with a woeful wrath that matched the fury of a burning volcano.

"If you don't want to help, just say so, and leave," Lorvin stated, before walking over to his hammock and laying down. "I'm tired of watching you for Vourden. Go do whatever you want. I'll do this myself."

Zakosa took a step towards the monk, his mouth opening to speak, but Kortyx growled and slammed one of her winged arms into the soil between the druid and the kobold. The protective growl turned quickly into a furious shriek as the scarlet eyes of the great beast focused on the small figure of the kobold.

"She'll kill you if you get any closer," Lorvin said coldly, rolling onto his side. "If you're still here in the morning, then I'm going to assume that she didn't eat you, and that you've decided to prove us all wrong. Though I won't be bothered if you were gone, as well."

With complete disregard for the kobold, Lorvin found sleep, though his thoughts were plagued with doubts and anxiety. His dreams drifted from his friends and people in his past, to images of a horrible world ran by the Onyx Spire and its lust for power. He tossed and turned, often waking up only to see the massive figure of Kortyx lying next to him, her left wing draped over his hammock, then drifted back to a fussy slumber.

The sun hadn't quite broken over the hills when the catfolk finally gave up on getting peaceful sleep and rolled off the hammock. His silver eyes scanned the camp, seeing no sign of the kobold, and shook his head a bit. After waking Kortyx with a firm massage to the sides of her face and neck, he sent the wyvern off to hunt for her breakfast while he prepared his own meal. Dried berries, oats, rice, and a bit of honey were turned into a thick hot porridge over the fire. He also put a hefty trout from the river over the flames, roasting it as he finished and ate the sweet porridge. By the time he had devoured half the fish, Kortyx returned with a killed deer, eating it greedily next to the river as the naetari worked on the remaining fish meat. It was a quiet morning, one that went unspoiled by the presence of the complaining kobold.

After breaking down the camp and securing packs to the harness around Kortyx, they took to the air once more. He didn't bother looking, or even calling for, the missing druid. Lorvin couldn't be troubled with it. He would find help in Anslater, as surely someone there knew about the grove. Lorvin knew about the grove and the druids, but he wasn't sure where to find it himself, as he had only met members when their paths crossed during his travels. He didn't need the kobold, and felt as though his life would be easier without Zakosa around.

He didn't just feel like it, he knew it would be easier.

As expected with Kortyx, the trip went without any problems for the rest of the day. Without the kobold complaining about his legs hurting from sitting so long, Lorvin could fly all day without stopping, which was easy for the powerful wyvern as well. A light lunch of unleavened bread and dried meat was eaten in the air as the scents from the sea air began to rise into the nostrils of the naetari. It was a briny, salty scent that reeked of dead fish, seaweed, and fair weather. By the time evening settled over the land, Lorvin and Kortyx were enjoying the soft summer breeze over the coast.

Another night, another camp was made. Kortyx was used to snatch a couple large fish from the ocean. One for himself, and one for the wyvern. With enough meat for both his dinner and breakfast, Lorvin made himself lazy around the camp after the sun faded from view. He drank down a couple cups of hot tea, stretched out next to the warm fire, and drifted asleep.

The following day was much the same. Lorvin had Kortyx follow the coast south and east, flying over small fishing villages and expansive vineyards as they drew closer to Vansenhul. With clear skies and pleasant weather, the trip was simple, and without the nagging of the druid, it went quietly. Only the movement of the wyvern's wings and the sound of the wind whipping by reached the ears of the naetari as they soared over the shore.

Once the sprawling coastal city of Vansenhul came into view, the naetari had the wyvern sweep out over the water, circling the city in an exhilarating rush as he looked for a place to set the great beast down. He knew people down below saw the spectacle of the wyvern flying at the edges of their city, but he didn't care, unless they became hostile. With the rarity of seeing a living wyvern, much less one with a rider, the likelihood of being attacked was slim, as most people were shocked and excited at the sight.

A large crater, obviously the ruins of a once impressive building, stained a hill in the center of the great city. Under the wyvern, people were pointing and looking as the circling beast drew closer to the city. With the crater in view, Lorvin directed the powerful reptile towards the hill, urging the great beast to slow as they dropped over Ostenfel Castle. Like a butterfly preparing to land on a fresh bloom, Kortyx slowed her wings to descend gracefully, and gently within the ruins of the destroyed building.

Three guards, and a man clad in mysterious reddish gold armor rushed into the ruins as Lorvin leapt from the back of Kortyx. Before he could take five steps, two swords and a glaive were pointed at the chest of the naetari.

"I don't mean you any harm," Lorvin said, using his right hand to push the glaive away before gesturing to the wyvern, "and she's housebroken."

"Who are you?" the man in the strange armor demanded, slapping the feline's hand with the glaive.

"A wyvern?" a female voice called loudly, her eager excitement stopping the answer from leaving Lorvin's throat as his lips began to move. "Is that a wyvern? Here? In the flesh?"

"Cerulla," the blonde-haired man in the strange armor spoke, turning to a voluptuous woman approaching from behind him.

"He's a wyvern tamer," she replied, putting a hand on the man's right shoulder as she reached him.

Lorvin shook his head, pushing away the glaive once more. "Sorry, ma'am, I'm just a humble monk of the land. I'm Lorvin Dendrostone, and this is my companion, Kortyx."

Without any hesitation, Cerulla stepped over to the great beast in the ruins. Her eyes, like fire opals, shimmered with excitement as she reached her hands out towards the powerful flying reptile.

"Hold on," the man spoke up, quickly grabbing the left wrist of the curvy woman. "You don't know what this thing, or this cat, will do."

"If I wanted to cause a problem," Lorvin responded, crossing his arms over his chest as he watched the two near Kortyx, "you would've been her lunch the moment you drew your weapons. The lady is fine, as long as my companion and I can remain unmolested in this city. We're just here to take a break, get some supplies, and then get back to our journey."

"He's right," Cerulla spoke up with a warm smile. "If they wanted to hurt us, they could've done so already."

Without waiting for a protest from the blonde man with the glaive, the woman reached up and put her hands on the sides of Kortyx's face. The touch was gentle, and as the woman closed her eyes, so did the wyvern. As she enjoyed the closeness with the wyvern, the soldiers put away their weapons, giving Lorvin a bit of space.

"She's beautiful," Cerulla commented with a warm smile as her fingers caressed the scales of the wyvern's head, "and she loves you very much, monk."

The familiarity that the woman showed with Kortyx struck Lorvin as odd, but the two seemed to be completely comfortable around each other. Most people stayed clear of the wyvern, mostly out of fear of being eaten, but this strange woman with the indigo hair seemed to be genuinely happy to see the large beast. The way she approached and touched the massive reptile, and the way she talked, it was like…

"You're not human, are you?" Lorvin inquired, the previous thought drifting out with his words.

Cerulla's eyes opened slowly as she threw a small smile to the naetari. "You're a rather perceptive one, aren't you?"

"I'm a monk of the land, ma'am," Lorvin grinned, moving to take a couple packs off the harness around Kortyx. "I didn't live this long with a wyvern because I'm blind and careless."

Despite the indignant glance of the man with the glaive, the woman moved over to Lorvin and put a hand against his forehead. Her touch was warm and pleasant, like a physical form of pure kindness. Lorvin closed his eyes, relaxed by the gentleness of the woman's hand against his face, but before he could get too comfortable, she yanked her fingers away.

"He knows your sister, my prince," she blurted, speaking to the man in the reddish-gold armor. "I can see it in his connection to nature."

"He knows her?" the man's eyes went wide.

"Who?" Lorvin asked with a confused smile. "I've met several sisters over the years, but none of them have struck my fancy."

"We need to talk," the man stated, before slightly bowing to the feline. "First, I wish to apologize for approaching you so aggressively. We've had some rather foul luck involving strangers lately, and with the wedding tomorrow, we're not taking any chances. Please, come with us to the castle. You'll be treated as an honored guest until you wish to depart."

12.

Elsewhere in the city of Vansenhul, Dorho stood on the balcony of the inn. Corina was sprawled out naked on the bed in the room behind him when he saw the circling wyvern over the city. He only knew one man crazy enough to fly with such a massive beast, and the rogue's heart jumped with excitement with the sight of the powerful creature overhead.

"Get dressed," he spoke hurriedly, downing the last of the onyx tea in his mug as he turned back to the room. "We need to go look into something."

"What is it, sweetie?" Corina called back, rolling onto her stomach with a wry grin.

"A wyvern, with a rider," Dorho said as he fetched his violet tunic and black leather vest. "I have a feeling I might know who it is. I hope you don't mind cats."

"Cats?" The young woman lifted her brow in curiosity as she slid closer to the rogue who sat on the bed to get dressed.

For a moment, Dorho's dark eyes scanned over the slender figure of the woman before he cupped her cheeks and kissed her deeply. "What are we doing?" he asked with a small laugh. "I'm married, and I'm pretty certain your father is going to be furious."

Corina laughed and nuzzled into his hands fondly. "It's fate. I've been dreaming of you, just as you've been dreaming of me. This was supposed to happen. Also, I don't think my father will mind much, as long as he knows I'm with you. He respects you. If anyone should be upset, it's me."

"Why you?" Dorho asked, before kissing her lips again.

"I couldn't meet the man of my dreams until after he got married," she answered, putting her arms around his waist gently. "Now, I'm lying in bed naked, being kissed by a foreign noble who's been plaguing my dreams for years, but he's spoken for."

"I'm just as much to blame," Dorho admitted with a soft sigh. "All those dreams I had where you were reaching out for me, and I can finally grab your hand in person. I can't seem to get enough of you. I'm a married man, I should hold back, but I just can't. Not with you. I need you."

"I love you," Corina smiled honestly, "and I always knew I would."

"Come on," he kissed her a third time, before slipping his tunic on and grabbing his boots, "I want to go see if I'm right about that wyvern's rider."

They quickly got dressed, with Dorho grabbing his hat, swords, and cloak. Corina wore the jade dress she picked up in Wayfarer's Folly. They shared another quick kiss and then stepped downstairs and out onto the street.

The city was bustling with visitors eager for the wedding, making the streets busy as the two walked hand-in-hand. Dorho saw the wyvern finally dip down near the college area, so he kept moving in that direction. They stopped for a meal of hot meat pies and sweetened tea at a small shop near the harbor, then got moving again. After what felt like almost an hour of wandering through the city streets, and letting Corina get distracted by items offered in store windows, the pair found themselves on the road leading to the college hill.

"Kortyx!" Dorho shouted, spotting the massive beast in the crater and ruins of a large structure near the center of the college district, once he managed to get through the rest of the crowd that gathered to see the rare being.

"You know that thing?" Corina asked as she hid behind the rogue, seeing the sheer size of the great creature.

Dorho grinned, looking from the young woman to the wyvern. "That harness is unmistakable. I helped Lorvin find the crafter who made it."

The powerful creature stirred from her slumber and crimson eyes gazed over the rogue before the nose of the beast sniffed at the man and woman. A low hiss escaped the mouth full of fangs, and then the wyvern nudged the rogue with the tip of her snout. Dorho ran his hand over the top of the creature's head, then threw his arms around the wyvern's neck in a tight hug.

"It's good to see you," the rogue said. "Where's your furry buddy?"

"Furry buddy?" Corina inquired while she carefully stepped closer to the beast, but stayed out of reach of the powerful mouth.

"Lorvin," Dorho answered, his eyes looking about for the naetari. "He's the rider of this wyvern, but last I heard, he was locked up for arson in the Calinsahr Duchy."

"Sir?" a youthful man in a hooded scholar's robe the color of mossy earth spoke up. "Are you talking about the cat-man?"

Dorho turned to the man, smiling wide. "Yes! I'm wondering why his companion is here."

"A trio of guards from the castle came and got him," the man replied. "The prince and Lady Cerulla were with them as well."

Dorho shook his head and laughed softly. "What has that damned cat gotten himself into now?"

"I didn't hear what they were talking about," the young scholar responded as he gestured towards the main academy. "I was just leaving my lessons for the day when I saw them taking him away."

"Thank you," the rogue shook the scholar's hands in gratitude before turning to Corina. "Are you ready to visit the castle?"

"I thought we were going to wait until the wedding, and talk to them during the reception?" Corina questioned, as Dorho took her hand once more.

"I might need to bail a cat out of the animal shelter," the count chuckled.

Dorho patted the side of Kortyx's thick neck and grinned, truly happy to see the magnificent beast, then started heading towards the grand castle. Sitting on a stony ledge overlooking the harbor, the sprawling grey marble and crimson tile roofs of the expansive castle appeared more like a grand mansion than anything else, but on a much larger scale. A single road of silver cobblestone climbed the slope from the city to the castle gate, where four guards, each wearing blue and black gambesons stood ready to intercept the pair.

"Halt!" an older guard held up his hand as Dorho approached the tall, iron gate. "Who are you?"

"Count Dorho Maizen," the rogue bowed respectfully. "I come with the hope to speak to the prince, or anyone who might know about the wyvern's rider."

"Is anyone expecting you?" the guard inquired, examining Dorho's attire carefully through weary blue eyes.

"Not yet," Count Maizen confessed with a disarming smile, "we originally came for the wedding, but the cat might want his bail paid."

The guards took a moment to converse with one another before one dashed off towards the castle through the courtyard. As the sun was descending for the evening, the rogue and the farmer's daughter waited patiently.

"Might I ask what he did this time?" Dorho spoke up as the minutes dragged by.

The old guard shrugged. "Not for me to know, nor do I care to ask. He was picked up by the prince and a few others shortly after that little stunt with his big lizard."

"Is that so?" Dorho chuckled. "That cat is well known for his strange stunts. I'm sorry your city is having to deal with him."

"It's not the worst thing to happen," the guard shifted his weight to lean against the stone wall by the grand iron gate. "The Onyx Spire attacked the Sages Arcanum, we're at war with the neighboring kingdom, and Lady Cerulla is finally getting married. A naetari flying around on a wyvern is hardly our biggest concern right now."

As the guard finished talking, three figures approached from the castle. One was the younger guard that had been sent inside. The one in the middle was a curvy woman with strikingly opal-like eyes that mimicked glowing embers. Next to her was a catfolk clothed in slate-hued robes and pants, with black and grey fur that matched his mischievous silvery eyes.

"By the gods," Dorho called out, a wide grin breaking on his face as he spotted the naetari. "It is you."

Lorvin stopped as the gate was cranked open with heavy chains running through massive gears, his eyes looking over Dorho with utmost suspicion. "This can't be. There's no way. Vourden, Ansha, everyone, they all said you were killed. You're dead. They saw you die. I've seen your grave. I've seen them mourn whenever they spoke of you."

Immediately, the guards began clutching at their weapons, unsure what was going on.

"That's true," Dorho replied, keeping his hands out where they could be seen by the guards. "I did die, but it's a long story, my friend. Last I heard, you were in jail for burning down some farms, then I saw Kortyx in the sky earlier today. I had to know if it was really you."

The naetari shook his head. "I find this incredibly hard to believe," the monk began. "I'm not sure what to say. I've seen your grave. I've met people who are grieving your death. How can you be here?"

"The harness on Kortyx," Dorho stated, forcing a smile, "you and I went to a leatherworker in Hafordein to get it made. His name was Volfin, and he offered to make it if we cleared some orcs from a cave north of town. You brought the entire cave down on the bloodthirsty bastards. You were upset because you hated killing them, but we would've been killed otherwise."

"You remember all that?" Lorvin chuckled and then quickly grabbed the rogue in a tight, friendly hug. "Then, it must really be you, but I still don't understand. How are you still alive?"

"It's been a long few weeks, it seems," Dorho chuckled, giving a hug of kinship in return, "I can't say being dead would've been worse than the mess I've been drawn into."

"It is a pleasure to meet you again, Miss Knepiri," the indigo-haired woman spoke up. "It would appear the man from your dreams has finally come to you."

"Lady Cerulla," Corina smiled warmly as she greeted the curvy woman. "Indeed, it seems my visions have brought me to your house this time."

"Shall we go inside and talk?" Cerulla suggested with a welcoming smile, "We've been expecting you, Dorho."

"Expecting me?" The rogue blinked, baffled by the admission, but ended up following the woman and one of the guards towards the castle, despite his confusion.

"I can't believe you're really here," Lorvin said excitedly as he looked over the count carefully before turning towards Corina. "Who is this lovely creature?"

"Lorvin," Dorho grinned from his joy of seeing the familiar naetari, "this is Corina Knepiri. She's my guide and companion here in Anslater."

"She's a practitioner of the Atheian Way," Cerulla added, "and despite her young age, is one of the best healers in the region."

"Count Maizen here," Corina spoke up, wrapping her left arm around Dorho's right bicep, "ended up on my family's farm. I've been keeping him out of trouble until he gets home."

"A pleasure to meet you, Miss Knepiri," the catfolk said with a kind bow. "I still can't believe you're alive, Dorho. Escaping death isn't like me checking out of the inn under Artinburg Castle. Did you annoy Dimorta that much with your endless tales?"

As they walked through the courtyard, and followed the fiery-eyed sage to the main entrance of the castle, Dorho spoke of how he ended up at the Knepiri farm. He talked about how it all started by just wanting to take Lynsia home to Euthrox, and resulted in the death of not only himself, but Vourden's wife as well. Lorvin discussed how he escaped from Goldenveil, met Vourden and the others in Ameribelle, and was sent to find the druids with the kobold. While traversing the halls of the great castle, Corina mentioned how she had found Dorho lying in the field near the farm, and how the count had protected her in Wayfarer's Folly. The voluptuous woman remained silent, listening carefully to the stories of each person following her.

Eventually, they arrived at a grand dining hall where the royal family was seated. Without delay, the woman made her way to a seat next to a man with shoulder-length blonde hair and honest blue eyes. The king and queen were an older couple, but their gaze might've well been made with steel daggers, as it pierced through Dorho with quick, unspoken judgment. The rogue felt the hand of the farmer's daughter slip into his own, giving his fingers a nervous squeeze.

"To the court of Anslater and the Galheam family, might I introduce Count Dorho Maizen of Golden Bow Gulch, Miss Corina Knepiri of Knepiri Brewery, and you already met Lorvin Dendrostone, the wandering monk. Come, sit down," the indigo-haired woman spoke up, gesturing to a series of chairs gathered at the moon-shaped table. "We should get to know each other." As the last word fell from her emerald-stained lips, the woman sat down gracefully.

The room itself was circular with a high, vaulted ceiling formed by a series of grand stone arches. Tapestries depicting either family lineage or Anslater history hung from ten of the twelve walls, while a grand door of birch and brass decorated the southernmost wall, and another, matching door graced the northernmost wall. Like the rest of the castle, the floors were created from tiles of red marble, while the walls were carved from polished white limestone. Shaped like a crescent moon, the iron-banded oak table bent away from the southern door, while a small dais between the door and table contained four seats occupied by court bards.

A maid stepped across the room, escorted Lorvin to a seat next to the curvy woman they had followed, while Dorho and Corina were seated beside the queen on the opposite end of the table. Glasses of sweet wine made from persimmons, and garnished with an edible hibiscus flower, were placed before the visitors, as the royal family had already been handed their drinks. Dorho took off his hat, hanging it carefully from the ear of the chair before picking up the drink he had been offered.

"I never thought I'd ever be having dinner with the king and queen of the land," Corina admitted quietly, whispering to Dorho as she looked anxiously at the yam-hued wine.

"My life tends to lead to many unexpected situations," Dorho said with a smile, sipping from the goblet of wine set before him.

"Golden Bow Gulch?" King Galheam inquired, his voice gruff, yet kind at the same time as his blue eyes took in the attire of the count. "Isn't that part of Elgrahm Hold? Might I ask what a noble from Thornbror is doing in my castle? I thought our borders were closed to the likes of you."

Dorho took another drink of the sweet wine as he considered how to answer, his eyes darting to Corina briefly before turning his attention back to the king. "I won't lie, now that I'm here. This is going to sound crazy, no matter how many times I repeat it. I was escorting a Sidhe-Vein to meet a faerie in the Faulkendor Mountains, when I was attacked and killed in Albinasky Keep. Oddly, I woke up a few days ago on the Knepiri farm with Corina standing over me. It's hard to explain, but I was given a second chance, but in trade I was told to find a second Sidhe-Vein to bring an end to the Onyx Spire's plans. That's what brings me to your court, King Galheam."

The king's aging eyes turned towards the woman seated next to Lorvin and pursed his lips a moment before speaking. "Cerulla? You're the court's sage, and warden over the land, what do you say of this man's words?"

"I have heard of this man's arrival through the whispers in nature's energy," the castle's sage spoke without delay. "It is also confirmed by the naetari seated here with us. They apparently know each other. Though, I also fear his arrival is a warning of dark times ahead for not just our land, but the world as a whole. Especially if the gods themselves were so concerned, they nullified his death."

"Excuse me, Lady Cerulla," Lorvin interrupted, poking his forehead with his left fingers. "Maybe you can do that thing you did with me earlier. You figured out I had met Lynsia. Can't you do that with Dorho?"

"I," Cerulla paused, then stood up as she shot a smile to the feline. "I could, if that's okay with him, of course."

"That is fine with me," Dorho replied, before looking over at the others at the table, "especially if it will ease the worries of others here."

The king nodded in agreement. "I believe it would help put aside our concerns. You're the sage of Anslater, Cerulla, your word in matters like this is regarded to be penultimate."

"My love?" Cerulla called, looking at the blonde man next to her seat.

The man nodded and offered a kind smile. "Do it. A man returning from the grave is a suspicious story, no matter how much others might believe it."

Cerulla's soundless footsteps were quick and deliberate as she moved closer to Dorho. She urged him to sit still as she stood behind his chair, putting one hand on his forehead, the other resting upon his left shoulder. As her eyes, like dulled fire opals, closed, the rogue felt his own body relax and he allowed his own dark eyes to shut leisurely as well. It was as though he were being embraced by a long-lost friend, as the relaxing warmth of her mysterious energy flowed through his body and lulled him into a state nearly akin to a peaceful slumber.

There was a brilliant flash in the back of Dorho's mind as his thoughts raced at lightning speed. He thought about Ansha, Lynsia, Kendira, Vourden, and others he had met through his travels. For a moment, he even saw things that he didn't fully understand. Deep in his visions, there was a great island floating in the sky above, while he stood in a small village next to Cerulla and Corina. Fire erupted from the village and the island came crashing down violently. Like someone was rapidly flipping through a book of memories, the images growing in his mind fluttered and shifted like a blur, but with a strange calm, he was forced to bear witness to it all. Suddenly, the hooded monstrosity with the pick-like weapon appeared, and everything he saw in his mind went black.

The sting from Dimorta's energy pulsed sharply under the skin of the count's right arm abruptly, drawing a gasp from the sage as she hastily took several steps back. Tears filled Cerulla's opal eyes, while she rubbed her arms as though she had just been touched by an offensive stranger. Meanwhile, Dorho clenched his fists tightly, trying to push the rush of death's magic to a faraway place within his body. It felt like someone was taking needles and jamming them through his flesh, but from the inside out.

"Cerulla?" Prince Jolson called as he quickly got up from his chair and pulled the woman against his chest. "Are you alright?"

"I'm fine," she muttered, taking a couple deep breaths to try and fight the tears falling down her cheeks. "I saw things. Terrible things. This man, he is equally blessed and cursed, both by faerie and death alike. Looking through his connection to nature, it's like walking along a stone wall between a haunted graveyard and an enchanted grove. Each step he takes, threatens to pull him one way or the other. He not only knows the other Sidhe-Vein, but he's been touched by her magic, likely several times. He's also been bewitched directly by faerie magic, most likely I'raha herself, if I were to guess the origin. Then there is a darkness to him, one that reacted as soon as I began to probe deeper into what nature knows about him. He's not lying about being dead, but I couldn't get much beyond that. A dark energy, a horrific energy in fact, slapped me away before I could dive further. I'm sorry, my prince."

"You're certain he's the one from your vision?" the blonde man asked, guiding the sage gently back to her seat at the table. "Is he the one coming for me?"

"Yes," Cerulla answered, nearly collapsing into the chair before looking over at Dorho. "He's the one we've been waiting for."

Corina put her hand on Dorho's marked arm, and though her words were soundless, mouthed a swift prayer.

Her healing energy flowed like steam through his veins, pushing away the aggravated needles of Dimorta's dark magic. He hadn't said anything, but there she was, reaching out to help him once more. Silently whispering three words only shared between lovers, Dorho placed his left hand atop her hand which was still on his arm as he finally relaxed from the surge of wicked energy.

"So, Dorho," Lorvin shifted his gaze from the sage to the rogue, then pointed briefly to the hand upon the count's arm. "What's all that about?"

"She's a healer," Dorho answered. "A very good one, honestly."

Cerulla took a long look at the rogue and the farmer's daughter and then turned her eyes toward the naetari. "Corina is likely the only thing keeping him alive right now."

"What do you mean?" Lorvin tilted his head curiously.

"Your friend is like a hot pan over a fire right now. The magic coursing through his blood would be grease. As it gets hotter and hotter, it risks bursting into flames. When it does ignite, the other magic attempts to pour water over the fire to keep it from getting out of control," the sage commented.

Lorvin rubbed his chin in a quick moment of deep thought. "If you pour water on flaming grease, it only spreads the fire."

"Exactly," Cerulla spoke with a nod. "Which is why your friend needs Corina. The only way to properly extinguish a grease fire, is to use the lid to smother it. That woman, and her bloodline magic, is a lid to Dorho's burning pan. The count is fighting a battle inside himself between the faerie magic of I'raha and the death magic of Dimorta. Unless he somehow figures out how to force those two powers to live in harmony in his flesh, they will continue to tear him apart. Corina is keeping him alive."

"But," Lorvin's silvery eyes darted to the rogue and healer once more, "he's married. Shouldn't his wife—."

"He died," the sage spoke quickly and coldly, while still massaging her arms firmly. "That experience will change anyone. The fact he was given a second chance, is a miracle in itself, but I can guarantee it still took something from him. You're lucky he remembers you. I've seen resurrected people forget their own names and homes. He might remember you, his friends, even his wife, but," her eyes shifted to the rogue, "things have changed."

"Well," Dorho sighed, brushing his fingers over the woman's hand on his arm, "she's also been haunting my dreams for years. When I woke up in her field, I felt like I had already known her for years."

"Because you have," Cerulla remarked. "Part of looking into your connection with nature, I saw bits of your history. Not just your history, but what the magic of nature knows about your lineage. You've been tainted by I'raha's magic, which allowed me to see things others might miss, at least until your other magic pushed me away."

"See things?" Dorho asked, picking up the goblet once more to take a slow drink of the sweet wine. "What kind of things?"

"Just tell them, Cerulla," the king ordered, throwing a sideways glance to the sage. "Tell them who you really are."

"It's okay, my love," the prince said with a comforting nod. "They might as well know."

Cerulla looked around the room slowly then nodded in agreement.

"What is it?" Dorho probed.

"I'm not human," the sage replied, "but the cat figured that out when we first met. In fact, I'm a faerie. One of the seven left since the Enlightened Aeon. I watched with horror as Atlantis fell from the sky. I've seen you humans raise kingdoms, only to witness their destruction at the hands of your children. Even here in Anslater, I've been a part of the royal court since before this castle was built. Several times, I wondered how the world would survive a particular catastrophe brought on by you mortals, only to be surprised when a small group banded together to stop the darkness from taking over. You mortals are both terrifying, and remarkable with what you have done, can do, and hopefully will do. So, understand that I've lived a very, very long life, and have seen so much pain, suffering, rage, and joy in my time."

"I think I understand," Dorho hesitantly spoke, "but I don't see how that answers my question."

"Let the woman speak, sweetie," Corina whispered, giving Dorho's arm a quick squeeze. "I want to hear what she meant by saying we've met before."

"During the Enlightened Aeon," Cerulla continued with a thankful glance to the healer, "the mages of Atlantis were divided into houses. House Morticaine was dedicated to the darker arts of necromancy and studying death. Dourmond Morticaine was the heir to this house, a proper prince among the mages, though modest in temperament and ethics. House Avrora was their opposite. Knesis Avrora was their youngest daughter, but a true mage of light and life. She was the origin of the term 'white mage' and gave birth to the Atheian Way."

"When demons attacked Atlantis, and took the Silver Eye from the Tower of Magi, Dourmond and Knesis went with four others to retrieve it. Though that journey has no importance on yours, Dorho, it's what happened afterwards that gets us to today. The two mages, life and death, fell in love with one another during the adventure, and despite the opposition from their vastly different houses, forged a powerful bond together. Cast out by their families, Dourmond and Knesis left Atlantis, settling in a human village during the Era of Upbringing. As I do now, I oversaw the land as its warden, witnessing their beautiful relationship as it bloomed through the ages."

"They had two children, twin daughters. Phera and Phyra Morticaine, just before the Fall of Atlantis. During the witch-hunts following the collapse of the magical empire, Dourmond and Knesis were slain by the very humans they swore to protect, but their two small daughters were taken in by friends of the family. As time went on, the two daughters bred with human husbands, and from then on the bloodline became more and more diluted. Though the Atheian Way was passed down through Phera's lineage, as Knesis' magic would continue to find use among the mortals, Phyra's children gave up the practice of magic completely."

"So, what you're saying," Lorvin interrupted, finishing his wine, "is that the woman comes from Phera Morticaine's blood, and Dorho—."

"Is born from Phyra's lineage," Cerulla cut him off. "It's several millennia in the past, but these two have met before. Like moths to a flame, they've been drawn to each other once again. It all makes me really curious, though."

"How so?" Lorvin asked.

The faerie sighed and shook her head, looking over the goblet of wine that remained untouched before her. "The sudden rise of the Onyx Spire. The birth of not one, but two Sidhe-Vein. A man being killed and then returned by Dimorta. Two souls, strayed from one another for several millennia, only to be drawn together once again. Life and death, pulled together to aid the magic of faeries. It's as though the world itself is crying out in fear, and doing everything it can in a desperate attempt to survive."

"It's because of Xa'morhu," Dorho said, his tone filled with dread as he processed everything the faerie had spoken about. "She wants to return to the world. That's why Dimorta sent me back. It's what she wants me, and all of us, to prevent."

"We sealed her away," Cerulla narrowed her gaze upon the rogue. "Before the Rise of Atlantis, even before the Enlightened Aeon, we sealed her away. We hunted down her followers, killed them, and sealed her away."

"Who is Xa'morhu?" the king asked, lifting up his goblet for a long drink.

The faerie took a deep breath. "She is an anti-god. The opposite of divine creation. You mortals think death is tragic, but what Xa'morhu represents is much, much worse. Extinction, obliteration, destruction, annihilation, those words don't begin to explain what she can do. The best way to describe her, is that she is, and creates, absolutely nothing. She's a void filled with entropy and desolation. After we killed her disciples, we sealed her away, and broke the seal into multiple parts to be buried and forgotten."

"Like that book the Onyx Spire took before destroying the archives?" the prince questioned. "The Tome of Entropy. That's what they were after. Was that part of the seal?"

Cerulla finally picked up the goblet and took a quick sip. "Yes. The Tome of Entropy represents her knowledge and wisdom. The Slate of Nullification was forged from her voice and desires. Meanwhile, the Seal of Ourixys holds her magic, heart, and soul."

Dorho nodded his understanding, looking over the faerie cautiously. "This Seal of Ourixys, and the Slate of Nullification, do you know where they went? If we can reach them first, then we can stop the Onyx Spire completely, correct?"

"Many decades ago, a member of the Onyx Spire found the Slate," Cerulla said with a heavy sigh as she considered her answer carefully. "Which would explain how they found the Tome here in Vansenhul so quickly. The Seal was locked in a hidden vault in what would become the Galensteil Wastes. Even if you manage to find it first, getting through the vault itself would prove to be a challenge that would likely break your spirit. The World of Glass, as the vault was named, is an artifact crafted by Kyltress, the goddess of ice, Lunaris, the god of the moon, and Ayperia, the goddess of light and illusions. It is not a place meant for mortals."

"Cerulla, on the chance someone were to reunite all these parts," Corina spoke up cautiously, "what would happen?"

"They would need a body," "Cerulla answered. "A strong body capable of withstanding the onslaught of incredible power, but one they could control. Combine the knowledge of the Tome, with the soul of the Seal, the voice of the Slate, and a body of unfathomable potential. They could bring her back, in at least a limited form."

"Lynsia," Dorho muttered. "That's why the Onyx Spire needs Lynsia. I was supposed to protect her, but I died."

"She's in the capable hands of Orota, Urna, and Kendira," Lorvin added. "They are taking her to meet with I'raha."

"I should be with them," Dorho argued. "What about Ansha and Vourden? I figured they would have kept going as well."

Lorvin's calm expression faded to one of sadness as he considered what to say. "Vourden was ordered to stay with Lady Eisley and help with the rebellion," he spoke up after a moment.

"What about Ansha?" Dorho asked, noticing the hesitation in his friend's voice. "Did she stay behind as well?"

"Dorho?" Lorvin replied after a deep breath, standing up. "Can we talk outside?"

After looking over the others in the room, Dorho nodded and stood up and followed the feline out of the dining hall. Without a word, they strolled through a long corridor until they stopped on a balcony overlooking a sprawling garden in the south. While the coastal breeze brought the scents of the garden up to where they stood, the evening sun was fading behind wisps of clouds in the west. For quite a while, Lorvin leaned against the balustrade taking several deep breaths as he examined Dorho, and then looked out over the flowering garden.

"Well?" Dorho broke the silence as he eventually settled onto a bench against the rail overlooking the aromatic lawn. "What about Ansha?"

Lorvin said nothing at first, while digging into a pouch tied around his belt. He produced a small blue gem slightly larger than a pea, and held it out for Dorho to take. The surface of the gem was smooth, except for a rune containing three horizontal lines split by a single vertical one. A tiny red dot rested at the top of the vertically carved line, which looked to be either paint or blood.

"Focus on the color and the rune," Lorvin instructed. "It's a trinket Urna made. She calls it a saystone."

Dorho shook his head as he held the tiny stone in his hand, examining it carefully. "This doesn't answer my question, cat."

"It will," the monk replied quickly. "Trust me. It will."

Letting out a frustrated sigh, Dorho closed his eyes and directed his thoughts to the stone. He pictured the blue stone and the marking upon the round surface. His mind wandered a few times, wondering what the naetari was failing to tell him, but every time, he pulled his focus back to the stone in his hand.

"Lorvin?" A familiar voice called through the air, like an echo in an empty room. "Is that you?"

"Kendira?" Dorho spoke slowly, his eyes opening to look at the naetari. "I'm not exactly furry enough, but I might pretend to be the cat, if you pay me enough."

The shock was audible, even through the connection between the stones.

"Lorvin? You mind telling me what's going on?" Dorho requested.

The cat shook his head and gestured to the stone in the rogue's hand. "Ask her. I'll let her explain what's going on."

"D..." Kendira's voice faded into her emotions. "Dorho? How? Is this a joke? Please, say something."

Dorho chuckled at the situation. "Dimorta got tired of my company. I ended up in Anslater looking for a second Sidhe-Vein."

He continued to explain how he ended up in Vansenhul with Lorvin. The rogue spoke about meeting Corina in Petiora, the fight in Wayfarer's Folly, and ending up meeting the royal family of Anslater. Though it was silent through the stone's connection, he swore he could hear the tears of the woman falling from her face as he mentioned the talk with Cerulla and his visit with Dimorta. Finally, he spoke of how he missed everyone, and how he was eager to see Ansha, and everyone again soon.

"She's gone," the echoing voice of Kendira called through the magic. "I'm so sorry, Dorho. The Onyx Spire took her. They tried capturing Lynsia, and ended up kidnapping Ansha instead. We couldn't stop them."

If he hadn't already been seated, Dorho would've been dropped to his knees from the verbal blow to his mind.

"Dorho?" Kendira's distant voice echoed through the magic. "We'll get her back. I'm sorry. Especially now that you're back. At least, I hope you're back. If this is a joke, it's an awfully cruel one, so I hope you're really here."

His dark eyes threw a dangerous glance to the naetari standing against the balcony railing. "I'm here, and it's really me. We're going to rescue her. Just as soon as I finish my business here. Even if I have to borrow Kortyx to reach you, I'm coming to you once I contact the second Sidhe-Vein."

"A second Sidhe-Vein?" Kendira's voice asked after a pause.

Dorho nodded as though the bard was standing in front of him. "The prince of Anslater. I believe he's the second Sidhe-Vein. I just have to explain 'we're on our way to destroy the Onyx Spire' in such a way that he'll agree to come with us."

"You don't have to," a warm, but stern male voice called from behind Dorho.

The rogue looked up quickly, only to see the prince standing only a few steps away with the faerie next to him. He had been so focused on talking to the bard through the stone that he failed to hear them approach.

"Dorho?" Kendira's voice called through the stone's magic.

Without saying anything, the count handed the saystone back to the naetari.

"I'm a Sidhe-Vein," the prince continued. "That was explained to me many years ago. You came for me, just as my faerie foretold, and I see that our desire to bring down the Onyx Spire is a mutually-held goal. There is no need to explain anything else to me. Sure, we could spend hours, days even, arguing over the best way to do this, over how to convince one another of our benefit to the end goal, but we both know that it's going to conclude with us joining forces."

"That's pretty direct," Dorho forced a smile through his anxiety over the news about Ansha.

Prince Jolson shrugged as he held out his hand in greeting. "Sly words and petty feelings have no place in a time of crisis. Either we see the end of our enemies, or they will see to our own end."

"Temperance, huh?" Dorho stood up as he took the prince's hand with a firm shake. "I see we're going to get along splendidly."

"Why don't you come back inside?" Cerulla offered, cupping her hands around the left hand of the prince. "Supper will be delivered soon. I believe the castle's cook is making fried chicken cutlets and rice."

"Just," Dorho took a deep breath to try and steady his emotions. "Just give me a moment. Things have just been," he looked at the naetari who was pocketing the small blue gem, "complicated."

13.

The creature, clothed in ashen grey robes and a tattered violet cloak, pushed open the door to the bedchamber quietly. In its hands, a tray of dried meat, cheeses, and a bowl of stew rested. Without saying a word, the creature moved across the room and set the tray on a low table next to the bed.

Ansha rolled onto her side gingerly and looked at the food. She wasn't hungry, but the monster sent to her room picked up the spoon from the stew and offered her a bite regardless of her wordless protests. The countess looked at the spoonful of stew in the bony fingers of the strange creature, took a deep breath, and accepted the bite of food. It wasn't cold, but the food definitely wasn't warm, either. Though she chewed and swallowed the bite, it wasn't because she was hungry, it was only to keep herself alive.

Other than Caynderia, this monster was the only creature she had seen since being brought to the Onyx Spire. The creature was gaunt and pale, impossibly so. Large, faded golden eyes peered out from the sunken sockets in the elongated, narrow head, while the wide mouth, stitched loosely shut with black leather cords, gave the appearance of something not quite alive, but not exactly dead, either. Habitually hunched over, the creature was considerably shorter than the countess, though it's true size was evident by the length of its bone-thin limbs. Stains of what Ansha could only assume was dirt, ash, blood, and maybe oil marked the flesh and clothing of the creature, though she knew better than to ask questions. A heavy steel collar holding a silver pendant of a jawless skull hung around the throat of the creature, marking it clearly as property.

"Do I call you slave," Ansha spoke, realizing she hadn't spoken to anyone since being knocked out in Pershing's Ferry, "or do you have a name?"

The creature looked up from the tray of food, tilted its head slightly and shook its head. "Nit. Nit is Nit," it spoke in a raspy hiss, the mouth only moving enough to not pull on the leather stitches.

"Nit?" Ansha groaned, trying to sit up, but collapsed after feeling her entire body ache and the pull of the chain attached to her right leg.

Whoever had put her in the bed had been kind enough to drive a ring through her right ankle; it was just above her heel, wrapped around her tendon, and connected to a heavy iron chain that was locked to the foot of the bed. The same leg was held tightly in a firm splint, and wrapped in bandages, and the ache from the bones told her something was broken. More bandages had been applied to the deep gash across her head, though she had lost part of her ear from the blast of cobblestone that had struck her. Several pieces of stone had been removed from her left shoulder as well, though the reason she was being kept alive was a mystery to the countess.

Not just alive, but somewhat well-cared for. Nit brought her three meals a day, and a bowl of fruit just before midnight. The creature also regularly checked the bandages on her broken body, and made sure she had plenty of fresh water to drink. Despite her obvious status as a captive, she felt that the Onyx Spire was tending to her needs better than she expected of such a place.

"Thank you, Nit," she offered, even though she would've preferred being left alone at the moment.

"Nit is just doing what Nit was ordered to do," the creature shuffled its weight slightly, holding up a piece of the dried meat.

Ansha nodded, taking the meat and chewing on it slowly. It was salted, and peppery, but even though it was cold, it was better than the stew.

The countess sighed heavily as she looked at the monster feeding her. "What even are you?"

"Nit?" the gangly creature tilted its head curiously again. "Nit is a wight. Nit was created by Mistress Doreena to serve the Lead Coin Sect."

"So, you're a slave?" Ansha inquired as she took another bite of the dried meat. "Are you friendly?"

Nit shook his head as he answered, "Nit is neither your friend, nor your enemy. You would be well-off to remember that Nit is merely a humble servant."

Nit held up another spoonful of the mediocre stew, which the countess accepted gingerly. She couldn't even explain the amount of pain and discomfort she was in, but it was more than she had ever dealt with before. Not just pain, but a heavy, depressing, loneliness. Gone was the safety of Dorho, her father, her friends, and the place she called home. Only Nit came to see her, and that was only when he was coming to perform one of his tasks. Honestly, she didn't even know how long she had been a guest of the Spire, but she felt like it had been a few days already.

Her room had only one window, which didn't face the sun, and being unable to get out of the bed made it impossible to peer outside. It wasn't a small room, but neither was it grand and luxurious. It was just big enough for the bed that was nearly as wide as she was tall, a table made from darkened bog oak with two matching chairs, and a small armoire. The walls were constructed from bricks of basalt and slabs of diorite, while the floors and ceilings were made from charred pine timbers and violet marble. A single pennant featuring a jawless skull and a coiled viper hung next to the heavy iron door that kept Ansha locked and sealed away from the rest of the Spire.

She also had no idea where in the world she was, other than being a prisoner of the Onyx Spire. The occasional whiff of the sea could be detected on the air where it mixed with the distinct aroma of pine needles and alpine leaves, while the warmth of Elgrahm Hold was long gone. Ansha could only assume that she was somewhere far north of her home, given the chill that still bit into the air despite being the middle of summer. She was grateful for the bear fur blanket that covered her, as it provided even the slightest sense of comfort in the strange, vile place

Without knocking or even announcing herself, a youthful girl pushed open the heavy iron door and stepped in, escorted by two large, thin, pale men in dark robes. If it hadn't been for the noise of the door creaking, Ansha would've missed the steps of the trio as they approached the side of the bed opposite of Nit. The girl, who couldn't have been more than seventeen years of age, stood next to the bed, holding her hands behind her back in a relaxed manner, while her two escorts took up positions next to the door.

"Nit, you can leave," the young-looking girl spoke, then gestured to the table near the window. "Leave the tray, as our guest may become hungry."

Nit backed away from the bed without question. "Yes, of course, Mistress Nadriah," the ghastly creature spoke in a murmured hiss before setting the tray upon the table as requested.

"Nadriah," Ansha mouthed, glancing from the strange creature to the young girl standing next to her. "I don't think we've met, but why does that sound familiar?"

As soon as Nit slipped from the room, and the door closed again, the young woman grinned slightly with indigo-stained lips, looking over the blanket-covered countess. "What can I say? I must be popular."

Her body was young, but there was a great depth of wisdom lurking behind the obsidian eyes Nadriah used to examine Ansha. Like strands of midnight-hued silk, her long, tightly braided hair fell elegantly behind her shoulders, while those dark eyes peered out from under a thin azure veil. Nadriah's entire body was short, lean, and looked younger than even Lynsia, but there was a hint in her posture of someone who had seen more years than Ansha dared to count. A sleeveless frock of crimson silk decorated with buttons of onyx and strands of platinum in the hem was draped tightly over a sheer black chemise, highlighting the slender, but young-looking body of the girl. Pale skin, like sun-dried parchment, and slightly pointed ears were enough for Ansha to know that the girl was more than just a mere human.

"You may call me Nadriah," the girl spoke warmly, though there was an air of ill-intent to her voice. "I am the High Tzar of the Onyx Spire. The ultimate ruler of this citadel you currently call home."

Ansha started to move away from the girl, but the ring through her ankle, and the pain shooting through her body forced her to stop. "What do you want from me?" she asked finally, struggling to sit upright.

"I made a deal with Cayn and her Whisper Troupe," Nadriah said calmly while walking around the bed, then adjusting the pillows behind Ansha to make it easier for her to sit up. "She would run some errands for me, and in trade, I would keep you alive."

"Me?" Ansha scoffed in disbelief. "Why me? Don't you want the Sidhe-Vein?"

The girl shrugged before sitting gently on the edge of the bed nearest to the countess. "I don't know why. The Lead Coin Sect, which Cayn and her group are a part of, have said you aren't to be killed. Well, not you precisely, just your unborn child. I thought about cutting her out of you and putting her in one of the nurturing chambers, but for now, keeping you alive is the easiest method. I would suggest not letting me regret that choice."

"How do you know about me?" Ansha eased into the adjusted pillows, though her eyes narrowed dangerously. "How did you know about my child?"

A wry smile appeared under the azure veil of the High Tzar as she glanced sideways at the countess. "A little birdy sang me a song. There's much I know about you all. I know who you are, where you're all going, and even about that husband of yours that was killed. Such a pity. He died protecting you and that troublesome girl, only for you to end up in my care. Such a pointless death."

"It wasn't pointless!" Ansha snapped harshly. "He was a good man, and he won't get to see his daughter grow up, because of you and your stupid games."

"Do you want him back?" Nadriah asked, her tone suggesting she had completely ignored Ansha's words. "I can do that for you."

Ansha would've struck the girl, if she had the ability in her body to do so. "No. I don't want anything from you. I just want to go home."

"That's a shame," the High Tzar said with blatantly fake sympathy. "I could have made a deal with you, just as I have with so many others."

"Never," the countess nearly spat on the High Tzar out of anger. "Not with you. Not with the Onyx Spire.

Nadriah sighed and shook her head at the willfulness of the countess. "I can only offer, it seems. I just hope you remember," she said with that damned sly smirk once more.

"Remember what?" Ansha glared.

"That I only offered to keep you alive for the sake of your child," Nadriah spoke as she leaned closer to the injured countess, "but I'm only keeping you alive because using one of our nurturing chambers requires more resources on our part. You best pray that Cayn can keep her end of the deal, because if she fails me, I no longer have to abide by our agreement. Do not think for one moment, that you, or your child, have any value to me or my goals."

"Is that why you came to see me?" the countess fumed, wishing she had the strength to wrap her hands around the girl's throat. "Just to mock me? I've lost my home, my father, my husband, and been through unimaginable horror because of you and your ilk."

"You haven't even touched the surface of horror, yet, princess," Nadriah smiled amusingly. "I only offered to keep you alive for the sake of your child, on behalf of the Lead Coin Sect. There is an entire realm of pain and suffering I can show you, and I'm looking forward to breaking that spirit of yours."

Abruptly, the girl stood up and looked at the two hooded figures standing next to the door. Her feet were nearly silent upon the stone floor as Nadriah walked away from the bed, a soft, but insidious laughter escaping her lips as she moved.

"What's so funny?" Ansha demanded.

"Your husband is alive," Nadriah stated with a scornful smirk. "It's amazing the things one can find out for the right price."

"What do you mean?" the countess nearly jumped from the bed. "He's dead. Don't you dare torment me with such things!"

The High Tzar of the Onyx Spire turned about on her heels and snickered wickedly. "As I said, a little birdy sings to me. Apparently your husband is alive and traveling in Anslater."

"That's not possible!" Ansha pushed herself towards the edge of the bed. "Your monster killed him! You're lying to me!"

"Believe me," Nadriah shrugged and smiled, "or don't. Doesn't matter to me. All I know is what my spy tells me."

"Then why even bother to ask if I wanted him back?" Ansha demanded to know. "If you already knew, then why?"

"It would've made things much simpler for you," Nadriah touched the arm of the robed figure on her left, "and for me, if you had just agreed to work with me."

"I would never align myself with the likes of you or your damned kindred," Ansha snarled.

"Gharrik," the girl addressed the figure she touched, "do as you please, but remember, you can't kill her. I'll send Nit back in the morning to feed the princess."

The girl and her other escort departed the room, slamming the door and locking it behind them as they left Gharrik alone with Ansha.

"Don't you dare touch me," the countess ordered immediately.

Ignoring Ansha, the tall man tossed his robes to the floor and crawled onto the bed wearing just a set of crimson breeches. The countess swung at his face, but he was quick, and far stronger than he appeared, grabbing her wrists and pinning them to the pillows as he straddled her waist. His tall, pale body pressed down against Ansha's slender form, while dull, pewter-colored eyes peered over the furious face of the woman. Wild, unkempt hair the same hue as dirty slate draped from the man's scalp in an untamed mess as he leaned closer to the face of the struggling countess.

"Let go!" Ansha pleaded, trying to push against the man, but her body was weak, and he was incredibly powerful.

A grin crossed the man's ashen lips, exposing the four long, razor sharp fangs.

Ansha gasped and pushed harder, "a vampire?"

The lips of the powerful man descended to the left side of Ansha's throat, and despite her trying to jerk away, she couldn't prevent the piercing bite into her neck. Pain surged through her body as the fangs sank deep into her flesh, drawing out the blood that flowed underneath. Suddenly the pain was washed away in a euphoric sense of warmth and tingling that flooded her entire body. In the moment before she fell unconscious, she could feel the hands of the vampire moving to explore her body under the bear fur blanket. Her ability to fight and push back faded into the exhilarated sensation from the bite in her skin, her eyes closed, and the world went black as she gave in to the unusual feelings that swamped her injured form.

14.

    Jolson stood in his bedroom, working with one of the butlers and his squire to put on his armor for the ceremony. He had considered wearing a royal garment like his father had suggested, but as a knight of the kingdom, he felt it was more appropriate to appear before the people clad in his paladin attire. A beige gambeson protected his skin from the reddish-gold links in his chainmail, while a new crimson hooded surcoat was placed over a vest of red and silver brigandine armor. Upon the scarlet cloth of the surcoat, an ivory griffon taking to the sky was embroidered, his link to the temple of justice and Hralgaer, the god of law and order. The hem of the doublet was woven with silver thread, and wrapped in golden ribbons of silk, enhancing the elegance of the outfit.

    "We all wondered how long it would be before you two went public with your little affair," the butler spoke as he helped put greaves over the shins and calves of the prince.

    "We didn't really do well at keeping it a secret, did we?" Jolson laughed as a pair of sabatons matching his chainmail were secured over his leather boots.

    "Everyone in the castle knew," the squire responded sheepishly, but with a grin.

    "Just the proclamation and decision of the wedding day was," the butler added, "just a little sudden. The queen was rather upset at the lack of time to do much planning."

    "We're at war, Dresden," Jolson answered after a nod of understanding. "We've been attacked and harassed by King Borlhauf and the Onyx Spire for quite a while now, and after that brazen attack on the Sages Arcanum, the people need a reason to relax and smile. I doubt throwing a massive, grandiose wedding worth several wagon loads of gold would have gone over well with the citizens, but they need a little positivity in their lives at the moment. If I can use my wedding to the castle's sage to put the people at ease, then so be it."

"Always putting the kingdom and its people before yourself," the king spoke up from where he sat across the room, "even on your wedding day. It's why the people respect you so much. You're going to be a fine leader of Anslater someday, and I'm proud to have raised you into becoming such a good man. I just hope that the world outside of Vansenhul won't crush that kindness when you depart with Count Maizen."

Jolson sighed thoughtfully, but managed to keep his hopeful smile as he glanced over to the king. "You taught me well, so did mother, and I can't forget about Cerulla and the others in the castle. I appreciate everything you all have done for me, and the lessons I was able to learn. Sadly, we'll be taking the fight to the Onyx Spire, and I doubt it will be a pleasant road paved with happy thoughts and silver coins. I don't know what the count's plan is yet, but he seems certain we can bring down that wretched place, which is long overdue."

The squire and butler worked together to place the reddish-gold pauldrons over the chainmail of the prince. They featured an eagle on the left shoulder, and a wolf on the right, taken from the Galheam family crest. Over his exposed forearms, a pair of dark gauntlets were bound around his wrists, with bracers matching the rest of his armor secured over the leather that covered his skin. For a moment, Jolson moved and flexed, testing the agility of the armor, then nodded his approval as his assistants finished checking the ties and straps used to hold the attire together.

"Though you refused to wear a proper formal outfit," the king commented from his seat, "you do look more natural in the armor."

Made of narrow bands of platinum, gold, and bronze, featuring a trio of polished round opals, the prince's crown was placed gently upon his head by the butler. As the butler finished checking the armor for fit and appearance, the squire retrieved the paladin's short sword, with its heavy, wide blade, slipped it into the elegant black scabbard, and then secured it to the right side of Jolson's waist with a dark leather belt.

"I would've been just fine in a pair of trousers and a cotton tunic, father," Jolson commented as he glanced over the armor momentarily.

"You are the prince of this kingdom, one of its knights, my son, and my heir," the king stated with a warm smile. "You should look the part, especially at your own wedding. It's just one day. You'll have plenty of time to lounge around in your comfortable vestments after the ceremony."

"I'll wear the cavalier shirt and doublet to the reception," the prince said with a kind expression. "The armor is for the common man who may be watching, that they are given hope and peace in these troubling times. When it comes time to mingle with the other nobles, I'll dress the part, don't you worry father."

King Galheam nodded happily. "Just do me one favor, Jolson?"

The prince turned his gaze to his father as he checked the position of the sword on his hip. "What would that be?"

"Have a good time," the king requested calmly. "Enjoy yourself. This is a big day for you, but don't forget what this means for Cerulla. She's the warden of the land, but after today, she'll officially be part of the royal family. This day is just as much for you as it is for her. She's always had a large role in this kingdom, and today that role becomes bigger to her."

"I haven't forgotten about her," Jolson chuckled slightly. "Trust me, I don't think she'd allow me to."

Once everyone was satisfied with his attire, Jolson was escorted from his bedroom by the butler and squire, with the king following a short distance behind. A royal carriage was waiting for them all as they stepped from the main entrance of the castle. Out of respect for his position, the king was allowed to get into the horse-drawn wagon first, followed by the prince and the others. The driver put the horses into motion, and from the castle courtyard, the royal carriage was guided into the streets of Vansenhul.

Citizens and nobles alike lined the path leading from the castle to the great temple near the harbor. They all came out to cheer and applaud the prince, while Jolson waved and shouted his praise from the window of the wagon. Though a few clouds had gathered over the city, the sun's light hadn't been deterred, making for a pleasant day on the coast. Only a slight breeze, blowing in off the sea, and carrying with it a faintly salty aroma, threatened the mood of the day, but it was nothing to be concerned about. Jolson allowed himself to relax and enjoy the sights and sounds of the people that had gathered to see the carriage arrive at the temple.

"I'm guessing that mother will be arriving with Cerulla?" Jolson asked as he looked at the grand stone structure that served as the primary temple in Vansenhul.

"Yes," the king answered as a pair of knights in polished steel chainmail and blue surcoats proceeded to open the carriage door, "she wanted to ensure that our beloved sage wasn't alone on this glorious day."

Jolson nodded with an understanding smile. "That's good. Cerulla deserves happiness. She's given so much to our kingdom, and never asked for anything in return."

"She's happiest when she's with you," the king replied, nudging the prince with his elbow. "Especially after you confessed how you felt about her. We all knew, but you just had to be honest with her, and yourself. I never considered this as a possibility when we asked her to conjure us an heir, but here we are. I wanted you to marry King Borlhauf's daughter, but that ignorant pile of excrement made that impossible."

"Good thing, too," Jolson grinned to his father, "I didn't like Liliana anyway. She only cares about wealth, power, and what others can do for her. She'll never be a great leader, and has no place in Anslater."

Through the crowd that gathered around the temple, the knights took the king, Jolson, the butler, and the squire up the marble stairs and into the towering structure dedicated to the many gods and goddesses worshiped in the city. The temple was crafted from carefully sculpted white marble and polished green granite, with obelisk-style pillars both inside and out. High, arching ceilings and octagonal patterns dominated the interior, with many different statues and tapestries dedicated to various deities. It was the kind of opulent, extravagant structure one would expect to find in the capital of the kingdom.

After entering the temple, Jolson and his entourage were ushered up a set of stairs to the balcony that overlooked the grand marble stairs they had ascended just moments before. The elder priest of the temple was waiting at the doors to the balcony, dressed in his finest alabaster robes, holding a pendant featuring the feather-wrapped heart motif of Daeva, the goddess of love. He dropped the pendant into the hands of the prince, who looked over the silver medallion before placing the chain around his neck loosely.

A trumpet sounded loudly from the street level, and where his carriage had been, a similar one, but colored like ivory with ribbons and streamers, pulled up to the stairs of the temple. Two knights, just as before, stepped forward and opened the doors of the luxurious wagon, and offered their hands to the occupants. First, the queen stepped out and looked up to where Jolson and the king were waiting. The prince took a deep breath and smiled a greeting to his mother.

Then, Cerulla appeared from the depths of the carriage. Covered in a long, sheer white dress, coupled with a navy blue bodice that enhanced her voluptuous figure, the prince's bride looked stunning in the late morning sun. Over the dress, a robe of dark purple silk was draped, while a thin ivory veil hid her facial features from those gathered around the temple steps. A single red rose clutched in the fingerless white gauntlets made of the finest sheer cloth proved a stark contrast to the other colors that adorned the kingdom's sage. Briefly, the faerie peered upwards to the balcony, and though he couldn't see it, Jolson could sense the warm smile hidden behind the white veil.

Just as they had done before, the two knights escorted the queen, the sage, and their two attendants into the temple. While he waited for Cerulla to step out onto the balcony with him, the prince looked out over the crowd, trying to find Count Maizen or the strange naetari monk. It took him a few moments, but eventually he spotted the black-clad noble and his lovely blonde escort sitting at the café across the street. The prince offered a friendly wave from the temple's balcony, but wasn't sure if the count had seen him.

"Are you ready?" the king asked, putting a hand on the shoulder of the prince. "There's no changing your mind once it starts."

Jolson nodded and slowly turned around, his sapphire-like eyes catching sight of Cerulla stepping out onto the balcony. "I made her a promise. She is the warden over the land, but at the end of the day, she's my faerie."

The mighty brass bells held within the tower of the temple rang out loudly twice over the crowd, drawing the attention of the masses gathered to witness the wedding. Jolson took a deep breath to steady his emotions, and moved to where the elder priest waited in the center of the wide, semicircular balcony. Standing two steps in front of him, Cerulla joined the prince at the small dais prepared for the ceremony. The king and queen stood a few steps behind the prince, while the butler and other attendants remained by the doors leading to the interior of the temple. Cerulla held out her right hand, and Jolson took it in his left, before they both turned to face the priest, who cupped their entwined hands in his own. Again, the bells rang out, three times in slow succession, with time given for each thunderous tolling to end.

"Today," the elder priest spoke up, his aging voice loud, slow, but full of authority, "we all gather here in the city of Vansenhul, under the light of Solarea, and within view of all the gods and goddesses, to witness the joining of Prince Jolson Galheam and High Sage Cerulla Cloudrain in blessed matrimony."

Jolson beamed wide as his eyes glanced at the blushing cheeks of his bride. Under the grip of the priest's hands, he could feel the fingers of the faerie tightening around his own, while her other hand held the crimson rose up to her lips to shield her grin from view.

The priest continued, smiling at the couple. "Prince Jolson Galheam of Anslater, you have dedicated your life to protecting this kingdom and her people, even becoming a devoted paladin of justice and donning the mantle of Hralgaer. You are also the only child of the royal family, and the sole heir of the kingdom."

"This is me," Jolson responded with a kind smile on his lips.

"And you," the priest turned his eyes to the faerie, "High Sage Cerulla Cloudrain, you have been born of nature and served as the fair and just warden over the land of Anslater. You have given this kingdom and her people many years of your service as a trusted voice for the natural world around us."

"This is me," Cerulla agreed, then shot a quick, pleased glance to her groom.

"King Vimor Galheam," the priest then turned slightly to face the ruler of the kingdom, "the fate of your kingdom, and the succession of your lands rests upon the shoulders of your only son. We are gathered here to join your son to a woman of his choosing. Do you agree that these two should be wed? Will you agree to leave your kingdom, and the people of Anslater, to these two and their offspring?"

Jolson's father looked at the couple, then approached them from behind slowly as his face twisted with the thoughts going through his mind. Heavily, he slapped his hands onto the forearms of the pair and gripped them tightly as he looked at his son, then the faerie, and finally rested his gaze upon the priest.

"I," the man stated with a nod, "King Vimor Galheam of Anslater, entrust my son to the love of our castle's loyal sage. When the time comes, they will inherit this kingdom, its land, and its people. I would trust no one else with such a daunting future, but I wholeheartedly believe their joining will be a benefit to the kingdom as a whole."

The elder priest smiled with a nod of his aging head. "Is there anyone gathered to witness this joining who would oppose the marriage of our brave prince and the beautiful sage?"

For a moment, the crowd remained silent. When no one spoke up, the king released his grip, and stepped back to stand next to the queen. The priest allowed the silence to continue for a brief moment, then let go of the couple's hands gently and offered a polite bow to the pair before taking a single step back.

"Prince Jolson Galheam," the priest began again, his voice booming so it could be heard down on the street, "do you agree to take this woman as your wife, to hold and protect until parted by Dimorta's cold embrace? Will you live side by side, as a pair made one, ruling this kingdom as partners, until separated only by death?"

Jolson let go of Cerulla's hand and turned to face her directly. He slipped the token of Daeva from his neck, gently laying it around the faerie's throat, then placed a single kiss to the forehead of the bride.

"I take this woman as my wife," the prince announced, unable to hide joy behind his smile, "to protect, hold, and live as one until the end of our days."

"High Sage Cerulla Cloudrain," the priest shifted slightly to speak to the faerie, "do you agree to be wed to this man, to be his safe harbor during dark storms, to keep him warm when nights grow cold, and live side by side, as a pair made one, until divided by Dimorta's hands?"

Cerulla beamed with pure happiness as she looked over Jolson, then reached out, put the rose in his hands, and curled his fingers around the stem carefully. Once he had a decent hold of the rose, she leaned forward and pressed a kiss to the back of his right hand.

"I proudly accept being married to this man," the sage answered, as tears of joy appeared in her eyes, "to be his rock in rough waters, to bring him a smile in times of strife, to bear him heirs, and to live as one until the end of our days."

An acolyte dressed in all white stepped onto the dais next to the priest, holding a goblet of red wine and a small silver knife. The priest took up the knife from the younger man, held it aloft as he offered up a silent prayer, and then held out his empty hand towards the prince.

"You two have both agreed to this union in the eyes of the gods," the elder priest spoke slowly. "By this knife, you will bleed, but you will bleed as one."

Jolson offered his left hand, resting it in the empty hand of the priest as he took a steady breath. The pain was quick, sharp, and followed by a deep, warm, throbbing sensation as the knife's blade was stuck into the pad of his middle finger. As blood dripped from the fresh wound, the acolyte held the goblet under the injured digit, letting the crimson stain the dark wine. Once five drops had been collected, the priest wrapped Jolson's finger in gauze and turned to the faerie. The same was done to Cerulla, in the same manner. A quick stab, and five drops of her blood were leaked into the wine, and her finger was swiftly wrapped in a bit of gauze. While the couple held the bandages tightly to their wounded fingers, the priest exchanged the knife for the goblet the acolyte held.

As the priest stirred the bloodstained wine with a silver spoon, he looked over the couple, who were holding hands and facing him once more. "By drinking from this goblet, you become one. By consuming this wine, you agree to share troubles, heartaches, blessings, joy, and laughter, until parted only by death. By sharing this drink, stirred with your blood, you place your lives in each other's hands, and promise to honor one another as husband and wife."

Jolson took the goblet first, glanced at Cerulla, smiled softly, and then drank half the contents from the vessel. "From this day forth, I take this woman as my beloved wife, as two joined into one."

Taking the goblet from the groom, Cerulla let her gaze examine the figure of the prince standing with her at the dais, then drank the remaining half of wine. "From this day forth, I accept this man as my husband, as two joined into one."

After taking the goblet from the faerie, the priest turned it upside down over the balcony's railing, showing that the wine had been consumed by the couple. He then lifted the silver vessel over the heads of the pair standing before him, as though he were offering it to the sun above.

"Daeva, goddess of love," the priest spoke loudly, "protect these two as they step forward into their life as husband and wife. Per'ita, goddess of hearth and home, protect these two as they make a life together, grant them peace and a grand family. Atheia, goddess of life, protect these two as they prepare to live as one, grant them many years of vibrant health to share with each other."

With the prayer finished, the priest handed the goblet back to the acolyte, who stepped off the dais quietly. The aging man then stepped closer to the couple, placing a hand on each of their foreheads. For a moment, everyone remained silent, as though they were waiting for a rebuttal from the gods.

"Then, with the king's blessing," the priest stepped back once more and looked over to the king and queen.

"I bless this wedding, as the king of Anslater," the king replied without delay. "I wish my son and his bride many years of happiness, and hope that with each other, they are able to share that happiness with the people of this kingdom."

The priest nodded and turned to the crowd that gathered below the balcony. "With the blessing of the gods, and the blessing of the king, I formally announce the marriage of Prince Jolson Galheam and Princess Cerulla Galheam, to the people of this great kingdom. From this moment forward, they will forever be known as husband and wife, not only in our eyes, but in the eyes of the gods who witnessed this joining."

Gracefully, the priest turned again to look upon the couple that joined him on the dais. "Before you take that first step as husband and wife, it is only proper to seal this wedding with a kiss."

Jolson didn't need to be told twice, as he stepped towards Cerulla and pushed her veil aside with his right hand. His left hand found itself on her waist as his fingers caressed the back of her neck softly. Without delay, he pressed a firm kiss to the lips of his new wife, pulling her close into his embrace. Her arms coiled around his shoulders as she returned with a kiss of her own, fighting to hold back the passion that welled up behind her eyes. Cheers and clapping climbed from the crowd gathered below the balcony as the husband and wife embraced on the dais under the late morning sun.

The temple bells chimed again, booming loudly over the gathered crowd as Jolson pulled his wife against his chest in a tight hug. Tears of joy from the faerie stained the surcoat as she pressed herself against his chest, Jolson knew that the vast majority of those who saw them embracing on the dais didn't understand what it meant for Cerulla to be married to him, but he did.

"You have nothing to fear," he whispered into her ear, inhaling the floral scent from her skin, "I will be by your side always."

"You have no idea," she replied quietly, kissing his neck. "I was alive during the rise and fall of Atlantis. I saw your people come crawling out of the dust created by the destruction of the Lost Era. I've seen the birth of your kingdom, and the first generations of your royal family. Finally, after so much time has passed, I found someone worth loving. I found someone I was willing to give up my immortality for, and you accepted the burden of loving a faerie."

Jolson kissed her a second time. "I love you. Always have, and always will," he spoke confidently as he stepped down from the dais.

"I love you too," Cerulla responded without hesitation, stepping with her husband as they turned as one towards the interior of the temple.

The temple bells clanged loudly a final time as Prince Jolson pulled his wife against him once more, and took her lips with a deeply passionate kiss.

15.

It almost went unnoticed as the prince kissed his wife again, but the crowd had suddenly fallen silent. A horrid shriek rose up from the voices below, and the sound of something heavy landing on the balcony broke through the loving mood that had filled the air. The priest gasped loudly before Jolson could even turn his eyes away from Cerulla.

Only mere inches from the neck of the prince, an arrow was clutched tightly in the grip of a grey-furred naetari.

"That was close," Lorvin spoke, breathing heavily as though he had been running a marathon.

"Assassins?" the prince uttered, stepping back out of shock as he pulled Cerulla behind himself.

Before the feline could answer, a sharp hum resounded through the air like a faint whisper, and Lorvin lunged towards the king and queen, who were already moving to the interior of the temple. With unmatched reflexes and speed, the monk snagged another arrow with a leaf-like point from the air, snapped the shaft, and threw the projectile to the ground. Another arrow slammed into the right side of the fleeing priest while the naetari urgently pushed the royal family through the doors and away from the balcony. As several more leaf-tipped arrows crashed into the stone of the temple's walls, Lorvin grabbed the hand of the fallen priest and yanked him through the entrance before the butler and squire could slam the heavy iron doors shut.

"What's going on?" the king demanded, as he aided the monk in getting the elder priest to his feet.

"King Borlhauf sent you a wedding gift," Lorvin spoke through exhausted breaths.

Prince Jolson looked over at the priest, then turned his anger-filled eyes to the naetari. "How many?"

Lorvin brushed his fingers through the hair of his chin, then shook his head in disdain. "At least two dozen from Unnamed Few and the Bladed Rumors. I spotted their barrel boats this morning while training on the pier. I wanted to reach you sooner, but you had already left the castle. I'm sorry, between the crowds and keeping track of their archers, I couldn't move any faster."

"No, don't be hard on yourself," Jolson cut the naetari short with a wave of his hands. "I owe you," he began, but was silenced by the king putting a strong hand on his right shoulder.

"We are indebted to you, monk," the king stated before bowing respectfully.

Lorvin shook his head and laughed nervously. "No, not at all. It's just something anyone would've done."

"You saved us," Cerulla bowed as well, before nudging her husband.

The prince bowed respectfully as well to the monk. "They are right, we owe you our lives. You acted selflessly on our behalf. This will not be forgotten."

"Please, don't," Lorvin nearly pleaded. "I'm just a humble monk of the land."

"We need to get going," the butler spoke up, using his shoulder to keep the priest standing.

Lorvin nodded eagerly. "Yes. Yes we do."

Jolson sighed and looked over the others. "Please, get my wife and parents to the castle, I need to protect the people of this city."

"My love?" Cerulla whined.

"I have a duty to this city," Jolson argued, brushing a hand through her hair.

"They're assassins," Lorvin gestured to the world outside. "You're one of the targets. Going out there will be like putting a steak on a plate in front of a pack of hungry dogs."

"He has a point," the butler grumbled.

"You can," the priest spoke weakly, "go through the tunnels under the reliquary."

A terrible explosion echoed from the street outside, and the shocked shrieks from the crowd turned into dreaded wailing mixed with horrified screams. The temple shook with the force of the blast, despite the solid construction of stone and heavy wood. Before the royal family could brace themselves, another explosion ripped through the front of the temple, throwing the heavy iron doors from the face of the great building and shattering the windows that gazed upon the balcony. As glass rained down from the broken windows, and dust from the shaken structure fell about the group, feral squeals of violence could be heard entering the main foyer of the temple.

"Now what?" Lorvin grumbled as he shuffled to a spot where he could look down into the temple's foyer from the walkway attached to the balcony's doors.

"We need to get moving," Jolson answered without delay, drawing the sword that was strapped to his hip.

Lorvin nodded in agreement as he pulled the meteor hammer free that had been crossed in an X over his chest. "I normally detest violence, but I don't believe we've been given a choice."

With two knights leading the way, and two more bringing up the rear, the group made their way to the far end of the walkway where it skirted along the walls over the temple's foyer, narthex, and main sanctuary chamber. Moving as quickly as they could, while trying to remain unnoticed, the royal family kept low along the terrace overlooking the sanctuary as the excited cheers of their hunters called out with violent intent. At least a dozen men poured into the temple through the hole where the doors once stood, and almost immediately they spotted their targets trying to flee along the higher walkway. Orders were shouted, and several men went up the stairs in the foyer, while others bolted for the doors across the sanctuary and under the terrace.

"Hurry!" Jolson urged, motioning for the wooden door at the end of the walkway.

In a rush, the knights ahead of the royal family burst through the door to the upper levels of the areas behind the temple's main dais and altars. They entered quickly into the building's private library, while the assassins moved about the bookshelves on the lower floor. With shouts rising up from the dark-clad murderers, the royal family and their escorts darted along the mezzanine. The two knights ahead of the group rushed down the stairs to the lower level first, encountering a trio of attackers bearing the matte black masks and dark cloaks of the Unnamed Few.

"Go!" Jolson ordered as the knights pushed the attackers back enough to give the royal family room to pass.

A fourth assailant, wielding a katiss, charged from behind a wall of books. The weighted brass orb at the end of the meteor hammer smashed the mask into dust, sending the attacker backwards as weapon and ceramic shards were forced into his flesh. Using the chain as a garrote around the assassin's throat, Lorvin used his running momentum to hurl the member of the Unnamed Few into an old wooden table.

Jolson almost stopped to aid the knights at the bottom of the stairs when he spotted a man with a dagger rushing to intercept his new wife. With his short sword held ready, the prince lunged at the charging attacker, shoving the blade of his sword up and under the ribs of the assassin as he yanked the man away from the faerie. The failed assassin sputtered and wailed, but with a backhanded swing, the blade of the short sword brought a swift end to the cries of the dying man.

"I thought you said there were only two dozen," Jolson growled as he rejoined the others dashing for the door to the reliquary.

"I didn't have time to get an accurate count," Lorvin shrugged nonchalantly. "I only guessed from the size of the barrel boats I saw."

The butler, still carrying the weight of the wounded priest, reached the door first, but as he went to grab the handle, it exploded open in a flash of crimson light. Fragments of wood and stone ripped through the servant's body, dropping him almost immediately as three more attackers sprinted out of the fresh hole in the wall. In the dust that clouded the air, Jolson spotted a dark figure lurking behind the three new assailants, a wide-brimmed hat atop the visage's head.

Before the trio could figure out who to attack first, Dorho's own katiss tore through the chest of the villain on the left, and then immediately brought his second sword violently across the neck of the man on the right. It was like watching a dance of blood and ferocity as the count dispatched the two attackers with ease and zero remorse.

The orb and chain of Lorvin's weapon wrapped about the right ankle of the remaining assailant, with the heavy ball slamming into the leg with a dreadful crunch of bone. A fierce tug from the chain yanked the man off his feet, and a deft thrust of the prince's sword drove the wicked man's body into the ground in a lifeless heap.

"I was wondering when you planned on joining the fun," Lorvin commented as he freed his meteor hammer from the defeated goon.

Dorho rolled his eyes at the attitude of the naetari. "Someone had to handle those archers."

"We need to get out of here," the king spoke urgently, motioning towards the reliquary beyond the ruined wall.

"Corina is waiting in the tunnel," Dorho replied with a nod, before darting back through the blasted hole.

Lorvin checked on the butler, but quickly discovered the man was dead, but the priest was still clinging to a thread of life. With help from the squire, they lifted the aging man and carried him into the reliquary, where a large rug had been pulled back to reveal a hidden door. Jolson ensured the king, queen, and his wife made it down the stairs and into the tunnel below before helping Lorvin move the wounded priest.

A deafening explosion thundered through the temple, and the two knights who had been handling the attackers at the base of the stairs were thrown through the air like straw dolls. Jolson only had time to count at least six attackers charging the hole through the reliquary wall before Lorvin and the remaining two knights nearly pushed him into the tunnel. He watched as the squire drew his own rapier and prepared to defend the hidden door.

"Go, master!" the squire shouted, putting his left foot forward as he readied his sword. "I'll do my best!"

"Like hells you will!" a high-pitched hiss screamed through the reliquary.

Green light ripped through the dim light of the temple under siege, and the squire was thrown down the stairs into the tunnel. Through the chaos that followed, Jolson made out the shape of a child-sized creature with a reptilian tail standing at the top of the stairs with a staff capped with a cat's skull. Stone spikes and thick brambles broke instantly shredded through the walls and floor of the reliquary, tangling and crushing the charging attackers. Screams of men were drowned out by the sound of wood and marble being crumpled together as though the earth itself was swallowing the assailants.

As the emerald-hued light faded, the creature at the top of the stairs leapt down into the tunnel, while a net of thorny vines and broken temple stones formed a seal over the hidden door.

"I tolds you," the small creature spoke coldly as it shuffled through the darkness towards Lorvin, "I is not the spy."

"I don't," Jolson felt around in the darkness until he reached Cerulla, pulling her behind him protectively. "I don't understand."

"Zakosa?" Dorho called from where he stood with Corina near the wounded priest. "What are you doing here?"

As the faerie used her magic to form three orbs of soft, amber light, Jolson could clearly see the kobold standing only a few steps away, looking dumbfounded at Count Maizen.

"The better questions," Zakosa tilted his head suspiciously, "is, whats are you doings here?"

"We don't have time for this," Lorvin spoke up. "We should get moving."

Corina shook her head as she knelt down next to the priest. "Let me tend to his injuries, then we can move."

"Agreed," the king responded, dropping onto a bench in one of the many alcoves that lined the tunnel. "We should gather our thoughts and take time to breathe for a moment."

"We don't have long, though," Jolson pointed to the barrier that closed the entrance to the tunnels. "They'll blast that apart eventually."

Dorho nodded, then looked at the farmer's daughter with a reassuring smile. "Go ahead. If we don't have to carry him, we can move faster."

"You didn't answers me," Zakosa argued, moving closer to Count Maizen as the blonde woman put her hands over the wound of the priest.

"You didn't answer me, either, kobold," Dorho smirked, watching the squire gently remove the arrow from the side of the wounded man.

Healing jade-hued light poured from the hands of the woman as she whispered a silent prayer to the goddess Atheia. As she worked, the ragged, shallow breaths of the elder priest became steady and calm. Blood stopped oozing from the deep wound, and after only a few moments, what had once been a grievous injury only looked like a minor cut. Corina took several deep breaths, and with a slightly painful wince, stood back up, looking on as the remaining two knights got the priest to his feet.

"Are you okay?" Dorho asked, letting the woman lean on him for a moment.

She nodded, then shot the man a soft smile. "I'll be fine, and so will he."

"Whats are you doing here?" Zakosa inquired sharply, prodding Dorho's chest with his skull-topped staff. "You died. I saws you get buried. I saws that monster from the Onyx Spire kills you."

Ignoring the kobold, Dorho took the arrow from the squire and sighed. His eyes scanned the black shaft, orange helical fletching, and the serrated, leaf-shaped tip. Without hesitation, he snapped the arrow in half and threw it to the ground, then gazed over to where the royal family was resting in the alcove.

"The Bladed Rumors, huh?" Dorho shook his head. "King Borlhauf and the Onyx Spire have turned them against you as well?"

Corina's sapphire eyes looked at where the arrow lay on the stone floor. "Aren't they bandits from the Galensteil Wastes?"

Dorho sighed unhappily. "They're why the guild in Kaenaan won't operate in Anslater. They're a nomadic group of rogues, bandits, thieves, goons, and assassins. Most likely, it was their barrel boats the cat spotted this morning. Probably arrived under the cover of darkness to avoid having those semi submersible ships spotted."

"Makes sense, though," Lorvin spoke as he picked up the arrow tip to look it over as well. "With Elgrahm Hold turning against the rest of the Thornbror Kingdom, you've forced King Borlhauf to fight a war with multiple enemies at once. He likely needed the extra forces."

"That's not the point the count is trying to make," King Galheam said after a deep breath.

Prince Jolson glanced at his father. "What do you mean?"

"Sometimes, as a ruler, you have to make pacts with various groups in order to keep the peace and accomplish goals," the king explained. "Because of the expansive desolation of the Galensteil Wastes, it's impossible to properly secure the entire region. So we've been having the Bladed Rumors operating as the peacekeepers of that region."

"In trade, you turned a blind eye to certain actions of their group," Dorho added bluntly. "As part of the guild in Kaenaan, I am familiar with how the Bladed Rumors operate out here. It's why we don't come into your lands unless it is absolutely necessary. Somehow, either the Onyx Spire or King Borlhauf made it worth it to them to turn against you."

"You're not just a simple noble, are you?" the king threw a damning gaze at Count Maizen as he spoke.

Lorvin chuckled and slapped his hand across Dorho's back jovially. "Not at all. This here is the Lord of Rogues, the venerated bandit lord from the city of Kaenaan. Everyone from the Thornbror Kingdom, the lands of Ordenstød, and even parts of the Youikan Kingdom know and respect this man."

"I've heard rumors of him," the king nodded. "Just never thought I'd meet him, and just assumed they were just stories told by the bards and minstrels."

"Damned bards," Dorho grumbled. "They'll be the death of me."

"That doesn't answers my questions," Zakosa insisted, his voice ripe with frustration. "Why are you nots dead?"

"I told Dimorta I was bored," Dorho grinned. "Now, why are you here? I thought you were helping take Lynsia to meet I'raha."

Zakosa scoffed at the answer, then shot a temperamental glance towards the feline. "Vourden thoughts I was a spy, so he sends me with this cat and his big lizard."

Dorho nodded, then shifted his dark eyes to Lorvin. "Is that true?"

"Aye," Lorvin stated without hesitation. "I was tasked with bringing him down here to find the druids of the Red Aspen Grove while the others took Lynsia to the Faulkendor Mountains. Vourden didn't want him costing us any more lives."

"He's not the spy," Dorho stated matter-of-factly.

"He can't be," Cerulla stated, cutting off Dorho's words with her own. "I'm the one that offered his service to I'raha. Before Count Maizen got involved, she was looking for a faithful follower, someone dedicated to her purpose who could help protect her Sidhe-Vein, and I suggested the kobold."

"You knew about him?" Dorho nearly spat the words with an incredulous tone.

Princess Cerulla nodded. "I knew he would be perfect for her, as he always talked about wanting to clean his home from the monsters that took it over, and she wanted someone who could benefit from forming a pact with her, but she insisted on having a druid."

"And you," Dorho pointed to the kobold. "You failed to mention this?"

"Everyone was so busy sayings I was the spy," Zakosa narrowed his gaze in a challenging manner, "that I never bothered. I tolds you I was sent you by the faeries, but you fails to listen."

"This would've been important information," Dorho grumbled. "Especially considering what we're up against."

"Talking about the things we're up against," Jolson sighed, and pointed further down the tunnel. "We should get moving before they blow open the tunnels."

Lorvin started walking away from the sealed stairwell that went up into the ruined reliquary. "I agree. We can hash out this argument later when we have the time, and some whiskey."

Jolson followed the feline, with his wife, father, and mother between himself and Count Maizen. The remaining knights brought up the rear, keeping themselves behind the priest and squire. They made their way through the blackness of the old stone tunnels, their path lit by the floating orbs of amber light produced by Cerulla's magic. The scent of the ocean washed through the tunnels in the musky air, proof that they were getting closer to the harbor with each step.

As they reached a split in the path, Lorvin stopped and waited for the others to move by as he etched some runes into the stone walls. He started with a sigil of a broken rock, then added a symbol for fire to the middle of the design. After a quick prayer to Chaugnah, the symbols carved into the walls flared to life and began to hum with a faint white light before fading to darkness once more.

"What was that?" Jolson asked as the feline jogged to catch back up to the rest of the group.

"A precautionary measure," Lorvin grinned.

Dorho shook his head and sighed. "I hope there's nothing of value above these tunnels."

The group turned left at the split in the tunnel as a terrifying explosion tore through the mess of vines and rock that covered the hidden stairwell. Shouts and cheers echoed along the stone-walled path, causing Jolson and the rest of his party to speed up their own movements. The priest ordered them to head right into a narrow alcove, and upon doing so, Jolson was greeted with a constricted hallway that ran for roughly twenty paces and ended at a heavy wooden door.

Without hesitation, the prince pushed and pulled on the door, but it refused to budge.

A brilliant flash of light filled the tunnels behind the group, and the shrieks of wounded men filled the damp air as Lorvin's runes detonated. Rocks, dirt, and fire could be heard crushing out the lives of those caught within the powerful blast. Panicked by the sound of the explosion, Jolson tried the door again, but it still didn't move.

"We're stuck!" Jolson tried the door a third time, but to no avail.

"No we're not," Cerulla looked to the prince and gave him a confident smile. "You can get us out of here."

The prince sighed and closed his eyes. "You're right, I'm not trying hard enough. I was just hoping to avoid using those powers."

The castle's sage shook her head and kissed his cheek. "I don't think you have a choice. You can rest when we get back to the castle."

A warmth, like a fond caress, began cascading through the body of the prince as he focused his thoughts inward. Despite the tension in the air, and the stress of the moment, his mind relaxed, his body felt rested, and his emotions steadied. The exhaustion and strain in his muscles faded while he pulled the faerie magic from the depths of his core, washing his flesh in a faint azure glow as the power came alive. He opened his eyes again and took a couple deep breaths as he felt the magic taking over his body slowly, like a protective cloak wrapping around his skin and filling his blood with courage and strength.

"What's he doing?" Corina questioned, looking from Cerulla to the prince and back again.

"This is what it means to be a Sidhe-Vein," the faerie answered with a proud smile.

Prince Jolson reared back, and slammed the heel of his right foot into the door, just below the handle. Blue light burst from the impact, wood splintered, carved stones cracked, and in an instant, the door was thrown from its rusted hinges. As the dust settled from the force of the door's destruction, the prince found himself looking into an old storeroom filled with barrels, crates, and jars with layers of forgotten grime over them.

"Lynsia just screams," Dorho remarked, stepping through the ruined doorway, "and things die."

"She's probably untrained," Cerulla commented as she moved to catch up to her new husband. "I expected as much from I'raha. She is rather reckless and prone to flights of fancy. It took the prince many years of training to learn how to control his powers like this."

"Where are we headed now, priest?" Jolson inquired, waiting for the others to join him in the stairwell as he scanned the wooden stairs leading up from a corner of the room.

"We're under an old bakery that served at the castle's kitchen in the time of King Vimor's grandfather," the priest responded, looking around the dark room.

"The Tin Biscuit?" Cerulla tilted her head and smiled slightly. "They have the best cakes, but why is this storeroom abandoned?"

The priest sighed as he answered, "The king's grandfather ordered access to those tunnels sealed when the family took up residence at Ostenfel Castle."

Before the conversation could continue, Jolson had broken through the door at the top of the stairs, knocking over a shelf of pastry ingredients in the process, and gaining access to the bakery's kitchen. Closed for the wedding, as they supplied the cake and pastries for the reception, the building was lifeless and vacant while the group slowly moved through the different rooms towards a rear exit that would take them to an alley behind the store. Flinging open the lock, the Sidhe-Vein pushed the door open and stepped out into the alley, finding himself only a few buildings away from the ravaged temple.

He looked back to his wife and parents. "We still have to get to the castle, come—."

Like a twisted mix between a dangerous big cat and a feral man running on all fours, the darkoyle slammed into the prince without remorse. Flesh, covered in what could only be seen as charred leather, rippled and pulsed with the beast's muscles as it threw the Sidhe-Vein to the ground. Although vicious spines protruded from the skin along the back and skull of the monster, it brought the long claws of its fingers to bear against the sprawled man in the alley. On wings that resembled twin blankets of midnight's darkness, two more of the devilish creatures descended into the narrow space between buildings. Each creature eyed the prince with four eyes that looked like burning embers wrapped in brilliant bands of gold.

    Dorho hurled himself at the one pinning the prince to the ground, driving both of his swords into the back of the vile monster and wrenching backwards until the creature screamed with fury. Ochre blood splashed across the limestone bricks of the ground when the rogue yanked his blades free from the terrible beast and proceeded to drive his left foot into the back of the monster's right knee.

    Shrieks of wrath filled the air from the other two darkoyles rushed the rogue and prince, claws ready to tear through the flesh of the men. The meteor hammer sparkled under the noon sun as it raced through the air, wrapping around the throat of one of the uninjured beasts. The heavy ball slammed into the side of the monster's head as the monk pulled the chain towards himself. Howling with rage, the wicked beast conjured up a flash of eerie green magic, throwing a trio of bone-like spikes at the naetari. With a strange grin on his face, the feline deftly sidestepped the brazen attack, catching one of the flying spikes in his right hand.

    Gnarled vines cursed with vicious thorns shattered the ground around the third beast, snapping into the air as they coiled like vipers around the neck and arms of the huge, black monstrosity. As spines bit into the flesh, the brambles tightened quickly and yanked the fiend onto its back upon the broken stones of the alley.

    The prince leapt to his feet once more, and from a burst of the sapphire energy around him, summoned a glaive to his hands. With a silver blade like a sharpened cutlass at the end of a long staff of red-stained wood, the weapon flickered with tendrils of the faerie's magic along its length. He charged the bleeding darkoyle that had tackled him, spinning the heavy weapon above his head quickly, then bringing the wide blade down towards the creature's neck, he lunged forward, aided by the boost from the flow of magic through his veins.

Brought to its knees from the assault by the rogue, the darkoyle swung with powerful claws at the figure of the prince. Dorho continued his own assault, driving the blades of his twin swords under the ribs of the mighty brute, and slashed outwards, spilling more of the ochre blood. The beast shrieked and twisted away from the prince to direct its fury at the count, but was cut silent by the glowing blade of the glaive separating its head from its body.

With the chain of the meteor hammer still wrapped around its throat, the last standing darkoyle snarled loudly as it gripped the metal links connecting it to the naetari. A quick jerk from the potent arms of the darkoyle pulled the feline into striking range of the devastating claws. Lorvin spun left, blocking the first strike with his right forearm as he drove the captured spike into the ground under the beast's feet. Deftly, he ducked under the second swipe of the mighty claws, sliding away from the creature as he offered a quick prayer to the god of stone.

Like a flameless volcano, the alley under the terrible monster erupted in an overwhelming explosion. The beast vanished into the dust and debris that filled the air, collapsing into the hole opened up by the intense detonation. Enraged growls and screams of pain from the wounded beast flooded the alley while the crumbling ceiling of the escape tunnel fell on top of it. Unfortunately for Lorvin, the chain wrapped around the monster went taut, pulling him into the hole as well, much to the horror of Jolson and the others.

"Dammit!" Dorho shouted as he saw the feline get yanked into an open hole in the ground.

"I'll get him!" Jolson yelled, leaping through the hole into the tunnels below with his glaive ready to be driven through the monster below.

Landing hard upon the chest of the rubble-covered monstrosity, Jolson wasted no time in plunging the blade of his weapon through the chest of the furious beast. Azure light poured out from the glaive, burning through flesh and bone with sheer abandon. When the brute tried getting up, Lorvin drove his chain-wrapped fist into the feral face of the darkoyle, forcing it to stay down and succumb to the Sidhe-Vein's magic.

"Are you hurt?" Jolson asked, looking over the feline as he withdrew the glaive's blade from the lifeless darkoyle.

"Just my pride," Lorvin grinned proudly, but quickly lost the cheer in his expression as he glanced over the fallen monster. "I would've preferred not ending a life."

"That thing," Jolson said as he started climbing back out of the hole, "would've killed you without hesitation. This is how it goes fighting the Onyx Spire."

When they got to the alley once again, Dorho had his right hand clutched to the throat of the monster held down by a mess of brambles. Violet lightning ripped through the skin and burned away the leathery flesh of the pinned creature. Pure, unadulterated rage flickered in the eyes of the count as he watched the life of the fiend come to a gruesome end under his grip. The black, tough skin turned pale, and the eyes went white as the dark magic seemed to scorch away the very soul of the vile beast.

"We need to get to the castle," Jolson stated, looking from the count to the others huddled next to the bakery.

Dorho pulled his right hand away from the dead creature as the violet light faded from the markings on his arm, nodding to the prince. "The sooner, the better, I think."

Flexing his right arm, and wincing quite noticeably, the count drove his heel into the pinned head of the vile monster. Corina ran to the rogue's side, grabbing onto his right arm securely as the others began heading north through one of the alleys behind the bakery. Clenching his fist and rubbing his arm as though he had been burned, Dorho and the farmer's daughter followed the king and queen, as they let the prince and monk lead the way through the city.

The stench of fire and destruction plagued the air as they pushed closer to the cliffs holding Ostenfel Castle over the harbor. Soldiers could be heard clashing with the attackers in the streets while the prince and the others darted through the corridors between buildings like rats fleeing a prowling feline. For the armored prince, it felt like the entire city had been plunged into a dark world of chaos, and they were merely prolonging the inevitable.

But what was their goal? He wondered. The Onyx Spire had already destroyed the Sages Arcanum, and taken the book, and it would take more than a few dozen assassins to take down the entire kingdom. Did they simply want to disrupt the wedding, or kill the royal family? It was the only motive that made sense, at least to the mind of the paladin.

"There is a tunnel in the harbor's main trading office and warehouse," the king spoke up, his voice feeling the strain of the stress and running. "It will take us into the cliffs and then up into the castle. It's supposed to be used if the castle needs to be evacuated, but I believe we can use it to do the opposite."

"I don't think we have a choice," Jolson nodded to the words of his father, "but to try."

"Hold on, I have an idea," Dorho called quickly, grabbing the arm of the naetari firmly as they waited near an herb and spice shop for the prince to check the next alley for assailants. "Lorvin?"

"What is it?" the feline responded with a curious tilt to his brow.

"How much can Kortyx lift?" Count Maizen asked abruptly, glancing at the royal family. "If we can get them to the castle quickly, I can take everyone else with me and meet you there later. Our highest priority is the safety of the Galheam family, since they are the targets."

Lorvin brushed a hand through the fur atop his head briefly as he thought it over. "Given her size, she could probably lift three, maybe four people, including myself, without much trouble."

"Prince Jolson," Dorho turned to the paladin hastily. "Can you get us to a roof?"

"Hey," Lorvin protested, "I said she could, I never said she would, nor did I ever say I would allow you to use her like that."

Dorho put a hand on the shoulder of the naetari and sighed, "The longer we spend running around these streets, the more danger we'll be in. If we can get the royal family to safety quicker, the attackers will have to pull back sooner. Can you call her?"

"I'll get us to a good place," Jolson glanced back to the monk with a pleading look, "if you don't mind calling your pet to our aid."

"I mind," Lorvin scoffed, clearly offended at the request that would put Kortyx in danger, "but I also understand what's at stake."

As the naetari picked up a wayward pebble from the ground and offered a quiet prayer to the god of stone, Prince Jolson scanned the surrounding buildings. A structure made of limestone and birch wood loomed across the street, colorful banners and silver sigils on full display from the front of the four-story construction.

"The guild hall," Jolson offered, pointing to the banners swaying in the afternoon breeze. "We can use their roof."

While the others bolted for the main entrance of the building, Lorvin hurled the pebble towards the roof of the structure. Like an angry bird, a loud whistle escaped from the stone as it flew, before exploding with a loud crackling noise near the top of the limestone construction.

Four attackers poured into the street from an alley only a couple buildings away from where Jolson escorted the others across the street. Before he could react, a trio of arrows hummed through the warm air, aiming for the fleeing family. Lorvin shouted, but the process of throwing the enchanted pebble left the monk too far away to do anything. Out of sheer instinct, Prince Jolson yanked Cerulla against his chest as he turned away from the speeding projectiles.

A loud grunt belted from the lungs of the king as the queen shrieked in terror. Corina screamed for the count, and the sounds of stones and earth being shattered filled the air. Through all of the pandemonium, the paladin could hear the cheers of their assailants being turned into fierce cries of panic.

When he turned around, the prince saw his father, two arrows protruding from his chest, hunched over in the middle of the street. The third arrow had found its home in the left shoulder of Count Maizen, who had tackled the queen to shield her from the attack. Green light flared out from the skull atop the druid's staff, while the ground beneath the assailants crumbled to dust, swallowing the four men whole without remorse.

"Father!" he yelled loudly, rushing to the king's side.

Shouts rose up from other attackers as two more darkoyles appeared in the sky near the harbor. Jolson carefully hoisted his bleeding father onto his shoulders and began climbing the limestone steps to the mahogany doors of the guild hall. Cerulla stepped back to help the squire get the queen to her feet while Corina aided the wounded Count Maizen. The world felt like it was being swallowed by chaos as the monk ran forward to yank open the doors of the building. Bringing up the rear was the druid, who summoned vicious brambles to bring down assailants that crept into view.

Inside, the guild hall was nearly devoid of life, as most members had left to attend the wedding or defend the city. Only a few workers remained behind to tend to the cleaning and cooking needed to keep the structure in decent shape, but a couple of them dropped their tasks to aid the group in navigating the hallways and stairwells to the roof.

Deep in his core, Jolson could feel the aching burn of his magic throbbing and churning slowly. It pumped through his veins and gave him the strength to push forward, regardless of any exhaustion that filled his body, but there was a limit to how long and how much he could channel through his figure. Cerulla had warned him several times to never use too much, to be careful how often and how hard he relied on the power she had used to create him, and he could feel it was about to break apart soon. It would fade and he would be left unconscious and weak, or worse, but he had to keep going.

Everyone was depending on him. His father and mother, his wife, his new friends, they were all counting on his bravery and decisions, but there was a limit to his abilities. Jolson took a deep breath, looked at the blood dripping from the king upon his armor and the floor of the guild hall, and shook his head at the fear that crept into his thoughts.

"You can't keep going," Cerulla called from a distance, seeing the look on his face as they raced up the final stairs to the roof. "You know that. I know that."

"I have to try," Prince Jolson replied, masking his true feelings with a hue of determination. "We'll get you and my parents to the castle, that's my priority."

Only a few heartbeats passed before the heavy wings of the wyvern could be heard overhead, and like a reptilian angel, the great creature quickly landed on the roof that was frequently used as a sparring arena by the various guilds. From the arch at the top of the stairs, Lorvin grinned happily and rushed out to greet the powerful beast by throwing his arms around the mighty neck and running his fingers along the thorny head of the huge reptile.

"Hurry!" the monk shouted, motioning towards the prince. "I will have her take you and your family first."

Jolson nodded eagerly, but only after a few steps, he felt the rush of faerie magic shatter like glass within his body. His knees gave way and he immediately felt nauseous and extremely fatigued all at once. Like a bag of stones, he collapsed to the ground, barely catching himself before setting the king down gingerly. The face of his father was pale, and his breathing was ragged, slow, and forced. His own body ached and strained with just the ability to remain awake.

His blue eyes looked over to the wyvern just in time to see the first darkoyle rise up over the building's northern wall. A green orb of devilish magic formed instantly in the clawed hands of the monster, and a swarm of bony spikes were hurled at those gathered on the roof.

"Come on," the naetari began to shout before one of the spines ripped through his waist, drawing a growl of agony from the monk.

As another of the spikes found a home in the right arm of the paladin, the druid was suddenly standing beside him, the skull-capped staff raised high while a barrier of jade-hued light pushed away the rest of the summoned darts. The light faded almost as quickly as it appeared, and the first darkoyle was joined by six others, meanwhile cheers and shouts for violence filled the afternoon air from assailants charging the building from the ground.

Was this it? Jolson looked around himself, at everyone that had followed him. His father was bleeding profusely, and his mother was terrified. Count Maizen was wounded, and Corina was a mere healer caught in the middle of this. The monk was gasping and clutching heavily to the deep wound in his side, while the squire was essentially untrained and ill prepared for such danger. Was this the final stand for the royal family of Vansenhul? Was this how everything would end?

"Sorry," Lorvin managed to growl as he turned his eyes to the gathering darkoyles, "I might've underestimated the enemy's numbers."

"No," Jolson groaned, looking at the spike driven through his arm, "I should've planned and prepared for this."

"You hush," Cerulla spoke suddenly, her feet tracing a deliberate path towards the kobold. "You both did everything you could."

The seven darkoyles all began summoning their orbs of eerie green magic, and Jolson felt a tear of dread forming in his eyes, unable to prevent what was coming. From all around the city, the roar of chaos wailed in a deafening song, and for once in his life, Jolson felt absolutely, and truly helpless to do anything.

"Druid," Cerulla called to the kobold, who turned to her immediately, "come to me."

16.

The darkoyles unleashed the rain of bony thorns like a cascade of death upon the group gathered on the roof. Again, the druid lifted his staff high, and a rush of wind ripped through the air, pushing the spikes away like they were merely leaves on a river. Tossed about by the breezy gusts summoned by the small kobold, the darkoyles quickly landed with noticeable force upon the surface of the sparring arena. Claws and fangs were made ready to rend through the flesh of the men and women that huddled weak, tired, and wounded upon the roof.

Cerulla put a hand on the back of the kobold and sighed heavily. "I do not ask this softly, but will you be my crossbow in this desperate time? Allow my magic to meld with yours, and cast these fiends away?"

The faerie could crush the entire city with her power, it would be easy enough to turn the entire region into a sprawling forest, or bury it in the sea, but she needed her magic to be pinpoint accurate. For that, she needed a way to direct her energy into their enemies with utmost discretion. Not only that, but she knew that faerie magic, especially her own, wasn't directly offensive, as it was mostly used to alter and protect the landscape itself, so she needed something to turn it into an arrow to attack with. For this, she needed the magic of the druid to give her energy the means to be used as a terrifying offensive weapon.

"I wills do as you please," Zakosa calmly stated, turning only a slight glance to the faerie who knelt behind him. "If it is needed, I will serves you unflinchingly."

"I am sorry," Cerulla spoke softly, resting her forehead on the back of the small creature's head as she began to conjure her own magic. "Please, forgive me."

Kortyx shrieked with anger and lunged at one of the darkoyles to protect the injured monk, and like a pack of hungry stray dogs, three of the monsters swarmed the great beast. The powerful jaws of the wyvern snapped upon the body of one of the vile creatures, ochre blood sprayed over the ground while the powerful teeth of the monk's companion ripped through the bones and flesh of the darkoyle. Pouncing like wild cats, darkoyles assaulted the snarling wyvern without hesitation, their long claws and razor-like fangs seeking any weakness in the reptile's scales they could find. Shrieking with fury, the wyvern slapped at one of the ferocious beasts with her mighty tail, throwing the monster from the roof like she was a child throwing a rock into the water just to watch the waves.

As the other darkoyles prepared to bring an end to the royal family, Cerulla poured her magic into the body of the kobold. Her eyes flickered with the amber light of her ancient power, as she felt her own energy coiling like a pair of mating snakes with the magic of the druid. As their powers combined in an instantaneous rush, she saw the kobold's hopes and dreams, his history and everything nature knew about his lineage. She witnessed everything that made Zakosa who he was, and still flooded his body, mind, and soul with her own potent magic. Their enemies were powerful, and even the great wyvern couldn't keep them at bay for long, so she had no choice but to make use of the small reptile and his bond with nature.

"I'm sorry, Zakosa," she said again, tears forming in her eyes as she felt the heat and fury of her magic blending with his protective, yet deliberate energy. "Someday, you will forgive me."

"I am a being of natures," the kobold said calmly, "I am yours to use."

"Focus your magic on the darkoyles," the faerie commanded, putting both hands on the shoulders of the druid. "We'll take them all down in one strike."

Without delay, Zakosa swung his gnarled staff above his head, then pointed the skull at the closest monster. The emerald-like glow of his magic radiated like a lamp from the eyes of the feline skull, causing even the bright light of the afternoon to seem dark and lifeless.

Like a torrent of nature's raw fury, Cerulla flooded the kobold's magic with her own. Through the mixing of their magic, she saw not just the darkoyles on the roof, but the rest of them hunting through the city. She also saw their Onyx Spire masters, the fiends in the black masks known as the Unnamed Few. Through the flow of magic, she could see them all, and there was only one thing she desired in that very moment.

Exploding from the skull atop the druid's staff, fiery orange tentacles burst forth, crushing through the hearts of the darkoyles on the roof. Like a vine of thorns, traces of jade-hued magic wrapped around the violent energy, threatening to tear apart anything they came in touch with. The brilliant tiger-colored tendrils of faerie magic instantly wrapped around the bodies of the darkoyles, burning them to ash almost immediately before exploding into a spread of lightning that drove into the depths of the city. As though they were crossbow bolts seeking only death, the bolts of swirling orange magic and emerald thorns tore through the city, slamming into every darkoyle sent by the Onyx Spire.

Each time a darkoyle was turned to a pile of ash, the ferocious chain of energy split, seeking out more targets in a swift wave through the city. Before they could react, even the members of the Unnamed Few were caught by the fierce, burning tendrils of horrifying magic. Their bodies were crushed, thrown aside like straw dolls, and left smoldering by the devastating whips of natural power. None of Cerulla's enemies were spared from her wrath as she sent the serpents of her magic into every nook and cranny of the city, striking death and agony into every minion of the Onyx Spire.

The brilliance of the magic made the day seem as dark as night, while the thunderous roar of the ferocious energy drowned out even the loudest scream of her victims. It crackled and burned through the air, and even the breeze off the sea did nothing to cool the heat that radiated from the rage-driven magic that raced through the city, killing everything it touched.

"I'm," she took a quick, steadying breath as she hugged the kobold tightly, "so very sorry."

As quickly as the magic had blasted through the city from the top of Zakosa's gnarled staff, the brilliant light faded from view. Soundlessly, the druid slumped backwards against the faerie, who held him tightly. The eyes of the kobold became dull and colorless, while the twisted wood of his staff clattered against the ground, shattering the feline skull that once graced the top of the old branch. His face, once proud, determined, and a bit quirky, was now devoid of any emotion, though a hint of realization of what had happened lingered until the kobold's arms fell lifelessly to his sides.

"We'll meet again," Cerulla muttered sadly as she held the kobold against her chest. "Please, forgive me. I know you'll understand eventually."

Taking several, long, deep breaths to keep herself from breaking down emotionally, Cerulla laid the body of the kobold gently upon the ground next to his staff. She barely noticed Jolson had moved to kneel beside her as she whispered a few more apologies to the kobold, holding onto the left hand of the small reptile.

"What happened?" the prince asked through a ragged breath.

Before she could answer, the body of the kobold began to crumble and decay, turning to dust, dirt, and ash that scattered through the breeze of the early afternoon. Even the druid's bones gave way to the price of such terrible magic being channeled through his body, leaving just a shell of tattered fur robes and the few trinkets worn by the kobold on the arena floor. Cerulla ran her hands through the mound of dust that had once been Zakosa, and clutched at a small object no bigger than a dried pea. She quickly pulled the item against her chest and closed her eyes.

"He sacrificed himself," the faerie spoke softly, not bothering to wipe at the tears that ran down her cheeks. "He gave his life for all of you."

Without being asked, Jolson wrapped his wife in a tight hug and kissed her cheek, ignoring his own pain and exhaustion that threatened to pull him into a terrible slumber. "I'm sorry," he whispered into her ear.

Gently, Cerulla put the tiny object in her hands into the hands of her husband. "When the time comes, take this seed to the Endless Tomb, so that Zakosa's dream can become a reality."

"I hate to break things up," Dorho spoke up with a wince as he moved to check on the monk, "but some of us are injured. We should really get going."

Jolson nodded, taking the tiny emerald-tinted seed from his wife. "Agreed. Take my father and the monk, the rest of us can walk."

"You go too," Cerulla insisted, picking up the druid's staff as she stood up, looking at the others carefully. "You're not going to last much longer after your own magic dissipates."

With the help of Corina and the squire, Cerulla and Dorho placed the wounded king and the monk onto the back of the wyvern. Barely able to move himself, they aided the prince as well as he sat behind the powerful wings of the great beast.

"You should go as well," Corina argued, nudging Count Maizen.

He shook his head stubbornly. "I'll be fine. Plus, she can fly faster without my added weight."

With a heavy groan of pain, Lorvin slapped the side of Kortyx's dense neck and uttered a quick command to the powerful wyvern. The creature spread her wings and with a great leap, took to the air before the farmer's daughter could protest further. With Cerulla, Corina, Dorho, the queen, and the squire left on the roof, the winged beast soared high into the afternoon sky, circling over the city on a path towards the castle on the cliffs overlooking the harbor.

"Are sure they're all dead?" Dorho asked, his voice cold and distant as his dark eyes gazed to the spot where Zakosa had died.

Cerulla nodded confidently. "It was a terrible price for him to pay, but he understood. We'll be able to travel safely back to the castle from here."

"My husband," the queen murmured sadly, fighting through her emotions. "My son. We need to find a carriage and get back quickly."

"I'll go look, your highness," the squire bowed diligently and then gave a hasty glance towards the others before darting away.

Cerulla watched the squire leave, then turned her ruby gaze towards the queen and took the woman's hands in her own as she spoke. "Your family will be fine. I'll take care of your son, just as I always have."

Corina stepped cautiously up to the count and put her left hand on his right arm, while her other hand grasped the arrow still stuck in his back. With a swift movement, she yanked the arrow from his flesh and immediately began flooding his body with the healing light of her magic. Before the wound could close completely, he put his arms around the woman and hugged her tightly to his chest. Cerulla failed to hear what the man said, but she could make a few good guesses when Corina buried her head into his chest and hugged him back.

"We owe you," Cerulla commented as the couple started walking towards the path back down to the street. "If not for Lorvin, Zakosa, Corina, and yourself, we likely wouldn't have survived."

Dorho stopped abruptly, glanced to where the druid's body had disintegrated, and shook his head. "You call this surviving?"

"Hey, sweetie," Corina grabbed his sleeve and pulled the rogue after her, "let's just focus on getting back to the castle for now. You need to rest. We all need to rest."

"Sure," Dorho nearly spat the word before following the woman, "we can go rest."

Quietly, they descended back into the guild hall, and by the time they arrived at the stairs leading to the entrance, the wagon Prince Jolson had used earlier came to a stop on the street. It didn't take long for everyone to get loaded into the carriage and find a place to sit before the horses began to pull the vessel toward the castle. Several of the city's knights bowed their heads in respect when the carriage went by them, a few saluted the queen and princess, but most of them quickly went back to getting control over the chaos that had engulfed Vansenhul.

Cerulla watched the others silently as the wagon moved through the city. Dorho was easy to read, he was angry and frustrated with how things were turning out, but there were things bothering him that he refused to talk about. The queen was a mess of worried emotions, clinging to the right arm of the faerie for some semblance of security in her shaken world. Corina was terrified, the faerie could see it in the way the woman hugged herself close to Count Maizen, but she was wearing a mask of strength and pride to keep the rogue from being concerned about her. Everyone was consumed by their own emotions, and it was as though a blanket of dark depression had been thrown over the city as a whole.

The faerie ended up looking at her own hands. She knew that the kobold's body wouldn't keep up with the flow of magic, especially her own energy, but she had used him anyway. He had known the danger, and he had been willing to let her use him, but she still felt like had murdered him. Zakosa had trusted her, and she ended up taking his life in order to save everyone else. Somewhere, deep in her mind, she realized Dorho was blaming her for the death of the druid, and to be honest, she blamed herself as well.

"If I hadn't," she muttered as the gates to the castle's courtyard came into view, "we would've died."

"You didn't give him much of a choice," Count Maizen refused to look Cerulla in the eye as he spoke angrily. "You knew he would follow your words, no matter what."

Cerulla sighed and gazed over the others quickly. "What would you have wanted me to do? Let the monsters win? You were in no shape to fight that many."

"You could've used me," Dorho grumbled through his frustration. "Or did you forget I've got I'raha's power in me as well?"

"Magic you barely know how to use," Princess Cerulla retorted, fighting back tears that yearned to fall from her eyes. "It would've killed you too, regardless."

The rogue turned just enough to meet the princess eye to eye before speaking again. "He didn't sacrifice himself for everyone else, you killed him to save us. I don't care how you paint it. You never gave the poor kobold a choice in the matter. Now, you can explain to I'raha why the druid you sent to help her Sidhe-Vein, was killed by your own hands."

"We all would've died if I hadn't," the sage protested. "I wasn't given much of a choice. My husband was done, you were injured, and the monk had been wounded. Would you have preferred death?"

"I've already died once," Dorho scoffed while the gates to the castle's grounds were opened and the wagon allowed through. "The way I see things now, we've already lost this fight. The Onyx Spire has us injured and licking our wounds in Vansenhul, meanwhile they're hunting for Lynsia up north. They already captured my wife, and let's not forget about that book from your library. I don't see a scenario in which we win."

"Relax," Corina interrupted, pressing a kiss to the count's cheek. "We lived. That means we get a second chance. This isn't over."

Cerulla wiped her cheeks as the carriage slowed to a halt in front of the castle's main entrance. "You're both right. I didn't give Zakosa a choice, I killed him, but I did it because now we get a second chance to strike back at the Onyx Spire and stop their plans."

Before the wagon came to a complete stop, Dorho forced the door open and left abruptly. With a heavy, defeated sigh, Corina followed him once the carriage finished moving. Cerulla could only watch as they headed away from the castle. She wanted to ask them to stay and rest at the castle, but she knew Dorho needed some time and space to process the events of the day.

After the others exited the carriage, they were hastily escorted into the castle, where maids and other servants were quick to greet them. Cerulla and the queen were taken to the bedroom the princess now shared with her husband, where a healer and a surgeon were tending to Prince Jolson. The faerie carefully placed the druid's burnt, twisted staff against the wall closest to the door, then sat upon the bed next to the Sidhe-Vein. Her wedding gown was a tattered mess from the day, and though the day had started out with a cheerful, celebratory mood, it seemed to be ending with just the opposite.

"How are you feeling?" Cerulla asked quietly, putting her hand on her husband's lap.

He had already been stripped of his armor, and was dressed in just loose-fitting trousers and a tunic while the surgeon and healer were closing up the large wound in his arm. The healer, who was part of the local temple, was using her mild magic to ease the prince's pain while the surgeon applied a series of tight sutures to close the deep injury.

Prince Jolson glanced over his wife for a moment before shaking his head. "It was supposed to be a great day of pleasant celebration, but now look at us."

"And the king?" his wife inquired, throwing a concerned glance to where the queen was seated at a small table.

"Honestly?" the Sidhe-Vein sighed heavily. "He's not doing well. He was injured pretty badly, and lost a lot of blood. The doctors are doing what they can, but I was told to prepare for the worst."

"Can I see him?" the queen pleaded.

Again, Jolson shook his head. "Sadly, no. I tried to stay by his side, but I was only in the way of the doctors, so I was brought in here."

Jolson's mother put her head into her hands as a maid left to fetch a cup of tea. "He's my husband, they need to let me see him," she muttered.

After a slight wince crossed his face, Jolson sighed with a defeated expression on his face. "He's my father, and right now, he needs us to give the doctors the space to do their jobs. We can see him once they are finished and he's able to rest, they assured me of such."

"You need to rest and heal as well," Cerulla insisted, moving her hand to his long blonde hair. "Using your magic that much will take its toll. Please don't wear yourself down unnecessarily."

"And you?" the exhausted prince questioned. "It was a rough day for you as well."

"I'm in better shape than you," Cerulla insisted defiantly. "I will be just fine. It's not the first time I've been in a dangerous scrape, but it was easier when I didn't have to worry about being mortal."

"Iria, Paesla," Jolson gestured with his good hand towards two of the maids remaining in the room, "please take my wife down to the baths and wash this terrible day from her skin."

With a wordless bow, the young women stepped towards the faerie with their arms outstretched.

"I'm fine," Cerulla insisted again.

Jolson shook his head. "You've been through a lot today. You should go get cleaned up and relax. I'll be here waiting for you to return."

"You aren't going to let me argue this, are you?" Princess Cerulla spoke as she stood up slowly from the bed that was like a giant soft sack filled with grain.

"I may be the embodiment of temperance," Jolson managed a weak smile, "but your well-being is not something I intend to take lightly. Go get washed up and I'll have someone bring you clean clothes. You're my wife, and part of the royal family now, so you're just as important to this castle as I am, if not more so, considering your history here."

Grumbling a silent argument, Cerulla allowed the maids to escort her from the bedroom. She went with them down the castle's grand staircase, and then down a narrow, spiraling set of stairs to the rooms under the castle. They followed a lamp-lit hallway lined with limestone brick walls and a floor made from hewn granite until they reached a set of double oak doors banded with iron. Creaking heavily, the doors were pushed open by the young maids, who stepped aside to allow the faerie to enter the bathing chamber first.

Inside, a pool of heated water waited, which had been a gift to the castle from the faerie just after construction started on the royal family's home. Cerulla glanced over the room quietly, slightly thankful that she was alone while the maids set about removing the dirty, stained dress from her body. The round pool's diameter was nearly three times her height, and the water easily came up to her shoulders whenever she stood in the cornflower-scented liquid. A large, domed ceiling loomed over the pool, the limestone arches embedded with palm-sized topaz orbs that glowed with a welcoming amber hue. Around the white granite pool, holding up the great arches, seven pillars of green marble stood like soldiers at the edge of the water.

Stripped of her cumbersome, ruined wedding gown, the princess descended the six steps into the steaming water. She dunked her head under the aromatic waves for a moment, drenching her indigo hair with the heated fluid, and then came back up as one of the maids set out a tray of soaps and oils near the edge of the pool. Iria, the younger of the two maids, undressed herself and followed the faerie into the pool, holding a clean washcloth in her right hand.

"You always were my favorite," Cerulla commented, forcing a smile through her swirling mess of emotions and exhaustion.

The strawberry blonde maid offered a kind expression as she soaked the cloth in the scented water of the pool. "The prince wants me to be your personal attendant, now that you're part of the royal family, princess. He knows you enjoy my company."

The castle's sage sighed, then dunked her head once more under the water. "Can I ask you something?" she inquired, shaking the excess liquid from her midnight-hued hair.

Iria shook her head as she began scrubbing the neck and shoulders of the princess. "Do as you please. You don't need to ask my permission to say anything to me. I'm just a maid, sweet fae."

"Someone important was sacrificed today," Cerulla spoke after a moment, leaning into the massaging hands and cloth of the maid. "They died so the rest of us could live."

"That's quite honorable, princess," the maid replied softly, working her damp fingers against the pale skin of the faerie.

"Usually, yes, it is," the princess sighed as she pictured the kobold in her mind. "Yet, I feel guilty. I asked him to be the foci for my magic, without telling him what the danger would be. I knew he trusted me enough to agree to anything I would ask, and I thought I was making the right decision, but now I feel like I made a terrible mistake. What do you think?"

"While it is not my position to question the logic of those I serve," Iria stated as she placed a bit of lavender-infused soap onto the cloth, "I see that you and the prince survived, as did many others. Our enemies were defeated, and now our people can return home to their families and work to regain their lost peace. Though a death, any death, should be mourned respectfully and avoided if possible, we do not live in peaceful, nor simple times, my lady. If one person's death means so many more can continue living, then that person should be hailed as a hero, rather than treated as a regret."

"Maybe so," Cerulla closed her eyes as the maid began wiping the grime of the day from her face, "but I still killed him. I've lived for eons, sweet girl, and yet of all the lives I've seen ended in my time, this one cut the deepest in my soul. I had no right to demand his sacrifice, not without giving him the chance to back out of the decision."

Iria lathered up the princess' hair firmly, making sure to run her fingers through the long length of the dark, cerulean hair. "Again, it is not my position to question your logic or reasoning, but I will say that I believe if the person could talk to you now, they would understand the choice you made. From what Prince Jolson said upon his return, it sounded as if you were given few options for survival. I'm sorry for the loss of your friend, and you have my sympathies for the choice you had to make, but look at those who lived because of that sacrifice. Look at everyone and everything you would've lost if you hadn't made your choice. Your friend would be proud of the bravery you showed in your decision."

"People are upset with me," the faerie stated, feeling the touch of the young maid massaging her scalp. "Normally this wouldn't bother me, but these people are angry over my decision, and they're important to our kingdom. Most of all, they're right in that I need to shoulder the blame for sacrificing our friend."

"Now," Iria picked up a bronze ladle to begin washing the soap from the sage's hair, "you know I can't give advice on matters of politics, but today was a rough day for the entire city. Many lives were affected by the tragedy that struck Vansenhul on what was supposed to be a day of celebration and smiles. People will need time to process what happened in their own way, just as you will do the same. I suggest some lengthy rest and relaxation, sweet fae. Maybe spend a few days locked in a room with your new husband?"

"He's injured, and his father is gravely wounded," Cerulla sighed heavily, despite the kind words of the maid. "I doubt he's going to have much time or patience to help me. At least, not for a while, I suppose."

"Then you need to be each other's safe harbor in these troublesome times," Iria suggested with a soft smile. "You two have been together for years, and most of us wondered how long it would be until you got married. Even the older staff don't remember seeing you as happy as you've been with Prince Jolson. They all say the same thing, you stuck to yourself and only appeared for official duties. If you didn't go with him, you were the first one waiting to see him return from his trips around the kingdom. The world has become a turbulent river, flooded with the waters of chaos and war, and the love you two share should be a rock to cling to in the middle of these vicious waves."

The princess turned slowly and hugged the maid tightly. "Thank you, Iria, I know I can always count on you when things seem dark around me. You're an amazing friend."

Wearing nothing but a warm smile, the maid gave the princess a comforting hug of her own. "Let's finish getting you cleaned up. Paesla should be back soon with some fresh clothes, and I know your husband is waiting for you."

Without complaint, Cerulla allowed the maid to continue scrubbing her down and rinsing her pale flesh. Just as Iria had predicted, the brunette pixie known as Paesla returned with a white robe and a green hooded cloak made of crushed velvet. With her body and hair washed and cleaned from the chaos of the day, Cerulla stepped out of the heated pool, her usual graceful steps hindered by the stress and fatigue that plagued her muscles. The princess slipped into the fresh clothes after Iria ran a dry towel over her voluptuous figure, letting the maids do their duty as they wrapped the garments about her waist with a silver silk sash.

Using a small, dry cloth, Iria dabbed a bit of rose-scented oil onto the faerie's neck and wrists, then dried herself before donning her maid garb once more. Following the two young maids, the faerie made her way back up into the main floors of the castle. It was a quiet trek through the grand building for the trio as they approached the bedroom the princess shared with her husband once more.

"Feel better?" Jolson asked as soon as Cerulla stepped through the door.

"Much better," she answered with a slight smile, "thank you for insisting."

"My father is waiting for us," the man stood up from the bed, rubbing the bandage around his arm lightly. "We should go see him."

"How is he?" Cerulla inquired, greeting her husband with a quick embrace from her arms as he approached her.

Jolson shook his head slowly. "Not well. My mother already went ahead of us, and I told her we would be right behind her."

Taking her hand in a comforting gesture, Jolson guided his wife from the bedroom. They walked, side by side, down the wide hall towards the bedchamber that held the king. Jolson's squire waited by the large set of oak doors, bowed to the prince in greeting, and then opened the entrance with a hefty tug on the iron rings that served as handles.

Surrounded by doctors, healers, and various other attendants, the king was laid upon his back on the grand bed. The queen sat by his side in an elegant chair made of oak gilded with gold and silver. Several bandages and scraps of cloth were piled, stained heavily with wet crimson, in a bowl held by one of the doctors. An older man, one of the city's chief surgeons, approached the prince with a grim expression worn on his round, but honest face.

"There's only so much we can do," the lead surgeon spoke up, looking over to the prince and the faerie. "If we remove the arrow in his chest, his lung will fail and he'll bleed out."

"This is my father," Jolson said, the news from the surgeon draining the color from his face. "He's the ruler of this country. You can do more, certainly?"

"Unfortunately," the surgeon shook his head in disappointment, "there's nothing much we can do without a strong jolt of healing magic. Something stronger than these healers can do."

"Where is Corina?" Jolson turned abruptly towards his wife, his face reflecting the surge of fear and determination in his heart. "She's a practitioner of the Atheian Way."

Cerulla glanced away in an attempt to hide her emotions from her husband. "I'm sorry, Dorho and Corina decided to go back to the inn."

"Send someone to get them!" he ordered, his blue eyes shifting to the castle's servants. "Your king needs a powerful healer!"

"My son," the king whispered, his voice ravaged by his physical weakness. "You need... to lead... this kingdom."

Jolson wheeled about quickly, then dropped to a knee next to his wounded father, scooping up the hand of the king in his own. "I can't. We'll get someone here who can help you. You just need to hold on a little longer."

The ragged breath of the king came out like a wind across a graveyard as he spoke to his son. "Heed... heed your mother... and your wife."

"Would you go get Corina?" the prince nearly shouted to the maids that escorted himself and the faerie to the king's chamber. "Do something! Save your king!"

Giving hesitant glances to the princess, the two young maids darted away.

"I can't allow that," Cerulla spoke up suddenly, her voice escaping after a deep breath to calm her mind and heart. "Corina saved the priest, and kept Dorho alive. The amount of damage she's absorbed into her own body through her magic today is astonishing, but asking her to do more, would be putting her life at risk. Especially with as far gone as the king is. She likely wouldn't survive."

"Let me go," the king mumbled, a heavy wince of agony washing over his entire body. "You need... you need to rule... rule with kindness... fair and just."

"I'm not ready," Jolson argued resolutely. "You're my father, the king, and you will take the throne once you heal and get some rest."

"I'm afraid," his father groaned, "I won't heal from this, my son."

Jolson shook his head defiantly. "Cerulla, I need you to convince Corina to help us. This is for the sake of the kingdom."

The princess took a single step back, clutching at the sleeves of her robe as she moved. "I can't. I already sacrificed one person for the sake of the kingdom today. I can't ask another to do the same. Not like this. I won't do it. I'm sorry, my love."

"This is my father," Jolson asserted adamantly. "We have to do something."

"And I already sentenced one innocent soul to death today," Cerulla fought back the tears that threatened to stain her face once more. "I won't keep killing our friends for this damned kingdom!"

As much as she wanted to remain by the side of her husband, the faerie ran from the king's bedchamber. Inside, her emotions were a knot of chaotic fire, and she wanted to just get away from everything for the moment. Her feet were quick, taking her back to the bedroom she shared with the prince. Throwing open the chamber's door, the faerie threw herself into the softness of the quilts covering the bed. Unable to hold back any further, she wept loudly into the buckwheat-stuffed pillows. She wanted nothing more than to help her husband with his own emotional turmoil, but she had been fighting to hide her own tsunami of grief ever since she sacrificed Zakosa.

She let the tears fall freely, curling into the quilts and pillows that decorated the sack-like bed. It was like a giant bag filled with dried grain or beans, soft, yet firm, and it conformed to the body like a welcoming embrace. After what felt like only a few sorrow-filled breaths, the faerie was buried under the blankets in a nest near the center of the squishy bed.

So absorbed by her own guilt-driven emotional release, she never saw or even heard her husband enter the room. It wasn't until he sat upon the edge of the bed, that she noticed him looking at her, sadness and concern in his deep blue eyes.

"I'm sorry," Jolson sighed heavily as he put a hand on her shoulder. "I shouldn't have pushed you. I never stopped to consider you in all of this."

"No," Cerulla spoke softly, "I should apologize to you. You're my husband, and I refused to help you in your time of need. What kind of wife rejects her husband when he's trying to save his family?"

"A brave one," he replied, brushing his fingers through her long indigo hair. "The brave one that I married. One with more common sense than the rest of the castle at the moment. You've been through enough today, I shouldn't have pushed you like that."

"He's your father," Cerulla began to sit up, wiping her eyes, "you have every right to do everything to try and save him."

"It's too late," Jolson shook his head and took a deep breath. "He's gone. I had the surgeon remove the arrow so he could pass swiftly without prolonged suffering."

Her eyes went wide upon hearing his words, throwing her arms around his shoulders in a tight hug. "Oh, I'm so sorry, my love."

"I realized, after you left, that you were right," the prince embraced his wife firmly, sobbing into her shoulder. "I couldn't ask more people to die for us, and neither should you."

Cerulla allowed herself to fall backwards into the bed, pulling her husband with her as she held him to her chest. "So, now what do we do?"

"We get some rest," the prince admitted, his voice torn by the weight of his emotions. "There's nothing much we can do at this point."

Together, the couple embraced upon the bed, letting themselves spill their emotions as a single soul. Cerulla succumbed to the torment of Zakosa's death, while her husband grieved the loss of his father. Wrapped in each other's arms, and caressed by the soft quilts of the bed, the two gave in to their exhaustion and inner suffering. Sleep took them quickly, luring them away from the concerns that plagued their minds while they found peace in one another's arms.

17.

It had been five days since Kendira and the others reached the small community of Euthrox. A sprawling cluster of farms and orchards surrounding a temple, a tavern, an inn, a government office, and a trading hub, Euthrox was the quintessential quaint hamlet set against an idyllic backdrop of pine forests and towering mountains. Though the residents had buried Lynsia's father and her brother shortly after their murder, the house itself was still in shambles from the attack of the king's men.

The bard and her group had spent the first three days organizing the house and cleaning up the destruction left by the soldiers sent by King Borlhauf. The following days were used to appropriately recover from dealing with the agents of the Onyx Spire, while also allowing Lynsia to properly grieve the loss of her family. Late in the fourth day, Dorho and Lorvin messaged through the enchanted stone, updating the bard on what had happened in Vansenhul. They told her how the druid had died, and that the king of Anslater had passed away as a result of the assault on the city. They spoke briefly on the condition of Lynsia and the plans for getting the girl to I'raha, then his voice faded into the depths of the gem once more. From that point on, the women dedicated themselves to recuperating and relaxing before they felt up to continuing with the journey north.

"Do you think Ansha is alive?" Kendira asked as she sipped from a mug containing a mixture of fruit brandy and tea stirred with cherry preserves.

"If they wanted her dead," Urna commented as she drank slowly from a bowl of onyx tea, "they would've killed her in the street. They're keeping her alive, for some reason. However, there's something I would like to know, Kendira."

"What's that?" the bard cocked her head to the side slightly with a bit of a drunken smile.

"I've been thinking," the reptilian woman tapped her fingers on the exterior of the bowl in her hands, "is someone leaking information to the Onyx Spire?"

Kendira sat upright quickly as she set down her mug. "What do you mean?"

Without a single ounce of hesitation, Urna reached across the table and grasped the front of the bard's tunic, nearly yanking the woman from her seat. Urna's eyes, like twin orbs of chartreuse gems burning with rage, looked upon the face of the bard with frustration and suspicion.

The lizard woman's voice was a harsh growl as she spoke to the startled bard. "Dracamori, the attack on Ameribelle, and let's not forget our fun little rendezvous in Pershing's Ferry. I get the distinct feeling that someone is feeding Nadriah information on where to find Lynsia. Who would be dumb enough to endanger this entire journey, and why is it you?"

Kendira forcefully pushed the slithzerkai away, narrowing her eyes dangerously as she straightened her shirt. "I don't know why you think it would be me. I love that girl, and I despise the Onyx Spire. How do I know it isn't you? You used to live there, after all. You could very well still be loyal to that terrible place."

"Did you sign your contract with Nadriah before," Urna persisted, "or after she saved your life?"

"It's not me," Kendira stated confidently. "It was probably that kobold, or Vourden. It could even be someone tied to Lady Eisley's court. How am I supposed to know?"

Urna shook her head and stood up before finishing her onyx tea in a single gulp. "The kobold is dead, and Vourden has already lost enough in his world. He wouldn't be brazen enough to throw it all away, not after he just got his daughter back. You, on the other hand..."

The slithzerkai let her thoughts trail away with her voice before departing the house, leaving the bard alone at the dining table. Kendira scoffed at the attitude of the reptile, and went back to her warm beverage, glancing through the window at the setting sun. The rain had stopped on their first day in Euthrox, and an air of tranquility had settled over their group as they had busied themselves with restoring Lynsia's home. As the bard looked at the door the slithzerkai had left through, she felt like the calm was about to be a thing left in the past, and that uncertainty and hostility were going to become commonplace in her life.

"What was that about?" Lynsia said as she stepped into the house, holding a basket of carrots, beans, radishes, beets, and cabbage against her slender waist.

"Urna?" Kendira shook her head a bit to dismiss the ill feelings about the slithzerkai. "She's just upset with how long this trip is taking. Don't let her bother you, my sweet birdy."

Lynsia nodded cautiously, then set the basket of fresh vegetables on a table in the kitchen. "I hope so. Any ideas how we're going to find I'raha once we leave Euthrox?"

"I was hoping we could find something among your father's stuff," the bard answered, before taking a long drink from her beverage. "Unfortunately, it appears either he didn't make any notes about how he found her, or they were lost over time. Any ideas from you?"

Lyn shrugged as she sorted the vegetables carefully. "Zakosa said he was supposed to help us, but everyone was worried that he was a spy, so Vourden sent him with Lorvin. Dorho told us he had spoken with I'raha, but he's not here to help us now."

"The Faulkendor Mountains are a vast region, we need something to start with," Kendira stated, interrupting the girl's thoughts with her own.

"She was able to tell Dorho about my father and brother," Lynsia added. "Which means, she knew about it somehow."

"You mentioned before," Kendira looked over the petite figure of the girl in the kitchen as she considered how to find the faerie, "that I'raha is seen as some kind of witch, and she protects the spring that feeds the fields here. Is that correct?"

Lynsia nodded and managed a small smile. "Yes, but it is only folklore. Stories to entertain small children. I don't know how true that all is."

"Luckily, I'm a bard," Kendira grinned as she stood up slowly, moving to help Lynsia with the basket of fresh produce. "My kind specializes in stories. It's what gives us life. If there's one thing I know is true here, it's that every story is built on a bed of truth, no matter how insane it sounds. If she's the protector of the spring that feeds these fields, then we just need to follow the water. What do you think?"

"It's a decent place to start," the Sidhe-Vein agreed with a warm smile, giving the bard a swift kiss to her cheek. "I just hope we can get there without running into more trouble."

"Are you nervous?" Kendira asked suddenly. "About meeting I'raha, the faerie that created you. Does that bother you at all?"

The girl pulled a knife from a nearby rack of tools, and began cutting up a couple carrots into small cubes. "A little. She made me into this," Lynsia gestured at herself, "creature. Whatever, and whoever I am, is because of her. All of this trouble we're in, is because she agreed to make me."

"Don't say that," Kendira offered a fond smile. "I like having you around. Sure, things have been rough, but I would've died without you."

"You wouldn't have been involved if it weren't for me being me," Lynsia responded quickly.

"And, if so," the bard found a cooking pan as she spoke, fetching an onion from a bowl next to the stove before returning to where Lynsia was working, "I wouldn't have met my beautiful little birdy. You have no idea how glad I am to have you in my life."

The Sidhe-Vein smiled kindly as she pulled a wrapped mutton loin from the bottom of the basket, speaking as she prepared to cut it into cubes as well. "You have been far too nice to me, considering all the trouble I've brought you. I remember when we first met, and Dorho was adamant that you shouldn't be with us. He was worried you were bad luck, or that you'd cause something terrible to happen. Little did we know that we'd get so close to one another, instead."

After putting diced onions and carrots into the pan, Kendira put her arms around the girl and kissed the back of her neck softly. "I'm glad we got to spend that time together at the Moonstone Observatory. Hopefully, once all this is over, we can stay by each other's side."

Abruptly, Lynsia turned around to steal a kiss from Kendira's lips, giving a sly grin as she returned back to working with the meat. "I love you, my beautiful bard."

"And I love you," Kendira giggled softly as she moved to prepare a mixture of rice and beans, "my beloved little birdy."

Together, the two finished preparing the evening meal. Tarragon, sage, and basil were added to the pan of meat and vegetables, while seasonings like turmeric, dried spicy peppers, and paprika were added to the rice and bean pot. The bard and the Sidhe-Vein relaxed as the supper simmered over a fire fueled by chunks of birch and alder. Drinking from cups of apricot wine stirred with tea, they lounged in one another's arms in a nest of large pillows near the house's main hearth.

The slithzerkai never returned to the house, allowing a feeling of calm to settle over the property once more as the evening progressed. Orota, Kendira, and Lyn ate quietly once the large northern woman finished splitting wood. Lynsia spoke of her trip to visit the various neighbors, and how she agreed to let them work her family's fields until she could return to handle the affairs of the estate. Kendira discussed leaving the farm in the next couple days, once everyone felt they were healed up and rested enough to handle the trip into the mountains. Overall, the night moved on peacefully, with the hot meal being eaten gladly before Orota retired to a bedroom long after the sun was removed from the sky. Figuring the reptile had returned to the wagon, Kendira didn't bother checking on Urna before following Lynsia to her bed. Sleep came quickly, finding the bard and Sidhe-Vein embracing one another lovingly under the blankets of the comfortable bed.

Long after the sun crawled into the sky, Kendira slowly pulled herself from the arms of the girl and got dressed. Wearing her long dress the color of the cloudless sky, and a loose-fitting beige sleeveless tunic, the bard stepped from the bedroom quietly. Her mind was set on preparing a decent breakfast for the others, which had become her task since starting this cursed journey, while her bare feet almost danced happily over the wood floors.

Then a man's voice broke through the morning silence in the large house. It was a deep voice, speaking words in a hushed tone as something rattled in the kitchen. For a moment, Kendira paused, having left her enchanted bracelets in the bedroom with the Sidhe-Vein. Her heart raced with the thought that the house had been broken into during the night.

"Urna," the voice spoke again, the bard close enough to hear the apprehensive tone clearly, "I'm sorry it took me this long to get here. I came as soon as I heard about what happened in Pershing's Ferry."

As she turned the corner from the hall leading to the bedrooms, Kendira's green eyes watched as Vourden placed a small plate of biscuits topped with eggs and gravy in front of the lizard woman at the dining table. His own emerald orbs scanned over the bard for a moment, a brief hesitation in his movements. After taking a quick breath, Justiciar Leustren swiftly approached the bard and pulled her into his strong arms.

"You look like hell," his voice called to Kendira's ears as he hugged the woman tightly.

Like his hug had yanked on a lever in her body, Kendira nearly collapsed into his arms, immediately sobbing against his tunic. She was shocked to see him, but she was so thankful that he had arrived at all, and her emotions broke through in an instant. All she could do was cry as he held her, clutching at his chest like a frightened child clings to a doll. She couldn't tell if it was relief, or longing, but Kendira took his lips with a feverish kiss as tears streaked her cheeks.

"News reached the castle about the attack in Pershing's Ferry," Vourden spoke softly, brushing his fingers through the soft ribbons of dark hair that fell about her shoulders, "and I came as soon as I could."

"You didn't come alone," another man's voice called from the pillows by the hearth.

Wearing dark leather armor patterned like a dragon's scales and held together with brass studs, the large figure of Halvene offered a concerned smile to the bard. The muscular man lifted a hefty mug of hot onyx tea to his lips and took a long drink before turning his attention back to the plate of eggs and sausage he had been eating from.

"I don't understand," Kendira looked them both over as though they were mere illusions, wiping her eyes with her hands. "I thought Lady Eisley needed you?"

Vourden placed a fond kiss to the woman's forehead before guiding her over to the dining table. "She isn't happy that we left, but she understands why we came to help."

"I failed to protect Ansha once," Halvene added between bites of sausage. "With her husband murdered, it would've been wrong to not offer my assistance as a form of atonement."

"What about our children?" Kendira inquired, running her right hand over Vourden's arm before he stepped back towards the stove.

Vourden gave a facetious shake of his head. "With your parents. They were more than willing to watch them once I explained you were in danger up here."

Urna set down her mug of herbal tea as her gimlet eyes settled upon the bard. "What luck you have, Kendira. Just as things were looking grim, two knights in shining armor appeared. Hopefully things will go smoother from this point on. It would be a shame if the spy ruined things again."

"I sent the kobold with Lorvin," Vourden stated, pouring a fresh mug of onyx tea for Kendira. "I was hoping that would solve our problem with him."

"Seems that problem," Urna glanced from the justiciar to the bard and smirked knowingly, "as you called him, Vourden, has been handled."

Kendira sighed and lifted the mug to her lips, inhaling the sweet aroma of honey that had been stirred into the black liquid. "We were told that Vansenhul was attacked by the Onyx Spire, and Zakosa was killed as a result." Her words fought through the mess of released emotions she felt upon seeing Vourden.

"The Onyx Spire attacked the capital of Anslater?" Vourden paused while preparing a plate of sausage, eggs, biscuits, and gravy. "This is one hell of a mess we've dug ourselves into, but at least our little troublemaker can't keep feeding information to the Spire. Hopefully Lorvin is doing well."

"He is," Kendira nodded, fidgeting with the mug in her hands, "so is Dorho, and they found another Sidhe-Vein."

Vourden blinked and gasped sharply. "What did you just say?"

"Dorho is alive," Kendira stared into her mug. "At least, that's what Lorvin says. I've talked to him myself. I don't know whether to believe it or not, but for some reason he's alive and well, exploring Anslater with Lorvin now. According to them both, they found a second Sidhe-Vein, as well."

"Dorho is alive?" Vourden's voice was immediately suspicious. "That's impossible. I saw him die. We all watched him get killed in Ameribelle. Anyway, if he is, why is he in Anslater, instead of up here helping us?"

The bard shrugged. "I don't know. He said he was given some kind of important task by the person who resurrected him. He wants to meet us up here once they are finished down there."

"I still don't believe any of that," Vourden scoffed dismissively. "I'll have to see it with my own eyes. You and I both know we saw him get killed by Lynsia's magic, so I find this hard to have faith in."

"My magic did what?" Lynsia's voice called from the hallway, her sapphire eyes peering over at the bard, the fear and shock from her voice mirrored in the blue orbs.

"Dammit," Kendira muttered as the Sidhe-Vein bolted for the door to outside.

The bard immediately gave chase, dashing from the table in a worried frenzy.

"No!" Lynsia shouted in anger as Kendira grabbed the girl's arm and pulled her back against her chest. "You told me that monster killed Dorho!"

"Because it did," Kendira insisted, forcing the girl into a firm hug on the patio just outside the house. "That monster killed our friend."

"Don't lie to me!" Lynsia nearly screamed, yanking herself away from the bard and stumbling backwards off the patio. "Who killed Dorho?"

"You did," Vourden spoke up, his feet coming to a halt next to Kendira. "We weren't supposed to tell you, and for that, I'm sorry. He was caught in the blast of magic that destroyed that monster, but he did so willingly. If he hadn't stopped that vile creature, it would've reached you, and everyone else. He gave you the chance you needed to save us all. He sacrificed himself, so the rest of us could live."

"Is that true?" Lynsia stepped away from Kendira as the bard moved closer.

"Kendira," Vourden's voice came stern, yet comforting, "just tell her. She has a right to know. I'm sorry for saying it out loud, but she should know the truth."

Kendira sighed, looking at the justiciar with an expression of contempt. She was so very glad to see him here in Euthrox, but now she was furious that he had spoken so openly about Dorho's death. Her gaze shifted to the terrified Sidhe-Vein that was moving away from the house.

"Yes," the bard finally spoke. "He's right. Your magic was the thing that killed Dorho, but he sacrificed himself so we could live and continue this journey. Without his bravery, you would've been taken from us."

Vourden nodded. "We have to keep going, for his sake. We should've told you sooner."

"No one wanted to hurt you further," Kendira added. "You had a terrible experience in the throne room when those monsters from the Onyx Spire appeared. We didn't want you to feel guilty."

The sapphires of the Sidhe-Vein's eyes flickered with the torrent of magic that formed her core. Kendira stopped moving, fully expecting to get hammered by an explosion of the furious girl's faerie magic as Lynsia's eyes glowed faintly with a hint of jade.

"Careful," Vourden reached out and put a hand on his lover's shoulder. "I think we just need to let her calm down."

"I didn't want to hurt anyone else," Lynsia's voice was sharp and full of cynicism. "You should've just told me. I killed someone. I killed my friend. I killed Dorho, and you lied to me!"

In less time than it took to blink, a scorching wind rose up, stirred by the flow of magic from the girl. The hot, dry gusts ripped at the soil and everyone standing on the patio. With such force that it threatened to shove Kendira to the ground, the rush of heated air threw dust and debris high into the morning light.

Kendira ignored the danger and broke away from Vourden, her feet rushing towards the frightened Sidhe-Vein. As the dreaded shriek began to escape the lips of the girl, the bard lunged at the furious Lynsia. Wind like fire, and magic thrown like daggers, pummeled the body of the woman as her arms wrapped around the shoulders of the enraged Sidhe-Vein. With no hesitation, Kendira pressed a loving kiss to the girl, hoping to bring her back from this dangerous edge. She couldn't lose her little birdy. Not like this.

It felt like a giant had swung a tree into her chest as the blast of magic from Lynsia pounded into Kendira's body. Her ears picked up the screams of Vourden standing on the patio still, but the rest of her senses were consumed by the thundering of ferocious magic tearing through her flesh. It felt like a demon had been given life deep within her core, and it was clawing its way out of her chest through her ribs, but she refused to give up on the girl.

"Stop this!" Kendira begged, ignoring the burning pain that ran through her veins, clutching Lynsia tightly to her chest.

A brilliant flash of emerald light exploded, and Kendira found herself on her backside, laying in a patch of charred ground cover. Her eyes, which felt like they were spinning, looked at the few wispy clouds in the sky, trying to focus on a single streak of white among the morning blue. The ears of the bard were ringing loudly, and even the shouts of Vourden and Halvene had been silenced, though the two were suddenly standing over her, trying to get Kendira to her feet.

Their hands hoisted the bard to her feet, but her body refused to obey her desires to stand and walk. It was like something had shut off her bones and muscles completely. Deep in her chest, a burning sensation was devouring her organs, at least that's what she believed from the pain that wracked her body.

Standing only a few paces away, a girl with long silver hair and deeply tanned skin stood where Lynsia had been. She wore the same pale blue dress and dark green cloak as the Sidhe-Vein, but the blue eyes of the girl were a very distinct platinum hue. Unable to focus her vision, Kendira stumbled forward on wobbly legs, and threw her arms around the strange girl who stood in Lynsia's place.

"I promised to protect you!" the bard wailed, ignoring the burning ache that clutched at her heart and lungs.

"I shouldn't have been created," the strange girl mumbled, the voice sounding vaguely like an exhausted Lynsia. "Why did you stop me?"

"Because I love you," Kendira answered, her voice a ragged whisper while her muscles and joints refused to keep her up.

With platinum eyes staring at her like twin needles striking out at her very soul, Kendira collapsed to the ground once more. Tears flooded her eyes, her voice lost as she found it harder to breathe with each breath she took. She felt the arms of Vourden around her sides, picking her up into a worried and emotionally devastated embrace, as her hazy green eyes watched the strange girl turn away from her.

The girl stopped walking, turning briefly to gaze upon the bard once more coldly. "You love me? Look what that did to you."

Kendira took a sharp breath as she felt the arms of Vourden wrap around her torso. The ache in her body, fed by the fatigue that suddenly ripped through her bones, left her unable to scream or argue while the silver-haired girl darted out of her view. Frustrated voices of concern filled her mind and ears, but those soon became as silent as death itself as the bard closed her eyes, succumbing to the terrible fury assaulting her core. Before falling into the bleakness of unwelcomed unconsciousness, Kendira felt a loving kiss upon her lips, one that seemed to pull her mind briefly from the despair that filled her heart.

18.

"Luckily, her body is used to magic," Urna spoke with a complete lack of concern, "so she should be fine after some rest."

"What exactly happened?" Vourden questioned, brushing a hand through the hair of the bard gently.

Urna pulled her hands away from the wrists of Kendira, her gimlet eyes looking over the justiciar carefully. "She absorbed the magic of the Sidhe-Vein. Kendira used her connection with Lynsia, and her own magic, to draw the fury of the faerie's magic into her body. She's lucky it didn't kill her, but she'll be changed forever."

Vourden nodded as he looked at Kendira unconscious in the bed. She was breathing, but something was wrong. Something was deeply, and terribly wrong with the bard. Like the Sidhe-Vein, her luxurious black hair had been turned into a strange silvery tone. Her once brilliant emerald-like eyes had become hazy and stained with a sheen of golden iridescence. Even her skin, once flawless and beautifully tanned, appeared cracked with a faint hint of jade-tinted light radiating from a few of the deeper wounds. Kendira had acquired a few cuts and scrapes from confronting the Sidhe-Vein's magic, but these were different, like cracks in a porcelain cup's surface.

"I hope she'll be fine," the justiciar commented pensively.

"We need to find the girl," Halvene stated from where he was leaning against the bedroom wall, arms crossed over his chest. "I almost forgot how much trouble she was."

"Indeed," Vourden sighed heavily. "Urna, please stay here with Kendira. You know more about these kinds of reactions to magic than I do."

"Before you go, Vourden," Urna stepped over to the justiciar, throwing a cautious look to the resting bard, "can we talk?"

He glanced at the woman in the bed, then shifted his green eyes to the slithzerkai before nodding. "I'm guessing in private?"

Urna gestured to the hallway with a firm expression. "Indeed."

Following the reptilian woman, Vourden stepped out of the bedroom, making sure the door was closed as they wandered out towards the kitchen. Remnants of the breakfast that was half-eaten and never cleaned up rested around the stove and table, signs that they had all forgotten to finish the meal in the morning's chaos.

"What's this about?" Vourden asked bluntly, watching the door to the bedroom as he leaned against the dining table.

"I don't think Zakosa was our spy," Urna stated, not bothering with politeness or subtleness.

Vourden took a heavy breath. "You think it was Kendira? What makes you think this?"

The reptile took a seat where she had been enjoying her tea earlier as she visibly thought over the words. "From what I got out of Ansha in our talks, is that the bard basically forced Dorho to let her tag along. As soon as you all returned to the Moonstone Observatory to get her and the Sidhe-Vein, you and your soldiers were attacked. You were attacked again in Dracamori, and upon returning to Ameribelle, the castle was attacked as though the Onyx Spire was lying in wait. After the assault on the castle, she drops into your life once more, giving you your daughter back, but Ansha said Kendira was furious the moment she saw you at the mage's castle. Everything seems to be going well again. Lives were getting back to normal. We got to rest, relax, and recover. Upon restarting this cursed journey, we were immediately attacked in Pershing's Ferry."

"And you think it was because of Kendira?" Vourden rubbed his neatly trimmed goatee for a moment as he processed the woman's words.

"It was a torrential rainstorm, Vourden." Urna's voice was direct and lacking any trace of friendly warmth. "There was no reason for anyone to be randomly out and about. Yet, the Onyx Spire not only knew we were there, but knew which tavern we were at, and knew they had to knock Lynsia out if they didn't want her using her powers. Zakosa was in the south with Lorvin, he could've guessed our route and timeline, but not as precisely as the Onyx Spire was able to."

Vourden took a sharp breath as she talked. "So, you suspect it was someone with you at the time? Which leaves Ansha, Kendira, and Orota?"

"And myself," Urna spoke with a quick nod. "I can't let you take me out of the line of suspects. You're the justiciar here, not myself. Ansha was captured by the Onyx Spire, which I still don't understand."

"Orota would condemn the entire Den of Red Venom if she made a pact with the Onyx Spire," Vourden rubbed his goatee again thoughtfully. "That's not something she would do. Especially not after helping us defend the castle."

Urna smiled slightly. "I lost my husband, my business, my customers, my pride, and some of my sanity, but I can assure you that it isn't me. I want Nadriah dead for what she did to me."

A tight feeling started coiling around Vourden's guts as he processed the words they were discussing. "And what about Kendira?"

"She's the only one of us," Urna looked over the man carefully, "who hasn't lost anything to the Onyx Spire. In fact, she's already won. Your wife was killed, and she got you back. Now she has her family reunited. You saw how relieved she was to see you here, right?"

Vourden closed his eyes for a moment, not wanting to believe anything he was hearing. "That doesn't make sense though. Why would she side with such an evil group? Plus, she has Lynsia, who loves her deeply. She wouldn't do this to her, would she?"

Urna shook her head slowly. "I don't understand everything, my friend, but I do understand women. We're unreasonable, illogical creatures driven by emotion over logic. Though, I would be willing to bet that she signed her contract with the Onyx Spire before she fell for Lynsia. Now, she's stuck with her decision, because Nadriah isn't the type to just let one of her pets go because they want freedom."

"If this turns out to be true," Vourden glanced over to the reptilian woman woefully, "what do you suggest I do?"

Urna shrugged with a deflective expression. "I'm not sure. You're the justiciar, and her lover. You can either work to free her from her contract, or you can make her pay the price for her sins. If this turns out to be the truth, you're going to have to search your own soul for the answer to this problem, my friend."

Vourden took a deep breath to try to push away the heavy ache that was swelling in his chest. He didn't want to believe the slithzerkai, but he also didn't feel she had any reason to deceive him.

"My only advice to you," Urna said as she played with her leftover tea, "is to tread carefully as we continue this journey. Do not let your heart cloud your mind. I don't want to see your son lose his father the same way he lost his mother."

"We need to go find that girl," Vourden stood upright and straightened his tunic. "One step at a time, and the sooner we can finish this damned quest, the better off we'll all be."

"Go," Urna urged, flashing a small smile of confidence, "I'll keep Kendira safe. We'll keep this discussion between us, Vourden."

"We will," he commented before moving down the hall to knock on the bedroom door. "Let's get going."

With Halvene, the justiciar of Elgrahm Hold went outside, where Orota was waiting by the wagon. Curled up at the feet of the burly woman was the larscot, Bies, appearing bored with the day.

"We don't have a faithful hound to follow the scent," Orota spoke as the two men drew closer, "so this guy will have to do."

"Any idea where to start?" Vourden looked at the others before scanning the landscape around the house.

Orota pointed west, towards the creek that meandered through the grain fields. "I saw her heading that way while you took the bard inside. We should take the larscot over there."

"Be careful, Vourden," Urna spoke as she stepped out onto the patio. "If my suspicions are correct, her magic has taken over and is threatening to break her apart. At the Spire, we called these types of creatures a Catalyst. They're walking on a razor's edge with their magic, as they've exceeded the limits of their physical form. It will either totally obliterate the physical body eventually, or it will turn her into a monster of unimaginable power if the magic is able to be restrained and controlled within the flesh. Provoking her won't end well, either way."

"I'm guessing this is why the Onyx Spire is so interested in the girl?" Vourden inquired.

The slithzerkai nodded solemnly. "A stable Catalyst capable of being controlled is a terrifying weapon."

"You heard the lizard," Vourden announced with a pensive sigh, "don't agitate the girl unnecessarily."

Orota patted one of her belt pouches and smiled, "I've got a way of calming unruly folks down, don't worry about that."

The trio, following the faithful larscot, headed out through the fields towards the creek. Dogwoods, poplar, and birch trees lined both sides of the waterway like a dense forest fed by the wet volcanic soil. A narrow trail, likely used by local wild game, ran along the rocks and among the trees, which Bies quickly began following northward. It didn't take long until they encountered the first set of footprints in the damp soil, indicating they were on the proper path, and proving that Bies was more than just a bed-warmer.

Shortly after the trail began to turn east, they spotted the Sidhe-Vein standing on a boulder, looking in the direction of Euthrox's center. She threw a sideways glance towards the group approaching her from the meandering path, flashed a sinister grin, and leapt from her perch. In a full sprint, Lynsia's new silvery hair was a blur through the woods as she darted for the taverns and trading depots at the core of the small community.

"What is she doing?" Halvene asked, startled by the speed of the small girl.

"I thought her magic was supposed to be all love and butterflies," Vourden sneered, hastily giving chase to the Sidhe-Vein. "We need to stop her!"

"We'll never catch her!" Orota stated obviously, though they all ran through the underbrush after the silver-haired girl.

Bies darted away through the dense woods, unbothered by the overgrowth spawned by the rich soil. By the time the trio broke through the forest along the creek, the larscot, and the girl, were already halfway to the town's center. For a moment, Vourden wondered if the large, weasel-like creature understood what they needed to do. The two men and the northern woman definitely couldn't keep up with the girl, leaving the justiciar worried as he felt like all he could do was watch the larscot bolt through the field ahead of them.

Just short of the rear of the inn, Bies caught up to the fleeing girl. Like a cat, the beast pounced heavily, tackling the Sidhe-Vein as his jaws latched onto the back of her clothes. The girl was quickly knocked to the ground, while the large, weasel-like animal tugged and pulled, preventing her from rising to her feet. Lynsia wheeled about, struggling to get free from the larscot, but with each movement, the creature only seemed to tighten his grip.

"Leave me alone!" Lynsia bellowed, her eyes a mix of fury and grief.

"Not going to happen," Vourden replied, finally catching up to where the larscot had the girl held down.

The eyes of the Sidhe-Vein flared a brilliant hue of white as she brought her hands up, palms aimed towards the justiciar.

"Nope," Vourden quipped quickly, landing a swift kick to the girl's temple. "You're coming with us."

Like a sack of potatoes, the girl slumped to the ground from the blow to her head. Heavily dazed and almost unconscious, Lynsia fought to get to her feet, though her movements were far too slow and sluggish to be of any benefit. Orota produced a vial of dark red fluid from a pouch on her belt, and handed it to Vourden with a nod.

"Th'charola extract mixed with a few other carefully chosen goodies," the muscular woman gave a knowing smile. "Might calm her down, considerably."

"Awfully bold of you," the justiciar looked at the scarlet slime that sloshed around inside the tiny vial, "handing illegal drugs to an officer of the law."

Orota scoffed and rolled her eyes. "I'm bigger than you, tiny southern man."

Halvene chuckled a bit.

Vourden looked over the small vial, then glanced at the girl. For a moment, he considered his other options. He could tie Lynsia up and gag her, but he was supposed to be a symbol of the law in Elgrahm Hold. His mind replayed the warning from Urna over and over, knowing he had to keep the girl from being provoked into using her magic. What would Kendira say if she found out he had given potent narcotics to the Sidhe-Vein? Did he have many other choices to keep everyone safe?

"Hold her down," Vourden requested, popping the cork from the small amber vial.

"Dorho would kill us for this," Halvene commented as he knelt down, grabbing the head of the dizzy girl who was still fighting against the larscot.

The justiciar shrugged, though a regretful ache burned in his belly. "He'll just have to forgive us. We need to keep her calm and keep everyone else alive."

Bies released the girl's clothes while Orota helped Halvene hold the girl down and open her mouth. Swiftly, Vourden emptied the contents of the vial down Lynsia's throat, followed by Orota holding the Sidhe-Vein's jaws closed until she swallowed the crimson slime.

"Now, what were you doing?" Vourden asked, kneeling down in front of the dazed girl.

"I," she spat, though none of the red potion came out, and her voice struggled through the dizziness from the blow to her head. "I want to kill the faerie. She made me into this monster. She created this demon. I'm going to kill her."

Vourden almost fell onto his backside with the confession of the girl. It was like her shy, timid, quiet self had been removed. In her platinum eyes, nothing but hate and emotional pain swirled, having replaced the fear and hope he was used to seeing. He remembered the expressions of love and longing on her face whenever Kendira was around, but now, it looked as though those traits had been long forgotten as he gazed over her figure. She was absolutely furious, with a gleam of malicious intent flickering in the expression thrown from her eyes.

"Kendira," Vourden sighed, "she loves you, dearly. She never wanted to see you get hurt. She definitely wouldn't want you acting like this."

Lynsia tried standing up, but it was clear that the effects of the narcotics were beginning to take hold. She was still obviously stunned from the strike to her temple, but her movements were becoming more relaxed and apathetic.

"I killed," the Sidhe-Vein took a deep breath as she tried to force her eyes to focus upon the justiciar. "I killed Dorho. Now, I hurt Kendira. This is all because of that faerie. If I had just stayed dead, this never would've happened."

"Let's get her back to the house," Vourden stated, standing up slowly. "Hopefully she calms down after sleeping that extract off."

"No," Lynsia protested, though her voice was getting heavy and slow with the intrusion of Orota's contraband. "I have... I have to..."

"You have to get back to the house," Vourden said firmly. "Kendira will be worried sick if she wakes up and you're gone."

As if the girl weighed nothing, Halvene lifted Lynsia over his shoulder and started walking in the direction of the girl's home. While Orota and Halvene moved away, Vourden looked over to where Bies was waiting patiently.

"I've been wondering why you were with us," the justiciar commented, bending over to run his hands through the fur along the creature's neck. "Thank you."

The weasel-like animal trilled happily and nuzzled the hands of the man before trotting after the others. Making sure to avoid the center of the Euthrox community, the group carried the drugged girl back to the Octivalin estate, with Vourden explaining to anyone who happened to pause and look, that they were conducting official business on behalf of Lady Eisley. By the time they reached the house, the girl was heavily under the control of the tincture provided by Orota, even her eyes were glazed over in a delirious stupor.

"We have a problem," Vourden spoke upon seeing the slithzerkai cleaning the kitchen.

Urna turned, glanced at the girl being carried like a sack of grain over the shoulder of Halvene, then focused her eyes on the justiciar. "Do I dare ask?"

"She wants to kill the faerie that created her," the man stated, before gesturing for the larger guard to drop the girl in the same room with Kendira.

The reptilian woman nodded her understanding of the situation. "That does complicate a few things, doesn't it?"

Following Orota and Bies, Vourden planted himself among the pillows gathered near the hearth. He freed his feet from his road-weathered boots and loosened his black leather jerkin before letting out a sigh of relief. From a pocket on the front of his worn green tunic, the justiciar produced a thin cigar, and after lighting it with a twig pulled from the low fire, took a long drag. He would've enjoyed a decent drink of whiskey or brandy, but Vourden didn't know if he had the energy to fetch the bottle in the old knapsack he brought with him.

Only a few months prior, he was enjoying life with his wife, waiting for the arrival of their first child. Things were calm and peaceful. He knew what each day would bring back then, and he missed it. He wanted it all back. Then Dorho showed up with the Sidhe-Vein, and his life had been turned upside down.

The justiciar found himself wondering if the girl was worth all the trouble they were putting into keeping her safe. Maybe, the best option would've been for Lady Eisley and himself to ignore the actions of King Borlhauf's men when they first captured the girl? Would the war for independence have started? Would Paisley still be alive to help him raise their son? For a moment, while he smoked the cigar, he understood the emotional confusion going on within Lynsia. She had just as many questions as he did, and wondered similar things about herself.

Except she wanted to undo her own creation. She regretted her life. Vourden had seen that in the girl when they first met. The allies of Elgrahm Hold wanted to save the girl, while the Onyx Spire and King Borlhauf wanted to use the girl, but in the end, Lynsia simply wanted to die to prevent further tragedies.

"Should we execute her?" Vourden asked as he noticed Halvene's return to the home's main room. "She wants to undo everything the faerie did and end her life. Would that solve any problems?"

Orota blinked before looking over the justiciar with a bewildered expression. "You're the sheriff of this land," she spoke up, "and you're asking if we are okay with murdering that girl? Did I just hear you right?"

"Dorho fought like hell to protect her, and his wife worked hard to get Lynsia this far," Urna commented as she brought over a platter holding mugs of herbal tea stirred with cream and honey. "It would be a shame to let all that progress fall through."

"I'm not opposed to the idea," Halvene spoke abruptly. "I won't lie, I never liked the girl. She's been far more trouble than she's worth since she first came to Kaenaan, and now, Ansha's been captured by the Onyx Spire. I was hired to protect the Caldavos family, and without that girl, Ansha and her father would still be safe in their manor."

"Since Dorho brought her back to Elgrahm Hold," Vourden sighed heavily as he recounted the events in his mind, "I've lost my wife, almost lost my son, and almost died a few times myself. Let's not forget about everyone lost during the attack on the castle. Dorho was killed, his wife is now a hostage, and war disrupts the lives of the citizens I swore to protect. Wouldn't granting her wish for death end the list of tragedies?"

Urna shook her head. "She's innocent in all of this. Yes, the Onyx Spire hunting her has created a long list of trouble for everyone involved, but we can't take out our frustration on her for it."

"You lost your husband, your business, your entire life," Vourden said as he took one of the mugs of tea, "all because that girl fell into your tavern in Kaenaan. What would you give to have it all back?"

The reptilian woman took a deep breath, handing Orota another of the mugs before answering the justiciar. "There's not an hour that goes by where I don't think about my losses, but one cannot change the past. It's exactly that, the past, and nothing can change it. I would love to have it all back, but there's not a damned thing I can do about it. I need to focus on pushing forward and getting justice for the wrongs that were done to me. Murdering that girl won't change the past, Vourden. Your wife will still be dead, and Lady Eisley's land will still be torn apart with war."

Vourden found himself taking a few heavy breaths to prevent himself from losing his temper with the woman as she spoke so casually about the death of his wife.

"It would prevent future problems," Halvene offered. "We can't fix the past, but we can prevent future events. I'm okay with putting an end to the girl, if it means peace slowly returns to the world. What is one life when compared to the lives of everyone who will be affected by her existence?"

"So you would sacrifice that one girl," Orota looked at the two men suspiciously, "for the sake of the future?"

"Why not?" Vourden answered coldly.

"Why not?" Urna responded after giving a mug of tea to Halvene. "Because the Onyx Spire won't forgive you. They want that girl, and they were willing to get involved in a war to get their way. Killing her may stop their plans, but it will only enrage them. The Onyx Spire would not let you forget that you dared to cross them and ruin whatever they have planned. They will shift their focus to you and everyone you care about."

Vourden shrugged. "I don't see how that changes the danger we're already in, but at least then we could face their threat as a proper enemy, with the full knowledge they intend to destroy us. We can stop skirting around their antics like frightened dogs, and face them directly."

Urna sipped from her own mug as she took a seat between Halvene and Vourden. "That doesn't change the fact that they still have Ansha, and that I fully intend to repay them for what they did to the Rock Chaser. Killing the girl and going to war against the Onyx Spire doesn't undo the things they've already done, only gives them the opportunity to be rather blatant with their intentions against you. They would spare nothing in their reach to grab you."

"Then what would you do?" Halvene inquired.

"As frustrating as it is," the reptile scanned the larger man carefully with her chartreuse eyes, "I would protect that girl. Keep her alive, and use her against the Spire. She has an extremely potent magic within her, one that the Spire needs for some reason. I would take her to the faerie and let I'raha do whatever it is she needs to do with the girl, then unleash her full potential against the Onyx Spire."

"Assuming she survives being a Catalyst, correct?" Vourden tilted his brow with intrigue.

"While we can't prevent her current state as a Catalyst," Urna replied with a hefty sigh, "we can take her to the faerie, and hope I'raha has a solution that puts the girl's magic in sync with her physical body."

"Dorho was supposed to drop the girl in Euthrox and return to Kaenaan," Halvene interrupted. "What ever happened to that plan? How did this become a babysitting endeavor where we're taking that troublesome girl to meet a faerie?"

Vourden chuckled, despite the seriousness of the discussion. "Dorho's a good man, that's what happened. He wanted to make sure the girl was safe, and knew how to use her magic properly. The rest of us got dragged along for the ride, and now we're the ones holding up the mission because we're a bunch of loyal idiots who refuse to let his dream die."

"So if we execute the girl," Halvene gave a sideways glance to the justiciar, "we can just engage in an all-out war against the Onyx Spire, and forgo this entire mess of a quest? Seems like the more direct path, if you were to ask me."

"Agreed," Vourden nodded slightly, while looking over to the bedroom door to ensure Lynsia wasn't listening in like she had before.

"Sheriff," Orota called from where she was seated on the other side of Halvene. "Could you bring yourself to murdering that girl? That's what I want to know. Do you have the cold, heartless ability to slit the throat of the girl Kendira loves so much? Can you honestly draw your blade against the Sidhe-Vein, and still respect yourself as an official of Lady Eisley's law? Or, do you want me to turn my back as the man who harassed the Den for years commits such a heinous act?"

And there it was, the truth spoken by the leader of a band of murderers and thieves. Vourden knew he couldn't murder the girl. Not only did he hold a respected position in Elgrahm Hold, but he wanted to keep Dorho's goal alive. He knew if he allowed himself to succumb to such thoughts as killing Lynsia, he would be tarnishing his badge of office, and letting his good friend down. Failing Dorho would be the harder blow to handle, and the justiciar knew it, even if he didn't want to openly admit it. Vourden had made a promise to Dorho, and gave that same promise to Ansha when her husband was killed, that he would do everything in his power to help them reach their goal.

"Thank you, Orota," Vourden spoke up after thinking over her words carefully. "I needed that."

The burly woman nodded. "I've lived around murderers, liars, and thieves since joining the Den of Red Venom. I've seen what it takes to end a life without provocation, and you don't have it in you."

"I know," the justiciar said with a thoughtful sigh.

"This one, on the other hand," Orota gestured towards Halvene as she spoke, "wouldn't break a sweat beating the girl with a rock without so much as a second thought."

"What does that mean?" Halvene scoffed, startled by the words of the northern woman.

"I've seen you training around the castle," she smirked coyly before standing up and offering her hand to the larger man. "Come on, put those muscles and anger to work."

Halvene took the hand carefully as he stood up. "You want to spar or something? Can't it wait? We just got back from chasing that girl."

"Or something," Orota laughed deeply. "I've spent over a week in a wagon with a bunch of soft southern girls talking about their men, been blasted by vile magic, and was forced to chase a girl through the fields today. I need to work through some aggression," she suddenly pointed to Vourden, "and he's taken by the bard."

"Don't scream for help, Halvene," Vourden chuckled, "no one will come to your aid."

Once Orota had essentially dragged Halvene out to the wagon, Vourden ran his left hand through the fur of Bies, who had curled up next to his hip. His mind wandered back to the issues regarding Lynsia and the journey as a whole.

"You clearly know more about magic than I do, Urna," the justiciar stated calmly as he took a slow pull from his cigar. "Do you mind explaining the Catalyst thing to me? How do we keep her from putting herself, and us, in danger?"

Urna took a long drink from her mug as her reptilian tail wrapped about her waist, gimlet eyes lost in thought as she scanned over the man for a moment.

"I'm feeling lost in all of this," Vourden said in the silence as he waited for Urna to decide what to tell him, "and I'm not even recovered from losing Paisley yet. I'm supposed to be a symbol of law and order in this land, and here I sit, drinking tea in the home of a girl whose family was murdered, and I did nothing to prevent it. Now that girl has turned into some kind of magic-fueled demon, and I don't know what I'm supposed to do in all of this. Dorho and Ansha, who brought this mission to my door, have both been taken by enemies that would see Elgrahm Hold reduced to ash. You tell me that we have a duty to protect Lynsia, to keep her out of the hands of the Onyx Spire, only because you desire to use her as a weapon yourself. Where do we draw the line between acceptable loss and honorable duty? I feel like we're all being devoured by a mess of chaos, madness, evil, and absolute darkness, and we're just fighting an impossible battle."

"Vourden," Urna finally spoke up as she set her mug upon the floor at her feet, "there is nothing I can say or do that will ease your burdens. If you want someone to be kind, and tell you it will be fine, then you need to look elsewhere, because I will only be honest with you. There are pawns and schemes being moved and played with that I can't even begin to warn you about properly, because I don't know what Nadriah has planned. If I had known when Lynsia first appeared at the Rock Chaser, that she would cause this much trouble and tragedy, I would've ended her life then, before it dragged so many of us into the web of the Onyx Spire. Now, it's too late. We're involved, and we're on the Spire's list of targets. Our only choice now is to fight against the waters of the dark river we find ourselves in. I fear what we've seen so far is only a minor taste of the hell that awaits us, and I dread even thinking about what will happen if we fail."

"So, tell me everything you know about Catalysts and magic," the man requested with a heavy sigh. "Maybe that will help us get an idea of how to approach our biggest problem."

"I can do that," the reptilian woman nodded with confidence. "But this is in no way, a lesson on how to use it."

Vourden took another pull from the cigar and gracefully flicked the smoldering remains into the hearth. "I don't care to learn how to use it. Unlike Dorho, I don't dislike magic-users, I just don't trust magic itself. It's a strange concept to me, and frankly, it's always sounded outright diabolical."

Urna managed a small, wry smile at the comments from the justiciar. "Then I will begin by telling you there are three types of magic. First, there is divine power, which is pulled from a connection to the gods and their realms. Second, we have natural magic, which is drawn from a strong link to nature and the energy of the world. Finally, there is arcane magic, which is what you would consider diabolical, as it comes from a person's own internal energy and channeled through a foci. Arcane magic can take many forms, but at its core, it is driven by the willpower and soul of the user. Our Sidhe-Vein is able to channel the magic of the faerie that created her, which is a form of natural power, while your beloved bard pulls power from her spirit, through the foci in those bracelets, to use her arcane magic. Healers tend to draw from a connection to Atheia, which would make their magic have a divine source."

"I think I understand," Vourden responded, gently petting the larscot sleeping next to him.

The reptilian woman sipped quietly upon her tea before speaking again. "But it is not the blessing some people think it is. The ability to use magic comes with a price. It's like a parasite pretending to be a symbiotic entity. Like running, climbing, fighting, or anything else you do, the use of magic consumes energy. It needs fuel to work. Usually it just draws from the host's mental focus or physical endurance, but if pushed too far, it can actually devour the physical body of the magic-user. Everyone is different, some with abilities to use different magnitudes of magic, and some can tolerate more of the power's feeding upon them than others. It is a balancing game, where one needs to figure out how much you're willing to feed the parasite in order to get the desired results."

"Dorho and yourself," the woman continued, "aren't exactly in harmony with the energy required to use magic. It only manifested in Dorho once he came in contact with I'raha; she forced it to awaken within him, but she didn't take the time to train him how to use it properly. His rapier was his foci, giving him a way to channel the natural magic from his body. It's also more likely to manifest freely in women than men, some like to joke that it is because women tend to be less logical creatures, but don't let that fool you into thinking men can't become formidable wielders of magic, either. Plenty of men have become dangerous spell-casters, there's just a difference between females and males that makes the parasite more likely to find a home in a woman's body."

"Kind of makes me feel relieved that it would rather take you than me," Vourden said with a small smile.

"Oh hush," Urna smirked. "It's not all sunshine and butterflies, you know."

The justiciar snickered lightly. "So far, I've not seen any sunshine and butterflies, just death and destruction."

Urna nodded as her chartreuse eyes glanced over the man slowly. "Sadly, that tends to be the truth and the final end for most of those cursed with the parasite known as magic."

"How does Lynsia being a Catalyst factor into all this?" Vourden inquired with a heavy sigh.

The lizard woman stretched out upon the cluster of pillows by the hearth, her gaze shifting to watch the dancing flames that ate at the offered chunks of birch. "Sometimes, when a person has an incredibly high tolerance for the abuse that using magic requires, they reach a point where they have to fight the parasite for control of their body. Basically, their power has become a mighty python, wrapping around their heart, soul, and mind with its full strength, seeking to become the master of the body. If someone reaches this point, they are living on a dangerous edge, as I described earlier. If they fall one way, the magic will destroy them absolutely, but if they manage to wrangle this fully unleashed level of power, they can become a truly horrific powerhouse among legendary spell-casters."

"So, we need to help her reign in her runaway power?" Vourden asked as he ruffled the fur behind Bies' ears.

"Indeed," Urna spoke intently, "because if we don't, who knows what her next blast of magic will do. She tore apart a dreadmage and turned him into a burnt husk. Even I would've had trouble getting through that creature's magical defenses. I also doubt Dorho could've done it on his own. Her magic is untamed, unrestrained, and now it's boiling under her skin at full strength. If not for Kendira absorbing the power through their connection and her own magic, likely we would've all been killed this morning."

The woman sighed before continuing the discussion. "That girl has become a Catalyst. She's on the cusp of either total self-annihilation, or becoming more powerful than we could ever imagine. The Onyx Spire gains a sick thrill by taking talented spell-casters and driving them to the point they become a Catalyst, only to see which way they fall from that ledge. When someone becomes a Catalyst, they can change, often so drastically they appear to be a different person, but in truth they are just struggling to control themselves and the power that threatens to rip them apart. They become irrational, desperate, and frequently allow the magic to guide their actions. Nadriah would love nothing more than to have a Sidhe-Vein that turned into a Catalyst under her control. No wonder she's willing to go to such ridiculous lengths to get the girl. In this aspect, I do sympathize with Lynsia."

"You sympathize with her?" Vourden tilted his head. "Why?"

"Poor Lynsia has no choice in any of this," Urna answered without delay. "She was created to help heal her father's broken heart, and that creation put her on this path. In a way, I understand her rage aimed at the faerie. Maybe for her, and the sake of the entire world, it would have been best if the faerie hadn't created her. Although, now it's too late to argue such things. She was given life, the Onyx Spire found out about her, Nadriah got her hands on King Borlhauf, and here we are. She had no say in her creation, and she's not been given much of a say in how she lives her life, but as long as she's with us, she'll be free from the Onyx Spire."

"And you think," the man rubbed his chin thoughtfully, "if we gave into her wish, and executed her, that wouldn't end our troubles?"

Urna shook her head slowly. "It might make things easier to handle, but in the end, it wouldn't fix things.

Nadriah will only focus all her fury onto those who ruined her schemes, because I can guarantee that whatever she has planned, it wasn't cooked up overnight in a drunken haze. You wouldn't be cutting a man's purse and running away, you'd be burning down his house and robbing his business at the same time. The Onyx Spire wouldn't have dedicated so many resources and made such an effort to capture this girl, if they were willing to just let her get pulled out of their grasp. Plus, if we can get I'raha to help Lynsia, we might be able to turn the tides against the Onyx Spire, get Ansha back, and take revenge for everyone they've ever crossed."

"We prevent her becoming a weapon for the Onyx Spire," Vourden smirked at the thought in his head, "only to use her as a weapon ourselves? Talk about irony."

Urna shrugged. "The girl's fate was sealed when she was made. If she had remained undiscovered by the Onyx Spire, things might've been different, but as things are now, her only choice is to decide who she wants to fight for. For some reason, Nadriah found out about the Sidhe-Vein, and built an entire campaign to take possession of the girl. I've not been a part of the Onyx Spire for years now, but Nadriah wouldn't have made these moves unless she had a plan to use the girl's powers for something terrible. I don't know about you, but I don't plan on finding out what those plans are."

"I don't want to find out, either," the justiciar commented, looking down at the larscot sleeping against his leg, "but how many more people have to be harmed to keep her alive?"

"As many as it takes," Urna said coldly, as if she had already thought about this long ago. "The Onyx Spire has only ever wanted one thing, absolute total dominance over the land and its people. Surely they've found a way to do that, and it involves that girl, and I don't plan on standing by idly while they run amok. The Spire is long overdue for being turned to a pile of dust and rubble. Whoever that girl decides to side with is going to win this war, and that's the truth of things, Vourden. Killing her would just prolong the destruction, cause more deaths, and allow the Spire to continue to be a malicious cancer in this world."

"But, we could take the fight to them, with an army," Vourden argued.

The reptile shook her head and pulled the blue saystone from one of her pockets, spinning the marked gem in her fingers as she examined the light of the fire through the stone. "What army? Elgrahm Hold is currently at war for their independence, fighting King Borlhauf who has already aligned himself with the Onyx Spire. Your army is already busy in the south. Gathering more allies to march north on the Spire would require time, resources, and personnel that I don't think you can spare right now. If I know this, trust me, Nadriah knows it as well. They don't teach us to be optimistic at the Onyx Spire, just honest and realistic with how we see things."

"Then what would you do?" he questioned peacefully.

"You want someone to give you advice?" Urna tossed the pea-sized gem over to the justiciar. "Talk to the man who started this quest. Dorho is the better adventurer than I am."

Vourden caught the tiny stone deftly, looking over the enchanted trinket for a moment before taking a heavy breath. "So, you're saying he really is alive?"

Again, Urna shrugged. "I won't say he is or not until I see him in the flesh, but I have heard his voice through that stone. Use it, and maybe you'll get the answer you need, to both your questions."

The justiciar held the tiny gem up, thinking about what he would ask Dorho if they were to speak again, when the door to the bedroom was yanked open and slammed shut. Kendira rushed from the room as Vourden and Urna leapt to their feet, seeing the look of sheer panic and disbelief on the woman's face. The bard's cheeks were stained with a cascade of tears, her feet carrying her swiftly into the arms of the justiciar.

"What's wrong?" Vourden asked, pulling the bard tightly against his chest in a comforting hug.

No sounds came from her lips as Kendira's mouth twisted in horror and grief. He could tell she wanted to say something, with the way she moved, but there was nothing reaching Vourden's ears. Tenderly, the justiciar ran his hands through the ashen white hair of the woman, unsure of what to say or do as she trembled in his arms.

"I don't think she can talk," Urna spoke up, cautiously drawing closer to where Vourden stood with the other woman in his arms.

Kendira grasped at her throat, and then clawed at her ears furiously. Tears poured down her face as she took a step back and collapsed to her knees upon the pillows by the hearth. Vourden dropped down next to the frightened bard and grabbed her hands before she ripped her own ears from her skull. The shock in his eyes at her behavior mirrored the pure terror on the woman's face when she threw herself into his arms once more.

Urna slowly lowered herself to her haunches a few steps away as she watched the justiciar and the bard. "Something's terribly amiss. What is it?"

Vourden could feel his own tears forming at the edges of his eyes while he held onto the bard tightly. "She's done as a bard," he said with the heavy weight of sorrow in his voice.

The reptilian woman sighed and hesitantly reached out to put a hand on the back of Vourden's left shoulder. "I'm sorry," she offered solemnly.

The justiciar tried his hardest to fight back the emotions that tore through his heart as he felt the woman weeping against his chest. "She can't hear you," Vourden finally said, keeping Kendira's hands away from her ears and throat. "She's deaf and mute."

19.

Nadriah walked through the smoldering ruins of the tavern as Revenant looked on with a prideful smile. White walls of granite and limestone had been turned to slabs of rubble under the fury of her minions. Blood and burnt streaks stained the ground under her feet as she strolled in a lightweight ebony dress that fit loosely to the curves of her young figure.

"You did great, Revenant," she said with a dark smile. "Who knew you could plan this out?"

Wearing a set of black armor forged from dragon scales, and covered by a hooded leather cloak, the monster lurked a few steps behind its creator. "I only do as you desire, High Tzar. You wanted me to pursue the Seal of Ourixys, and we are pushing south into the Galensteil Wastes to secure your treasure."

Nadriah laughed softly, picked up a severed arm from a table near the bar, and jabbed her monster's chest with the limp fingers. "But, to use the royal family's wedding as a distraction? That's devilish. You even managed to kill the king, I hear."

"By attacking the wedding, they were forced to pull their forces towards the capitol," Revenant spoke though its gravelly, genderless voice. "With the madness drawing the attention of the royal family and their soldiers, we punched through their border like it was nothing. We lost a few underlings in the attack, but it was worth it."

"Well worth it," the High Tzar smirked before tossing the arm aside. "I knew keeping you around would prove beneficial to me."

"I am honored by your words, High Tzar," Revenant bowed slightly.

Just as Nadriah turned to leave, two of King Borlhauf's soldiers appeared, clutching a tall, curvy, redheaded woman. The High Tzar could tell that this woman didn't shy away from a good meal or hard labor, but her teal eyes were filled with rage and fear upon seeing Nadriah and the monster. Her short-sleeved, jade-colored tunic was ripped down the left side, and her navy blue skirt was stained with soot and dirt, clear signs of the struggle she had hiding from Revenant's forces.

"Ya'll are monsters!" the woman screamed, her voice torn by pure fury.

"We're monsters?" Nadriah turned slightly to face the woman, a small smile crossing her lips as she spoke.

The woman twisted and pulled against the men holding her arms behind her back, but couldn't free herself. "Let me go! I don't have a thing fer ya! Yer monsters already trashed our tavern!"

Without hesitation, the woman spat at the High Tzar. Like a protective hound, Revenant rushed forward, but froze immediately when Nadriah put her hand up.

"Let her go," Nadriah ordered, the smile on her face seeming to ignore the spit that landed on her dress.

The two soldiers glanced at one another, then nodded to the High Tzar before releasing the woman.

"Tell me your name," Nadriah demanded as her obsidian eyes scanned over the redheaded woman before her.

"Go ta hell!" the woman shouted, backing away from the High Tzar and the others. "Ya'll are filthy monsters!"

Nadriah looked over to where Revenant stood ready to strike the woman down. "Have I not been polite? Did I not ask the soldiers to let her go?"

Revenant's voice was a low growl as the monster replied, "she should learn to respect you, High Tzar."

The High Tzar nodded before turning back to the woman who was several steps away already. "I am High Tzar Nadriah of the Onyx Spire, I apologize, as I should have introduced myself first. You have no reason to fear us, woman."

"Stuff it," the woman snarled, "ya'll destroyed my home."

Again, Nadriah glanced to Revenant and shrugged. "I thought I was being polite, and she chooses rudeness."

"Rudeness?" the woman gestured to the ruined tavern around her. "Ya'll want ta teach me about rudeness?"

Nadriah sighed her disapproval of the woman's attitude, then pointed her right index finger at the redhead who was still slowly backing away. "Then I will teach you about Xa'morhu, instead, vile human."

An explosion of blackness swirled around the flesh of the woman, who shrieked in terror, but only for a brief instant. As if she had been pulled apart by millions of invisible ropes, the entire body of the woman buckled, yanked violently into a swirling black ball where her chest had once been. Nadriah opened her right hand, then immediately clenched it into a tight fist, and her divine magic forced the apple-sized orb of darkness to detonate sadistically. Blood sprayed through the air from the lightless blast as wisps of black magic blew through the ruined structure like flying snakes. While a wicked smile formed on the green-painted lips of the High Tzar, the threads of dark energy became absorbed into her body, drawing a pleased breath from her lungs as she embraced the rush of the Xa'morhu's power through her flesh.

"By the gods," one of the soldiers muttered, shocked by the blatant display of power.

"So, that's the High Tzar's power?" the other asked, putting a bit more distance between himself and the members of the Onyx Spire.

Nadriah shook her head. "That's not my power. That was merely a miniscule fraction of my goddess' power, which she allows me to borrow."

Without further explanation, the High Tzar left the broken husk of the tavern, ignoring the droplets of blood that had splattered across her face. Behind her, Revenant followed, like a hulking sentinel eager to protect a dainty princess. Through the streets of the town, they walked, examining the destruction that had befallen the residents and their pathetic attempts to defend themselves. Countless bodies were broken and bloodied in the streets, though some had been impaled and left on display by the minions of the

Onyx Spire, creating a grisly reminder for anyone else who dared to challenge the High Tzar or her followers. Buildings had been recklessly destroyed, leaving no structure unscathed from the one-sided battle that had been fought through the streets of the town.

From the southern gates of the town, they wandered, following the path of terror and death the army had left through Anslater. The evening was growing late, and the breeze over the grain fields filled the air with a warm, welcoming scent, mixed with the distinct aroma of warfare. Mages and darkoyles from the Onyx Spire offered their respectful greetings to the High Tzar, even if they were stunned to see Nadriah visiting the war-ravaged land. Other monsters, most of them created or summoned by the minions of the Spire, simply watched as the youthful figure and the lumbering Revenant strolled by. Soldiers sent by King Borlhauf, dressed in their scarlet surcoats, paused to bow to Revenant, though most had no idea who Nadriah was, as she only visited with the monster on special occasions.

She felt today was special enough, though. With Vansenhul distracted by the chaos unleashed by the attack on their royal family, Revenant and the army were able to punch through the border and take the town of Petiora. It was a key victory in what was to be a string of defeats for the kingdom of Anslater. They had shown both King Galheam and King Borlhauf what the Onyx Spire was capable of, and left no doubt in what they intended to do now that they were here.

On a hill surrounded by various fields of grain, a large house sat next to a barn engulfed in a hellish inferno. Nihilings, scrawny creatures that looked like malnourished gnomes with black, bark-like skin and the faces of pit vipers, scurried around the property, chasing a woman and her children. A group of four crimson-clad soldiers held an older man at the end of their spears, laughing at the antics of the Onyx Spire's minions.

"I am Nadriah, the High Tzar of the Onyx Spire," the youthful mage called as she moved in front of the old farmer. "Might I know who we have captured?"

"I own this farm," the old man stammered through the fear and sadness that was shown on his face. "I am Jonsal Knepiri. Please, let my family go. I'll do whatever you ask."

"Whatever I ask?" Nadriah tapped the fingers of her left hand against her chin as her solid black eyes scanned over the man carefully. "Now what would I want with an old farmer? The children, however, have promise. Can I have them, if I spare you and your wife?"

"What kind of monster are you?" Jonsal protested, narrowing his gaze dangerously at the High Tzar. "Seriously, you cannot expect me to give up my own children. That's insane."

"Again, with the monster business," the young-looking mage shook her head. "I am offering you a chance to escape. All you have to do is let me send your children to the Onyx Spire. You can always make more."

"And if I refuse?" Jonsal growled, though he was seated against a barrel with his arms and chest bound to the cask with tight cords.

Nadriah shrugged, glancing from the man, to Revenant, then back to the man. "Then I will allow my companion here to kill everyone on this farm in any manner it sees fit."

Jonsal snarled and fought to get to his feet, but a jab from one of the spears against his right side kept him seated. "Afraid to get your own hands dirty? Do you always send your pets to do your dirty work?"

The High Tzar watched the Nihilings chasing the rest of the family off to her left, and without a single breath of hesitation, raised her right hand out in front of herself. She closed her eyes momentarily, whispered a prayer to Xa'morhu, and snapped her fingers. Screams of pain filled her ears, but only for a brief instant as the woman and children exploded cruelly into what appeared to be a cloud of black ash and blood. The Nihilings cheered and hollered their praise for the High Tzar, while the evening wind carried the scarlet mist and flakes of dark ash to where Nadriah stood with the bound farmer.

"They did nothing to you!" Jonsal wailed, tears of grief and rage filling his eyes. "They were innocent! How can you do that?"

"Simple," Nadriah replied with a neutral smile on her face, "I gave you the chance to save everyone here, and you chose to forsake them all out of selfishness. I ended their suffering by snuffing out their mortality. Now, you no longer have to worry about them."

"Then kill me too," Jonsal cried as he slumped against the barrel helplessly. "You might as well, you damned monster."

"Monster?" the High Tzar knelt down to look into the old man's eyes. "I offered you mercy, and you declined. Who is the real monster here? I only ended their misery because you refused to save them."

Footsteps rushed towards the group near the farmhouse, drawing Nadriah's attention away from the old man. Two Nihilings and two of the red-garbed soldiers nearly slid to a stop only a short distance from the High Tzar and Revenant, giving both a respectful bow.

"What is it?" Nadriah asked, straightening her posture as she examined the men winded from their run.

"Reinforcements from Vansenhul," one of the soldiers spoke purposefully and confidently. "They'll be here within an hour."

"How many?" Revenant inquired, his movements seeming to radiate his excitement for more battle.

"At least three hundred cavalry, two hundred archers, and two hundred heavily armored infantry," the soldier reported.

Nadriah turned slowly to look at Revenant with a smile. "Took them long enough to respond, but the majority of our forces have already moved south to push into the Galensteil Wastes. Will this be a problem, childe?"

"Not at all, High Tzar," Revenant replied without delay. "We might only have a couple hundred remaining in Petiora, but that is more than enough to crush those soldiers."

The youthful mage nodded with a wry smirk as she turned to the farmer once more. "You might be useful still, old man."

"Go to hell," Jonsal growled furiously. "You really think I'm going to help you?"

Nadriah shook her head and brushed her hands over the man's face in a mocking gesture. "This time, I'm not giving you a choice," she spoke before turning to Revenant with a wicked grin on her verdant lips. "Do you have any explosives left with this group?"

20.

Dorho, Jolson, and Lorvin rode out with the army as soon as they heard about the attack on Petiora. Corina and several others had been stationed in Wayfarer's Folly to treat any wounded that returned from the expedition to the town. Lorvin stayed high in the evening sky on the back of Kortyx, watching the road ahead of the main force, while Dorho and Jolson rode between the cavalry and archers.

The rogue had been preparing to join Lorvin in heading to the druids when the news of the attack reached the throne room. Jolson insisted that they ride with him and the army, plus Cerulla refused to let her husband leave the castle unless Dorho acted as his escort. No one in the castle wanted the new king to head into battle, but the man insisted, claiming it was his duty as a paladin of justice and a soldier of the kingdom. For Dorho, it meant facing the Onyx Spire again, after only barely surviving an encounter with their minions a few days before. The healers and Corina had done their best after the assault on the royal family, but no one had completely recovered from the attack, and Dorho could feel the tension, anxiety, and desperation radiating from everyone around him in the formation.

From what Dorho had heard, after two attacks on the capitol city, forces were pulled back to provide better defense for the castle and the royal family. This knee-jerk reaction from the generals left the front lines and borders gravely understaffed, and King Borlhauf's army, supported by the Onyx Spire, was able to punch through like a lance. It was the distraction and reaction that their enemies had been expecting, and they took the chance to pounce when their target was already weakened and frightened.

Now, as the smoldering town of Petiora came into view, Dorho could feel a heavy weight upon his chest as he felt they were just riding into a trap. What choice did Vansenhul have, though? He wondered. The town was attacked, and the military was expected to respond quickly. Jolson hoped that the majority of the Spire's forces would've left soon after the assault, leaving only a basic rear guard behind, allowing the Anslater army the chance to cut off the enemy's supply route. Sadly, with his experiences with fighting against the forces of the Onyx Spire, Dorho felt the enemy would anticipate this reaction, and be prepared. He knew they were a diabolical group with zero remorse, but they weren't stupid, either. Unfortunately, his protests had gone ignored, mostly because he didn't have a decent alternative plan.

In truth, he wanted to ignore the attack completely, and try to get ahead of the Onyx Spire and whatever goal they had in mind. For the rogue, heading to Petiora was like stepping backwards in a vain attempt to get the upper hand on a cunning enemy. Originally, he and Lorvin were going to fly to the druids with Kortyx, then head south to the Galensteil Wastes to try and reach the Seal of Ourixys first. He didn't care about the warnings regarding the World of Glass, Dorho just had to try to finally get a step ahead of the Onyx Spire.

A voice cried out through the warm summer air, causing several men to glance towards the farm on the hill south of town.

"Did you hear that?" Jolson asked, pulling his steed closer to the rogue's.

Dorho nodded. "That's the Knepiri Farm, it's the home of Corina's family. We should probably check it out. She would want to know what happened here, but I don't expect to find anything good."

Jolson agreed silently, then ordered one of the commanders to take a group over to the farm. Dorho broke away with the commander's group of twenty infantry and twelve archers, following them up to the flaming remains of the barn. It didn't take them long to spot Jonsal tied to a barrel near the main entrance of the house. The old man was squirming and trying to stand up, but the cords around his chest and arms kept him tightly bound to the cask.

"No, don't come near!" Jonsal begged, spotting the soldiers drawing close with their horses.

"Tell me," Dorho slid off his horse and slowly approached the old farmer, "what happened here, Jonsal?"

"Is my daughter safe?" the farmer demanded, pain and terror filling his eyes with fresh tears.

Dorho offered a kind smile. "Yes, she's perfectly fine. She's waiting for you in Wayfarer's Folly. Let's get you out of here."

The commander and five of his soldiers walked towards the old farmer, who only grew more frantic as the men from Vansenhul drew near.

"No!" Jonsal shouted. "It's a—."

But it was too late. Dorho was thrown like a doll through the air as the barrel exploded with a mighty blast of crimson flames. Anslater's blue-clad soldiers could be heard shrieking in agony and surprise as debris and fire ripped through the ground and air from the terrifying discharge. The entire front of the house had been removed in the explosion, and vile flames licked at the exposed interior as though it were made of hungry parasites. Black smoke and acrid dust filled the evening air with the distinct scent of blood and death.

Jonsal was gone, completely vaporized when the barrel detonated, and the commander and his five men were torn asunder, dead, and spread over the crater like broken toys. The intense ringing in his ears, and the dizzying effects of the vicious blast kept Dorho from hearing the bloodthirsty cheers rising up from the monsters in the town, but his eyes could make out the dark shapes charging the army from Vansenhul. The others that had followed the commander up to the farm were wounded, startled, and scattered from the force of the explosion. Dorho grabbed his hat from where it had landed, then forced himself to his feet with a grimace on his face.

"Are you hurt?" Jolson shouted as he approached Dorho and the others, the first real sound the rogue had heard since the bomb went off.

"I'll live," Dorho grumbled, trying to shake the dizziness from his eyes.

The cavalry from Vansenhul charged the oncoming enemies that poured out of the town of Petiora, while archers let the fury of their crossbows rage against the furthest targets. Following their new king, the infantry swarmed around the destroyed Knepiri Farm, preparing to face the onslaught of anything that broke through the front lines.

She comes for you, a faint whisper echoed through Dorho's mind, and just for a quick moment, he saw an illusion of Dimorta standing before him.

Dorho drew both of his swords in a heartbeat, his dark eyes scanning the terrain around the farm as the visage of death faded from his vision. Though he could tell that the army from Vansenhul outnumbered the enemy forces, he could also sense they were in grave danger. He couldn't explain it with words, but Count Maizen felt like a pair of eyes had been watching him ever since the blast executed Jonsal. It was a familiar feeling, but one he couldn't place exactly with a source.

"Tell your men to withdraw," Dorho requested, moving to stand next to the paladin. "Something feels wrong about this all."

Jolson glanced around the ruined farm, and the enemies tangled with his cavalry. "We have them outnumbered. They might have the benefit of magic and those monsters, but we came here to take this town back."

As Count Maizen prepared to explain his feelings, his eyes watched in horror as the blood splattered around the ground from the explosion began to move. Slowly, it crept along the ground, as though the crimson liquid was being pulled from the soil itself and drawn into thin streams. Where the old farmer once sat, the fluid was pulled into a pool that shimmered and rippled while more blood oozed out of the ground and into the tiny streams feeding the puddle.

"We need to get back," Dorho pulled on the king's armor urgently.

"Infantry," King Jolson ordered upon seeing the movement of the blood on the ground, "fall back!"

A vicious detonation sent the pooled blood into the air in a fine mist, spraying everyone who stood around the farm with the crimson of the fallen. From the center of the cloud of blood, a burst of vile red flames swirled and died in an instant, leaving two figures standing where the farmer had died.

One was a hulking behemoth of a man, or it might have been made from several men, Dorho assumed. It was a monster of impressive size, and from what he could see through gaps in the armor and cloak, was a patchwork of different types of flesh held together with a dark metal. Milky eyes the shade of dusty emeralds peered out from under a cowl of dark leather. Under the cloak, Dorho could clearly spot the armor forged from reptilian scales that glistened in the evening light.

Next to the monstrosity stood a girl who looked no more than sixteen summers in age. She was petite and lean, with a young face framed with braided hair like strands of midnight. Eyes, like a pair of polished obsidian orbs, were a stark contrast to the ashen skin as they peered over those sent from Vansenhul. Her green-stained lips, thin and dainty, curled into a wicked smile while she stepped towards Dorho first.

"Hold on," the growling, genderless voice of the monster called out as the bloody mist settled upon the ground. "I know this one. He died in Ameribelle."

The girl paused her movements, turned to the looming creature behind her, flashed a sly grin, and took three more steps towards the rogue. "Is that so? I am High Tzar Nadriah of the Onyx Spire. Do you have a name, mortal?"

The sounds of the nearby battle seemed to fade away as Dorho looked upon the petite girl. She could easily be mistaken for a child, and for a moment, he didn't want to believe that the person standing before him was the most powerful mage in the Spire.

"I'm Count Dorho Maizen," the rogue answered, putting one of his swords between himself and the High Tzar.

"Count Dorho Maizen?" the girl tilted her head curiously, then reached out and poked the tip of his sword with her right index finger. "Any relation to a Countess Ansha Maizen?"

Dorho lunged purely out of instinct, but the girl vanished in less time than it took him to blink. He slid to a stop only a couple steps from the hulking monstrosity that had appeared with the girl.

"I killed you once," the voice, like dozens of people crushed into a single sound, called to the rogue from the fiend.

"Well, I don't remember you," Count Maizen proclaimed, jumping away from the black-clad creature.

Red fire erupted from the fingers of the massive constructed man, forming a weapon resembling a two-handed mining pick reinforced for combat. As the flames dispersed into the air around the behemoth, runes etched into the curved spike of the weapon flickered with an eerie amber light. The monster's pale eyes gazed over the rogue before it took a step forward and vanished into a burst of crimson light.

"Dorho!" Jolson shouted, summoning his glaive from the faerie's magic as he had done on the streets of Vansenhul.

The ground under the rogue's feet exploded, throwing the count upwards just as he saw the behemoth reappear to his left, and its vicious pick raised and ready to strike. Left sprawling from the eruption under his legs, Dorho could only watch as Jolson rushed the behemoth, blocking the heavy pick with his glaive while simultaneously driving his shoulder into the chest of the vile creature. As the monster staggered backwards from the blow, the king in the reddish-orange armor thrust the glowing tip of the glaive towards the chest of the wretched creation.

Another blast of red fire threw the king aside like he was just a stone thrown by an angry child, though unlike the rogue, Jolson remained standing. Several of the soldiers rushed to their king's aid, weapons drawn as they made to attack the monstrosity with the pick. Dorho leapt to his feet once more, looking around for the girl, wondering where she had taken off to.

The snap of fingers answered the rogue's curiosity faster than he could spot Nadriah with his eyes. Shrieks of pain and howls of shock rose up from the soldiers dressed in the blue surcoats of Anslater, and in an instant, were snuffed out as their bodies were turned to bursts of black ash and blood.

"We didn't call for help," Nadriah explained coldly, stepping out from behind the monstrous creation holding the pick. "Why should you?"

"What kind of creature are you?" Dorho asked, putting himself between the enemies and the king.

Nadriah walked slowly towards the rogue, brushing one of her braids behind her left shoulder while she moved. "I've been nice enough to keep your wife alive, Count Maizen. Surely, you can show me a little more respect than this."

"Respect?" Dorho replied, shocked that she would even suggest such a thing. "You destroy homes, murder innocent people, and you demand that I respect you?"

"Hit me," the girl demanded, standing not even two steps from Count Maizen, her hands behind her back.

"High Tzar," the monster growled from behind her.

She shook her head. "No, it's only fair, Revenant. I've been disrespectful to these people. He should be given the chance to strike me in revenge."

Without pause, Dorho feigned a slice with his left sword, only to thrust with the one in his right hand, aiming for the girl's neck.

For a moment, it felt like time stopped for the rogue, as the High Tzar vanished yet again from his vision. Only, this time, she appeared almost immediately to his right, next to his thrusting arm. Nadriah's right hand grasped his wrist, while the fingers of her left hand coiled around Dorho's throat. A blast of entropic darkness filled the senses of the rogue as he was hurled to the ground like a discarded table scrap. The magic burned and coursed through his veins like vile lightning, flooding his eyes with blackness for a brief moment as Nadriah looked on with an eerie grin.

Not my scion, not yet, Dimorta's voice whispered into the corners of Dorho's consciousness as he winced from the sting of magic assaulting his body.

"You lived?" the High Tzar asked, visibly puzzled as she stood over the rogue.

Jolson charged the duo while Dorho crawled back to his feet, taking deep breaths as he pushed back the feeling of having the girl's magic burning through his blood. A reptilian shriek from the heavens filled the war-torn air around the farm, and Kortyx slammed into the towering monster before the paladin could reach it. Wyvern and vile creation tumbled and wrestled as Lorvin's companion dragged the behemoth to the ground with her might. Kortyx pinned the monster with her powerful legs as she attempted to crush it with her jaws, but the creature repeatedly swung with the rune-covered pick, driving the reptile off, but only briefly.

The brass orb of the meteor hammer hurled towards Nadriah, just as Lorvin appeared to Dorho's left. Once more, the girl vanished from view. The ground began to shake, and the sun's light faded as a dark mist swirled up from around Dorho's group. In less time than it took for the trio to breathe, the farm had been taken from their view as the girl's laughter echoed through the churning mess of darkness.

You. You are the scion of death, the whispers of the goddess spilled through the mind of the rogue.

He was supposed to protect Ansha, and now she was captured by the Onyx Spire. He was supposed to protect Lynsia, and now he couldn't even save himself. He once made a promise to protect Breja, and now she was dead. He had made a promise to Jonsal that he'd protect Corina, and now her family was dead, while these monsters roamed freely through her homeland. How many more people did he plan to fail? Dorho clenched his fists as he visited each face he had failed in his mind. He had even told Cerulla he would protect Jolson during this mission to Petiora, and now they were all about to be crushed by the Onyx Spire.

You are my scion of death.

Lorvin had broken out of jail to help him. Vourden had lost his wife in his attempt to help him. Kendira took up her own weapons once more in her desire to help him. Orota had helped him change the path of the Den of Red Venom. Zakosa has been killed in order to keep him and so many others alive. Ansha gave up her gentle life in the manor in order to help his quest. Urna had lost everything that had meaning to her, and still found the strength to join his mission. Corina and the royal family of Anslater had been almost eager to become part of his quest.

You are my scion of death.

What had he done so far? He had brought a cursed girl from Kaenaan to the court of Lady Eisley. Then he died. Dorho had fought so hard, and been through so much, only for everyone he met to pay the price for his inability to protect others and keep promises. He needed to get stronger. He needed to get better.

You are my scion of death, the whispers of Dimorta had turned into a desperate growl in his mind.

He had always been a thief, an assassin, a seeker of the hard-to-find. Count Maizen was the Lord of Rogues, and he had never felt like a job was too much for him, but this was different. This wasn't just a normal job. It wasn't simply taking a trinket from one man and giving it to another for a hefty profit. Sure, it had started out as a simple request to take Lynsia back home, which was beyond easy, but it had become something much more. Lives had been lost, lives had been changed, entire nations were at war, and for once, there was much more on the line than simply being branded a thief or murderer if he failed. It wasn't a client counting on him to succeed, but it felt like the entire world was watching him, waiting with nervous breath to see what he could do. If he failed before, he could simply hide for a little while until the heat died down from the law. This mission was vastly different. If he failed, the Onyx Spire would destroy everything.

You are my scion of death, the growls were becoming a commanding voice, mocking him for his weakness.

If he failed, he would be failing Dimorta. The Onyx Spire would grab onto Lynsia and use her to bring back a creature capable of erasing everything. He thought of I'raha and her request to protect Lynsia, and then of Dimorta and her request that he bring an end to the Onyx Spire's plan. They were one and the same. They both wanted him to work against the Spire to keep them from their goals. They both expected him to succeed, but each time he faced the Onyx Spire, he was met with defeat. Lynsia had to save him during the fight with the darkoyle, and he was killed during the attack on Ameribelle. After Dimorta brought him back for her own needs, he only survived the assault on Vansenhul because the faerie sacrificed Zakosa as her weapon. Now here he was, back where he had been returned to life, only to be defeated yet again.

You are my scion of death, the voice was urging him forward, demanding he show the goddess what he was made of.

Dorho had been born from a slave, raised to be nothing more than a slave's child. He had been beaten and abused, harassed and taunted until he found his calling in Kaenaan. There, he became the Lord of Rogues, and met Ansha Caldavos. He made genuine friends there, like Vourden and Kendira, who he considered to be his family. He had gained the respect of several nobles, including Lady Eisley, and became Count Dorho Maizen, sheriff of Golden Bow Gulch in Elgrahm Hold. People were counting on him, and he hadn't come up from nothing only to be beaten back down by the likes of Nadriah and her minions.

You are—

"The scion of death!" Dorho shouted through the darkness that pulsed and swirled around him.

The markings on his right arm surged with heat as his flesh was engulfed in wicked violet flames.

"What did you say?" Jolson spoke cautiously.

"Lorvin," Dorho called loudly, "we need Kortyx. We need to get out of here."

Lorvin nodded, picking up a pebble as he had in Vansenhul, hurling it through the mess of black clouds. The enchanted stone whistled and screamed through the air before exploding with a crack that vibrated through the churning dark energy.

Nadriah appeared again, standing only a handful of steps away. "A scion, you say? That explains quite a lot, honestly."

"I'm done playing your games, bitch," Dorho growled, pointing the sword in his right hand at the figure of the girl.

"Is that so?" the High Tzar tilted her head, making a gesture with her left hand that summoned two hovering spears of vibrating black energy above the youthful mage. "I will forget your rudeness if you agree to join me."

"Why would I do that?" Count Maizen spat.

"Think about it," she mused, "the scions of void and death, working together for a better future. Sounds romantic, doesn't it? Nothing could stop us. We're gods to the pathetic mortals that surround us."

Dorho rushed the girl, prepared to drive the blade of his sword through her chest, but in an instant, he lost. The twin spears flew through the air like black bolts of lightning, striking both Jolson and Lorvin in the chest. Their screams rose through the air as the black clouds lifted from the farm, and as the swirling darkness vanished, so did the rogue's friends. Not even a drop of their blood hit the ground before they were gone, leaving Dorho standing alone, face to face with the High Tzar of the Onyx Spire.

"Pity," she commented, flexing her left hand as the last tendrils of black energy faded into the sky. "Look what happened. I took your friends away. You won't turn me down again, will you?"

"I would rather die than join your side," the rogue tightened his grip on the twin swords.

"So be it," Nadriah shrugged, raising her right hand as she prepared to snap her fingers again, "but die knowing that you had the chance to change the world by my side."

Kortyx swooped in, her skin battered, cut, and bruised as she suddenly yanked Dorho from the ground before she soared over the head of the High Tzar, knocking the petite mage to the ground in the process. As he climbed carefully to the back of the powerful beast, he could hear the laughter of Nadriah following him into the sky. Yet again, he had lived while people he knew paid the price for his failures. The rogue slumped against the back of the flying wyvern, the rush of Dimorta's energy leaving him nearly catatonic and exhausted as it faded from his flesh. In every way he could imagine, he felt defeated.

It was well after dark when the beast landed near the stables in Wayfarer's Folly. Count Maizen nearly fell from the back of the injured creature while Corina and several other military staff rushed to greet him.

"What happened?" Corina asked, her voice rife with concern as she grabbed onto the rogue and held him to her chest.

As he looked into her soft blue eyes, his memories flashed with the explosion that killed her father, the tremendous monster that said it knew him, the disappearance of Lorvin and Jolson, but mostly, he remembered the eerie, callous, malicious look on Nadriah's face. He had to get stronger, and he had to get better, because he was the scion of death, and he had a job to do.

21.

Jolson dropped hard upon the floor built from cobbled together slate slabs while the last fragments of the churning black clouds faded from his view. From all around him, he could hear pitiful cries and painful moans, which mixed with the sounds of metal chains being rattled and iron bars getting slapped with various tools. Lorvin was lying on the ground next to him, clutching his chest in agony, though no wound could be seen. The king remembered being impaled by those ebony spears, but just as quickly the magic projectile had struck his armor, it had vanished and the two of them appeared in this strange location.

"Prince," a weak voice called from behind Jolson while he checked on the naetari monk. "I mean, King Jolson, they got you too? By the gods, how bad have things gotten?"

The paladin turned to face the man, the blacksmith of Petiora, and couldn't even fake a smile with the current situation. "Clearly we didn't die, but things aren't good for us, or our friends back home. Where are we?"

"We're somewhere under the Onyx Spire," the man replied, before gesturing to the other people sitting in small huddled groups around the spherical chamber. "Those of us that were captured were sent here. The vampires have taken a few already for their personal food bags, but most of us are just waiting to be killed."

"Under the Onyx Spire?" Jolson glanced around, noticing there were no windows, and only a single, heavy, dark metal door to the chamber.

"How are you fine?" Lorvin coughed, rolling to his knees slowly as he grabbed at his chest.

Tapping his armor, Jolson smiled weakly as he answered, "this gift from my wife. Because my magic comes from her faerie powers, it reacts badly to iron. So, she had my armor made from orichalcum and had it blessed by the temple I serve. Used in combination with my magic as a Sidhe-Vein, it helps protect me from injuries that should otherwise kill me."

"That was a pain to make," the blacksmith remarked. "Getting the combination of copper, zinc, silver, and adamantium just right wasn't easy, my king."

Despite the situation around them, Jolson chuckled. "I'm sure Cerulla was hard to please with such a task, she can be very precise in her desires. Regardless, you did a great job."

"Your praise means more than you know, my king," the shorter, older man offered a hesitant smile.

"If we're under the Onyx Spire," Lorvin commented, crawling towards the door as he coughed heavily. "We need to try and reach Dorho's wife. Then we can form a plan to get out of here."

"Good to see we think alike, monk," Jolson added, putting a hand to the heavy metallic door. "Luckily, it looks like the magic that brought us here didn't bother to disarm us."

Jolson took a deep breath and began drawing the magic from his core, which flared to life as a faint azure glow to his eyes and skin. Without hesitation, he reared back and drove his heel into the large door. His magic exploded upon impact, rumbling through the solid metal of the door. Like a sneeze to rid itself of problematic dust, the door reacted, blasting the magic back to the paladin, throwing him away like he was unwanted trash.

"I can't believe you thought it would be that easy," Lorvin said as he looked over to where the king landed on his back. "This is a prison under an evil mage's castle."

"Then what's your plan?" Jolson asked, sitting upright gingerly as he gasped from the pain that wracked his legs.

Lorvin brushed his left hand over the door, then glanced at the citizens of Petiora gathered in the wide chamber with himself and the king. "Patience. This wouldn't be my first jailbreak. If you're the aspect of temperance this should be easy for you."

"Being born from temperance, and a paladin of justice," King Jolson stated, watching the feline carefully, "doesn't mean I'm not in a hurry to get out of here. Nor does it mean I'm not furious about being here in the first place."

Lorvin nodded his understanding while he moved to where the blacksmith was seated against the wall of the unlit chamber. "How often does anyone come by? Any routines you might be aware of?"

The blacksmith sighed and pointed to a hole in the ceiling. "Every once in a while, they lower down buckets of questionable water or bowls filled with flavorless gruel. Whenever the vampires come by, they always come with armed escorts to drag away their next victim, but we never know when that will be."

"We don't even know what time of day it is," a woman's voice called with a wrathful tone from a spot farthest from the door.

Jolson grumbled with his frustration as he managed to stand up again. "When we were taken from Petiora, it was evening, if that helps. Though, I doubt the passage of time means anything to the monsters in the Onyx Spire. That girl who sent us here, I get the feeling she's much older than she appears."

"Nadriah?" the woman spoke up again. "Good luck with that one. She's just as cruel as she is kind. Those vampires are her faithful hounds in this place."

"That's Rei Inhala," the blacksmith spoke up, "she was here before any of us from Petiora."

The woman crawled up to where the light that leaked through the slot in the door could reach her, revealing a calico naetari with fierce eyes like twin topaz gems. She was dressed in a battered grey robe, matching knee-length leggings, with a navy purple hooded cloak draped over her body. Even with the loose-fitted clothing, it was easy to tell she was rather slender and petite, but also muscular and rather athletic. Around her neck, a silver choker held a tiny brass gear pierced by a golden hammer, the sigil of Vulkania, the goddess who ruled over flames, forges, and those who built machines.

Even Jolson heard Lorvin catch his breath upon seeing the other feline.

"You're a naetari?" Lorvin inquired, kneeling close to the woman.

"Aye," she answered with a smirk. "When King Borlhauf's emissaries came looking for aid from the Bladed Rumors, my clan opposed their offer. Most of my clan was killed, and those that weren't, were sent here by that vile woman. I haven't seen my other kin for weeks now, as we were split up into different cells here. What clan are you from, ishkafu?"

Lorvin shrugged. "I don't have a clan anymore, asakifu. I'm just a monk of the land. My clan was killed years ago, when I was still small, and I was raised by the monks of Chaydenhall."

Rei scoffed. "Clanless and a monk? You are a naetari with no heritage. Such a shame."

"I don't think any of us are in a position to be prideful, asakifu," Lorvin suggested, sitting cross-legged in front of the other catfolk.

Without warning, and without remorse or hesitation, the female balled up her right fist and struck Lorvin's chin with every ounce of strength she could muster. The monk fell backwards, but quickly sat back up as Rei prepared to strike him again. Jolson rushed forward, swiftly moving to tackle the female naetari to protect the monk.

"No," Lorvin urged, catching the flying fist with his left hand as he gestured for the paladin to halt with his right. "It is not my place to strike an asakifu, therefore I cannot allow you to do the same."

"What?" the king inquired, confused by the statement from the monk. "But she just hit you."

Lorvin sighed as he eased his grip on the woman's fist. "In naetari culture, the males are required to be submissive to the females. They are the creators of the next generation, and should be cherished, protected, and respected as such. It would be improper if I allowed myself or anyone else to harm her in my presence."

"So, you haven't forgotten where you came from," Rei commented before a small smile cracked her lips. "There might be hope for you still, ishkafu. Do you have a name?"

The monk bowed low, placing his hands flat against the slate floor. "I am Lorvin Dendrostone, born from Clan Akothas."

Slowly, the other naetari reached her right hand out, and ran her slender fingers through the fur atop Lorvin's head as she listened to his answer. "Son of Clan Akothas, I am Rei Inhala, from Clan Laak'mah."

"Laak'mah?" Lorvin sat upright again, tilting his head. "Then you're..."

"We were born as enemies, ishkafu," Rei stated coldly, pulling her hand away from his head. "Now, it looks like we must work together."

"Agreed," Jolson spoke up as he examined the rest of the dome-shaped cell they were in, "but I don't really grasp what you two are doing."

Rei stood up slowly, turning her gaze from Lorvin to the paladin instead. "My clan was responsible for exterminating his own, but down here, we cannot afford to be enemies. I will help however I can to get us out of here, if you have a plan."

King Jolson paced around the cell, circling the hole where the blacksmith mentioned food and water was delivered through. His sapphire eyes scanned the walls and door independently, then glanced to where Lorvin still sat upon the slate floor.

The paladin of justice frowned as he finally replied. "I think patience is the best answer here. We need to figure out each person's strengths, and figure out how to best work together in order to free ourselves."

"I'm just a blacksmith," the old man answered quietly. "Unfortunately, I have none of my tools, nor my forge."

"But you still understand metal, correct, Shalltic?" Rei called over as her tail twitched in the damp air of the cell.

The old man laughed darkly. "Well, of course! I might be without my tools, but I still know my trade, Rei."

"And you, asakifu?" Lorvin inquired, standing up next to the female naetari. "What is it you do?"

Rei crossed her arms over her chest as she examined Lorvin carefully through her topaz eyes. "I'm a follower of Vulkania," she flicked the brass trinket dangling from her choker mockingly. "I have a few other skills, but we can discuss those later, ishkafu."

"We have a blacksmith," Jolson commented as he looked over the dozen or so people locked in the cell with him, "a monk, a paladin, and a woman from the church of fire and metal. Do we have any others we can add to this cluster of misfits?"

Lorvin nodded and pointed upwards. "We have a skilled archer if we can reach Countess Maizen."

"We don't even know where she is in this hellish place," Jolson added.

"Then that is our first goal," the king replied with a forced smile.

Rei shook her head. "Correction, our first goal is getting through that door."

"The vampires have been using these people as a food supply, right, asakifu?" Lorvin rubbed his chin as he considered everyone else in the cell.

The other feline nodded. "Indeed, ishkafu. I don't see how that helps us though."

"It helps us plenty," the monk managed a small grin. "They won't want their food battered, beaten, and bruised, or worse."

Jolson narrowed his gaze at the two felines. "Are you suggesting we start a fight in here?"

"Let's work on what we need to do once we get out of this cell," the blacksmith recommended, "but I can see what the cats are plotting already."

Sitting in the dark, away from the door, Jolson gathered several people in the cell as they worked over the scheme in near silence. Lorvin, sitting between the paladin and Rei, was quick to dismiss using magic, as it would draw the attention of the mages in the Onyx Spire. Rei was stern in her assumption that they would be overwhelmed and outnumbered swiftly if they worked too loudly, and would have to stick to small groups operating from the shadows. Through the discussion, and talking individually, it was made obvious to the king that most of the people in the cell were farmers, shopkeepers, and other residents of the town with little to no combat experience.

They had no idea of telling how much time had passed, but eventually a bucket of stagnant water was lowered from the smooth hole in the ceiling. Cautiously, some of the residents of Petiora scooped the scum from the top of the water and took small drinks of the water using their hands as cups. A little later, a large bowl of chunky gruel was sent down the hole as well. It was nothing more than potatoes, oats, rice, and amaranth mashed together crudely into a thick paste with a few chunks of cod thrown in for the sake of having meat. There was no heat coming off the colorless food, and no seasonings apparent in its appearance. Hesitantly, a few of the farmers locked in the cell ate small portions of the gruel with their hands, but stopped after only a few bites.

"Even the jail in Goldenveil was nicer than this," Lorvin commented as he looked at the disheartening offerings of food and water.

"This is the Onyx Spire, ishkafu," Rei replied with a defeated tone. "They want you broken and in despair. I've heard a couple of my kin being dragged away, having lost their minds from the treatment here. You can't let the oppressive discomfort and callus torture get to you."

Using her left hand, Rei scooped a handful of the colorless gruel and cupped her right hand over the mess. Silently, she offered a prayer to Vulkania, and several flashes of brilliant yellow fire raced between her hands. When the feline opened her hands, she held a toasted croquette made from the ball of gruel, which she offered to Lorvin, though she refused to look him in the eyes as she held out the warm food.

"It's all in making the most of a bad situation, ishkafu," Rei said while the other naetari took the offered toasted gruel from her hand gently.

"You know, with you being the asakifu in this cell," Lorvin chuckled a little as he toyed with the hot ball of food in his hands, "I'll be expected to follow your lead, over anyone else here."

"Strange, isn't it?" Rei allowed a small smile to cross her face as she threw a sideways glance to the male. "Here we are enemies, united for a common cause, and your place in our society means you'll have to protect me. You'll have a fun story for your own mari-asakifu when we get out of here. What I wouldn't give to watch that discussion."

Lorvin devoured the fish-flavored croquette without further delay and shrugged dismissively. "Going to be an awfully short conversation, though. Would be boring to watch."

"We're notorious for being incredibly jealous women, Lorvin," the female grinned before picking up another ball of gruel and repeating her baking process to form another croquette for herself. "What makes you think I wouldn't enjoy watching an enemy ishkafu get beat by his own mari-asakifu?"

"I don't have a mari-asakifu," Lorvin stated as he watched her work. "Not unless you count the wyvern I travel with, and I don't think she'll care unless I simply didn't return from this hell."

"At least you have someone waiting for you," Rei turned her eyes away from Lorvin and sighed, her expression shifting to saddened memories.

"You two can continue this banter once we get out of here," Jolson interrupted.

The paladin almost chuckled, seeing the eyes of Rei examine Lorvin's body before biting into the warmed croquette in her hand. The look she had given the other naetari made Jolson think about his wife, who would soon be getting news of his capture. His mind worked over the memories of the last few weeks, since the attack on the Sages

Arcanum, and he wished for nothing more than to be back home in his bed with Cerulla.

"Hey, Lorvin?" Jolson suddenly called out after a moment of silence fell over the cell. "Do you still have that little blue gem?"

The monk patted his robes quickly, then pulled the saystone from a pouch tied to his belt. "What good will this do us?"

"You can use it to reach your other friends, right?" King Jolson asked, looking at the tiny blue stone with the rune carved into its surface.

Lorvin nodded then tilted his head suspiciously. "I don't see what good it will do. We're locked under the Onyx Spire. Urna and the others are somewhere near Euthrox, hunting for a faerie with the Sidhe-Vein. I can't reach out to Dorho or your wife with it, if that's what you are wondering."

"That's fine," Jolson admitted as he considered what to do. "That just means we can coordinate our efforts in here with people on the outside. One of them is an unrestricted Sidhe-Vein."

The naetari scratched his head in confusion as he tucked the stone back into the pouch. "I'm not following your words, Jolson."

"It means you were right," King Jolson threw a knowing glance to the feline as he cracked a slight smile.

"About what?"

"Patience," the paladin spoke warmly. "We need to show patience and temperance here."

22.

"We'll be heading south into the Galensteil Wastes," Dorho announced, kneeling respectfully in front of Queen Cerulla.

He wasn't fully recovered from his encounter with Nadriah, but he wanted to get moving. Corina and the other healers had done what they could in the four days following the expedition to Petiora, but less than half of the force that left Vansenhul had returned alive. Jolson and Lorvin had vanished into those clouds of darkness, and countless others had simply been erased by the magic of the High Tzar. His loyalty to his friends made Dorho want to stay in the capitol and help with the war effort, but he knew he needed to get ahead of the Onyx Spire and beat them to the vault.

"I was hoping you would stay," Cerulla spoke sadly, her opal-like eyes peering over the rogue and his blonde companion. "We can use a strong fighter like yourself in our court."

"I appreciate the offer," Dorho replied with bated breath, "but if we are to stop the Onyx Spire, we need to get ahead of them. We've been playing catch-up ever since this all started, and it's time we took the lead. If we can get the Seal before they do, they'll have to play by our rules."

Cerulla sighed as she examined the count kneeling before her. "My husband is still alive, I know it. If this allows us to bring him, and everyone else home, then so be it. Do you know where to find the World of Glass?"

"The Galensteil Wastes," Dorho admitted, then shook his head, "but from there, I would have no idea. I was hoping you would have some insight on where it might be located."

"As you know, I am the faerie of these lands," Cerulla held out her right hand, with the palm flat facing the ceiling as tendrils of green and blue magic began spinning and twisting together from her fingers. "I am the warden of the land, and it is my job to know everything that happens across my territory. Luckily for you, I have yet to sense anyone disturbing the vault, but that doesn't mean they aren't on their way already. Fly your wyvern south, and after crossing the Canteace Mountains, turn west until you reach the Ashtooth Canyon, then head south once more. You will see the Dasniva Oasis. Take this, and when you look north from the cliffs above the oasis, you will see the entrance to the World of Glass."

The magic in her hand sputtered and danced, then faded as a sheer lens of amethyst dropped into the faerie's palm.

"It is the only help I can give you," Queen Cerulla offered, rising from her throne to tuck the thin disc into Dorho's hands. "It will allow you to see through the illusions that mask the vault from view. I only hope that you fully understand that you will not find joy or happiness in the World of Glass, as nothing is meant to ever come out of that vault. What you seek to do will not be easy, and it may indeed prove to be impossible, but you have my blessing."

"I am honored, your majesty," Dorho bowed before rising to his feet with the violet lens in his hands. "I'm the scion of death, Dimorta's chosen body for this mission, and I trust in her power to see me through this test. She wouldn't have blessed me if she didn't feel I could do this."

"I hope you are right, for your sake," the faerie stated as she returned to her throne. "Go, my friend, don't waste more time with idle chatter. We have people to bring home, and a High Tzar to upset."

Dorho nodded as he turned to Corina, who waited several steps behind him. He considered offering some comforting words regarding the loss of King Jolson, but he knew the only thing the queen wanted was to see her husband returned to her side. The rogue felt he had already done and said enough over the past few days, anyway, and that anything else would be a waste of time and effort. He needed to get moving, to prove to Dimorta, and everyone else, that he was the right choice for the mission.

They departed the castle, finding Kortyx ready to go as she harassed a couple guards in the courtyard. For the rogue, it was strange to be taking the magnificent beast without the naetari present, but they had no choice. He had to rely on the speed of the great reptile, and the little bit of trust they had in each other from the few times they traveled together. Unlike Lorvin, the rogue knew he lacked the skills to recall the powerful wyvern if they got separated, so he planned to take special care to keep the lizard close.

"Do you need anything before we leave?" Dorho asked, looking over Corina as they walked up to the wyvern together.

"No, I'm good," she replied, grabbing onto the harness around the great lizard and pulling herself up onto the beast's back. "I just wish I could've seen my family one last time."

"I do too," Dorho replied, taking a position behind the woman while Kortyx trilled with the excitement of the flight to come. "When this is all over, I will help you in any way I can, Corina."

The woman turned her head as she leaned back against his chest in order to press a fond kiss to his cheek.

After he had returned from Petiora, more and more wounded began to arrive in Wayfarer's Folly as the Anslater army withdrew from their attempt to take the town. Even after they had come back to Vansenhul, the woman barely had any time where she wasn't helping tend to the wounded. This left her with no time to grieve her own loss, and Dorho could see it in her eyes that all she wanted to do was break down emotionally, but she was being stubbornly strong for the sake of everyone around her. Dorho wanted to tell her that everyone was going to be fine, but he knew better than to make that promise. Not now, and not to her.

He pressed a kiss to Corina's neck and pulled her close as Kortyx took to the sky with a mighty leap. The wings of the powerful wyvern soared out over the city of Vansenhul gracefully while the summer breeze off the ocean battered the two riders. Kortyx flew a wide circle over the expanse of the city on the coast, then after a nudge from the rogue, began to race southward. Grasslands, forests of birch and poplar, and wetlands spread out before the great creature, though all were quickly forgotten as the speed of the wyvern outpaced any horse on the ground.

For two and a half days they flew south, only stopping to eat, let Kortyx rest, and get some sleep. The deserts and grasslands of the Ela Warein region were scarred by deep river canyons, stalwart bluffs, and ancient craters left by stones from the heavens many eons ago that had filled with water since their creation. Towns and villages came and went, which the rogue had little interest in visiting. At one point, they flew a little too low over the top of a hill, startling a group of nomadic gypsies who had settled down for the night. It was a decent pace, which Dorho appreciated.

When the black rocks and the dehydrated pines of the Canteace Mountains came into view, the wyvern was directed west, following the tooth-like ridges that often threatened to reach up and grasp the flying lizard with their height. From the back of Kortyx, Dorho could see the vastness of the Galensteil Wastes that spread out from the southernmost rocks of the mountains. They were skirting the border of a land that no one wanted to call home, but some were forced to.

The bone-dry soil was cracked and wrought with eons of forgotten devastation. Through some miracle, patches of dried shrubs and dead grass rose from the bleak landscape, their brown, lifeless fingers lifted to the sky in a desperate plea for moisture. Crags of basalt, lumps of jagged orange limestone, and pillars of red granite dotted the arid land, standing like towering giants over the windswept valleys and shifting dunes of red sand. Other than the wind pushing dead brush around, and the swirling of dirt in the oppressive heat, nothing moved. Not even birds dared to fly over the barren soil while the sun was up.

During the day, Dorho had Kortyx take shelter among the nooks, crannies, and caves offered by the Canteace Mountains, and shifted their flights to the cooler temperatures of the night. The two riders used whatever shade they could find, hopefully with a slight breeze, to get as much sleep as they could while they hid from the burning light in the sky. They kept daytime activities limited to prevent spending too much time in the lethal heat of the hellish landscape, while rationing their water so it would last them until they reached the next source of fresh refills.

It was during the late morning of the fifth day of travel that Dorho first spotted a sign of the Onyx Spire's intrusion into the Galensteil Wastes. A camp had been placed on the edge of a plateau where the mountains met the volcanic rocks of the Ashtooth Canyon. Wagons featuring banners of the Spire mixed with crimson flags from Thornbror rested in a loose cluster around a smoldering fire. Two darkoyles and several soldiers scurried about lazily, seeming to be waiting impatiently for someone to arrive. As he watched from their alcove among the mountains, Dorho pondered letting his rage loose upon the small camp, but he held himself steady, keeping an eye on the movements of his enemies through a spyglass he had picked up after returning to Vansenhul.

"They're already here," he whispered, leaning against the rocks next to Corina. "It's going to be a race to get to the vault first."

"Sweetie, we haven't talked much since you returned from Petiora," Corina mentioned, resting her head on his shoulder as he observed the enemy camp.

"What is there to talk about?" Dorho asked honestly, putting his arm around the woman gently. "I have a job to do, and the world is going to hell around us."

"Something's changed in you," Corina stated wholeheartedly, "and I don't like it. You've become colder, distant, and I'm wondering what really happened in Petiora. Was the High Tzar really that terrifying?"

"She's a monster," he answered, glancing to where Kortyx was resting in the shade of a rocky outcropping, enjoying a freshly killed goat she had slain. "I've fought orcs, elves, and dwarves, even had a few encounters with golems and zombies, but none of that compares to that girl. There's a rawness to her power that I don't think anyone is ready for, and a ruthlessness that not even I can match. I watched her slaughter an entire group of infantry without even a bead of sweat breaking on her brow. It was like facing off against a true deity, and I think I finally understand what it means to be a scion."

Corina put her arms around the rogue's chest lightly and sighed as she listened to him talk. "Do you think we can beat her?"

Dorho shook his head with disappointment in himself. "I don't think so. I need to get stronger as a scion. I need to be able to match her power. I'm not able to even stand in her shadow right now, and I was forced to come face to face with that weakness. I'm sorry if I've been distant, but I've been trying to focus on the task at hand, and find ways to improve myself as a scion. I have a goddess counting on me."

"Is there anything I can do to help?" Corina spoke while her lips brushed against the skin of his throat.

A smile crossed Dorho's face as he felt her touch. "Just be there for me if I drift too close to the Undertow. If I had my rapier, I could use I'raha's magic alongside Dimorta's, and it might be enough to put a scratch on the High Tzar. As it stands, I don't even know where my sword is."

"Do you even need your sword?" Corina sat upright, looking at Dorho's right arm and the markings burned into his skin. "Cerulla said you were bewitched by faerie magic, which means she could see in you, even without your rapier. Surely, the magic is in you, not the sword. The sword only worked as a foci. What if we found you another foci?"

"Like what?" Dorho lifted his brow in suspicion. "I don't even understand how magic works."

Corina smiled fondly and captured his lips with a deft kiss. "Lucky for you, I know how to use magic."

"Then what do you suggest?" Dorho inquired as the woman straddled his lap with her knees.

"Close your eyes," the blonde woman whispered, resting her forehead against his own. "Think about the last time you used the rapier. How did it feel? Focus on that feeling. Pull it from your memories. Burn that feeling into your thoughts. Just focus. No talking."

So Dorho did as she commanded. He closed his eyes and relaxed against the rocks behind him. The last time he had used the sword's magic, he had been fighting the dreadmage in the battle for Ameribelle. Every time he struck the vile creature, the power from the faerie's magic screamed through his blood, rushing out through the blade of the sword and tearing into the body of his victim. He replayed the battle over and over in his mind, memorizing each swing and lunge with the scalloped blade. Each time he encountered a memory of using the sword with the faerie's magic, he remembered how he felt bolder, stronger, and absolutely fearless. He felt unstoppable whenever the magic flowed through his body and into the sword.

"There you go," Corina whispered affectionately, as Dorho realized her hands were caressing his forearms tenderly.

The blade in Dorho's mind glowed with that brilliant green magic each time he used it. As he struck the dreadmage, the verdant light exploded violently, tearing hungrily at the wicked creature. He focused on that feeling, wanting to pull it closer, wanting to make it his current reality. Dorho wanted nothing more than to have the power to put down the minions of the Onyx Spire like that once again. Lynsia had used her own magic to decimate the dreadmage, but it was Dorho and his sword that kept the monster from reaching its goal. As he delved deeper into the memories and feelings, he found himself wanting to get stronger, if only it meant protecting those he cared about.

"Pull it forward," the woman's voice called softly to the ears of the rogue.

His mind shifted slowly, keeping the thoughts of that magic at the front of his memories as he pondered what Corina meant with her words. Through his web of thoughts, he suddenly saw all the lives he had ended with the magic from Dimorta. Dorho remembered the sting of magic burning through his skin each time he channeled the dark powers that extinguished life. It reacted to his desires in those moments, and that desire was death. In those moments, he only wanted to see his enemies drained of their life and left as a dead husk. Whenever he used his rapier, it was to protect someone.

So he turned his mind to how it felt to draw on Dimorta's powers, but with the memories of protecting Lynsia and his friends playing through his deepest thoughts.

"Give it form," the healer spoke gently. "Remember how Jolson created his glaive from nothing? Give your magic a shape. Be your own foci."

Almost out of instinct, Dorho, with his eyes still closed, stretched his right arm out as if he were holding his lost rapier. He wanted to protect everyone he cared about, and he wanted to remember that feeling of I'raha's magic rushing through his blood. He had no foci, so he had to make one from within himself. He had to become his own foci, forged of his memories and desires. Dorho's mind raced, seeing all the faces of people he promised to protect, but had failed. His thoughts forced him to witness everyone he had ever laid low with his own hands. Like a ragged whisper, heat churned and bubbled within his right hand, and the more he delved into his memories of everything that brought him to this point, the burning intensified. Finally, he spotted the hulking monstrosity with the pick he encountered near Corina's home. Seeing the wretched creation in his mind made his rage boil, as though the behemoth were standing directly in front of him at that very moment. He pictured plunging the glowing blade of his rapier through the chest of that terrible fiend, with all of his fury and desire to protect those he loved.

The heat in his hand erupted, becoming something solid and tangible that crackled and sputtered in the air under the rocks that protected them from the sun. When Dorho opened his eyes, a rapier forged from polished black bones rested in his grip. Around his hand sat a protective basket made from a hollowed-out wolf's skull, while a rigid blade of dark fossils featuring a wickedly serrated spine sprang forth from the top of the skull-shaped guard. Dancing along the blade, traces of green lightning and violet fire entwined, stirring together like forbidden lovers. At the ricasso of the blade, a pair of pale, white eyes, one on each side, stared at the rogue as if they were waiting for him to do something. Dorho's hand clutched at the sword's grip, which appeared to be some kind of leather-wrapped rib that curved perfectly into the fingers of the rogue. It was just as grisly as it was beautiful to Count Maizen, and matched his desires perfectly, he thought.

Corina tilted her head, looking over the sword in her lover's hand with a proud smile. "You did it. Now, just remember this feeling. You can only grow from this point. Cerulla said you would have to figure out how to get both the faerie and death magic to work together, and this is your first step. It's not that you're not strong enough to beat Nadriah, but rather you lack the confidence in yourself. You've been hurt, far too deeply, far too often, and you don't see what others see."

Dorho gazed over the terrifying rapier that rested in his hand before meeting the sapphire eyes of Corina. "What do you see?"

Corina shifted her weight slightly, resting on her haunches upon his thighs as she considered his words carefully. "What do I see? I see a man destined for greatness. I see the reason my heart will ache once your quest is done."

Count Maizen took a deep breath, and envisioned the power that swelled through his body being pushed into a dark hole in his core. As quickly as it appeared, the grisly rapier of black bones vanished into a churning cloud of jade light and violet fire. Dorho flexed his fingers, feeling the ache burning through his hand as the last traces of magic dispersed into the air around him.

"Why would you ache?" he asked finally, putting his arms around the woman's waist.

She leaned against his chest, sadness flickering to life in her deeply blue eyes as she pressed herself against his body. "You'll go back to your wife and Elgrahm Hold. I'll be here in Anslater, alone, knowing that what I have now, I can never have again. I honestly don't think it's fair, sweetie."

Dorho watched as a tear ran down her cheek, causing him to hug the woman tightly. "What would you do if I stayed in Anslater after everything was finished?"

"You know that's not possible," the healer nuzzled against his shoulder. "You have a life and duty waiting for you. I... I have nothing waiting for me..."

He hadn't thought about that. Corina had lost everything when Petiora was razed. Her home and family were gone. The only reason she had been spared, was because she had been sent with the count to escort him to Vansenhul. If they could somehow end the Onyx Spire, and bring an end to the war that plagued their lands, she would be returning to a destroyed farm alone.

"How do you feel about living in Elgrahm Hold?" Dorho asked, feeling her hands tighten against his shirt as she sobbed from the loss of her family.

The woman blinked a few times and gazed into his dark eyes while she wiped the tears from her cheeks. "What? Surely, you're joking, yes?"

Dorho shook his head confidently. "I'm inviting you to come live in Elgrahm Hold. I dragged you into this mess, it should be my responsibility to see that you are taken care of afterwards. I'm absolutely serious."

"But, your wife, and your friends," Corina bit her lower lip nervously as Dorho could see she was fighting back a torrent of emotions.

Count Maizen shrugged and sighed. "It's not like we haven't been sleeping together all this time. It's not going to be easy, and definitely won't be smooth, but we'll work things out somehow. You've been harassing me in my dreams for years, and I love you, Corina."

There was no hesitation in the body of the woman as she took his lips in a deep kiss. "I love you, Dorho. Don't let me go."

"You do know," Dorho snickered between attacks from the woman's lips, "the enemy is literally just down the mountain from us. They could be watching."

Her hands unclasped the belt around the rogue's waist and a wry smile crossed the healer's face. "Let them watch," she purred before kissing him again.

22.

Vourden watched the fire near the wagon as he leaned against an old lodgepole pine, a smoldering cigar hanging from his lips. Kendira was eating a dinner of roasted pheasant and rice seated on her bunk in the wagon, while Urna and Orota conversed about the expectations of the journey ahead of them. Halvene occupied himself with splitting wood for the fire, and flexing for Orota's entertainment, which got the larger woman laughing a few times. Lynsia sat at the edge of the fire's light, her knees clutched to her chest while her platinum eyes nervously scanned the faces around her. It had been a rough few days, the justiciar though, as he peered around the camp, lost in his thoughts.

Not only was Kendira covered in a roadmap of scars after looking like a badly cracked clay pot when she absorbed the magic from Lynsia with her own, but she had been rendered deaf and mute. She could still see just fine, but the magic tearing through her body had taken her voice and hearing completely, the price she paid for loving the Sidhe-Vein. Her career as a bard had been terminated the moment she used herself as a lightning rod for Lynsia's magic. Seeing the bard torn up and broken left an empty hole in the heart of the justiciar as it rained memories of losing Paisley into his thoughts.

As expected, Lynsia took the blame on herself, though she also threw rage-filled words at the faerie that had given her life. The girl had turned into a conflagration of emotions that threatened to undo the entire mission. Against his desires as an officer of the law, Vourden allowed Orota to occasionally slip some of her narcotics into the drinks of the Sidhe-Vein, hoping it would keep the girl docile enough to see the mission finished. So far, it was working. Lynsia was still a ball of fury and self-destruction, but she lacked the energy to do anything out of the ordinary.

After the bard had lost her ability to sing and hear music, Urna never returned to the subject of the spy among the group, though she kept a weary gaze upon Kendira. Though he considered the warnings of the lizard carefully, Vourden just wanted to finish the quest and get back to Ameribelle. He didn't want to see Kendira suffer more than she had to, mostly for the sake of their children. Deep down, in the back of his mind, the justiciar knew the bard was done with the mission, regardless of her role in everything, and he was fine with that idea.

Orota and Halvene tried their best to keep the spirits of everyone up, but it was a fruitless endeavor. Vourden was beyond the point of wishing the journey was over, and from the pain in Kendira's eyes, he knew she felt the same. With everything that had happened in the last month or so, he no longer cared what happened to Lynsia, he just wanted this business finished. Urna had become the foundation for common sense among the group, as she had the most experience with magic and the Onyx Spire. The lizard wanted to destroy the Spire, a fact she repeated often through her discussions with others, and sometimes Vourden wondered if that was the only reason she was with them.

He took a long drag off the cigar and blew the smoke into the night air as his eyes shifted to the stream they were following into Faulkendor Mountains. It was their only lead on finding the faerie. Local myths said I'raha was an ageless witch that protected the waters that fed the fields of Euthrox, so Urna and Vourden agreed to follow the main waterway northwest from the town. If it didn't work out the way they hoped, the justiciar was quite open to the primary idea of the Caldavos' guard.

Halvene wanted to execute Lynsia to prevent the Onyx Spire from getting her, and bring an end to their journey. In many ways, Vourden agreed, but he currently felt like entertaining the ideas of Urna and Kendira. He also didn't want to let Ansha and Dorho down by giving into such drastic solutions. So, for now, the Sidhe-Vein was allowed to live.

Vourden fetched the tiny blue gem from his shirt pocket and held it up to the moonlight that was being overtaken by the threat of an incoming storm. He hadn't had the time or focus to use the trinket since Urna gave it to him. She had removed it from Kendira after the bard was rendered unconscious by the Sidhe-Vein, and gave it to him while they talked in the home of Lynsia's family. The mage wanted him to talk to Dorho through it, but he didn't know what he was supposed to say or ask.

"Now is better than never," he spoke to himself, closing his eyes to focus on the rune carved into the blue gem, and turning his thoughts to the color of the stone in his hand.

After what felt like several minutes of nothing, a voice echoed through the saystone's magic. There was a slight disconnect, like a wall of stone had been placed between Vourden and whoever he had reached. He couldn't explain it, as his understanding of magic was underwhelming and not even subpar by basic standards, but Vourden could sense the other party was trying harder than normal to reach through the barrier erected between the stones.

"Urna?" the voice called sheepishly, though clearly it wasn't Dorho. "Kendira?"

Vourden shook his head, as if he expected the other person to see his reaction. "Neither. It's Vourden. Kendira's been retired."

For a long while, there was a pause on the other side of the connection. "Vourden? This... Lorvin, I... you were... Ameribelle... the war. How... are things that you... get involved?"

"You're hard to understand," Vourden grumbled, hearing the broken words through the magical connection between the stones. "Where are you?"

The frustration in the other's voice was palpable as they replied. "Decided... book a room... Onyx Spire's... hotel. It's not... but King Jolson and Rei... here."

"Urna?" Vourden called, motioning for the slithzerkai to join him by the tree as he held the saystone out for her. "I don't understand, am I doing something wrong?"

Without hesitation, the lizard woman took the enchanted gem from the justiciar and closed her eyes. It only took a few breaths before her gimlet eyes shot open in horror.

"It's Lorvin. They're in the Onyx Spire. They've been captured," Urna spoke urgently, narrowing her gaze as she looked upon Vourden. "I know the feeling of that magic anywhere. Come here, put your hand on the stone as well. I'll try to negate the barrier Nadriah has in place."

Vourden did as she suggested, and with the tiny blue gem in the woman's hand, he placed his own hand over the stone. "Lorvin?" he asked into the trinket.

"Vourden?" The voice came through the magic once more, this time it was clear and distinct, like that wall had been taken down and a stage curtain opened between the two saystones.

"I was told to talk to Dorho," the justiciar spoke. "Is he really alive? Is he there with you?"

Even through the connection in the gems, Vourden could feel the mood drop from the other end as Lorvin responded. "He was with us in Petiora, but he's not with us here. I don't know what happened to him."

"But, you did see him?" Vourden asked.

"Most certainly," Lorvin answered with a tone of optimism. "He was in Anslater looking for a second Sidhe-Vein, but now Jolson is sitting next to me in the Onyx Spire's grand hotel."

"We'll come get you when we're finished here," Vourden offered.

"I'll—."

The gem in Urna's hand popped violently, turning into a cloud of blue shards and wicked sparks. Vourden winced, reeling from the tiny thorns of sapphire that got embedded in his hand in the sudden blast.

"Nadriah," Urna growled as she immediately began digging the diminutive pieces of the saystone from her palm. "This won't be good."

"What do you mean?" the justiciar asked, trying to pull the slivers of blue gem from his own hand.

"If she bothers to trace the magic," the reptile responded with a hiss, "she'll find us almost immediately."

"Then let's get moving," he stated, looking around the camp at the others. "We're leaving. Pack up. This isn't debatable!"

The others perked up as the justiciar barked his orders. Without question, Halvene and Orota began putting out the fire and gathering the gear they had used to cook the evening meal. Urna ushered Lynsia into the wagon, where the reptile did her best to relay what was happening to Kendira. Vourden gave his help to Halvene, extinguishing lamps and hastily packing equipment away. The very first drops of rain had only just hit the ground by the time Orota had the wagon moving along the trail.

With Bies by his side, Vourden sat on the rear of the wagon's roof, his eyes scanning the dense pine forest for signs of anyone following them. A fresh cigar was clenched between his lips as he used the hood of his green gambeson to protect his face from the droplets of rain that dampened the night around him. Nothing could be seen through his emerald eyes, but he could feel the sensation of something watching them from the darkness of the forest that swallowed the travelers.

"Keep going, Orota, follow the stream," he threw a command to the front of the wagon, where the bandit and the guard sat with the reins. "We're not stopping until we find that damned faerie!"

More than once, Vourden swore he saw something creeping through the trees at the edge of his vision. It was like a spider made of shadows, threatening to pounce upon the wagon, but between the speed of the horses and the pounding of rain, the justiciar wasn't sure if he saw anything at all. What he did understand, was that if they stopped, something would indeed catch them.

The path they were following grew treacherous, and several of the bumps they hit nearly threw the man and larscot from the rear of the wagon. Wind howled through the tall pines, causing the trees to sing with their creaks and groans in the darkness while the falling rain created a steady drumbeat of moisture. A flash of lightning burst to life across the clouded sky, throwing a wicked flash of light over the mountain trail that the horses trudged along.

"Wait!" Vourden barked, pointing to the west as the harsh path broke away from the stream. "We need to follow the water!"

"The wagon won't go that way!" Orota returned quickly.

Halvene shifted to look back at the justiciar. "We'd have to continue on foot if we kept following the water."

"Then we walk!" Vourden said before leaping from the back of the wagon as the horses were slowed to a halt. "Get everyone out."

Urna and Lynsia were the first ones to leave the wagon, wrapping themselves in heavy hooded cloaks. For a brief moment, Vourden considered leaving Kendira behind in her condition, as his eyes looked her over. He cursed the gods and motioned to her with a sense of urgency. She couldn't hear his words, nor could she raise her voice to complain, but he did his best to explain that they needed to head into the trees on foot. After throwing a crimson cloak around the shoulders of the bard, the justiciar pulled her from the wagon, while Orota and Halvene waited by the stream's edge. Bies followed Vourden, his eyes darting back and forth at whatever lurked in the forest around them.

"We keep moving," Vourden pointed to the water that tumbled over rocks and fallen logs. "This is our only chance to succeed! We're doing this for Dorho and Ansha!"

With the feeling of eyes peering into his soul from the darkness of the forest, Vourden took up the rear of the group, keeping one hand on Kendira's wrist as he moved through the trees. Orota and Halvene were up front, picking the path the rest would follow as they kept their eyes and weapons ready to intercept any threat that might escape the shadows of the night. That massive spider-like monster at the edge of his vision continued to pursue them, turning into tentacles of eerie blackness sneaking through the pines while the group pushed further up the ravine cut by the creek flooded with fresh rain.

Muddy soil gave way to rain-slick boulders and broken rocks littered with fallen trees the higher they climbed in the ravine, chasing the rain-fed water. Lightning blasted through the sky above, and thunder roared with anger, while the wind ripping through the trees offered no kindness to the fast-moving group. More than once, a swaying tree threatened to snap and fall upon the justiciar, only to be yanked away by the torrents in the wet air. The chill of the rain had quickly soaked through their clothes, but the urgency with which they moved kept them going, unwilling to submit to whatever might be behind them. With his claws and size, only the larscot seemed to be unhindered by the dreadful terrain, but kept himself within sight of the justiciar as he moved among the rocks and trees.

Vourden kept them going, kept barking orders to the front of their column from the rear. At the edge of his vision, hidden within the shadows of the forest, that black mass of horror crept along behind them, eager to destroy them all. Eyes unseen, but clearly felt upon his damp skin, watched everything they were doing with hungry anticipation, like wolves waiting for a wounded elk to collapse.

"Dammit!" Halvene shouted suddenly, as the first light of the morning began to hit the trees, though it was drenched in tones of grey from the raging storm.

"What?" Vourden demanded, before he saw the jagged cliff and tumbling cascade of water that roared from the top of the ledge.

"We can't go further!" Orota commented, pointing at the cliff and rain-soaked stones that blocked their path.

Urna spun about, facing the darkness of the forest as she raised her hands into the air, sparks of white light escaping from the tips of her fingers and racing into the heavy clouds above. Lightning exploded through the rain, barreling into the trees with furious intent as the bright flash tore through rocks and wood alike. Something screamed in the shadows, something else howled with agony and reeled away, slinking back into the darkness it came from.

In the bright flash, Vourden saw the cave behind the shattered rocks and waterfall. It only appeared for the instant the lightning struck out against whatever pursued them, but there was a path beyond the cliffs.

"Go!" the justiciar commanded with a growl. "Behind the waterfall! Just go!"

Again, Urna called down a thunderous blast of white light from the fierce storm, and again, unseen creatures screamed and whined from the explosion. Vourden drew his cutlass and prepared to stand and fight next to the slithzerkai while Orota and Halvene ushered the others into the cave. Bies remained by his side for a couple breaths, but eventually scampered away, giving chase to the Sidhe-Vein and the bard.

"No," Urna spoke coldly, shifting her gaze to the man beside her, "you need to go with them. I'll keep the Onyx Spire from following you. I'm the only one who can. You know this."

For a single beat of his heart, Vourden paused, but he knew the woman was right. He didn't have the skills to fight against an enemy like the Spire. "You better be right behind me," he spoke with a firm nod.

Without waiting for a reply, Vourden clambered over the rocks and into the cave, fighting through the sheets of water that plummeted from the top of the ravine. A ferocious explosion of blue fire and white lightning screamed through the drenched morning air, causing the stones of the cave to rattle and shake. Vourden could only hear something heavy crash into the ground just beyond the entrance of the cave, and the world went pitch black.

"Urna!" the justiciar yelled, starting to turn back to get the slithzerkai, but Orota's hand grabbing his right arm stopped him from moving.

"She'll be waiting for us," Halvene offered, helping pull Vourden to his feet. "We don't have time to worry about her."

"Where do we go?" Vourden asked, taking a deep breath as he looked back towards the cave entrance. "I can't see a thing in here."

"Follow him," Orota spoke, and almost on instinct, Bies trilled with excitement.

Like an obedient hound, the larscot began wandering through the cave, while the others followed closely behind, guided by the sounds of the large animal scraping over the rocks and dirt. While another explosion resounded from where they had invaded the cavern, which made Vourden consider going after Urna once more, the larscot pressed onward. The sounds of water trickling over the damp stones of the cave mixed with the occasional breath of fresh air through the narrow tunnels, but it was the movement of the weasel-like beast that kept everyone moving.

"I see light," Orota stated, her hands on Lynsia's shoulders.

Indeed, they climbed over a cluster of mossy rocks, and Vourden found himself looking at a pool of crystal-clear water among a gathering of glowing green gemstones. Vines, shrubs, and even grass grew around the shallow pond in the cave, while a crack in the ceiling allowed a soft wind from the world outside to caress the plants around the water. A small stream of clean water poured through the hole in the cavern's dome, splashing into the far end of the clear pool. As the justiciar looked on, several butterflies fluttered around some of the magenta, amber, and violet flowers that grew from the rocks and vines around the serene chamber.

"Where are we?" Vourden asked, crawling up to the edge of the water slowly, his body exhausted from running and climbing to get away from whatever followed them.

"Rest," a soft voice flowed through the cave's air like a song.

A woman, her body appearing slim and frail, draped in robes of moss and surrounded in sashes made from willow boughs, slowly rose from the clear water of the pool. Her eyes, glittering like dark sapphires in the dim light of the cavern, scanned the group from under a hood of roses and apple blossoms, as a sad smile crossed her berry-stained lips. Glowing as if lit by the midnight moon, her pale skin shimmered with the wetness that dripped from her slender figure.

"Who are you?" Vourden narrowed his gaze, reaching for his cutlass.

"Rest," the voice repeated, coming from the mouth of the woman as she stepped across the surface of the water, drawing closer to the group that gathered near the pond. "You've done well."

His eyes grew heavy, and Vourden found it impossible to get to his feet. He looked over the others with him, and like him, they were dropping to the ground, where the softness of the grass greeted their tired bodies. Kendira was already unconscious, while Lynsia fought defiantly to at least remain kneeling. Before he was thrown into a world of sleep and dreams, Vourden saw the eyes of the Sidhe-Vein close, though her mouth whispered a curse of disobedience.

"Rest," spoke the woman once more, as the justiciar was lulled into such a peaceful slumber that he never thought was possible.

23.

Dorho and Corina followed the Ashtooth Canyon like Cerulla had said. After ripping one of the wagons off the plateau using Kortyx's powerful legs, they soared southward for the better part of three nights. Even for the powerful darkoyles, the wyvern was impossible to catch as she raced through the winding canyon of volcanic rocks. Pools of stagnant water, broken apart by scorched riverbeds, were the only things that welcomed the rogue as the mighty lizard flew between the walls of the canyon. Like the walls of a natural castle, the crimson limestone and basalt of the ravine rose up over the flight of the reptile, often forming narrow arches and hallways the wyvern deftly navigated without any hesitation.

At the end of the canyon, they shot out of a thin corridor like a ballista bolt, Kortyx shrieking with glee as the lush grass, towering palm trees, and climbing wisteria scaled the red rocks around a pool of clear water. Ferns and tropical berry shrubs gathered around the edges of the azure lake, while dragonflies raced the wyvern over the surface of the water. After seeing the barren lands of the Galensteil Wastes, the vibrant shades of green grass, fuchsia wisteria blooms, and lively insects of this oasis were like something from a dream for the rogue.

"Let's fill our water supplies, then we can find the door to the vault," Dorho suggested, pointing to a family of basalt boulders in the southern part of the lake.

"Oh sweetie, this is beautiful," Corina spoke, her sapphire eyes scanning the oasis carefully while Kortyx circled the cluster of rocks before landing gently.

Not a moment was wasted as Dorho dropped from the back of the powerful beast, turning to catch the woman as she did the same. He untied the waterskins they had been rationing, and were almost completely dry, and tossed them down into the water one by one. With a laugh, the rogue pulled off his shirt and trousers, threw off his boots, and dove into the deep, clear water of the lake. Corina giggled, then followed his lead, shedding her clothes in the morning light before leaping from the rocks and into the cool water of the oasis.

"A small break can't hurt, can it?" Dorho asked, pulling the woman close as they enjoyed the refreshing feel of the cool waves lapping at their bodies.

Before Corina could answer, Kortyx dropped into the lake as well, using her powerful wings as fins as she splashed her riders. Dorho and Corina smiled and chuckled at the antics of the giant lizard enjoying the chance to cool off in the water. The wyvern swam slowly around the two, dunking her head repeatedly under the waves to wash the dust and dirt of the canyon from her scales. As he watched the great reptile swim, Dorho pushed Corina under the water as well, chuckling as he swam away before she returned to the surface.

"I'm your healer," Corina sputtered, snickering as she wiped the water from her eyes. "If you drown me, you'll be in big trouble, Count Maizen."

"If I drown you," he grinned, "I can keep all the food and water for myself."

"Oh hush," she giggled, splashing him with a wave of the cool water.

Dorho returned it with a splash of his own. "Come on, help me fill these waterskins. We can't forget that the Onyx Spire is looking for the same thing we are."

Corina sighed and nodded, grabbing one of the empty skins. "Can't have them finding us enjoying ourselves, can we?"

"Luckily," Dorho glanced around the shore of the lake as he filled one of the empty vessels with the cool water, "I think we got ahead of them. I just don't know how far ahead we are. I would rather not risk them strolling into our own work. It's just us out here, and who knows how many of them. We need to get into that vault and get out as quickly as we can."

"The World of Glass," Corina whispered, mostly to herself as she filled a second waterskin by dunking it under the water. "Are we ready for this? We don't even know what is in there."

Dorho nodded as he listened to her words. "I don't think we have a choice. If we don't go into that vault, the Onyx Spire will, and then we will just be another step behind them. I'm done following them. They're going to start catching up to us."

"We don't have a choice," the woman smiled confidently, hiding her fears behind her expression. "You're right. We need to do this, for everyone we lost."

"For everyone I've already failed," Count Maizen breathed.

They finished filling the waterskins, depositing the filled vessels on a slab of limestone next to the rocks they had landed upon. Once they were done, the couple enjoyed a swim around the lake, before collapsing onto the soft grass under the midmorning sun of the oasis.

The wisteria breathed a fresh aroma to the day as the two watched the wyvern enjoy her own time in the cool water of the lake. With a welcoming breeze through the swaying palms, and not a single hint of clouds in the sky, the heat of the sun quickly dried their bodies, allowing them to return to their clothes before noon. When he thought about the furious heat of the canyon and mountains the days before, Dorho felt like the oasis was somehow its own little world. Even with the sun high overhead, and knowing they were deep in the Galensteil Wastes, the air was comfortable and quite relaxing against his skin.

As though she were a giant dog, Kortyx sauntered from the water and shook the cool liquid from her scales, starting with her head and ending with her long tail. Dorho chuckled, as Corina had just finished putting on her blouse and trousers when she got splashed with the wayward water off the wyvern's body. The farmer's daughter, dripping with moisture, shoved Dorho off the basalt rocks and into the lake, grinning as he fell into the cool waves. Count Maizen grumbled as he pulled himself from the lake, drenched from hair to boot. He pondered throwing her in as well, but instead focused on securing the filled waterskins to the harness around Kortyx.

They grabbed a few of the wild berries from around the lake, eating them with a little of the dried meat they had packed in their rations, then rode Kortyx to the cliffs above the southern edge of the oasis. Dorho examined the land to the north, seeing the desolate landscape of the Galensteil Wastes stretching out beyond the rim of the oasis like a vision of hell threatening to swallow the paradise. A series of six limestone crags loomed far to the north, with a natural arch joining the two tallest spires about halfway up their impressive height. Even from the edge of the oasis, Dorho could see the bubbling lake of magma under the limestone bridge, churning and boiling like a bowl of liquid hatred.

Count Maizen produced the amethyst disc from his pocket, and held it up to his right eye. As he scanned the limestone sentinels looming over the lake of fire, he watched as the peak on the western side of the natural bridge shifted and shimmered, finally revealing itself to be a castle forged from black basalt and gold. When he pulled the lens from his eye, the mirage went back to being a simple mountain of crimson rocks over a pool of liquid rage.

"I found it," Dorho whispered with an optimistic grin, holding the lens back up to his eye to scan the mountains once more. "Now we just have to find our way in. Also, I hope you don't mind heights or extremely hot places."

The rogue patted the wyvern firmly upon the side of her neck, then motioned for her to take to the skies once more. Part of him wanted to rest and take the day to sleep, but they were this close, and he didn't know how close the Onyx Spire were. They hadn't seen any more signs of the enemy since they dropped into the Ashtooth Canyon, but that didn't mean anything to the hopeful rogue.

With impressive speed, Kortyx took flight once again. She soared across the oasis, giving the couple one final glimpse of paradise before turning north over the sun-scorched wasteland. They raced the wyvern's own shadow as the towering limestone guardians of the magma lake grew closer with each breath they took.

Three wagons appeared through the dust and dirt kicked up by the wind over the hellish landscape, one featuring the flag of King Borhauf, while another waved a tapestry of the Onyx Spire. With a smirk, Dorho nudged the wyvern down, letting her rip through the Thornbror wagon with her talons before driving back into the sky, out of reach of the enemy archers before they could react. He now knew how close the enemy was, and they were well aware of his presence. Dorho felt his anticipation swell in his chest, eager to reach the limestone bridge over the boiling lake of fire.

While the sun dipped down towards the late afternoon, Kortyx circled high over the crimson mountains around the burning lake of wrath, then swooped down to a spot Dorho had chosen on the western side of the bridge. Before he slid from the back of the wyvern, Dorho brought the amethyst lens to his right eye once more, gazing over the peak of the mountain that towered over them. Again, the illusion shifted, shimmered, and eventually faded from his view, revealing a grand palace of black basalt decorated with gold. An alcove etched from solid stone housed a single, but massive door carved from what appeared to be limestone banded with chunks of bone.

Dropping the lens, the door vanished from his view, replaced by a rocky outcropping with a cluster of haphazardly stacked boulders underneath. Dorho took a deep breath, looking over Corina carefully as he finally slid from the back of the wyvern. He had no idea what awaited them inside the vault, no idea what it would even look like, but they had no choice but to press forward now. The Onyx Spire was on their tail, and so far, the entrance to the World of Glass looked completely undisturbed.

The air above the lava was sweltering, and the sun was relentless, while Dorho helped Corina get down from the powerful mount. Quickly, he fetched two of the freshly filled skins of water, and grabbed a pack of supplies from the harness around the great lizard. He eyed Kortyx and then examined the mountains around them. Dorho knew the Onyx Spire would slaughter the loyal beast if they found her, and he wasn't certain if she'd be able to enter the vault with her size. With a heavy sigh from his chest, the rogue whistled sharply and pointed skyward. There was no delay from the wyvern as she leapt from the bridge and flew away, seeking refuge somewhere among the caves and crags in the nearby mountains.

"I hope she listens just as well when we come out of here," Dorho said, watching the reptile leave them behind.

"Where are we headed?" Corina wiped the sweat on her forehead as she followed the eyes of the rogue. "We need to get out of this heat. This is insane."

"Those rocks," Count Maizen stated, immediately walking towards the stack of boulders where he had seen the door through the lens.

Dorho went first, sliding into a small space between two of the largest stones, forced to move sideways through the tiny gap. After only a handful of steps, he had to drop down to all fours to scurry through a slender hole that dropped the rogue down a short ledge, onto his backside, into a dark pit. He had nearly climbed to his feet when Corina fell into his arms from the hole in the rocks above. Carved into the limestone before them, a rough mineshaft beckoned like the maw of a great devil, but it only dipped a short distance down into the mountain, and was barely tall enough for Corina to stand upright.

At the end of the mine, a sheer wall of metal greeted the couple. It was oddly out of place, and polished to a nearly mirror-like finish. There was no door, no windows, just a vertical wall of polished black metal, and their reflections staring back at them.

"Now what?" Corina tapped on the metallic surface with her right hand, and a slight hum echoed through the mineshaft.

"If it was easy," Dorho smiled, looking over the pure metal wall, "they wouldn't have sent me. Whoever built this, never meant for a regular human to find it, much less open it."

"What do you mean?" the healer pushed herself closer to the rogue, her eyes uneasy with their surroundings.

"I have the blessing of a goddess," Dorho said, pressing his right hand to the polished black wall. "I'm the scion of death. I am the Lord of Rogues. I came here to do what rogues do best, pilfer one of the greatest vaults known to our world."

The markings that had been etched into his skin flared to life with violet flames, which danced and caressed over the rest of his body slowly before they licked at the black metal of the wall. Almost immediately, the wall vibrated in response to the touch of Dimorta's magic. It shimmered and pulsed, like the surface of an obsidian lake assaulted by a winter breeze.

You are, the whisper of Dimorta's voice crawled through the memories and feelings in the rogue's mind.

"The scion of death," Dorho whispered, forcing the magic to pour into the rippling surface of the polished wall.

As though he had spoken some kind of password, the reflective black wall shattered abruptly, turning to dust as it fell about the couple standing before it. The purple flames vanished back into the scriptures carved into Dorho's arm, and he found himself standing before a door carved from red limestone and banded with bones. It wasn't nearly as massive or impressive as the one seen through the lens, but he knew it was the door they needed to find.

Dorho flexed his fingers, forcing the stinging sensation to subside before he reached for the door. Just before he touched it, the bone-clad limestone slab began to grind and shake, sliding into the ground at the rogue's feet. Beyond the ancient opening, a mysterious stairwell fell away into the depths of a black abyss. Orbs of hovering blue light flickered to life and glowed along the path, while a frozen wind instantly slammed the couple as they examined the opening. Other than the metallic stairs that descended for an unknown distance, and the azure orbs, the chamber beyond the door was nothing more than an infinite black void dotted with stars, like one might see in a clear night sky.

"Well," Dorho took a sharp breath, feeling the icy wind blasting from the depths of the strange realm beyond the door. "We can't turn away now."

Corina nodded her agreement, though the expression she wore mirrored the doubt Dorho felt creeping into his heart.

Together, they took their first step through the doorway. Dorho found the stairs were some kind of strange blue metal, covered in a thin layer of frost, but he had no issues keeping his footing on the surface. As he had seen from the outside, he couldn't detect any walls, just an endless expanse that fell away in every direction that was blacker than night and dotted with faint lights like stars. Even the hovering balls of blue light produced no heat, and the chill proved to be a startling contrast to the damning temperature of the limestone bridge just outside.

Were they actually inside, or outside? Dorho found himself wondering as they slowly descended the frozen steps. He couldn't tell.

It felt like they had gone down at least a hundred of the strange blue stairs into the depths of nothingness surrounded by hovering blue lights when an iron door materialized before the couple. Dorho hesitantly reached for the ring on the door, noting how simple the door looked as he considered their situation, and remembered they were dealing with an artifact assembled by the gods. He turned around, almost drawn by instinct, and saw that the door back to the mineshaft was only eight stairs behind them.

"I already don't like this," he commented, looking at Corina, then the mineshaft, before turning back to the iron door.

With a deep, anxious sigh, Dorho grabbed onto Corina's left hand prior to grasping the ring of the heavy iron door. There was a heavy rush of shockingly cold air as it felt like the entire world fell away. The stairs were gone, both doors vanished into the star-filled blackness, and only the floating sapphire lights remained, though they now formed a spinning ring around the pair.

Another blast of frozen wind threw Dorho from his feet, and he pulled Corina close to his chest as he tumbled, holding her protectively against whatever might happen. He closed his eyes tightly, feeling the sting of the icy gale against his face as they fell through the blackness of the strange realm they had entered. Bursts of freezing wind pushed the couple around like leaves in a storm, pulling a grimace from the lips of the rogue as the chamber's arctic fingers assailed any exposed flesh the air could find.

Something hard, and frigidly cold, slammed into the back of Count Maizen, knocking the air from his lungs as he gasped from the sudden blow. Snow and a dusting of frost fell around the couple as he finally opened his eyes, realizing their falling had stopped. Dorho coughed, rolling to his left, then sitting upright as his dark eyes examined the area around them, still holding a frightened Corina to his chest.

They were lying in a vacant tundra with frozen mountains of limestone and shale towering around them like disapproving guardians of the realm. Dorho and Corina had landed in a patch of knee-deep snow next to a single long-dead tree, from which a lone lantern was hung off one of the lifeless branches. The sky appeared to be a shifting grey mess of faded moonstone, with only the occasional dull pulse of green, blue, or white leaking through the churning jumble of clouds. Somewhere during their fall, the ring of azure orbs had disappeared, though the landscape was cursed with a dishearteningly dim sapphire glow that seemed to pour in from all directions at once.

Built into the mountain directly in front of him, a castle that had lost its war against the frozen environment, broke through the slate surface. Parapets and towers jutted from the snow-covered rocks in such a disorganized manner, that Dorho found it hard to believe anyone would actually construct such a monstrosity. Almost like it resembled a skull, the windows and main gate of the massive castle were lit with flickering torches of green fire, making the structure look like it was ready to consume whoever stepped inside next.

"We have to get out of this wind," Dorho observed, helping Corina get to her feet as he began moving towards the castle.

"There?" She commented, trying to hide the shiver in her voice.

"Do you have a better idea?" the rogue chuckled, holding her hand as they trudged through the dense snow. "We can get inside, and maybe we can rest before figuring out what this vault is all about."

"Where are we?" Corina asked, wrapping her arms around the waist of the rogue as they moved.

Dorho shrugged, scanning the mountains and castle with his dark eyes. "If I were to guess. This vault was made by the gods to hold part of another god. We're probably in some kind of world between worlds. Somewhere between our world and theirs, but that's just a guess, because I don't recognize anything around here."

"Is this what the Undertow was like?" her voice called as her eyes watched the walls and gates of the castle drawing closer slowly. "You said Dimorta sent you back, so I'm just curious."

Count Maizen chuckled and shook his head. "This is worse," he confessed after a moment. "The Undertow wasn't frozen, and there were creatures to talk to."

With their breath turning to frost in the air before their eyes, the couple reached the impressive black gates of the frozen palace. Dorho wrenched open the metal entry, yanking on the icy bars until they had enough room to pass through, then slipped into the courtyard of the long-forgotten castle carved from the snow-covered cliffs. Statues dedicated to different gods and goddesses stood in the courtyard, with only one of the figures smashed into indistinguishable pieces. The rogue recognized most of the deities represented, and assumed the broken one was shattered as a slight to Entropy.

Thunder ripped through the valley between the mountains, and hellish green lightning arced across the faded opal-like sky. The sound, and the flash of light, pulled Dorho's attention to the tree where they had landed just as a blast of emerald electricity slammed into the ground under the lantern. Snow was fiercely thrown into the air like ash from a crackling fire, while the verdant light streaked out over the frozen tundra in all directions.

"Compared to the Undertow, this is much worse," Dorho muttered, seeing the hooded behemoth that stood where the lightning had left a crater in the icy terrain.

"What's that?" Corina's voice trembled with fear, seeing the black-clad monster in the distance.

Count Maizen took a sharp breath and pushed her towards the entrance to the castle. "Remember when I told you about the girl from the Onyx Spire?"

The woman nodded, running through the courtyard until her hands clasped the heavy rings on the castle doors. "That's no girl, Dorho," her voice called back, shaking with concern.

"No, it's not," the rogue grimaced, helping the woman throw open the doors of the frozen keep. "She called that thing Revenant."

24.

Orota stirred awake, rolling onto her back as her eyes adjusted to the dim light of the cavern. The faint light from the glowing green gems met her eyes kindly, and her lungs were filled with the fresh scent of flowers and healthy grass. Nearby, water trickled from a hole in the cave's ceiling, spilling into a clear pool only a couple steps from where she was laying. Her emerald eyes looked about while she slowly sat up, realizing the others who had come with her into the cave were also waking up.

"How long were we asleep?" she asked timidly, flexing her arms and neck slowly.

"Five days," a soft, female voice answered almost immediately from a lone figure standing on the water of the underground pond.

She saw the justiciar leap to his feet, wide-eyed as he gazed upon the pale-skinned woman covered in moss and willow boughs. "Five days? Who are you?"

"You were exhausted, so I allowed you to rest without interruption," the woman's voice sang kindly. "Don't worry, you are perfectly safe here. Nothing can harm you in my temple. I am the faerie of these waters, your kind often call me I'raha Greyleaf."

"In here?" Vourden's green eyes darted around the cave. "What about Urna and the Onyx Spire? They were right behind us."

"You came to my temple," the faerie remarked softly, then pointed towards Lynsia, "and you brought my daughter. You are all safe in here."

"Go to hell!" Lynsia screamed, stomping into the water of the pool. "You created this mess! People have died because of you!"

"Lynsia!" Vourden grumbled, moving to grab the girl, but a motion from the strange woman caused him to stop abruptly.

A flash of green light burst from the faerie's sapphire-like eyes, as she grabbed Lynsia's forehead in a single swift motion with her right hand. The girl immediately went limp, like a lifeless doll, while I'raha lowered her gently into the depths of the pond. Even for Orota, it was a terrifying display of the faerie's power, but her body refused to move or react as she watched.

"What are you doing to her?" the justiciar managed to ask, fighting to move his legs against the power of the faerie.

"Her powers are out of control," the faerie spoke with a sorrow-filled tone while continuing to hold Lynsia under the water of the underground pool. "She's on the verge of destroying herself."

Orota backed away from the pond, her movements sluggish and forced while her gimlet eyes watched over the others with her. Kendira's face was washed with terror and panic, though no sounds escaped her broken throat as the bard reached for the Sidhe-Vein. Halvene sat quietly, a respectful distance from the edge of the pool, though his fingers slowly coiled around the handle of his mace. Behind the faerie, Bies was perched on a shelf of slate, munching happily on a fat squirrel, seeming unbothered by the faerie holding Lynsia under the pool's water.

Vourden shook his head and growled. "You're going to drown her! I didn't come all this way, watch my wife get murdered, see my best friend get killed, just so you can drown that girl."

"Nonsense," I'raha calmly said. "I'm merely encouraging her magic to run in sync with her body. I should have done this many years ago, but I had hoped she would never discover her truth. She was supposed to be a farmer's daughter, nothing more. I wanted her to just live her peaceful life, without my influence, but that was foolish. Her powers started waking up, and evil found her. Pushed and prodded, her magic grew and reacted to the stress she was under, and now, here we are."

Slowly the faerie let go of Lynsia's forehead, but the girl remained unconscious, face-up in the clear pool. I'raha moved closer to Vourden, her fingers reaching out to caress the man's face fondly. Her depthless blue eyes seemed to look right through the man's soul as she examined the justiciar. Never before, had Orota seen a man look so exposed, even when they had been stripped of their clothing in front of her. He trembled against the faerie's touch, while his movements appeared to be begging to get away, though his body refused to even flinch.

"You are not the man I entrusted to protect my daughter," I'raha commented with a saddened smile, "but you have done a great job so far."

Tears formed at the edges of the man's eyes as it looked like I'raha was reading the justiciar's soul like a book.

"You grow tired of this quest," the faerie stated, as though she had looked through the pages of his life. "You want to be done with it all, but you also realize that your role isn't completed yet."

Vourden shook his head and tried backing away. "I've lost too much already, because of you, your daughter, and this damned quest. You're right, I just want to be done with it all and go home to my children."

"I'm sorry this has taken so much from you," I'raha bowed her head politely and ended up pressing her forehead against the justiciar's chest tenderly. "You've been so strong for so long, and it's taking a toll on you."

"I'm done with this madness," Vourden insisted.

"You are done," I'raha nodded in agreement, before staring into the man's eyes once more, "but your journey is not over. There is a future for you, but not this version of you."

"What does that mean?" the justiciar managed to narrow his eyes in protest of the woman's words.

"I am the warden of the waters that feed the crops below my mountains. I am a faerie of growth and rebirth," I'raha stated calmly. "You have worked hard to bring my daughter to me, so I could correct the balance between her magic and her body. Now, I offer you a gift for your service to me and my daughter. May this help you push further, to reach the end of your quest, and bring you the solace you need in order to understand that your losses were not in vain."

"No," Vourden snapped, finally able to pull himself away from the touch of the faerie. "I have done enough. You trusted Dorho, and he's dead. Your daughter trusted Kendira, and now she's deaf and mute. I agreed to help, and it cost me my wife. My job here is done, so you can take your daughter and keep her from the hands of the Onyx Spire yourself."

Orota looked on from where she sat as I'raha lunged forward and reached for the face of the justiciar once more. Vourden stepped back, using his arms to block the advancing hands of the faerie. Before she could blink, Orota saw the woman grasp Vourden's wrists, push his arms away, and forced him to accept a kiss to his forehead.

"Your current form has lost so much, so I grant you the gift of rebirth," I'raha whispered into the air of the cave, as her sapphire-like eyes flickered with a brilliant green flash of light.

Tears poured down Vourden's face as he dropped to his knees, the arms of the faerie embracing his shoulders as water from the pool began to move. The clear pond shifted and shimmered, waves lapping at the edges of the pool where I'raha held the weeping justiciar. Water started reaching out, forming a shallow puddle under Vourden that swiftly soaked through his trousers.

The green energy from the eyes of the faerie appeared in the peaks and valleys of the water that collected around the justiciar. Kendira tried crawling closer to the man, but something kept her held in place, her face stained with the river of sadness flowing down her cheeks. Orota fought against the unknown forces working to hold her to the spot where she sat, her fingers caressing the length of her hammer's handle, though she found herself unable to draw it against the faerie.

A blast of verdant magic rushed through the pool, raced over the waves, and wrapped tightly around the body of the justiciar. As though he was nothing but a feather, I'raha pulled the man slowly into the middle of the pond, while the pulses of emerald light burned away his clothes. There was not a single ounce of struggle from the figure of Vourden as the faerie used her hands upon his wrists to lure him into the water. From where Orota sat, it almost appeared like the justiciar welcomed whatever was happening to him.

"Sleep, brave guardian," I'raha whispered, holding onto the man's arms tenderly. "Sleep, and be reborn with my gratitude."

With the rest of the group looking on in shock, and Lynsia still floating in the water, I'raha pushed Vourden under the waves, until not even his face could be seen. A brilliant ring of jade light erupted from the pond, raced around the underground temple like a bolt of lightning, then shot from the crack in the ceiling as though it were a prayer sent to the heavens. The faerie slowly removed her hands from the water, and the magic that flowed through the liquid silently vanished with a few gentle ripples. It took Orota several breaths to realize that she couldn't see the body of the man anymore, as though he had been completely erased from existence.

"What did you do?" Halvene demanded finally, forcing himself to his feet.

"I gave his body the rest he needed," I'raha spoke without remorse. "He sacrificed so much to get here, you all have, and after seeing what he had gone through, I decided to give him the chance of rebirth. You will meet again. Do not fret, brave warrior."

The faerie smiled sadly as she walked across the pond to reach the guard. Her feet leaving only the smallest of ripples over the surface of the pool.

"Do you have any idea how many people have been lost to protect your daughter?" Halvene unhooked the mace from his belt as the woman drew closer. "Was it all worth it?"

"Halvene, don't provoke her," Orota suggested. "We can't stand up to that kind of power."

"I don't care," the man bellowed, gazing over the approaching faerie dangerously. "We dragged that girl here, and she returned the favor by killing the sheriff?"

"Why did you come?" I'raha asked, stopping her feet only a couple steps from the figure of the guard. "You don't respect me or my daughter. What drives you?"

"Someone I care for," Halvene spoke harshly, "and I was instructed to protect, was captured while defending that girl. I'm only here because I am going to get Ansha back. I don't care for you or that girl you call a daughter. Your daughter wasn't worth the price others are paying for her safety, and that's a fact, damned faerie."

The faerie shook her head and sighed. "Then I owe you nothing, human," she spoke bluntly, before turning to face Orota.

"Vourden asked me to come, to lend my hammer, and my strength, to this journey," the jotunblöd stated without hesitation, withdrawing her hand from her weapon. "I only come to protect those who travel with the girl, and to bring honor to the Den of Red Venom."

"You will need to be stronger if you wish to protect them from the future," I'raha declared, holding out her hands. "Grant me your hammer, and I will see to it you have the ability to face the enemies that await you."

For a moment, Orota delayed, her eyes scanning over the others that joined her at the edge of the pool. Eventually, she sighed and pulled the hammer from her back, flipping it so that she was holding the heavy metallic head, and the handle was aimed at the faerie. Surprisingly, I'raha grasped the handle of the powerful weapon like it was weightless, dipped the blunt head of the hammer into the cool water of the pond, and then lifted it over her head.

Verdant light tore through the handle of the hammer, burning a floral pattern into the hardened wood before the green tendrils of electricity coiled around the hammer's head. The streaks of faerie magic crackled and fizzled through the air around the weapon, as the head of a stag was etched into the metal of the hammer's striking face. Silvery horns, curved like vicious antlers, formed from the emerald glow that caressed the heavy head of the hammer, and as the light faded, left a brutal-looking spike off the rear of the blunt face of the woman's weapon.

"Infused with my magic, and blessed by my temple," I'raha took a deep breath as she offered the weapon back to Orota, "take Stagbreaker, and use it to grow a new future for your people."

Orota grabbed the hammer gently, looking over the rebuilt weapon carefully before bowing compassionately to the faerie. "I am honored by your gift," she spoke, securing the heavy hammer to the hook on her back once more.

"As for you," I'raha nearly whispered as she knelt before Kendira, cupping the woman's tear-streaked cheeks lovingly in her hands. "Look at you. Broken by your love. Unfortunately, there is nothing I can offer you, for it appears you sealed your own fate. I only wish you find peace with yourself."

Kendira leaned into the touch of the faerie, her lips wanting to speak, but nothing came out. Instead, she merely wept into the arms of the mystical woman, throwing her arms around the shoulders of I'raha.

"Such a selfish creature," the faerie spoke softly, "masquerading as selfless. Little did you know what it would cost you. For love you have reached for the stars, but that love also condemned your soul. I only ask that you decide if you deserve to rise or fall, for the sake of my daughter, who has trusted you with her heart."

I'raha pulled herself away from the arms of the bard, who collapsed on the edge of the pond. While she returned to the center of the underground pool, Lynsia gradually sat upright, her platinum eyes scanning the faerie carefully.

"What happened?" Lynsia questioned, noticing that Vourden was missing, and Kendira was trembling with grief.

The faerie brushed a hand through the long, silvery hair of the Sidhe-Vein as she answered, "I took some of your excess power, and used it to give gifts to your friends. That is how I created a balance between your magic and your body. I gave one the ability to be reborn into a form that will grow vastly from what he is now, while the remaining excess of your magic was forged into a new hammer for your protector there."

Nodding, Lynsia seemed to understand as she knelt in the shallow waves of the pond under the crack in the ceiling. "And Kendira? I hurt her so badly, but I still love her dearly. Can you help her?"

I'raha shook her head and hugged her daughter tightly. "I cannot. She has already condemned herself. She understands what she needs to do, if she wants to remain by your side. I only hope she has the willpower to keep pushing forward."

As Lynsia stood up, giving the faerie a hug of her own, she sighed, glancing away from the woman who had created her. "I still don't forgive you. I didn't ask to get made. This is all because you gave me life."

"Understandable," I'raha breathed regretfully. "You have a job ahead of you, my daughter, you know that, right? You saw what you need to do, correct? When you are finished, if you are still angry, we will meet again."

"So that's it?" Orota tilted her head. "You fixed the girl?"

The faerie escorted Lynsia to where Kendira was seated at the edge of the water. "She still needs to learn how to properly use her magic, but she shouldn't be at risk of destroying herself now. You all know what lies ahead of you, even if I haven't said so directly. I've seen it in the memories of those of you I touched."

"The Onyx Spire?" the northern woman inquired, furrowing her brow as she glanced around the cave.

"Bies will take you out of here," I'raha stated. "Return to where you came from and once you are ready, you will begin hunting the hunters. Be warned, however, the path ahead is littered with darkness and death. I do not envy any of you."

Kendira, clutching tightly to the Sidhe-Vein, climbed to her feet as the faerie slowly returned to the center of the pond. Bies finished chewing on the squirrel, stretched his limbs and tail, and hopped down from the shelf he had occupied during the meeting. Orota put her hand on Halvene's shoulder, seeing the man was still upset over the way the faerie had treated him, and pulled him away from the pool.

"We'll bring her back to you," Orota offered, before turning to follow the wandering weasel-like creature.

"I hope you are all able to reach the goals you set for yourselves," I'raha bowed, giving a fond farewell to the travelers that visited her temple.

Bies guided them through the darkness, climbing higher into the cave system and away from the pool of the faerie. Going back the way they came meant risking running into the enemies that had followed them to the spring. The path the larscot picked lacked the streams of water and moss of the journey to I'raha's temple, which made it easier to follow than the way they had entered days before. As a group, they scaled a few short ledges, with Orota helping Lynsia and Kendira climb before following herself. It was a long, quiet trek through the seemingly infinite blackness of the cave's depths.

Light poured through a crack in the darkness after what seemed like several hours of climbing, crawling, and shuffling over loose rocks and hardened soil. It was warm and welcoming, like the glowing hearth of a home after a long hunting trip. Following the larscot, Halvene broke through the vines and grass that shielded the exit, then stepped into the light of the evening sun. Excited to get out of the cave, Orota almost pushed the Sidhe-Vein and the bard from the hole in the rocks, falling into a sea of soft grass herself as she stumbled from the crack.

A lush forest of tall pines, juniper, and a scattering of aspen trees spread out before the justiciar as he sprawled on the comfortable grass. They had stepped into a long, narrow crater with a deep, broad lake pushed against the western rim. Grass, like a carpet of emerald-hued feathers, greeted the feet of the travelers as they scanned their eyes over the friendly sight of the crater. Far in the south, a cabin that rested half-buried in the ground, relaxed with a turf roof sprouted with tiny blue flowers.

"It's real?" Lynsia mouthed, nearly silent by her awe of the scenery.

"What do you mean?" Orota asked before taking a deep breath of the alpine air.

The girl smiled wide and started sprinting towards the cabin. "My dreams. This is all from my dreams. The lake, the cabin, even the larscot."

"That's all great," Halvene scratched his chin out of concern, "but how do we get back home from here?"

Orota shrugged as her pale green eyes turned to the sky. "I say we make the most of this situation, and worry about our journey in the morning. Night is about to fall over these mountains."

"I agree," Halvene spoke, making his way slowly towards the cabin.

As night descended over the crater sanctuary, Lynsia made Kendira comfortable in the cabin while Halvene and Orota took to the woods and lake to fetch food. Bies fended for himself, hunting small rodents and birds around the cabin as his eyes kept a close watch on the forest. While the last breaths of the sun's light faded from the sky, Orota returned to the cabin with two grouse and a rabbit. Shortly after, Halvene reappeared from the darkness of the trees with firewood and wild berries.

Closed away in the shell of her emotions, Kendira only watched as the others worked to prepare the meal in the cabin's small hearth. Occasionally, Orota and Lynsia tried to encourage her to get involved, but the bard only shook her head and pulled her knees against her chest. They eventually gave up, then busied themselves with roasting the meat over the flames while a pot of tea made from herbs and berries steamed within a kettle found in the cabin.

The meal was warm, and more than welcomed among the small group that gathered under the roof of the secluded cabin. Without the bard able to sing, Orota told stories from her homeland in Jorundefel. Most of it was mythology involving local legends and gods, but it helped to relax the group as they ate and drank. It didn't take long until Halvene and Lynsia fell asleep, and after checking on Bies and Kendira, Orota made herself comfortable near the cabin's door and drifted into the land of dreams.

Early in the morning, just before the sun danced over the rim of the crater, Orota stretched and opened her eyes. As she worked on waking the guard and the Sidhe-Vein, Bies yawned and rolled onto his back. The northern woman laughed and rubbed the soft belly of the animal before looking over the interior of the cabin. She was about to ask where the bard had gone, when Kendira appeared in the doorway, her expression empty and seeming lost.

The group packed their few belongings and started walking from the cabin with Bies and Orota leading the way. They located a break in the crater's wall a short distance east of where they had spent the night, and slowly began their descent from their overnight sanctuary. Halfway through the day, they spotted the waterfall that had hid the faerie's temple from view, and saw that a massive landslide had collapsed the entrance completely. Trees were blasted and left in splinters and charred bodies lined the stream they had followed up a few days prior, a stark reminder of the hell that waited them outside the sanctuary offered by the faerie.

"I don't see Urna," Halvene whispered as he stepped up beside Orota, his green eyes glancing over the destruction in the ravine.

"It was just her, against whatever followed us," Orota replied, her tone hushed in the early afternoon air. "I'm guessing she was either captured or killed. Keep your eyes peeled for signs of danger. I doubt our enemies gave up easily."

Cautiously, Bies and Orota guided the others down through the rocks and broken trees. With a dreadful sigh, she kept them going, ignoring the trail of shattered, burned bodies that littered the waterway. The fight had been so intense, that she couldn't immediately determine what race the bodies were, only that most of them looked like elves, and others appeared to be twisted monsters created by cruel masters. Blood splashed against several of the rocks, partially washed away by the storm the battle took place under, but the stench filled the air, making Orota wishing they had stayed in the crater for another day or two.

Orota scanned the terrain, shaking her head at the destruction. "I can't believe—."

A black cloud of vile energy exploded under the feet of the northern woman suddenly, hurling her into the creek several steps from her path. Dirt, stone fragments, and dust were thrown high into the air, spraying over the group as it all rained down from the sky from the potent blast. Through the pandemonium, Orota saw Kendira get thrown from the path by a tall, slender figure clad in a robe the color of the midnight sky. Bies darted under a cluster of rocks, grunting angrily as another blast from the ground showered the larscot in clumps of soil and shattered stones.

Lynsia jumped back away from the woman in the matte black robes, her eyes instantly igniting with the brilliant white light of her ferocious magic. As if she anticipated the reaction from the Sidhe-Vein, the woman immediately lashed out with a whip, made to resemble a thorny rose, which had been concealed under her hooded blackberry-colored cloak. The barbed tail of the black whip wrapped around the throat of the girl, and just as quickly, the mysterious woman vanished into a cloud of shadows, only to instantly appear behind the Sidhe-Vein, grabbing the whip like a garrote.

"If you scream, I kill her," Caynderia whispered through the chaos, while tentacles of black fire wrapped around Kendira only a few steps from where she held Lynsia with the whip of thorns.

The Sidhe-Vein fell silent, dropping to her knees as she struggled to breathe with the whip coiled around her throat. Fire forged from pure darkness enveloped Kendira's chest and arms like mighty pythons, crushing her under the strength of the mage's magic, preventing her from focusing on the bracelets she wore. Halvene, stunned by the speed of the attack, spun about with his mace raised, only to be blasted by a spear of black fire from the midnight-clad mage. The guard stumbled backwards, and another blast of the dark energy tore through the ground under his feet, dropping him into the water next to Orota. He growled and started climbing to his feet, but the woman threw out a wave of crimson magic, which burned through the air like a glowing knife of fire. Howls of rage filled the forest from the lungs of the burly man as he was knocked into the rocks of the stream, clutching the bloodied stub where his hand with the mace had been.

Orota began moving towards the Sidhe-Vein, but a dark, reptilian hand violently grabbed her and tugged her behind a cluster of fire-blasted rocks.

"Urna!" the woman started to shout, before the slithzerkai slapped her hands over the woman's mouth.

From behind Caynderia, a short, petite girl approached wearing a robe of crimson silk covered by a cloak of wolf fur and a thin veil of violet over her face. Her skin, a dull shade of white, like the bark of ash trees in the winter, was a vivid contrast to the girl's tightly braided black hair that framed her head and shoulders in an inky cascade.

"Well done, Caynderia," the strange, petite girl spoke softly, stepping gently over to where Kendira was bound, being suffocated by the tendrils of black fire.

"Let," Lynsia begged as she clutched at the hands holding the whip around her throat. "Let... her go..."

"If I let her live," the girl turned to face the Sidhe-Vein, her hands folded behind her back in a polite gesture, "will you come with us peacefully?"

Lynsia nodded, gasping as the thorns of the black whip dug into the flesh of her neck. "Please... let her go..."

The girl in the red dress scanned the bard momentarily and then nodded finally. "Very well. Caynderia? Let the woman go. We'll take our prize and depart."

On command, the black flames around Kendira exploded and vanished into the afternoon air. Freed, but struggling to breathe, the bard collapsed into the dirt, barely able to move, much less retaliate against the attack. She couldn't scream, due to the damage on her throat, making her cries silent as she slowly reached for the Sidhe-Vein.

A black cloud swirled around Caynderia, and within only a breath or two, the mage and Lynsia were gone from the ravine. Orota prepared to strike the girl in red standing alone on the path, but Urna kept her grip on the muscular woman, shaking her head defiantly.

"Oh, Urna?" the girl with the braided hair called out, looking as though she was talking to the forest around her. "Let this be a warning to not bite the hands that used to feed you."

One of her pale, ashen hands extended towards Halvene who groaned while he clutched at the stump where his wrist used to be. As if it were fired from a crossbow, a bolt of red magic swirling with flaming lightning slammed into the squirming guard, blasting a hole through his ribs. The air turned foul with the stink of blood and cinders floating on the afternoon breeze while blood, bones, and chunks of flesh were thrown into the air like gruesome confetti. Flowing with boiling crimson, the stream beside Urna and Orota turned a grisly hue of red, then the veiled girl turned away from the ruined body of the guard to gaze upon Kendira once more.

"Everything you've already lost because of your twisted idea of love," the young-looking mage sneered, putting a hand over the eyes of the bard. "I should pay you, but instead, I would rather you simply remember this lesson."

A blast of red fire ripped across Kendira's face, drawing a sharp, but noiseless shriek from the broken bard. When her victim slumped to the ground, fighting to just breathe and move, the mage stood up straight and smiled wickedly. She gazed over the scene one final time from behind her silken violet veil, and stepped into the shadows of a nearby shattered tree. A cloud of darkness swirled about, and the girl vanished, leaving the forest a silent scene of death and destruction in her wake.

"Kendira!" Orota shouted, breaking away from Urna once she was certain the mages were gone.

She yanked the bard from the ground, who was barely breathing through the trauma that had been pounded into her body. The skin on her face, especially around the eyes, had been burned and boiled, with several areas turned black from the fierce magic of the youthful mage. Blood poured from the deep wounds where the bard's green eyes had once been, turning Kendira's tears of grief into a distressing shade of scarlet.

"We need to get her to a healer," Urna urged quickly, gesturing to the path down the ravine.

"What about Halvene?" Orota asked, tearing off part of her shirt to wrap the wounds on Kendira's face.

The reptilian woman shook her head. "He's dead. There's no surviving what Nadriah did to him. Let's go, before they decide to come back."

Clutching tightly to the terrified figure of Kendira, Orota immediately headed down the path to where they had left the wagon. With Urna's aid, Kendira and Bies were loaded into the carriage, and after doing a quick check on everything, Orota got them moving south towards Euthrox. They knew it would take several days to return to Ameribelle, and the wagon felt empty compared to when they left, making for a long, wordless trip.

Orota grimaced as the wagon bumped and rocked along the mountain path, her thoughts turned to how badly everything had gone. Kendira had been rendered blind, deaf, and mute. Ansha has been captured by the Onyx Spire. Halvene's body was left in the ravine where he had died. I'raha had taken Vourden with some promise of rebirth. Most of all, she thought about how the whole reason they had come up here, Lynsia the Sidhe-Vein, ended up being kidnapped by the mages. As her pale eyes glanced at the remaining people still in the wagon, she couldn't help but feel like they had lost a war.

25.

Vourden strolled through the kitchen of the house he shared with Paisley, kissed his wife's cheek and ruffled the hair of their infant son. He fetched the navy blue beret from a hook near the home's main entrance, slapped it onto his head, and grinned as he departed on his journey to visit Lady Eisley at the castle. Chatter around the capitol of Elgrahm Hold was all about the war against King Borlhauf, and being the region's justiciar, he was waist-deep in his duties related to keeping law and order for Lady Eisley.

The midmorning sun was already plenty warm as the justiciar moved through the streets in his sun-bleached white tunic and slate-colored trousers. A tabard of pale green, related to his allegiance to Elgrahm Hold, was draped over the scales of his leather cuirass. Boots of soft leather tapped against the stones of the road with each step Vourden took, echoing off the buildings around the narrow street leading to his home. From his left hip, the ebony scabbard that held the curved blade of his basket-hilt cutlass shimmered in the light, matching the badge that decorated the front of his beret.

He made his way through the market district, greeting several residents of Ameribelle who bothered to stop and speak to him. From a small shop, he purchased a trio of skewers, two were made from spice-rubbed chicken, and the final one was a sweet-glazed rabbit, but they were all grilled to perfection. Vourden ate as he walked, keeping Albinasky Keep in his vision as he moved through the crowds that gathered to do their morning shopping.

Respectfully, he greeted the guards at the castle gates with a kind gesture, then proceeded through after a brief moment to talk about the pleasant weather that had settled over the area. Like a blast of paint, the gardens that decorated the courtyard filled the morning air with vibrant colors and floral aromas, while the gentle breeze fluttered through the willows and cherry trees. One of the gardeners smiled and waved to the justiciar as he walked, causing him to pause and talk for a short while, which ended with the gardener offering to drop a few flowers off at Vourden's house for Paisley.

Once he was able to get into the castle, he headed directly for the throne room, knowing that Lady Eisley would be waiting for him, just as she always was. Vourden gave a swift greeting to the castle's herald, then threw open the great doors leading to the ten wide stairs that climbed into the round chamber of polished ivory marble. Like grass, a path of emerald-hued carpet lined with grand alabaster pillars led to where the throne sat upon a raised dais. Next to the main, ornate throne, were four slightly less-sophisticated chairs to each side, though only the primary seat was taken. A trio of minstrels played softly from a bench near the dais, one strumming on a lute, one with a set of pipes, and the third holding a psaltery.

Seated in the central throne was a tall, slender woman wearing a dress the color of fresh spring crops, with her long blonde hair pulled back into a trio of braids tied off with ribbons of white silk. Holding a grand ruby above her brow, a thin band of gold beads and sapphires decorated the woman's head, while she threw a welcoming grin to the justiciar that approached the dais. Lady Eisley certainly wasn't young, but she was by no means considered old, either, as she relaxed upon the throne, her blue eyes holding the wisdom that would lead Elgrahm Hold to a future of independence from the Thornbror Kingdom.

"You look well rested, Justiciar Leustren," Lady Eisley spoke kindly as she sipped from a goblet of dark wine. "You had me concerned when I was told some fishermen found you floating in the river by Dracamori."

"Yes, I've been resting at home the last three days. I'm still not certain how that happened," Vourden chuckled, rubbing the side of his neck nervously. "I must've slipped off some rocks while fishing. Good thing they found me."

"I'm certain your wife and son are glad to see you take a break," the tall, blonde noble commented warmly.

The man shrugged and smiled. "I think Paisley is tired of having me around so much. Though, something seems off. Am I forgetting anything important, Lady Eisley?"

The noble shifted in her seat, as if she meant to say something, but then shook her head dismissively. "Not at all. I am just glad to see you back. I was worried when you left with Halvene in such a hurry. Did you ever reach Urna and the others?"

"That's part of my problem," Vourden furrowed his brow in confusion, "I remember meeting them at a house in Euthrox. Things were tense and stressful there, but they were glad to see us arrive. The next thing I remember is being in the water of the river. I don't know what happened between those moments. I was hoping you could help."

Lady Eisley took a long drink from her goblet of wine, her eyes seeming to consider the words of the justiciar carefully. "I'm sorry, I've been busy with the war effort down here."

The man nodded, sighing through his mental frustrations before taking the seat immediately to the left of the noble. A crystal glass half-filled with brandy was brought to him by one of the castle's servants as he scanned the throne room slowly, listening to the soft hum of the music from the bards.

"I can send them away," Lady Eisley gestured to the minstrels, "if they are bothering you. I know how you feel about bards."

Vourden shook his head and laughed softly. "I don't mind. It's relaxing, honestly. You should get a fourth one. Have you considered finding one that can sing?"

"Are you sure," the noble gazed over the justiciar suspiciously, "that you're fine from your dip in the river?"

"Why do you ask?" Vourden beamed a confident grin.

Before Lady Eisley could respond, the great doors to the throne room were slammed open, and the herald sprinted up the stairs ahead of a muscular woman and a hooded reptilian. A larscot sauntered urgently behind them, the weasel-like creature trilling and chattering with excitement brought them all up the dais.

"That's," the burly woman froze in her movement before stepping onto the throne's stage, her pale green eyes settling upon the figure of the justiciar with an expression of pure shock.

"Lady Eisley!" the herald called, trying to keep ahead of the others. "These two come from the group that took the girl north. They have important news for your ears."

"Vourden?" The reptilian woman's head tilted slightly to the left as her gimlet eyes looked over the man seated next to the noble.

"Orota?" Vourden's smile quickly vanished as he watched the group approach. "Urna? Did something happen?"

Lady Eisley took a slow drink of her wine as she took in the scene around her, blue eyes filled with suspicious thoughts before she finally answered the call. "Please, let them speak. Thank you, herald. Justiciar Leustren will handle it from here."

"Why?" Orota said as she blatantly refused to get any closer to the justiciar, narrowing her eyes with angered concern. "How? I don't understand. The faerie... she took you into the water..."

"T'raha said we would meet again," Urna let out an exhausted breath, pulling back the hood of her cloak as she scanned the man on the dais. "I just didn't expect to see you here, or so soon. What did she do?"

Vourden shrugged as he stood up, setting the glass of liquor down gently upon a low table next to his seat. "I'm not sure what you're talking about, Urna. Last I remember, is meeting with everyone in Euthrox. Why don't you tell me what brings you here?"

Urna and Orota traded cautious glances as Bies sniffed the shins of the justiciar, who bent down to scratch the creature behind his ears. Lady Eisley motioned for the herald to escort the bards from the throne room, which he did hastily without complaint. As the doors to the throne room were closed, the northern woman and the lizard both turned their gaze upon the justiciar.

"We failed, Vourden." Urna sighed heavily, hanging her head in a defeated manner. "The Onyx Spire took Lynsia, Halvene was killed, and Kendira…"

Vourden nodded as the reptile's words trailed away while her eyes looked over the justiciar. "So the Onyx Spire got her? Can we get her back?"

Orota shook her head. "After the dust settled, it was just Urna and myself on the mountain. Well, Kendira too, but she might as well have been killed. The things she suffered were cruel, even by my standards."

"Can we get her back?" the justiciar stepped forward, looking over the two women. "Is there anything we can do?"

Urna gestured northward and took a deep breath. "We would have to assault the Onyx Spire itself. That would be suicide for just the three of us."

"Then we need to find more than just us three," Vourden announced.

Urna waved her hands dismissively. "You already know that Lorvin and Ansha have been taken by the Onyx Spire. We don't know where Dorho is. Unless you're hiding an available army somewhere, we don't stand much of a chance right now, Vourden. Even if we find an army, good luck convincing them that we need to storm the Onyx Spire for the sake of one girl."

"We're already occupied with King Borlhauf's forces south of the Free Region," Lady Eisley noted as she listened to the reptilian woman speak. "Otherwise, I would see if any of my men would be willing to help."

"So, the Onyx Spire is holding all the cards now?" Vourden paced uneasily upon the dais as he spoke. "Which means we are stuck waiting for them to act. Do we even know what they're going to do?"

"Nadriah saw to Lynsia's capture herself," Urna answered sternly. "If you consider that, and all the resources she was willing to throw at obtaining that girl, it tells us that she's up to something rather nefarious. Whatever she has planned, Lynsia is the key to the entire scheme."

"Then all of our sacrifices were for nothing?" Vourden scanned the northern woman and the slithzerkai slowly.

"Not yet," Urna urged with a hint of hope in her voice. "We aren't dead yet. We just have to figure out how to beat Nadriah at her own game. Maybe, if we can meet up with Dorho, he might know something we don't. Unfortunately, we can't reach him since Lorvin has the other saystone, and ours was shattered by Nadriah's barrier."

The justiciar picked up the glass of brandy and took a slow drink before setting it back down. "When we talked in Euthrox, you mentioned that Lorvin said Dorho was in Vansenhul with a second Sidhe-Vein, correct?"

Urna nodded as she responded. "That's correct, and he wanted to meet us up here when he was finished down there."

"Then our position is fixed, Urna," Vourden stated with a tone of modesty. "We're going to stay here and help with the war effort in Elgrahm Hold, at least until Dorho gets here. When we aren't giving the soldiers of Thornbror hell, we can be building a plan to attack the Onyx Spire."

"Orota?" Lady Eisley spoke up suddenly, nearly cutting the justiciar's words short. "Do you still have contacts within the region of Ordenstød?"

The northern woman stepped forward slowly, keeping her gaze upon the justiciar for a moment before shifting her pale eyes towards the noble. "Yes, I am the Hammer Princess of Jorundefel. My father is King Vargsten Faroe. I still have friends and allies in the northern lands. Why do you ask?"

"Justiciar Leustren?" Lady Eisley called to the man still pacing on the dais, throwing him a sideways glance.

"Yes?" the justiciar tilted his head, lost in his own thoughts.

Lady Eisley stood up and approached the northern woman confidently, putting a hand on the large woman's shoulder as her sapphire eyes skimmed over Vourden. "You will go with Orota Faroe as my ambassador. Head to the northern lands, see if they will aid us in our fight, and speak to them about the issue regarding the Onyx Spire. Meanwhile, Urna can remain here to help me with the war effort. Her knowledge and experience from the Onyx Spire might prove beneficial to keeping King Borlhauf out of my land."

"And if Dorho arrives while you two are gone, I can bring him up to speed on our situation," Urna smiled slightly, agreeing with the noble.

"Indeed," Lady Eisley offered a knowing gaze to the lizard woman.

Vourden nodded, appreciating the wisdom of the noblewoman. "That is a great idea. If they are willing to help, it would be a great boon to all of our problems."

"The warriors of the north are prideful folk," Orota added, "but they will want something in exchange for their assistance. Especially if you want them to join you in confronting the Onyx Spire."

"Get some rest, both of you," Lady Eisley spoke kindly. "You have been though an awful lot these last few weeks. I will work with my advisers and we will speak again soon, Orota, regarding what we can offer the people of the north."

"Meanwhile, Vourden," Urna shifted slightly on her feet, giving an uneasy expression to the justiciar, "you should go see Kendira. If there is anyone she would want near her right now, it would be you."

The man rubbed his goatee before directing his eyes to Lady Eisley. "She's the mother of my daughter, I should at least go talk to her. I will return shortly, Shallia."

With a nod from the noblewoman, Vourden finished the liquor in his glass, and followed Orota away from the dais. Urna stayed behind at the behest of Lady Eisley, joining the elegant noble in a stroll through the halls of the castle. The northern woman escorted the man through the courtyard and into the city that sprawled lazily around the castle's walls. Several times, the muscular woman gave suspicious glances to the justiciar, remaining just beyond his reach as they walked.

"Something amiss?" Vourden asked finally, refusing to ignore the strange looks from the large woman.

"The faerie," she spoke coldly, "dragged you into the water. You vanished before our eyes, and we couldn't stop her. Yet, here you stand. I'm confused. Are you really here?"

The justiciar shrugged as he walked beside the white-haired woman. "I don't remember that. The last thing I remember is going to bed in Euthrox. After that, I woke up on a fishing boat on the river. The crew said they found me floating in the water. I can only assume I went fishing and slipped into the water."

"You never went fishing," Orota narrowed her gaze somewhat. "You went with us to go meet the faerie in the cave. How do you not remember that?"

"I don't," he insisted. "I simply don't recall doing that. I woke up on that boat, and they brought me back to Ameribelle. Paisley was excited to see me come back, so at least—."

Orota stopped walking and shot the justiciar a startled expression. "Paisley? She's dead. I saw her get buried."

Vourden laughed faintly and shook his head. "She's just fine at home with our son. Trust me on this. She's quite alive and well. I don't know why you think she died. Lady Eisley said the same thing, but she came to visit for dinner two nights ago."

"No," Orota turned abruptly, snatching the collar of the justiciar's armor roughly. "You don't understand. Something is wrong here. Your wife was killed, and so were you. Kendira has been helping you raise your son for a while now. You're acting like none of that happened. Why?"

"Because it didn't happen," the man protested, pushing himself away from the powerful woman. "Paisley was injured by Garneil in Dracamori, but she recovered quickly and she's doing great. You are more than welcome to come visit if you would like to see for yourself. I believe my wife is making a mutton roast for dinner tonight. You'd enjoy it."

"What about Marle?" the woman inquired, her tone frustrated with the argument of the justiciar.

"What about her?" Vourden let out an annoyed sigh. "She's staying with Kendira's parents currently, and I visit her at least once a day. I would love for her to spend more time around her half-brother, but that's up to her mother."

Orota nodded, though her eyes showing that she only partly understood. "So, where does this leave Kendira? She loves you, and in the state she's in, she's going to need you more than ever."

"I don't know how you expect me to answer that," he replied. "She's a good woman, and an amazing mother, but I'm married to Paisley. I care about Kendira, but that ship sailed years ago."

"You might want to find a way to explain that to her," Orota suggested with a scowl that was only partially restrained.

Without waiting for the justiciar, the woman headed for the temple dedicated to Atheia, the goddess of life and healing. Vourden had to almost jog to keep up with the northern woman, an irritated grimace on his face. Offering a quick greeting to temple workers cleaning the foyer, the pair hustled up the white stone steps to the main entrance. A priest welcomed them hastily, then guided the northern woman and the justiciar to a room on an upper floor.

Upon opening the door, Vourden was greeted with the sight of Kendira sitting on a bed, her eyes wrapped in a heavy cloth, though she glanced at the window, clearly drawn by the light on her skin. Her long black hair had been turned a pale, ashen shade of white, and fell about her shoulders in a loose mess. Once flawless tanned skin had become a chaotic map, rivers of scars seemingly burned into her flesh in a haphazard fashion. For a long moment, Vourden wondered if it was the same woman who had given birth to his daughter all those years ago, but the twin bracelets she wore were definitely the property of the bard.

"Kendira?" Vourden called, slowly approaching the side of the bed furthest from the window.

"She can't hear you," the priest responded as he stood between Orota and the justiciar.

Vourden sighed with disappointment, then hesitantly reached out to touch the bard's hands. Immediately, she pulled away, but then slowly used her fingers to find the man's face. As Kendira's fingers brushed over his cheeks and lips, the man could see she wanted to cry, but nothing came from her throat, and any tears were absorbed by the bandages around her eyes.

"She can't speak," the priest added, seeing the woman wanting to sob. "It's also extremely unlikely that she'll ever see again, either."

"Who did this to her?" Vourden felt his heart drop into his gut as he felt the woman exploring his facial features slowly.

Orota crossed her arms over her chest and took a deep breath. "Nadriah from the Onyx Spire did this. Blasted the poor woman's head with her wicked magic. We were surprised she even survived, but she's got amazing willpower."

Out of instinct, Vourden hugged the bard tightly, caressing her hair with his hands as he held her. Her body seemed to collapse against his touch, her emotions letting go completely, though silently, into his right shoulder. There was a need for comfort in the way she embraced him with her arms, like a lost child who suddenly found their parent. Vourden felt her shift and move to press herself further against his chest, drawing several tears from his own eyes as he realized how absolutely terrified and helpless the woman was.

"We can't heal her," the priest commented quietly, "not completely. The injuries she's sustained are beyond our ability, so the best we can do is just make her comfortable in her condition."

"Then we'll find someone better," Vourden stated before pressing a kiss to Kendira's forehead. "We'll find someone who can restore her vision, hearing, and voice. She doesn't deserve this."

Shaking with the soundless weeping that took over her body, Kendira pushed herself away somewhat from the justiciar. Her slender fingers messed with the bracelets on her wrists until she was able to remove them, forcing them into the hands of Vourden. As she closed his fingers around the golden bands and gems, she delivered a wordless kiss to his lips.

Feeling the sadness pouring from his green eyes, Vourden hugged the bard once more. "I promise, Dira, regardless of what happens, I will make sure you can use these again someday. I won't forget you, and I won't let you be forgotten."

The bard hugged him tightly, nuzzling his neck fondly before leaning away slowly. Though no sounds left her lips, it was clear to the justiciar what she wanted to say.

"I love you too, Dira," he replied, feeling a smile crack his woeful features.

Kendira's hands moved to a small table next to the bed she was resting in, prodded a small leather envelope bound with a brilliant blue ribbon. She tucked the envelope close to her chest, then lifted it to give the ribbon a kiss before pushing it into the hands of the justiciar. With one hand holding the leather pouch in the grip of Vourden, she gestured to the window and nodded.

"I think she wants you to wait until you are outside to open it," Orota spoke up, leaning against the wall by the door.

Vourden looked over the lightly tanned leather pouch in his hands, along with the bracelets, and nodded. "I can wait. I'd rather just give her the company she wants for now."

So, for a long while, the justiciar just visited with the bard. He talked, even though he knew she couldn't hear him. She leaned against his chest, feeling his breath rise and fall as he spoke to her. Vourden told her about his last visit with Marle, and how he was going to head north with Orota. Then, he talked about events going on around the castle, and that he was excited to hopefully see Dorho again soon. Somehow, he felt like she understood, even if she couldn't see or hear him.

Eventually, Vourden departed with Orota, leaving the priest to attend to the needs of the wounded bard. Quietly, he walked through the temple, feeling his emotions burn through his chest and blood while he thought about Kendira. He was married, but something about visiting the bard, seeing her torn up like that, ripped a hole into his heart and felt like it wounded his soul with heavy stones. As he stepped out of the temple, and started to cross the street into the market district, Vourden pulled the ribbon-bound envelope from his pocket.

With a deep, solemn rock holding his heart deep in his gut, the justiciar untied the ribbon and opened the leather pouch. A tiny red gem only slightly larger than a pea, with a carved black rune, rolled into his left hand.

Orota's voice called from Vourden's left as he realized what he was holding. "Is that—."

A scream shook the air from behind the justiciar, causing him to wheel about immediately. Instantly, his eyes were drawn to a figure leaning out of a window high up along the southern wall of the temple. Before Vourden could shout, Kendira leapt from the window.

Made in the USA
Columbia, SC
12 February 2023